The Cthulhu Cycle

Thirteen Tentacles of Terror

Chaosium Fiction

CALL OF CTHULHU® FICTION

The Cthulhu Cycle

THIRTEEN TENTACLES OF TERROR

by

H. P. LOVECRAFT

DONALD R. BURLESON

LEONARD CARPENTER

PIERRE COMTOIS

AUGUST W. DERLETH

LORD DUNSANY

ALAN DEAN FOSTER

C. J. HENDERSON

M. R. JAMES

WILL MURRAY

STEVEN PAULSEN

DAVID C. SMITH

Selected and edited by ROBERT M. PRICE
Chapter decorations by EARL GEIER

A Chaosium Book

1996

FIRST EDITION
1 2 3 4 5 6 7 8 9 10

Chaosium Publication 6005. Published in July 1996.
ISBN 0-56882-045-3.

 PRINTED IN CANADA

CONTENTS

The Other Name of Azathoth

The Kraken

Below the thunders of the upper deep;
Far, far beneath in the abysmal sea,
His ancient, dreamless, uninvaded sleep
The Kraken sleepeth; faintest sunlights flee
About his shadowy sides; above him swell
Huge sponges of millennial growth and height;
And far away into the sickly light,
From many a wondrous grot and secret cell
Unnumber'd and enormous polypi
Winnow with giant arms the slumbering green.
There hath he lain for ages and will lie
Battening upon huge seaworms in his sleep;
Until the latter fire shall heat the deep;
Then once by man and angels to be seen,
In roaring he shall rise and on the surface die.

— Alfred Lord Tennyson

IN WHAT FOLLOWS we shall be busy seeking after the origins of Lovecraft's greatest mythopoeic creation, the octopus-headed titan Cthulhu. In the first place it is difficult to deny the cogency of Philip A. Shreffler's suggestion that the principle source of octopoid Cthulhu asleep in the deep is the poem of Alfred Lord Tennyson reproduced just above. The poem is based on a Norwegian legend, and as if in acknowledgement of his source, Lovecraft makes the sailor Johansen of all things a Norwegian. He might have been anything else. The Kraken and Cthulhu are both drowsing the ages away, Cthulhu dreaming, the Kraken dreamless, but even this difference is but a variation on the same theme. Both are due in their day to rise to the surface in an apocalyptic cataclysm, for all that for Tennyson the monster itself will meet doom, while for Lovecraft it is we who must say our prayers.

And what is the Kraken? Legend makes of him a giant octopus. Recent discoveries have suggested that fantastically huge octopus behemoths actually do lie at the root of the legend. Such beings do wash up on shore now and again. When the complete form is lacking, the size may be gauged by the size of the suckers, even when only a single tentacle survives. Shreffler's neglected suggestion gains even more force from the fact that in none of the several other traceable sources for "The Call of Cthulhu" do we find the crucial element of Cthulhu's octopus-like appearance. So we have started with the missing piece.

Another important literary source for "The Call of Cthulhu" (1926) is the fiction of Lord Dunsany. Indeed, the crucial influence of Dunsany upon this tale is enough to upset the distinction usually drawn between the Cthulhu Mythos tales and the Dunsanian tales of Lovecraft. In his article "The Emergence of 'Cthulhu'" (*Lovecraft Studies* 15, 1987) Steven J. Mariconda notes that on the same day in 1925 on which he hatched the plot for "The Call of Cthulhu", "Lovecraft read some of the ethereal phantasy of Lord Dunsany 'to stabilize my recovered creativeness of mood.'" In a footnote Mariconda comments, "Exactly what work of Dunsany Lovecraft read that day is unknown." But I am sure I know.

Lovecraft must have been rereading Dunsany's "A Shop in Go-by Street." He first read it in 1919, the same year he had a dream (see below) which formed the basis of the Wilcox episode. In Commonplace Book entry 24 we have a note referring to Dunsany's tale by name, while the very next entry is a capsule summary of the Wilcox dream. Though Lovecraft employed other motifs from "A Shop in Go-by Street" elsewhere in his fiction, what must have struck him in his 1925 rereading and led directly to the basic idea of "The Call of Cthulhu" was this passage (emphasis added), in which a keeper of a curio shop in a twilight dimension shows his wares, including:

> a dingy lumber-room full of idols: the near end was dingy and dark but at the far end was a blue caerulean glow in which stars seemed to be shining .... "This," said the fat old man in carpet slippers, "is the heaven of the gods who sleep." *I asked him what gods slept and he mentioned names that I had never heard* as well as names that I knew. "All those," he said, "that are not worshipped now are asleep."
>
> "Then does Time *not kill* the gods?" I said to him and he answered, "*No, but for three or four thousand years a god* is worshipped and for three or four he *sleeps*. Only Time is wakeful always."
>
> "But they that teach us of new gods," I said to him, "are they not new?"

> *"They hear the old ones stirring in their sleep being about to wake,* because the dawn is breaking and the priests crow. These are the happy prophets: *unhappy are they that hear some old god speak while he sleeps being still deep in slumber,* and prophesy and prophesy and no dawn comes ...."

No wonder HPL could say that "a new story plot ... had occurred to my awakening faculties ...." Here is the origin of the Old Ones who sleep for thousands of years, and whose faithful priests listen for the sounds of their reawakening, of the Old One Cthulhu who speaks in dreams while yet he slumbers, who "is not dead."

But there is another Dunsanian borrowing of equal importance. I am thinking of Dunsany's *The Gods of Pegana,* the acknowledged inspiration for Lovecraft to create his own pantheon. Here is the relevant passage:

> When MANA-YOOD-SUSHAI had made the gods and Skarl, Skarl made a drum, and began to beat upon it that he might drum for ever. Then because he was weary after the making the gods, and because of the drumming of Skarl, did MANA-YOOD-SUSHAI grow drowsy and fall asleep.
>
> And there fell a hush upon the gods when they saw that MANA rested, and there was silence on Pegana save for the drumming of Skarl. Skarl sitteth upon the mist before the feet of MANA-YOOD-SUSHAI, above the gods of Pegana, and there he beateth his drum. ...
>
> Sometimes the arm of Skarl grows weary; but still he beateth his drum, that the gods may do the work of the gods, and worlds go on, for if he cease for an instant then MANA-YOOD-SUSHAI will start awake, and there will be worlds nor gods no more.
>
> But, when at the last the arm of Skarl shall cease to beat his drum, silence shall startle Pegana like thunder in a cave, and MANA-YOOD-SUSHAI shall cease to rest.

In the introduction to another volume in this series, *The Azathoth Cycle,* I have argued that this section of *The Gods of Pegana,* "Of Skarl the Drummer", forms the basis of the pervasive Lovecraftian image of Azathoth (or Nyarlathotep) drowsing to the accompaniment of two amorphous idiot flute and/or drum players. Now I am suggesting that the same text provides the basis for the notion of Cthulhu dreaming till Doomsday. We have already seen that Dunsany spoke in "A Shop in Go-by Street" of forgotten gods who sleep on for ages, but they awaken only to receive worship again. Whence did Lovecraft derive the element of Cthulhu waking to bring an end to our world, as Robert Bloch depicts in *Strange Eons?* Not even from

Tennyson's "The Kraken", for that finny titan rises from sleep to his own doom at the final judgment.

No, Cthulhu's apocalyptic rising comes from Pegana's fear that MANA-YOOD-SUSHAI will awaken, and that the jig will be up when he does! Only here had Lovecraft preserved this aspect of Dunsany's mytheme: He has Azathoth lulled to sleep by his drummers, but only in "The Call of Cthulhu" do we hear that when the age-long sleep is over, the world will end. Ramsey Campbell, in one of his early tales, speaks breathlessly of "the other name of Azathoth!" That name is Cthulhu. The two are variations on the same theme, two versions of the same mytheme, a pair of Whateley twins, as it were, just like Azathoth and Nyarlathotep elsewhere in the fiction.

Once the story idea gelled from these Dunsanian ingredients Lovecraft decided he could at last make use of a dream transcript he had noted down in the same year as he first read "A Shop in Go-by Street." It reads as follows:

I was in a museum somewhere down town in Providence, trying to sell the curator a bas-relief which *I* had just fashioned from clay. He asked me if I were crazy, attempting to sell him something *modern* when the museum was devoted to antiquities? I replied to him in words which I remember *precisely*. "This," I said, "was fashioned in my dreams; and the dreams of man are older than brooding Egypt or the contemplative Sphinx or garden-girdled Babylon." The curator now bade me shew him my bas-relief, which I did gladly. Its design was that of a procession of Egyptian priests. As I shewed the sculpture, the old man's manner changed suddenly. His amusement gave way to vague *terror* - I can even now see his blue eyes bulging from beneath his snow-white brows - and he said slowly, softly, and distinctly - "WHO ARE YOU?" I can reproduce the awe and impressiveness of his low voice only in capitals. I replied very prosaically - "My name is Lovecraft - H.P. Lovecraft - grandson of Whipple V. Phillips." I fancied a man of his age could place my grandfather better than he could place me. But he answered impatiently, "No! No! - *before that*!" I answered that I could recall no other identity save in dreams. Then the aged curator offered me a high price for the Thing I had made from clay, but I refused it; for intuition told me that he meant to *destroy* it, whereas I wished it hung upon the wall of the museum. Then he asked me *how much* I would take for the bas-relief; and I jocularly replied, having now no mind to part with it, "*One million pounds sterling*." (Currency mixed!) To my amazement, the old man did not laugh. He seemed perplexed, dazed and frightened. Then he said in a quavering tone: "Call again in a week, please. I will consult with the directors of the corporation."

Obviously, this dream forms the basis for the episode of Henry Anthony Wilcox in the opening mini-story, "The Horror in Clay", in which a sculptor fashions an ancient artifact from his dreams. Only in HPL's own dream, the implication is that, if anything, the supramundane source for the bas-relief was his buried memories of a previous life, whereas Wilcox is the unwilling recipient of the dreams of another, Great Cthulhu himself. Here Lovecraft has appropriated another story element from the Commonplace Book in which he used to jot down ideas for just such use: "Power of wizard to influence dreams of others."

When he wrote the second episode of the "The Call of Cthulhu", "The Tale of Inspector Legrasse", Lovecraft saw the opportunity to place a few other Commonplace Book notes like individual tiles into the larger mosaic he was composing. For some time he had been waiting for the proper context for these two ideas:

> Lone lagoons & swamps of Louisiana - death demon - ancient house & gardens - moss-grown trees - festoons of Spanish moss.
>
> Ancient ruin in Alabama swamp - voodoo.

Of course we see here the origin of the raid by Legrasse and his boys in blue on the bayou sabbat. The white polypous thing worshiped by the degenerate cultists is a gratuitous leftover from the Commonplace Book note. He is the "death-demon." In "The Call of Cthulhu" we read that of this thing it was rumored that none who saw it lived much longer. There is really no place for this second-banana monster in the Cthulhu tale. The cultists are supposed to be worshipping *Cthulhu*, aren't they? Who then is *this*? He is like Tolkien's wizard Saruman, a pale echo of the main villain Sauron. What is he doing there at all? Unlike many of the Commonplace Book entries, this one was not a mere motif but more of a self-contained plot germ. Lovecraft liked the implicit mini-story and could not resist telling it, even though the result is something like Robert Bloch's "The Mannikin", where an abortive twin lives on grotesquely like a barnacle on the back of the twin more fully formed.

Once Legrasse starts interrogating the cultists, we see two more Commonplace Book items come into play. As the incredible tale of a worldwide secret cult using a litany in the dead language of R'lyeh surfaces, Lovecraft is plugging in these two:

> Hideous secret society - widespread - horrible rites in caverns under familiar scenes - one's own neighbor may belong.
>
> A secret language spoken by a few very old men in a wild country leads to hidden marvels & terrors still surviving.

The third episode, "The Madness from the Sea", owes a great debt to Lovecraft's early tale "Dagon" and may be viewed almost as a rewrite of it. It is what Raymond Chandler called "cannibalizing" one's own shorter fiction. Robert E. Howard did the same thing with "The Scarlet Citadel" when he rewrote it as part of *The Hour of the Dragon*. The link is acknowledged in "The Shadow over Innsmouth" when we learn that the Innsmouth Order of Dagon worships Cthulhu. Indeed in view of the analogous positions of Dagon and Cthulhu at the crucial points of both narratives, it is not impossible that Lovecraft intends Dagon in "The Shadow over Innsmouth" to be simply a biblical pseudonym for Cthulhu.

But here, too, Lovecraft found occasion to check off another Commonplace Book idea:

> Man abandon'd by ship - swimming in sea - pickt up hours later with strange story of undersea region he has visited - mad?

Finally, I think we must ask whether M. R. James's tale "Count Magnus", much admired by Lovecraft, was not perhaps a major source for the whole sequence in which the narrator Francis Wayland Thurston sails for Norway and comes away with the Johansen Narrative, the revelations of which eventually spell his own doom. In "Count Magnus" we have the similar premise of a narrator, unnamed, relating the contents of the memoirs of a Mr. Wraxall who traveled to Sweden, where he learned, to his subsequent and everlasting regret, of Count Magnus, who had once been on a trip south (the Black Pilgrimage to Chorazin, the nativity site of the future Antichrist). Count Magnus had returned with a demonic familiar which the hapless Wraxall manages to unleash again. In precisely the same way, Thurston, as recorded in his memoirs, had journeyed to Scandinavia (not Sweden, but Norway, again, in honor of the Kraken), to read the memoirs of a deceased predecessor's trip south from which he returned with knowledge of a monster, knowledge which winds up killing Thurston in the end, just as it killed Wraxall. And in both cases there is a tentacled monster from a tomb!

When one examines the various components making up "The Call of Cthulhu", it becomes evident just what a melange of disparate plot-germs and divers elements it is. We think of Derleth's *The Lurker at the Threshold*, which tries to incorporate far too much, using complex notes from what Lovecraft intended to be the premises for at least three different stories, one about the mysterious stone tower, another about Richard Billington and Ossadogowah, and a third about the rose window linking the viewer with creatures from other dimensions. What saves "The Call of Cthulhu" from seeming overburdened in the same way is the lack of any real narrative structure!

The "story" is really an anthology of three separate mini-stories for which the Thurston narrative is just an artificial framing device. Lovecraft used scraps of three abortive stories, not quite finally melding them into one. But the experiment is a success anyway. As with most of Lovecraft's major fiction, what we are reading is more in the nature of a paper or a treatise about events, not strictly a narrative of events (a fact of which most would-be Lovecraft pasticheurs would seem to be utterly oblivious).

What of the subsequent development of the Cthulhu character? In later stories Lovecraft might make Great Cthulhu the leader of this or that extra-terrestrial species, the object of worship by this or that ancient civilization. (For a catalogue of these developments, I refer you to my article, "Cthulhu Elsewhere in Lovecraft" in my collection *H. P. Lovecraft and the Cthulhu Mythos*, Borgo Press.) As is well known, August Derleth would ring his own far-reaching changes on the figure of Cthulhu. For one thing, though it is fairly trivial, he couldn't make up his mind what Cthulhu ought to look like. In "The House on Curwen Street" he is depicted pretty much as a haystack of tentacles. "The Black Island" presents him as a heap of tentacles with one cyclopean eye staring out. In "Something in Wood", the monster is described thusly:

> Its appearance suggested a body much longer than and different
> from that of an octopus, and its tentacular appendages issued not
> only from its face, as if from the place where a nose ought to be ...
> but also from its sides and from the central part of its body. The two
> appendages issuing from its face were clearly prehensile and were
> carved in an attitude of flaring outward, as if about to grasp .... Im-
> mediately above these two tentacles were deep-set eyes ....

It seems to me that the idea of a Cthulhu with no fixed or stable form is an attractive one. Otherwise we run the risk of picturing Cthulhu like a comic book character with a specific costume. Derleth may have taken a good thing a bit too far in his occasional suggestions that R'lyeh might move back and forth from the Pacific to the Atlantic like the Flying Dutchman.

But the more important point in Derleth's conception of Cthulhu was his notion that Cthulhu had been imprisoned beneath the waves by way of punishment by a race of more powerful beings. This idea Dirk Mosig ridiculed, pointing out that Cthulhu's octopoid features surely marked him as a water being, so what sense would it make for him to be *imprisoned* under the sea? Of course, this point cuts both ways: Mosig also repudiated Derleth's characterization of Cthulhu as a water elemental, but once we highlight his octopus features, this no longer sounds so absurd. In any case, it is certainly not out of the question for a water being to be imprisoned in water. The way Derleth saw it, Cthulhu's sleep, like Azathoth's stupor, was a punishment by the greater gods. (And, as we have seen, Derleth was onto something when he saw the parallel between torpid Azathoth and sleeping Cthulhu.) As he sleeps he is confined in a crypt in R'lyeh, not merely in the sea.

It is true, "The Call of Cthulhu" had R'lyeh sinking and Cthulhu nodding off simply as a result of the progress of the cosmic cycle measured by the position of the stars. In that story there was absolutely nothing about Cthulhu being punished by any greater beings, or about such beings period. But Derleth never claimed to be offering an exegesis of "The Call of Cthulhu" by itself. He was trying to harmonize all the data from the various stories (plus, admittedly, adding new ideas of his own), and the imprisonment motif he almost certainly derived, not from "The Call of Cthulhu", but rather from the *Necronomicon* passage given in "The Dunwich Horror." Here is what it says:

> The sunken isles of Ocean hold stones whereon Their seal is engraven, but who hath seen … the sealed tower long garlanded with seaweed and barnacles? Great Cthulhu is Their cousin, yet can he spy Them only dimly.

Here is what Derleth thought it meant:

> He was tak'n by Those Whom he had Defy'd, and thrust into ye Neth'rmost Deeps and und'r ye Sea, and placed within ye barnacled

Tower that is said to rise amidst ye great ruin that is ye Sunken city (R'lyeh), and seal'd within by ye Elder Sign ....

It is far from clear that Derleth's is a forced interpretation of the text. Certainly the idea of Cthulhu and his spawn engaging in warfare with rival races of space-devils is not foreign to Lovecraft, as we read of pretty much the same scenario in *At the Mountains of Madness*.

Finally, one may mention the shocking suggestion of Brian Lumley in *The Transition of Titus Crow* that the octopoid entity that pursues Johansen in "The Madness from the Sea" was not in fact Great Cthulhu himself but rather "merely" one of his Old Ones, or the Cthulhu-spawn of *At the Mountains of Madness*. Some damn Lumley for rank revisionism here, as if Lovecraft's story were a sacred text on which one dare not lay rough impious hands. But wait a moment! Lumley also catches flack for trivializing the transcendent Old Ones, impersonal cosmic forces in Lovecraft's reckoning, turning them into melodramatic comic opera villains who speak to humans like Titus Crow as to pestiferous nemeses and implicitly as equals, playing the Joker to Batman. Be that as it may, this time Lumley is doing the exact opposite. What Lumley has seen here is that, according to the philosophy of the Old Ones Mosig attributes to him, Lovecraft has made Great Cthulhu far too concrete in "The Call of Cthulhu", more like King Kong. In fact there are several startling similarities between "The Madness from the Sea" and *King Kong*. No cosmic power this! Lovecraft's Cthulhu, then, is not quite Great enough! Lumley has safeguarded his transcendence by removing him from the Godzilla-like spectacle of chasing a single escaping ship!

What follows is by no means an attempt to include all Cthulhu stories. There are too many of them. But the present collection does collect the foundational stories. Of Derleth's Cthulhu tales, only "The Black Island" is included. In some ways it seems to be his most direct attempt at a sequel. There are some rare reprints, a couple of new stories, and, in short, ample evidence that Cthulhu continues to send out his dreams.

Finally, let me express my thanks to Tani Jantsang, Paul Berglund, Randall Larson, Peter Cannon, and Larry Thomas for their help and suggestions.

— Robert M. Price

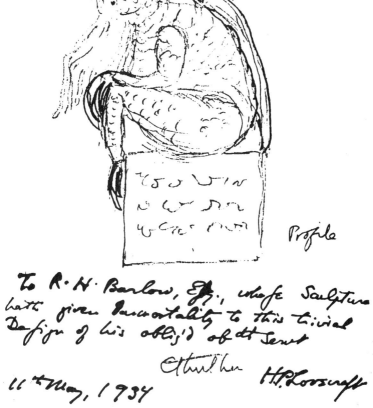

Cthulhu as drawn by H. P. Lovecraft.
(*Cthulhu*, A.Ms., John Hay Library, Providence.)

Dedicated to

S. T. Joshi,

friend and colleague,
reincarnation of H. P. Lovecraft

The Cthulhu Cycle

EDWARD JOHN MORETON DRAX PLUNKETT (1878-1957) became the eighteenth Baron of Dunsany in 1899. His castle was near Dublin. As a British aristocrat he distinguished himself in military service in the Boer War and thereafter spent much of his time on big game safaris in Africa. He played cricket and chess well. But best of all Lord Dunsany wrote fantasy fiction. Rather like Robert W. Chambers, he wrote a large amount of other work for which he is not remembered, but the fantasy work of Dunsany, like that of Chambers, was so effective, so haunting, so inspired, that it provided the basis for an important literary reputation. Dunsany was prophetic in his abilities, an obedient oracle of his muse. We are told that he would simply dictate stories off the top of his head as his wife wrote them down. He had the gift. If his literary contribution ill matches his worldly persona, we must not be surprised. When Socrates went about interviewing the leading figures of Athens trying to find a truly wise man, he crossed the poets off his list since they were indeed marvelously wise, but with a wisdom that came to them from beyond. So with Lord Dunsany.

The influence of Dunsany on Lovecraft is well known. Lovecraft wrote many short tales in imitation of Dunsany. "The White Ship" owes an obvious debt to Dunsany's "Idle Days on the Yann", to which "A Shop in Go-by Street" is a sequel. Naturally, those influenced by Lovecraft will have been influenced by Dunsany, too, almost as a matter of genetics. Henry Kuttner, Lin Carter, and Gary Myers all have their own canons of Dunsanian fictions. Dunsany's own work, nowadays hard to come by, is a feast and a delight. As L. Sprague de Camp observed, "An assortment of Dunsany is the foundation stone of any fantasy collection."

As for the present story, Dunsany confided that certain elements came from childhood memory. One day he and his father entered "into a long dark shop where an old man lolled in a chair at the end of it; and it was filled with strange things." The vast gorge between two vast precipices in the story, Dunsany recalled, was a fictional transformation of the gorge of the Avon in Clifton.

"A Shop in Go-by Street" first appeared in *Tales of Three Hemispheres* (Boston: John W. Luce and Company, 1919).

A Shop in Go-by Street

by Lord Dunsany

I SAID I MUST GO BACK to Yann again and see if *Bird of the River* still plies up and down and whether her bearded captain commands her still or whether he sits in the gate of fair Belzoond drinking at evening the marvellous yellow wine that the mountaineer brings down from the Hian Min. And I wanted to see the sailors again who came from Durl and Duz and to hear from their lips what befell Perdóndaris when its doom came up without warning from the hills and fell on that famous city. And I wanted to hear the sailors pray at night each one to his own god, and to feel the wind of the evening cooling arise when the sun went flaming away from that exotic river. For I thought never again to see the tide of Yann, but when I gave up politics not long ago the wings of my fancy strengthened, though they had erstwhile drooped, and I had hopes of coming behind the East once more where Yann like a proud white war-horse goes through the Lands of Dream.

Yet had I forgotten the way to those little cottages on the edge of the fields we know whose upper windows, though dim with antique cobwebs, look out on the fields we know not and are the starting point of all adventure in all the Lands of Dream.

I therefore made enquiries. And so I came to be directed to the shop of a dreamer who lives not far from the Embankment in the City. Among so many streets as there are in the city it is little wonder that there is one that has never been seen before; it is named Go-by Street and runs out of the Strand if you look very closely. Now when you enter this man's shop you do not go straight to the point but you ask him to sell you something, and if it is anything with which he can supply you he hands it to you and wishes you good-morning. It is his way. And many have been deceived by asking for some unlikely thing, such as the oyster-shell from which was taken one of those single pearls that made the gates of Heaven in Revelations, and finding that the old man had it in stock.

He was comatose when I went into his shop, his heavy lids almost covered his little eyes; he sat, and his mouth was open. I said "I want some of Abama and Pharpah, rivers of Damascus." "How much?" he said. "Two and a half yards of each, to be delivered at my flat." "That is very tiresome," he muttered, "very tiresome. We do not stock it in that quantity." "Then I will take all you have," I said.

He rose laboriously and looked among some bottles. I saw one labelled "Nilos, river of Aegyptos" and others Holy Ganges, Phlegethon, Jordan; I was almost afraid he had it, when I heard him mutter again, "This is very tiresome," and presently said, "We are out of it." "Then," I said, "I wish you to tell me the way to those little cottages in whose upper chambers poets look out upon the fields we know not, for I wish to go into the Lands of Dream and to sail once more upon mighty, sea-like Yann."

At that he moved heavily and slowly in way-worn carpet slippers, panting as he went, to the back part of his shop, and I went with him. This was a dingy lumber-room full of idols: the near end was dingy and dark but at the far end was a blue caerulean glow in which stars seemed to be shining and the heads of the idols glowed. "This," said the fat old man in carpet slippers, "is the heaven of the gods who sleep." I asked him what gods slept and he mentioned names that I had never heard as well as names that I knew. "All those," he said, "that are not worshipped now are asleep."

"Then does Time not kill the gods?" I said to him and he answered, "No. But for three or four thousand years a god is worshipped and for three or four he sleeps. Only Time is wakeful always."

"But they that teach us of new gods," I said to him, "are they not new?"

"They hear the old ones stirring in their sleep being about to wake, because the dawn is breaking and the priests crow. These are the happy prophets: unhappy are they that hear some old god speak while he sleeps being still deep in slumber, and prophesy and prophesy and no dawn comes, they are those that men stone saying, 'Prophesy where this stone shall hit you, and this.'"

"Then shall Time never slay the gods," I said. And he answered, "They shall die by the bedside of the last man. Then Time shall go mad in his solitude and shall not know his hours from his centuries of years and they shall clamor round him crying for recognition and he shall lay his stricken hands on their heads and stare at them blindly and say, 'My children, I do not know you from one another,' and at those words of Time empty worlds shall reel."

And for some while then I was silent, for my imagination went out into those far years and looked back at me and mocked me because I was the creature of a day.

Suddenly I was aware by the old man's heavy breathing that he had gone to sleep. It was not an ordinary shop: I feared lest one of his gods should wake and call for him: I feared many things, it was so dark, and one or two of those idols were something more than grotesque. I shook the old man hard by one of his arms.

"Tell me the way to the cottages," I said, "on the edge of the fields we know."

"I don't think we can do that," he said.

"Then supply me," I said, "with the goods."

That brought him to his senses. He said, "You go out by the back door and turn to the right," and he opened a little, old, dark door in the wall through which I went, and he wheezed and shut the door. The back of the shop was of incredible age. I saw in antique characters upon a mouldering board: "Licensed to sell weasels and jade earrings." The sun was setting now and shone on little golden spires that gleamed along the roof which had long ago been thatched and with a wonderful straw. I saw that the whole of Go-by Street had the same strange appearance when looked at from behind. The pavement was the same as the pavement of which I was weary and of which so many thousand miles lay the other side of those houses, but the street was of most pure untrampled grass with such marvellous flowers in it that they lured downward from great heights the flocks of butterflies as they travelled by, going I know not whence. The other side of the street there was pavement again but no houses of any kind, and what there was in place of them I did not stop to see, for I turned to my right and walked along the back of Go-by Street till I came to the open fields and the gardens of the cottages that I sought. Huge flowers went up out of those gardens like slow rockets and burst into purple blooms and stood there huge and radiant on six-foot stalks and softly sang strange songs. Others came up beside and bloomed and began singing too. A very old witch came out of her cottage by the back door and into the garden in which I stood.

"What are these wonderful flowers?" I said to her.

"Hush! Hush!" she said, "I am putting the poets to bed. These flowers are their dreams."

And in a lower voice I said: "What wonderful song are they singing?" and she said, "Be still and listen."

And I listened and found they were singing of my own childhood and of things that happened there so far away that I had forgotten them till I heard the wonderful song.

"Why is the song so faint?" I said to her.

"Dead voices," she said, "dead voices," and turned back again to her cottage saying: "Dead voices" still, but softly for fear that she should wake the poets. "They sleep so badly while they live," she said.

I stole on tiptoe upstairs to the little roof from whose windows, looking one way, we see the fields we know and, looking another, those hilly lands that I sought—almost I feared not to find them. I looked at once towards the mountains of faery: the afterglow of the sunset flamed on them, their avalanches flashed on their violet slopes coming down tremendous from emerald peaks of ice; and there was the old gap in the blue-grey hills above the precipice of amethyst whence one sees the Lands of Dream.

All was still in the room where the poets slept when I came quietly down. The old witch sat by a table with a lamp, knitting a splendid cloak of gold and green for a king that had been dead a thousand years.

"Is it any use," I said "to the king that is dead that you sit and knit him a cloak of gold and green?"

"Who knows?" she said.

"What a silly question to ask," said her old black cat who lay curled by the fluttering fire.

Already the stars were shining on that romantic land when I closed the witch's door; already the glow-worms were mounting guard for the night around those magical cottages. I turned and trudged for the gap in the blue-grey mountains.

Already when I arrived some colour began to show in the amethyst precipice below the gap although it was not yet morning. I heard a rattling and sometimes caught a flash from those golden dragons far away below me that are the triumph of the goldsmiths of Sirdoo and were given life by the ritual incantations of the conjurer Amargrarn. On the edge of the opposite cliff, too near I thought for safety, I saw the ivory palace of Singanee that mighty elephant-hunter; small lights appeared in windows, the slaves were awake and beginning with heavy eyelids the work of the day.

And now a ray of sunlight topped the world. Others than I must describe how it swept from the amethyst cliff the shadow of the black one that opposed it, how that one shaft of sunlight pierced the amethyst for leagues, and how the rejoicing colour leaped up to welcome the light and shot back a purple glow on the walls of the palace of ivory while down in that incredible ravine the golden dragons still played in the darkness.

At this moment a female slave came out by a door of the palace and tossed a basketful of sapphires over the edge. And when day was manifest on those marvelous heights and the flare of the amethyst precipice filled the abyss, then the elephant-hunter arose in his ivory palace and took his terrific spear and going out by a landward door went forth to avenge Perdondaris.

I turned then and looked upon the Lands of Dream, and the thin white mist that never rolls quite away was shifting in the morning. Rising like isles above it I saw the Hills of Hap and the city of copper, old, deserted Bethmoora, and the Utnar Vehi and Kyph and Mandaroon and the wandering leagues of Yann. Rather I guessed than saw the Hian Min whose imperturbable and aged heads scarce recognize for more than clustered mounds the round Acroctian hills, that are heaped about their feet and that shelter, as I remembered, Durl and Duz. But most clearly I discerned that ancient wood through which one going down to the bank of Yann whenever the moon is old may come on *Bird of the River* anchored there, waiting three days for travellers, as has been prophesied of her. And as it was now that season I hurried down from the gap in the blue-grey hills by an elfin path that was coeval with fable, and came by means of it to the edge of the wood. Black though the darkness was in that ancient wood the beasts that moved in it were blacker still. It is very seldom that any dreamer travelling in the Lands of Dream is ever seized by these beasts, and yet I ran; for if a man's spirit is seized in the Lands of Dream his body may survive it for many years and well know the beasts that mouthed him far away and the look in their little eyes and the smell of their breath; that is why the recreation field at Hanwell is so dreadfully trodden into restless paths.

And so I came at last to the sea-like flood of proud, tremendous Yann, with whom there tumbled streams from incredible lands— with these we went by singing. Singing he carried drift-wood and whole trees, fallen in far-away, unvisited forests, and swept them mightily by; but no sign was there either out in the river or in the olden anchorage near by of the ship I came to see.

And I built myself a hut and roofed it over with the huge abundant leaves of a marvellous weed and ate the meat that grows

on the targar-tree and waited there three days. And all day long the
river tumbled by and all night long the tolulu-bird sang on and the
huge fireflies had no other care than to pour past in torrents of
dancing sparks, and nothing rippled the surface of Yann by day and
nothing disturbed the tolulu-bird by night. I know not what I
feared for the ship I sought and its friendly captain who came from
fair Belzoond and its cheery sailors out of Durl and Duz; all day
long I looked for it on the river and listened for it by night until
the dancing fireflies danced me to sleep. Three times only in those
three nights the tolulu-bird was scared and stopped his song, and
each time I awoke with a start and found no ship and saw that he
was only scared by the dawn. Those indescribable dawns upon the
Yann came up like flames in some land over the hills where a
magician burns by secret means enormous amethysts in a copper
pot. I used to watch them in wonder while no bird sang—till all of
a sudden the sun came over a hill and every bird but one began to
sing, and the tolulu-bird slept fast, till out of an opening eye he saw
the stars.

I would have waited there for many days, but on the third day I
had gone in my loneliness to see the very spot where first I met *Bird
of the River* at her anchorage with her bearded captain sitting on the
deck. And as I looked at the black mud of the harbour and pictured
in my mind that band of sailors whom I had not seen for two years,
I saw an old hulk peeping from the mud. The lapse of centuries
seemed partly to have rotted and partly to have buried in the mud
all but the prow of the boat and on the prow I faintly saw a name.
I read it slowly—it was *Bird of the River*. And then I knew that,
while in Ireland and London two years had barely passed over my
head, ages had gone over the region of Yann and wrecked and rotted
that once familiar ship, and buried years ago the bones of the
youngest of my friends, who so often sang to me of Durl and Duz
or told the dragon-legends of Belzoond. For beyond the world we
know there roars a hurricane of centuries whose echo only troubles—though sorely—our fields; while elsewhere there is calm.

I stayed a moment by that battered hulk and said a prayer for
whatever may be immortal of those who were wont to sail it down
the Yann, and I prayed for them to the gods to whom they loved to
pray, to the little lesser gods that bless Belzoond. Then leaving the
hut that I built to those ravenous years I turned my back to the Yann
and entering the forest at evening just as its orchids were opening their
petals to perfume the night came out of it in the morning, and

passed that day along the amethyst gulf by the gap in the blue-grey
mountains. I wondered if Singanee, that mighty elephant-hunter,
had returned again with his spear to his lofty ivory palace or if his
doom had been one with that of Perdóndaris. I saw a merchant at a
small back door selling new sapphires as I passed the palace, then I
went on and came as twilight fell to those small cottages where the
elfin mountains are in sight of the fields we know. And I went to
the old witch that I had seen before and she sat in her parlour with
a red shawl round her shoulders still knitting the golden cloak, and
faintly through one of her windows the elfin mountains shone and
I saw again through another the fields we know.

"Tell me something," I said, "of this strange land?"

"How much do you know?" she said. "Do you know that dreams
are illusion?"

"Of course I do," I said, "Every one knows that."

"Oh no they don't," she said, "the mad don't know it."

"That is true," I said.

"And do you know," she said, "that Life is illusion?"

"Of course it is not," I said. "Life is real, Life is earnest—"

At that both the witch and her cat (who had not moved from her
old place by the hearth) burst into laughter. I stayed some time, for
there was much that I wished to ask, but when I saw that the
laughter would not stop I turned and went away.

MONTAGUE RHODES JAMES (1862-1936) is universally revered as the greatest practitioner of the traditional ghost story, a genre which seeks to invoke not great shapes of apocalyptic doom or visions of grotesque gore, but rather only a subtle chill of the numinous and the demonic. And as MRJ's many admirers and fans would attest, in this case less is definitely more. H. P. Lovecraft always spoke very highly of James, esteeming him a true literary man, a writer of weird spectral literature, not a pulp second-rater like himself and his circle. This, at least, was Lovecraft's own self-effacing comparison—though Monty James might well have shared it. We do not know that MRJ ever read any of Lovecraft's fiction, but he did peruse HPL's essay "Supernatural Horror in Literature" and had some hard words on the style evident there.

Lovecraft thought highly of "Count Magnus" and, as I have suggested, adapted elements of it for "The Call of Cthulhu." Beyond this, it is worth noting that "Count Magnus" is also the probable source of items we find tucked into other Lovecraftian tales. The appearance of the shambling, reeking Thing on Daniel Upton's doorstep seems to reflect the hunched, coat-shrouded familiar of Count Magnus, from whose sagging sleeve protruded no human hand. And the moment in "The Lurking Fear" when the narrator's assistant is found to have had his face chewed off by the Martense ghouls was surely inspired by the terrible fate of Anders Bjornsen, who had a similar cosmetic setback in "Count Magnus." Let's face it.

"Count Magnus" has left its mark on "The Rats in the Walls", too. While much of that story is derived from Sabine Baring-Gould's *Curious Myths of the Middle Ages* and Poe's "Ligeia", the element of the medieval tyrants with diabolical connections, the Barons Exham, seems to come from "Count Magnus." Note, too, that in his rewrite of William Lumley's draft of "The Diary of Alonzo Typer", Lovecraft places the haunted van der Heyl mansion in "dubious Chorazin" in New York state. Typer, too, has made a Black Pilgrimage to Chorazin, though it is a New World counterpart to the original.

"Count Magnus" first appeared in James' collection *Ghost Stories of an Antiquary* in 1904.

Count Magnus

by M. R. James

BY WHAT MEANS THE PAPERS out of which I have made a connected story came into my hands is the last point which the reader will learn from these pages. But it is necessary to prefix to my extracts from them a statement of the form in which I possess them.

They consist, then, partly of a series of collections for a book of travels, such a volume as was a common product of the forties and fifties. Horace Marryat's *Journal of a Residence in Jutland and the Danish Isles* is a fair specimen of the class to which I allude. These books usually treated of some unfamiliar district on the Continent. They were illustrated with wood cuts or steel plates. They gave details of hotel accommodation, and of means of communication, such as we now expect to find in any well-regulated guidebook, and they dealt largely in reported conversations with intelligent foreigners, racy innkeepers and garrulous peasants. In a word, they were chatty.

Begun with the idea of furnishing material for such a book, my papers as they progressed assumed the character of a record of one single personal experience, and this record was continued up to the very eve, almost, of its termination.

The writer was a Mr. Wraxall. For my knowledge of him I have to depend entirely on the evidence his writings afford, and from these I deduce that he was a man past middle age, possessed of some private means, and very much alone in the world. He had, it seems, no settled abode in England, but was a denizen of hotels and boarding-houses. It is probable that he entertained the idea of settling down at some future time which never came; and I think it also likely that the Pantechnicon fire in the early seventies must have destroyed a great deal that would have thrown light on his antecedents, for he refers once or twice to property of his that was warehoused in that establishment.

It is further apparent that Mr. Wraxall had published a book, and that it treated of a holiday he had once taken in Brittany. More than this I cannot say about his work, because a diligent search in bibliographical works has convinced me that it must have appeared either anonymously or under a pseudonym.

As to his character it is not difficult to form some superficial opinion. He must have been an intelligent and cultivated man. It seems that he was near being a Fellow of his college at Oxford—Brasenose as I judge from the Calendar. His besetting fault was pretty clearly that of over-inquisitiveness, possibly a good fault in a traveller, certainly a fault for which this traveller paid dearly enough in the end.

On what proved to be his last expedition, he was plotting another book. Scandinavia, a region not widely known to Englishmen forty years ago, had struck him as an interesting field. He must have lighted on some old books of Swedish history or memoirs, and the idea had struck him that there was room for a book descriptive of travel in Sweden, interspersed with episodes from the history of some of the great Swedish families. He procured letters of introduction, therefore, to some persons of quality in Sweden, and set out thither in the early summer of 1863.

Of his travels in the North there is no need to speak, nor of his residence of some weeks in Stockholm. I need only mention that some Savant resident there put him on the track of an important collection of family papers belonging to the proprietors of an ancient manor-house in Vestergothland, and obtained for him permission to examine them.

The manor-house, or *herrgard*, in question is to be called Råbäck (pronounced something like Roebeck), though that is not its name. It is one of the best buildings of its kind in all the country, and the picture of it in Dahlenberg's *Suecia antiqua et moderna*, engraved in 1694, shows it very much as the tourist may see it today. It was built soon after 1600, and is, roughly speaking, very much like an English house of that period in respect of material—red-brick with stone facings—and style. The man who built it was a scion of the great house of de la Gardie, and his descendants possess it still. De la Gardie is the name by which I will designate them when mention of them becomes necessary.

They received Mr. Wraxall with great kindness and courtesy, and pressed him to stay in the house as long as his researches lasted. But, preferring to be independent, and mistrusting of his powers of conversing in Swedish, he settled himself at the village inn, which turned out quite sufficiently comfortable, at any rate during the

summer months. This arrangement would entail a short walk daily
to and from the manor-house of something under a mile. The house
itself stood in a park, and was protected—we should say grown
up—with large old timber. Near it you found the walled garden,
and then entered a close wood fringing one of the small lakes with
which the whole country is pitted. Then came the wall of the
demesne, and you climbed a steep knoll—a knob of rock lightly
covered with soil—and on the top of this stood the church, fenced
in with tall dark trees. It was a curious building to English eyes.
The nave and aisles were low, and filled with pews and galleries. In
the western gallery stood the handsome old organ, gaily painted,
and with silver pipes. The ceiling was flat, and had been adorned
by a seventeenth-century artist with a strange and hideous 'Last
Judgment', full of lurid flames, falling cities, burning ships, trying
souls, and brown and smiling demons. Handsome brass coronae
hung from the roof; the pulpit was like a doll's-house, covered with
little painted wooden cherubs and saints; a stand with three hour-
glasses was hinged to the preacher's desk. Such sights as these may
be seen in many a church in Sweden now, but what distinguished
this one was an addition to the original building. At the eastern end
of the north aisle the builder of the manor-house had erected a
mausoleum for himself and his family. It was a largish eight-sided
building, lighted by a series of oval windows, and it had a domed
roof, topped by a kind of pumpkin-shaped object rising into a spire,
a form in which Swedish architects greatly delighted. The roof was
of copper externally, and was painted black, while the walls, in
common with those of the church, were staringly white. To this
mausoleum there was no access from the church. It had a portal and
steps of its own on the northern side.

Past the churchyard the path to the village goes, and not more
than three or four minutes bring you to the inn door.

On the first day of his stay at Råbäck Mr. Wraxall found the
church door open, and made those notes of the interior which I have
epitomized. Into the mausoleum, however, he could not make his
way. He could by looking through the keyhole just descry that there
were fine marble effigies and sarcophagi of copper, and a wealth of
armorial ornament, which made him very anxious to spend some
time in investigation.

The papers he had come to examine at the manor-house proved
to be of just the kind he wanted for his book. There were family
correspondence, journals, and account-books of the earliest owners

of the estate, very carefully kept and clearly written, full of amusing
and picturesque detail. The first de la Gardie appeared in them as
a strong and capable man. Shortly after the building of the mansion
there had been a period of distress in the district, and the peasants
had risen and attacked several chateaux and done some damage. The
owner of the Råbäck took a leading part in suppressing the trouble,
and there was reference to executions of ringleaders and severe
punishments inflicted with no sparing hand.

The portrait of this Magnus de la Gardie was one of the best in
the house, and Mr. Wraxall studied it with no little interest after
his day's work. He gives no detailed description of it, but I gather
that the face impressed him rather by its power than by its beauty
or goodness; in fact, he writes that Count Magnus was an almost
phenomenally ugly man.

On this day Mr. Wraxall took his supper with the family and
walked back in the late but still bright evening.

'I must remember,' he writes, 'to ask the sexton if he can let me
into the mausoleum at the church. He evidently has access to it
himself, for I saw him tonight standing on the steps, and as I
thought, locking or unlocking the door.'

I find that early on the following day Mr. Wraxall had some
conversation with his landlord. His setting it down at such length
as he does surprised me at first; but I soon realized that the papers
I was reading were, at least in their beginning, the materials for the
book he was meditating, and that it was to have been one of those
quasi-journalistic productions which admit of the introduction of
an admixture of conversational matter.

His object, he says, was to find out whether any traditions of
Count Magnus de la Gardie lingered on in the scenes of that
gentleman's activity, and whether the popular estimate of him were
favourable or not. He found that the Count was decidedly not a
favourite. If his tenants came late to their work on the days which
they owed to him as Lord of the Manor, they were set on the wooden
horse, or flogged and branded in the manor-house yard. One or two
cases there were of men who had occupied lands which encroached
on the lord's domain, and whose houses had been mysteriously burnt
on a winter's night, and the whole family inside. But what seemed
to dwell on the innkeeper's mind most—for he returned to the
subject more than once—was that the Count had been on the Black
Pilgrimage, and had brought something or someone back with him.

You will naturally inquire, as Mr. Wraxall did, what the Black Pilgrimage may have been. But your curiosity on the point must remain unsatisfied for the time being, just as his did. The landlord was evidently unwilling to give a full answer, or indeed any answer, on the point, and, being called out for a moment, trotted off with obvious alacrity, only putting his head in at the door a few minutes afterwards to say that he was called away to Skara, and should not be back till evening.

So Mr. Wraxall had to go unsatisfied to his day's work at the manor-house. The papers on which he was just then engaged soon put his thoughts into another channel, for he had to occupy himself with glancing over the correspondence between Sophia Albertina in Stockholm and her married cousin Ulrica Leonora at Råbäck in the years 1705-1710. The letters were of exceptional interest from the light they threw upon the culture of that period in Sweden, as anyone can testify who has read the full edition of them in the publications of the Swedish Historical Manuscripts Commission.

In the afternoon he had done with these, and after returning the boxes in which they were kept to their places on the shelf, he proceeded, very naturally, to take down some of the volumes nearest to them, in order to determine which of them had best be his principal subject of investigation next day. The shelf he had hit upon was occupied mostly by a collection of account-books in the writing of the first Count Magnus. But one among them was not an account-book, but a book of alchemical and other tracts in another sixteenth-century hand. Not being familiar with alchemical literature, Mr. Wraxall spends much space which he might have spared in setting out the names and beginnings of the various treatises: The book of the Phoenix, book of the Thirty Words, book of the Toad, book of Miriam, Turba philosophorum, and so forth; and then he announces with a good deal of circumstance his delight at finding, on a leaf originally left blank near the middle of the book, some writing of Count Magnus himself headed 'Liber nigrae peregrinatinis.' It is true that only a few lines were written, but there was quite enough to show that the landlord had that morning been referring to a belief at least as old as the time of Count Magnus, and probably shared by him. This is the English of what was written:

'If any man desires to obtain a long life, if he would obtain a faithful messenger and see the blood of his enemies, it is necessary that he should first go into the city of Chorazin, and there salute the prince ....' Here there was an erasure of one word, not very thoroughly done, so that Mr. Wraxall felt pretty sure that he was right in reading it as *aeris* ('of the air'). But there was no more of the text copied, only a line in Latin: '*Quaere reliqua hujus materiei inter secretiora*' (See the rest of this matter among the more private things).

It could not be denied that this threw a rather lurid light upon the tastes and beliefs of the Count; but to Mr. Wraxall, separated from him by nearly three centuries, the thought that he might have added to his general forcefulness alchemy, and to alchemy something like magic, only made him a more picturesque figure; and when, after a rather prolonged contemplation of his picture in the hall, Mr. Wraxall set out on his homeward way, his mind was full of the thought of Count Magnus. He had no eyes for his surrounding, no perception of the evening scents of the woods or the evening light on the lake; and when all of a sudden he pulled up short, he was astonished to find himself already at the gate of the churchyard, and within a few minutes of his dinner. His eyes fell on the mausoleum.

'Ah,' he said, 'Count Magnus, there you are. I should dearly like to see you.'

'Like many solitary men,' he writes, 'I have a habit of talking to myself aloud; and unlike some of the Greek and Latin particles, I do not expect an answer. Certainly, and perhaps fortunately in this case, there was neither voice nor any that regarded: only the woman who, I suppose, was cleaning up the church, dropped some metallic object on the floor, whose clang startled me. Count Magnus, I think, sleeps sound enough.'

That same evening the landlord of the inn, who had heard Mr. Wraxall say that he wished to see the clerk or deacon (as he would be called in Sweden) of the parish, introduced him to that official in the inn parlour. A visit to the de la Gardie tomb-house was soon arranged for the next day, and a little general conversation ensued.

Mr. Wraxall, remembering that one function of Scandinavian deacons is to teach candidates for Confirmation, thought he would refresh his own memory on a Biblical point.

'Can you tell me,' he said, 'anything about Chorazin?'

The deacon seemed startled, but readily reminded him how that village had once been denounced.

'To be sure,' said Mr. Wraxall; 'it is, I suppose, quite a ruin now?'

'So I expect,' replied the deacon. 'I have heard some of our old priests say that Antichrist is to be born there; and there are tales—'

'Ah! what tales are those?' Mr. Wraxall put in.

'Tales, I was going to say, which I have forgotten,' said the deacon; and soon after that he said good night.

The landlord was now alone, and at Mr. Wraxall's mercy; and that inquirer was not inclined to spare him.

'Herr Nielsen,' he said, 'I found out something about the Black Pilgrimage. You may as well tell me what you know. What did the Count bring back with him?' Swedes are habitually slow, perhaps, in answering, or perhaps the landlord was an exception. I am not sure; but Mr. Wraxall notes that the landlord spent at least one minute in looking at him before he said anything at all. Then he came close up to his guest, and with a good deal of effort he spoke:

'Mr. Wraxall, I can tell you this one little tale, and no more—not any more. You must not ask anything when I have done. In my grandfather's time—that is, ninety-two years ago—there were two men who said: "The Count is dead; we do not care for him. We will go tonight and have a free hunt in his wood."—the long wood on the hill that you have seen behind Råbäck. Well, those that heard them say this, they said: "No, do not go; we are sure you will meet with persons walking who should not be walking. They should be resting, not walking." These men laughed. There were no forest-men to keep the wood, because no one wished to hunt there. The family were not here at the house. These men could do what they wished.

'Very well, they go to the wood that night. My grandfather was sitting here in this room. It was the summer, and a light night. With the window open, he could see out to the wood, and hear.

'So he sat there, and two or three men with him, and they listened. At first they hear nothing at all; then they hear someone—you know how far away it is—they hear someone scream, just as if the most inside part of his soul was twisted out of him. All of them in the room caught hold of each other, and they sat so for three-quarters of an hour. Then they hear someone else, only about three hundred ells off. They hear him laugh out loud: it was not one of those two men that laughed, and, indeed, they have all of them said that it was not any man at all. After that they hear a great door shut.

'Then, when it was just light with the sun, they all went to the priest. They said to him:

'"Father, put on your gown and your ruff, and come to bury these men, Anders Bjornsen and Hans Thorbjorn."

'You understand that they were sure these men were dead. So they went to the wood—my grandfather never forgot this. He said they

were all like so many dead men themselves. The priest, too, he was
in a white fear. He said when they came to him:

"'I heard one cry in the night, and I heard one laugh afterwards.
If I cannot forget that, I shall not be able to sleep again."

'So they went to the wood, and they found these men on the edge
of the wood. Hans Thorbjorn was standing with his back against a
tree, and all the time he was pushing with his hands—pushing
something away from him which was not there. So he was not dead.
And they led him away, and took him to the house at Nykjoping,
and he died before the winter; but he went on pushing with his hands.
Also Anders Bjornsen was there; but he was dead. And I tell you
this about Anders Bjornsen, that he was once a beautiful man, but
now his face was not there, because the flesh of it was sucked away
off the bones. You understand that? My grandfather did not forget
that. And they laid him on the bier which they brought, and they
put a cloth over his head, and the priest walked before; and they
began to sing the psalm for the dead as well as they could. So, as
they were singing the end of the first verse, one fell down, who was
carrying the head of the bier, and the others looked back, and they
saw that the cloth had fallen off, and the eyes of Anders Bjornsen
were looking up, because there was nothing to close over them. And
this they could not bear. Therefore the priest laid the cloth upon
him, and sent for a spade, and they buried him in that place.'

The next day Mr. Wraxall records that the deacon called for him
soon after his breakfast, and took him to the church and mausoleum.
He noticed that the key of the latter was hung on a nail just by the
pulpit, and it occurred to him that, as the church door seemed to
be left unlocked as a rule, it would not be difficult for him to pay
a second and more private visit to the monuments if there proved
to be more of interest among them than could be digested at first.
The building, when he entered it, he found not unimposing. The
monuments, mostly large erections of the seventeenth and eighteenth centuries, were dignified if luxuriant, and the epitaphs and
heraldry were copious. The central space of the domed room was
occupied by three copper sarcophagi, covered with finely-engraved
ornament. Two of them had, as is commonly the case in Denmark
and Sweden, a large metal crucifix on the lid. The third, that of
Count Magnus, as it appeared, had, instead of that, a full-length
effigy engraved upon it, and round the edge were several bands of
similar ornament representing various scenes. One was a battle,
with cannon belching out smoke, and walled towns, and troops of

pikemen. Another showed an execution. In a third, among trees, was a man running at full speed, with flying hair and outstretched hands. After him followed a strange form; it would be hard to say whether the artist had intended it for a man, and was unable to give the requisite similitude, or whether it was intentionally made as monstrous as it looked. In view of the skill with which the rest of the drawing was done, Mr. Wraxall felt inclined to adopt the latter idea. The figure was unduly short, and was for the most part muffled in a hooded garment which swept the ground. The only part of the form which projected from that shelter was not shaped like any hand or arm. Mr. Wraxall compares it to the tentacle of a devil-fish, and continues; 'On seeing this, I said to myself, "This, then, which is evidently an allegorical representation of some kind—a fiend pursuing a hunted soul—may be the origin of the story of Count Magnus and his mysterious companion. Let us see how the huntsman is pictured: doubtless it will be a demon blowing his horn."' But, as it turned out, there was no such sensational figure, only the semblance of a cloaked man on a hillock, who stood leaning on a stick, and watching the hunt with an interest which the engraver had tried to express in his attitude.

Mr. Wraxall noted the finely-worked and massive steel padlocks—three in number—which secured the sarcophagus. One of them, he saw, was detached, and lay on the pavement. And then, unwilling to delay the deacon longer or to waste his own working-time, he made his way onward to the manor-house.

'It is curious,' he notes, 'how on retracing a familiar path one's thoughts engross one to the absolute exclusion of surrounding objects. Tonight, for the second time, I had entirely failed to notice where I was going (I had planned a private visit to the tomb-house to copy the epitaphs), when I suddenly, as it were, awoke to consciousness, and found myself (as before) turning in at the churchyard gate, and, I believe, singing or chanting some such words as, "Are you awake, Count Magnus? Are you asleep, Count Magnus?" and then something more which I have failed to recollect. It seemed to me that I must have been behaving in this nonsensical way for some time.'

He found the key to the mausoleum where he had expected to find it, and copied the greater part of what he wanted; in fact, he stayed until the light began to fail him.

'I must have been wrong,' he writes, 'in saying that one of the padlocks of my Count's sarcophagus was unfastened; I see tonight that two are loose. I picked up both, and laid them carefully on the window-ledge, after trying unsuccessfully to close them. The remaining one is still firm, and, though I take it to be a spring lock, I cannot guess how it is opened. Had I succeeded in undoing it, I am almost afraid I should have taken the liberty of opening the sarcophagus. It is strange, the interest I feel in the personality of this, I fear, somewhat ferocious and grim old noble.'

The day following was, as it turned out, the last of Mr. Wraxall's stay at Råbäck. He received letters connected with certain investments which made it desirable that he should return to England; his work among the papers was practically done, and travelling was slow. He decided, therefore, to make his farewells, put some finishing touches to his notes, and be off.

These finishing touches and farewells, as it turned out, took more time than he expected. The hospitable family insisted on his staying to dine with them—they dined at three—and it was verging on half-past six before he was outside the iron gates of Råbäck. He dwelt on every step of his walk by the lake, determined to saturate himself, now that he trod it for the last time, in the sentiment of the place and hour. And when he reached the summit of the churchyard knoll, he lingered for many minutes, gazing at the limitless prospect of woods near and distant, all dark beneath a sky of liquid green. When at last he turned to go, the thought struck him that surely he must bid farewell to Count Magnus as well as the rest of the de la Gardies. The church was but twenty yards away, and he knew where the key of the mausoleum hung. It was not long before he was standing over the great copper coffin, and, as usual, talking to himself aloud. 'You may have been a bit of a rascal in your time, Magnus,' he was saying, 'but for all that I should like to see you, or, rather—'

'Just at that instant,' he says, 'I felt a blow on my foot. Hastily enough I drew it back, and something fell on the pavement with a clash. It was the third, the last of the three padlocks which had fastened the sarcophagus. I stooped to pick it up, and—Heaven is my witness that I am writing only the bare truth—before I had raised myself there was a sound of metal hinges creaking, and I distinctly saw the lid shifting upwards. I may have behaved like a coward, but I could not for my life stay for one moment. I was outside that dreadful building in less time than I can write—almost as quickly as I could have said—the words; and what frightens me yet more, I could not turn the key in the lock. As I sit here in my room noting these facts, I ask myself (it was not twenty minutes ago) whether that noise of creaking metal continued, and I cannot tell whether it did or not. I only know that there was something more than I have written that alarmed me, but whether it was a sound or sight I am not able to remember. What is this that I have done?'

Poor Mr. Wraxall! He set out on his journey to England on the next day, as he had planned, and he reached England in safety; and yet, as I gather from his changed hand and inconsequent jottings, a broken man. One of several small notebooks that have come to me with his papers gives, not a key to, but a kind of inkling of, his experiences. Much of his journey was made by canal-boat, and I find not less than six painful attempts to enumerate and describe his fellow-passengers. The entries are of this kind:

24. Pastor of village in Skane. Usual black coat and soft black hat.

25. Commercial traveller from Stockholm going to Trollhattan. Black cloak, brown hat.

26. Man in long black cloak, broad-leafed hat, very old fashioned.

This entry is lined out, and a note added: 'Perhaps identical with No. 13. Have not yet seen his face.' On referring to No. 13, I find that he is a Roman priest in a cassock.

The net result of the reckoning is always the same. Twenty-eight people appear in the enumeration, one being always a man in a long black cloak and broad hat, and the other a short figure in dark cloak and hood. On the other hand, it is always noted that only twenty-six passengers appear at meals, and that the man in the cloak is perhaps absent and the short figure is certainly absent.

On reaching England, it appears that Mr. Wraxall landed at Harwich, and that he resolved at once to put himself out of the reach of some person or persons whom he never specifies, but whom he had evidently come to regard as his pursuers. Accordingly he took a vehicle—it was a closed fly—not trusting the railway, and drove across country to the village of Belchamp St. Paul. It was about nine o'clock on a moonlight August night when he neared the place. He was sitting forward, and looking out of the window at the fields and thickets—there was little else to be seen—racing past him. Suddenly he came to a cross-road. At the corner two figures were standing motionless; both were in dark cloaks; the taller one wore a hat, the shorter a hood. He had no time to see their faces, nor did they make any motion that he could discern. Yet the horse shied violently and broke into a gallop, and Mr. Wraxall sank back into his seat in something like desperation. He had seen them before.

Arrived at Belchamp St. Paul, he was fortunate enough to find a decent furnished lodging, and for the next twenty-four hours he lived, comparatively speaking, in peace. His last notes were written on this day. They were too disjointed and ejaculatory to be given here in full, but the substance of them is clear enough. He is expecting a visit from his pursuers—how or when he knows not— and his constant cry is 'What has he done?' and 'Is there not hope?' Doctors, he knows, would call him mad, policemen would laugh at him. The parson is away. What can he do but lock his door and cry to God?

People still remembered last year at Belchamp St. Paul how a strange gentleman came one evening in August years back; and how the next morning by one he was found dead, and there was an inquest; and the jury that viewed the body fainted, seven of 'em did, and none of 'em wouldn't speak to what they see, and the verdict was visitation of God; and how the people as kep' the 'ouse moved out that same week, and went away from that part. But they do not, I think, know that any glimmer of light has ever been thrown, or could be thrown, on the mystery. It so happened that last year the little house came into my hands as part of a legacy. It had stood empty since 1863, and there seemed no prospect of letting it; so I had it pulled down, and the papers of which I have given you an abstract were found in a forgotten cupboard under the window in the best bedroom.

WHAT IS THE FUNCTION of "in-jokes" in a story? Ironically, to lessen the story's effectiveness: If you get the joke, you are vividly reminded of the textuality of the text. It ceases to serve as a window through which you may view far-off things and becomes instead a two-dimensional flat surface with no depth. You become aware of the texture because of the knot of the in-joke. The in-joke tells you "Psst! This is only a story, and here's what I've smuggled into it, like graffiti on a wall. Those poor saps who are drawn into the story for its own sake remain oblivious of the joke, but you, yanked away from engagement with it, can join me in a secret laugh." The suspension of disbelief is dispelled. But, hell, it's dispelled anyway, we've read the story so many times. So here are the facts on a couple more of the in-jokes.

First, a few names: "George Gammell Angell" is derived from Angell Street in Providence. "Old Castro", the Mestizo sailor with tall tales to tell, was probably based on Lovecraft's revision client Adolphe DeCastro, originally Adolph Danziger, a jack of all trades who wrote unbelievably bad fiction and was a friend of Ambrose Bierce, from whom he once sought to steal credit for a story. He was a dentist by trade, though once he had been in the diplomatic corps. He changed his name to avoid anti-German sentiment in the Great War. Lovecraft's revisions for DeCastro include "The Electric Executioner" and "Clarendon's Last Test", as well as at least another tale, mentioning Tsathoggua, now lost. The unnamed Paterson, New Jersey geologist is closely based on Lovecraft's fellow Kalem Clubber James Ferdinand Morton.

The "hideous" Fleur-de-Lys house in which Wilcox resides is quite real and you can find it just where Lovecraft located it. In fact it was the published reference to it which prompted a local columnist who lived there to threaten to send HPL an avenging ghost at 3:00 a.m. This mock threat was in turn the occasion for Lovecraft's poem "The Messenger."

"The Call of Cthulhu" led to another Lovecraft poem as well, unless I miss my guess. The twentieth sonnet in the "Fungi from Yuggoth" cycle, "Night-Gaunts", seems to be a verse version of the description in "The Tale of Inspector Legrasse" of a "hidden lake unglimpsed by mortal sight, in which dwelt a huge, formless white polypous thing with luminous eyes; and squatters whispered that bat-winged devils flew up out of caverns in inner earth to worship it at midnight." Here is the relevant section of the poem: "Black, horned, and slender, with membraneous wings/That bear the bifid barb of hell." They take wing "down [to] the nether pits to that foul lake/Where puffed shoggoths splash in doubtful sleep." The only difference is whether you picture the bat-winged devils (night-gaunts) as flying to or from nighted caverns. This means that the tentacled thing in the bayou is the prototype for the shoggoths, maybe even that it is a shoggoth.

"Call of Cthulhu" first appeared in *Weird Tales* in February 1928.

The Call of Cthulhu

(Found Among the Papers of the Late Francis Wayland Thurston, of Boston)

by H. P. Lovecraft

> Of such great powers or beings there may be conceivably a survival
> ... a survival of a hugely remote period when ... consciousness was
> manifested, perhaps, in shapes and forms long since withdrawn before
> the tide of advancing humanity ... forms of which poetry and legend
> alone have caught a flying memory and called them gods, monsters,
> mythical beings of all sorts and kinds ....
>
> — Algernon Blackwood

I. The Horror in Clay

THE MOST MERCIFUL THING in the world, I think, is the inability of the human mind to correlate all its contents. We live on a placid island of ignorance in the midst of black seas of infinity, and it was not meant that we should voyage far. The sciences, each straining in its own direction, have hitherto harmed us little; but some day the piecing together of dissociated knowledge will open up such terrifying vistas of reality, and of our frightful position therein, that we shall either go mad from the revelation or flee from the deadly light into the peace and safety of a new dark age.

Theosophists have guessed at the awesome grandeur of the cosmic cycle wherein our world and human race form transient incidents. They have hinted at strange survivals in terms which would freeze the blood if not masked by a bland optimism. But it is not from them that there came the single glimpse of forbidden aeons which chills me when I think of it and maddens me when I dream of it. That glimpse, like all dread glimpses of truth, flashed out from an accidental piecing together of separated things—in this case an old newspaper item and the notes of a dead professor. I hope that no one else will accomplish this piecing out; certainly, if I live, I shall never knowingly supply a link in so hideous a chain. I think that the professor, too, intended to keep silent regarding the part he knew, and that he would have destroyed his notes had not sudden death seized him.

My knowledge of the thing began in the winter of 1926-27 with the death of my grand-uncle George Gammell Angell, Professor Emeritus of Semitic Languages in Brown University, Providence, Rhode Island. Professor Angell was widely known as an authority on ancient inscriptions, and had frequently been resorted to by the heads of prominent museums; so that his passing at the age of ninety-two may be recalled by many. Locally, interest was intensified by the obscurity of the cause of death. The professor had been stricken whilst returning from the Newport boat; falling suddenly, as witnesses said, after having been jostled by a nautical-looking Negro who had come from one of the queer dark courts on the precipitous hillside which formed a short cut from the waterfront to the deceased's home in Williams Street. Physicians were unable to find any visible disorder, but concluded after perplexed debate that some obscure lesion of the heart, induced by the brisk ascent of so steep a hill by so elderly a man, was responsible for the end. At the time I saw no reason to dissent from this dictum, but latterly I am inclined to wonder—and more than wonder.

As my grand-uncle's heir and executor, for he died a childless widower, I was expected to go over his papers with some thoroughness; and for that purpose moved his entire set of files and boxes to my quarters in Boston. Much of the material which I correlated will be later published by the American Archaeological Society, but there was one box which I found exceedingly puzzling, and which I felt much averse from shewing to other eyes. It had been locked, and I did not find the key till it occurred to me to examine the personal ring which the professor carried always in his pocket. Then indeed I succeeded in opening it, but when I did so seemed only to be confronted by a greater and more closely locked barrier. For what could be the meaning of the queer clay bas-relief and the disjointed jottings, ramblings, and cuttings which I found? Had my uncle, in his latter years, become credulous of the most superficial impostures? I resolved to search out the eccentric sculptor responsible for this apparent disturbance of an old man's peace of mind.

The bas-relief was a rough rectangle less than an inch thick and about five by six inches in area; obviously of modern origin. Its designs, however, were far from modern in atmosphere and suggestion; for although the vagaries of cubism and futurism are many and wild, they do not often reproduce that cryptic regularity which lurks in prehistoric writing. And writing of some kind the bulk of these designs seemed certainly to be; though my memory, despite much familiarity with the papers and collections of my uncle, failed in any way to identify this particular species, or even to hint at its remotest affiliations.

Above these apparent hieroglyphics was a figure of evidently pictorial intent, though its impressionistic execution forbade a very clear idea of its nature. It seemed to be a sort of monster, or symbol representing a monster, of a form which only a diseased fancy could conceive. If I say that my somewhat extravagant imagination yielded simultaneous pictures of an octopus, a dragon, and a human caricature, I shall not be unfaithful to the spirit of the thing. A pulpy, tentacled head surmounted a grotesque and scaly body with rudimentary wings; but it was the *general outline* of the whole which made it most shockingly frightful. Behind the figure was a vague suggestion of a Cyclopean architectural background.

The writing accompanying this oddity was, aside from a stack of press cuttings, in Professor Angell's most recent hand; and made no pretense to literary style. What seemed to be the main document was headed "CTHULHU CULT" in characters painstakingly printed to avoid the erroneous reading of a word so unheard-of. This manuscript was divided into two sections, the first of which was headed "1925-Dream and Dream Work of H. A. Wilcox, 7 Thomas St., Providence, R.I.", and the second, "Narrative of Inspector John R. Legrasse, 121 Bienville St., New Orleans, La., at 1908 A.A.S. Mtg.—Notes on Same, & Prof. Webb's Acct." The other manuscript papers were all brief notes, some of them accounts of the queer dreams of different persons, some of them citations from theosophical books and magazines (notably W. Scott Elliot's *Atlantis and the Lost Lemuria*), and the rest comments on long-surviving secret societies and hidden cults, with references to passages in such mythological and anthropological source-books as Frazer's *Golden Bough* and Miss Murray's *Witch-Cult in Western Europe*. The cuttings largely alluded to outré mental illnesses and outbreaks of group folly or mania in the spring of 1925.

The first half of the principal manuscript told a very peculiar tale. It appears that on March 1st, 1925, a thin, dark young man of neurotic and excited aspect had called upon Professor Angell bearing the singular clay bas-relief, which was then exceedingly damp and fresh. His card bore the name of Henry Anthony Wilcox, and my uncle had recognised him as the youngest son of an excellent family slightly known to him, who had latterly been studying sculpture at the Rhode Island School of Design and living alone at the Fleur-de-Lys Building near that institution. Wilcox was a precocious youth of known genius but great eccentricity, and had from childhood excited attention through the strange stories and odd dreams he was in the habit of relating. He called himself "psychically hypersensitive", but the staid folk of the ancient commercial city dismissed him as merely "queer." Never mingling much with his kind, he had dropped gradually from social visibility, and was now known only to a small group of aesthetes from other towns. Even the Providence Art Club, anxious to preserve its conservatism, had found him quite hopeless.

On the occasion of the visit, ran the professor's manuscript, the sculptor abruptly asked for the benefit of his host's archaeological knowledge in identifying the hieroglyphics on the bas-relief. He spoke in a dreamy, stilted manner which suggested pose and alienated sympathy; and my uncle shewed some sharpness in replying, for the conspicuous freshness of the tablet implied kinship with anything but archaeology. Young Wilcox's rejoinder, which impressed my uncle enough to make him recall and record it verbatim, was of a fantastically poetic cast which must have typified his whole conversation, and which I have since found highly characteristic of him. He said, "It is new, indeed, for I made it last night in a dream of strange cities; and dreams are older than brooding Tyre, or the contemplative Sphinx, or garden-girdled Babylon."

It was then that he began that rambling tale which suddenly played upon a sleeping memory and won the fevered interest of my uncle. There had been a slight earthquake tremor the night before, the most considerable felt in New England for some years; and Wilcox's imagination had been keenly affected. Upon retiring, he had had an unprecedented dream of great Cyclopean cities of titan blocks and sky-flung monoliths, all dripping with green ooze and sinister with latent horror. Hieroglyphics had covered the walls and pillars, and from some undetermined point below had come a voice that was not a voice; a chaotic sensation which only fancy could transmute into sound, but which he attempted to render by the almost unpronounceable jumble of letters, "*Cthulhu fhtagn.*"

This verbal jumble was the key to the recollection which excited and disturbed Professor Angell. He questioned the sculptor with scientific minuteness; and studied with almost frantic intensity the bas-relief on which the youth had found himself working, chilled and clad only in his night-clothes, when waking had stolen bewilderingly over him. My uncle blamed his old age, Wilcox afterward said, for his slowness in recognising both hieroglyphics and pictorial design. Many of his questions seemed highly out-of-place to his visitor, especially those which tried to connect the latter with strange cults or societies; and Wilcox could not understand the repeated promises of silence which he was offered in exchange for an admission of membership in some widespread mystical or paganly religious body. When Professor Angell became convinced that the sculptor was indeed ignorant of any cult or system of cryptic lore, he besieged his visitor with demands for future reports of dreams. This bore regular fruit, for after the first interview the manuscript records daily calls of the young man, during which he related startling fragments of nocturnal imagery whose burden was always some terrible Cyclopean vista of dark and dripping stone, with a subterrene voice or intelligence shouting monotonously in enigmatical sense-impacts uninscribable save as gibberish. The two sounds most frequently repeated are those rendered by the letters "*Cthulhu*" and "*R'lyeh.*"

On March 23rd, the manuscript continued, Wilcox failed to appear; and inquiries at his quarters revealed that he had been stricken with an obscure sort of fever and taken to the home of his family in Waterman Street. He had cried out in the night, arousing several other artists in the building, and had manifested since then only alternations of unconsciousness and delirium. My uncle at once telephoned the family, and from that time forward kept close watch of the case; calling often at the Thayer Street office of Dr. Tobey, whom he learned to be in charge. The youth's febrile mind, apparently, was dwelling on strange things; and the doctor shuddered now and then as he spoke of them. They included not only a repetition of what he had formerly dreamed, but touched wildly on a gigantic thing "miles high" which walked or lumbered about. He at no time fully described this object, but occasional frantic words, as repeated by Dr. Tobey, convinced the professor that it must be identical with the nameless monstrosity he had sought to depict in his dream-sculpture. Reference to this object, the doctor added, was invariably a prelude to the young man's subsidence into lethargy. His temperature, oddly enough, was not greatly above normal; but his whole condition was otherwise such as to suggest true fever rather than mental disorder.

On April 2nd at about 3 p.m. every trace of Wilcox's malady suddenly ceased. He sat upright in bed, astonished to find himself at home and completely ignorant of what had happened in dream or reality since the night of March 22nd. Pronounced well by his physician, he returned to his quarters in three days; but to Professor Angell he was of no further assistance. All traces of strange dreaming had vanished with his recovery, and my uncle kept no record of his night-thoughts after a week of pointless and irrelevant accounts of thoroughly usual visions.

Here the first part of the manuscript ended, but references to certain of the scattered notes gave me much material for thought—so much, in fact, that only the ingrained scepticism then forming my philosophy can account for my continued distrust of the artist. The notes in question were those descriptive of the dreams of various persons covering the same period as that in which young Wilcox had had his strange visitations. My uncle, it seems, had quickly instituted a prodigiously far-flung body of inquiries amongst nearly all the friends whom he could question without impertinence, asking for nightly reports of their dreams, and the dates of any notable visions for some time past. The reception of his request seems to have been varied; but he must, at the very least, have received more responses than any ordinary man could have handled without a secretary. This original correspondence was not preserved, but his notes formed a thorough and really significant digest. Average people in society and business—New England's traditional "salt of the earth"—gave an almost completely negative result, though scattered cases of uneasy but formless nocturnal impressions appear here and there, always between March 23rd and April 2nd—the period of young Wilcox's delirium. Scientific men were little more affected, though four cases of vague description suggest fugitive glimpses of strange landscapes, and in one case there is mentioned a dread of something abnormal.

It was from the artists and poets that the pertinent answers came, and I know that panic would have broken loose had they been able to compare notes. As it was, lacking their original letters, I half suspected the compiler of having asked leading questions, or of having edited the correspondence in corroboration of what he had latently resolved to see. That is why I continued to feel that Wilcox, somehow cognisant of the old data which my uncle had possessed, had been imposing on the veteran scientist. These responses from aesthetes told a disturbing tale. From February 28th to April 2nd a large proportion of them had dreamed very bizarre things, the intensity of the dreams being immeasurably the stronger during the period of the sculptor's delirium. Over a fourth of those who reported anything, reported scenes and half-sounds not unlike those which Wilcox had described; and some of the dreamers confessed acute fear of the gigantic nameless thing visible toward the last. One case, which the note describes with emphasis, was very sad. The subject, a widely known architect with leanings toward theosophy and occultism, went violently insane on the date of young Wilcox's seizure, and expired several months later after incessant screamings to be saved from some escaped denizen of hell. Had my uncle referred to these cases by name instead of merely by number, I should have attempted some corroboration and personal investigation; but as it was, I succeeded in tracing down only a few. All of these, however, bore out the notes in full. I have often wondered if all the objects of the professor's questioning felt as puzzled as did this fraction. It is well that no explanation shall ever reach them.

The press cuttings, as I have intimated, touched on cases of panic, mania, and eccentricity during the given period. Professor Angell must have employed a cutting bureau, for the number of extracts was tremendous and the sources scattered throughout the globe. Here was a nocturnal suicide in London, where a lone sleeper had leaped from a window after a shocking cry. Here likewise a rambling letter to the editor of a paper in South America, where a fanatic deduces a dire future from visions he has seen. A despatch from California describes a theosophist colony as donning white robes en masse for some "glorious fulfillment" which never arrives, whilst items from India speak guardedly of serious native unrest toward the end of March. Voodoo orgies multiply in Hayti, and African outposts report ominous mutterings. American officers in the Philippines find certain tribes bothersome at this time, and New York policemen are mobbed by hysterical Levantines on the night of March 22-23. The west of Ireland, too, is full of wild rumour and legendry, and a fantastic painter named Ardois-Bonnot hangs a blasphemous "Dream Landscape" in the Paris spring salon of 1926. And so numerous are the recorded troubles in insane asylums, that only a miracle can have stopped the medical fraternity from noting strange parallelisms and drawing mystified conclusions. A weird bunch of cuttings, all told; and I can at this date scarcely envisage the callous rationalism with which I set them aside. But I was then convinced that young Wilcox had known of the older matters mentioned by the professor.

II. The Tale of Inspector Legrasse.

The older matters which had made the sculptor's dream and bas-relief so significant to my uncle formed the subject of the second half of his long manuscript. Once before, it appears, Professor Angell had seen the hellish outlines of the nameless monstrosity, puzzled over the unknown hieroglyphics, and heard the ominous syllables which can be rendered only as "*Cthulhu*"; and all this in so stirring and horrible a connexion that it is small wonder he pursued young Wilcox with queries and demands for data.

This earlier experience had come in 1908, seventeen years before, when the American Archaeological Society held its annual meeting in St. Louis. Professor Angell, as befitted one of his authority and attainments, had had a prominent part in all the deliberations; and was one of the first to be approached by the several outsiders who took advantage of the convocation to offer questions for correct answering and problems for expert solution.

The chief of these outsiders, and in a short time the focus of interest for the entire meeting, was a commonplace-looking middle-aged man who had travelled all the way from New Orleans for certain special information unobtainable from any local source. His name was John Raymond Legrasse, and he was by profession an Inspector of Police. With him he bore the subject of his visit, a grotesque, repulsive, and apparently very ancient stone statuette whose origin he was at a loss to determine. It must not be fancied that Inspector Legrasse had the least interest in archaeology. On the contrary, his wish for enlightenment was prompted by purely professional considerations. The statuette, idol, fetish, or whatever it was, had been captured some months before in the wooded swamps south of New Orleans during a raid on a supposed voodoo meeting; and so singular and hideous were the rites connected with it, that the police could not but realise that they had stumbled on a dark cult totally unknown to them, and infinitely more diabolic than even the blackest of the African voodoo circles. Of its origin, apart from the erratic and unbelievable tales extorted from the captured members, absolutely nothing was to be discovered; hence the anxiety of the police for any antiquarian lore which might help them to place the frightful symbol, and through it track down the cult to its fountain-head.

Inspector Legrasse was scarcely prepared for the sensation which his offering created. One sight of the thing had been enough to throw the assembled men of science into a state of tense excitement, and they lost no time in crowding around him to gaze at the diminutive figure whose utter strangeness and air of genuinely abysmal antiquity hinted so potently at unopened and archaic vistas. No recognised school of sculpture had animated this terrible object, yet centuries and even thousands of years seemed recorded in its dim and greenish surface of unplaceable stone.

The figure, which was finally passed slowly from man to man for close and careful study, was between seven and eight inches in height, and of exquisitely artistic workmanship. It represented a monster of vaguely anthropoid outline, but with an octopus-like head whose face was a mass of feelers, a scaly, rubbery-looking body, prodigious claws on hind and fore feet, and long, narrow wings behind. This thing, which seemed instinct with a fearsome and unnatural malignancy, was of a somewhat bloated corpulence, and squatted evilly on a rectangular block or pedestal covered with undecipherable characters. The tips of the wings touched the back edge of the block, the seat occupied the centre, whilst the long, curved claws of the doubled-up, crouching hind legs gripped the front edge and extended a quarter of the way toward the bottom of the pedestal. The cephalopod head was bent forward, so that the ends of the facial feelers brushed the backs of huge fore paws which clasped the croucher's elevated knees. The aspect of the whole was abnormally life-like, and the more subtly fearful because its source was so totally unknown. Its vast, awesome, and incalculable age was unmistakable; yet not one link did it shew with any known type of art belonging to civilisation's youth—or indeed to any other time. Totally separate and apart, its very material was a mystery; for the soapy, greenish-black stone with its golden or iridescent flecks and striations resembled nothing familiar to geology or mineralogy. The characters along the base were equally baffling; and no member present, despite a representation of half the world's expert learning in this field, could form the least notion of even their remotest linguistic kinship. They, like the subject and material, belonged to something horribly remote and distinct from mankind as we know it; something frightfully suggestive of old and unhallowed cycles of life in which our world and our conceptions have no part.

And yet, as the members severally shook their heads and confessed defeat at the Inspector's problem, there was one man in that gathering who suspected a touch of bizarre familiarity in the monstrous shape and writing, and who presently told with some diffidence of the odd trifle he knew. This person was the late William Channing Webb, Professor of Anthropology in Princeton University, and an explorer of no slight note. Professor Webb had been engaged, forty-eight years before, in a tour of Greenland and Iceland in search of some Runic inscriptions which he failed to unearth; and whilst high up on the West Greenland coast had encountered a singular tribe or cult of degenerate Esquimaux whose religion, a curious form of devil-worship, chilled him with its deliberate bloodthirstiness and repulsiveness. It was a faith of which other Esquimaux knew little, and which they mentioned only with shudders, saying that it had come down from horribly ancient aeons before ever the world was made. Besides nameless rites and human sacrifices there were certain queer hereditary rituals addressed to a supreme elder devil or *tornasuk*; and of this Professor Webb had taken a careful phonetic copy from an aged *angekok* or wizard-priest, expressing the sounds in Roman letters as best he knew how. But just now of prime significance was the fetish which this cult had cherished, and around which they danced when the aurora leaped high over the ice cliffs. It was, the professor stated, a very crude bas-relief of stone, comprising a hideous picture and some cryptic writing. And so far as he could tell, it was a rough parallel in all essential features of the bestial thing now lying before the meeting.

This data, received with suspense and astonishment by the assembled members, proved doubly exciting to Inspector Legrasse; and he began at once to ply his informant with questions. Having noted and copied an oral ritual among the swamp cult-worshippers his men had arrested, he besought the professor to remember as best he might the syllables taken down amongst the diabolist Esquimaux. There then followed an exhaustive comparison of details, and a moment of really awed silence when both detective and scientist agreed on the virtual identity of the phrase common to two hellish rituals so many worlds of distance apart. What, in substance, both the Esquimaux wizards and the Louisiana swamp-priests had chanted to their kindred idols was something very like this—the word-divisions being guessed at from traditional breaks in the phrase as chanted aloud:

"Ph'nglui mglw'nafh Cthulhu R'lyeh wgah'nagl fhtagn."

Legrasse had one point in advance of Professor Webb, for several among his mongrel prisoners had repeated to him what older celebrants had told them the words meant. This text, as given, ran something like this:

"In his house at R'lyeh dead Cthulhu waits dreaming."

And now, in response to a general and urgent demand, Inspector Legrasse related as fully as possible his experience with the swamp worshippers; telling a story to which I could see my uncle attached profound significance. It savoured of the wildest dreams of myth-maker and theosophist, and disclosed an astonishing degree of cosmic imagination among such half-castes and pariahs as might be least expected to possess it.

On November 1st, 1907, there had come to the New Orleans police a frantic summons from the swamp and lagoon country to the south. The squatters there, mostly primitive but good-natured descendants of Lafitte's men, were in the grip of stark terror from an unknown thing which had stolen upon them in the night. It was voodoo, apparently, but voodoo of a more terrible sort than they had ever known; and some of their women and children had disappeared since the malevolent tom-tom had begun its incessant beating far within the black haunted woods where no dweller ventured. There were insane shouts and harrowing screams, soul-chilling chants and dancing devil-flames; and, the frightened messenger added, the people could stand it no more.

So a body of twenty police, filling two carriages and an automobile, had set out in the late afternoon with the shivering squatter as a guide. At the end of the passable road they alighted, and for miles splashed on in silence through the terrible cypress woods where day never came. Ugly roots and malignant hanging nooses of Spanish moss beset them, and now and then a pile of dank stones or fragment of a rotting wall intensified by its hint of morbid habitation a depression which every malformed tree and every fungous islet combined to create. At length the squatter settlement, a miserable huddle of huts, hove in sight; and hysterical dwellers ran out to cluster around the group of bobbing lanterns. The muffled beat of tom-toms was now faintly audible far, far ahead; and a curdling shriek came at infrequent intervals when the wind shifted. A reddish glare, too, seemed to filter through pale undergrowth beyond the endless avenues of forest night. Reluctant even to be left alone again, each one of the cowed squatters refused point-blank to advance another inch toward the scene of unholy worship, so Inspector Legrasse and his nineteen colleagues plunged on unguided into black arcades of horror that none of them had ever trod before.

The region now entered by the police was one of traditionally evil repute, substantially unknown and untraversed by white men. There were legends of a hidden lake unglimpsed by mortal sight, in which dwelt a huge, formless white polypous thing with luminous eyes; and squatters whispered that bat-winged devils flew up out of caverns in inner earth to worship it at midnight. They said it had been there before d'Iberville, before La Salle, before the Indians, and before even the wholesome beasts and birds of the woods. It was nightmare itself, and to see it was to die. But it made men dream, and so they knew enough to keep away. The present voodoo orgy was, indeed, on the merest fringe of this abhorred area, but that location was bad enough; hence perhaps the very place of the worship had terrified the squatters more than the shocking sounds and incidents.

Only poetry or madness could do justice to the noises heard by Legrasse's men as they ploughed on through the black morass toward the red glare and muffled tom-toms. There are vocal qualities peculiar to men, and vocal qualities peculiar to beasts; and it is terrible to hear the one when the source should yield the other. Animal fury and orgiastic license here whipped themselves to daemoniac heights by howls and squawking ecstacies that tore and reverberated through those nighted woods like pestilential tempests from the gulfs of hell. Now and then the less organized ululation would cease, and from what seemed a well-drilled chorus of hoarse voices would rise in sing-song chant that hideous phrase or ritual: "*Ph'nglui mglw'nafh Cthulhu R'lyeh wgah'nagl fhtagn.*"

Then the men, having reached a spot where the trees were thinner, came suddenly in sight of the spectacle itself. Four of them reeled, one fainted, and two were shaken into a frantic cry which the mad cacophony of the orgy fortunately deadened. Legrasse dashed swamp water on the face of the fainting man, and all stood trembling and nearly hypnotised with horror.

In a natural glade of the swamp stood a grassy island of perhaps an acre's extent, clear of trees and tolerably dry. On this now leaped and twisted a more indescribable horde of human abnormality than any but a Sime or an Angarola could paint. Void of clothing, this hybrid spawn were braying, bellowing, and writhing about a monstrous ring-shaped bonfire; in the centre of which, revealed by occasional rifts in the curtain of flame, stood a great granite monolith some eight feet in height; on top of which, incongruous in its diminutiveness, rested the noxious carven statuette. From a wide circle of ten scaffolds set up at regular intervals with the flame-girt monolith as a centre hung, head downward, the oddly marred bodies of the helpless squatters who had disappeared. It was inside this circle that the ring of worshippers jumped and roared, the general direction of the mass motion being from left to right in endless Bacchanal between the ring of bodies and the ring of fire.

It may have been only imagination and it may have been only echoes which induced one of the men, an excitable Spaniard, to fancy he heard antiphonal responses to the ritual from some far and unillumined spot deeper within the wood of ancient legendry and horror. This man, Joseph D. Galvez, I later met and questioned; and he proved distractingly imaginative. He indeed went so far as to hint of the faint beating of great wings, and of a glimpse of shining eyes and a mountainous white bulk beyond the remotest trees—but I suppose he had been hearing too much native superstition.

Actually, the horrified pause of the men was of comparatively brief duration. Duty came first; and although there must have been nearly a hundred mongrel celebrants in the throng, the police relied on their firearms and plunged determinedly into the nauseous rout. For five minutes the resultant din and chaos were beyond description. Wild blows were struck, shots were fired, and escapes were made; but in the end Legrasse was able to count some forty-seven sullen prisoners, whom he forced to dress in haste and fall into line between two rows of policemen. Five of the worshippers lay dead, and two severely wounded ones were carried away on improvised stretchers by their fellow-prisoners. The image on the monolith, of course, was carefully removed and carried back by Legrasse.

Examined at headquarters after a trip of intense strain and weariness, the prisoners all proved to be men of a very low, mixed-blooded, and mentally aberrant type. Most were seamen, and a sprinkling of Negroes and mulattoes, largely West Indians or Brava Portuguese from the Cape Verde Islands, gave a colouring of voodooism to the heterogeneous cult. But before many questions were asked, it became manifest that something far deeper and older than Negro fetichism was involved. Degraded and ignorant as they were, the creatures held with surprising consistency to the central idea of their loathsome faith.

They worshipped, so they said, the Great Old Ones who lived ages before there were any men, and who came to the young world out of the sky. Those Old Ones were gone now, inside the earth and under the sea; but their dead bodies had told their secrets in dreams to the first men, who formed a cult which had never died. This was that cult, and the prisoners said it had always existed and always would exist, hidden in distant wastes and dark places all over the world until the time when the great priest Cthulhu, from his dark house in the mighty city of R'lyeh under the waters, should rise and bring the earth again beneath his sway. Some day he would call, when the stars were ready, and the secret cult would always be waiting to liberate him.

Meanwhile no more must be told. There was a secret which even torture could not extract. Mankind was not absolutely alone among the conscious things of earth, for shapes came out of the dark to visit the faithful few. But these were not the Great Old Ones. No man had ever seen the Old Ones. The carven idol was great Cthulhu, but none might say whether or not the others were precisely like him. No one could read the old writing now, but things were told by word of mouth. The chanted ritual was not the secret—that was never spoken aloud, only whispered. The chant meant only this: "In his house at R'lyeh dead Cthulhu waits dreaming."

Only two of the prisoners were found sane enough to be hanged, and the rest were committed to various institutions. All denied a part in the ritual murders, and averred that the killing had been done by Black Winged Ones which had come to them from their immemorial meeting-place in the haunted wood. But of those mysterious allies no coherent account could ever be gained. What the police did extract, came mainly from the immensely aged mestizo named Castro, who claimed to have sailed to strange ports and talked with undying leaders of the cult in the mountains of China.

Old Castro remembered bits of hideous legend that paled the speculations of theosophists and made man and the world seem recent and transient indeed. There had been aeons when other

Things ruled on the earth, and They had had great cities. Remains of Them, he said the deathless Chinamen had told him, were still to be found as Cyclopean stones on islands in the Pacific. They all died vast epochs of time before men came, but there were arts which could revive Them when the stars had come round again to the right positions in the cycle of eternity. They had, indeed, come themselves from the stars, and brought Their images with Them.

These Great Old Ones, Castro continued, were not composed altogether of flesh and blood. They had shape—for did not this star-fashioned image prove it?—but that shape was not made of matter. When the stars were right, They could plunge from world to world through the sky; but when the stars were wrong, They could not live. But although They no longer lived, They would never really die. They all lay in stone houses in Their great city of R'lyeh, preserved by the spells of mighty Cthulhu for a glorious resurrection when the stars and the earth might once more be ready for Them. But at that time some force from outside must serve to liberate Their bodies. The spells that preserved Them intact likewise prevented Them from making an initial move, and They could only lie awake in the dark and think whilst uncounted millions of years rolled by. They knew all that was occurring in the universe, for Their mode of speech was transmitted thought. Even now They talked in Their tombs. When, after infinities of chaos, the first men came, the Great Old Ones spoke to the sensitive among them by moulding their dreams; for only thus could Their language reach the fleshly minds of mammals.

Then, whispered Castro, those first men formed the cult around small idols which the Great Ones shewed them; idols brought in dim eras from dark stars. That cult would never die till the stars came right again, and the secret priests would take great Cthulhu from His tomb to revive His subjects and resume His rule of earth. The time would be easy to know, for then mankind would have become as the Great Old Ones; free and wild and beyond good and evil, with laws and morals thrown aside and all men shouting and killing and revelling in joy. Then the liberated Old Ones would teach them new ways to shout and kill and revel and enjoy themselves, and all the earth would flame with a holocaust of ecstasy and freedom. Meanwhile the cult, by appropriate rites, must keep alive the memory of those ancient ways and shadow forth the prophecy of their return.

In the elder time chosen men had talked with the entombed Old Ones in dreams, but then something happened. The great stone city R'lyeh, with its monoliths and sepulchres, had sunk beneath the waves; and the deep waters, full of the one primal mystery through which not even thought can pass, had cut off the spectral intercourse. But memory never died, and the high-priests said that the city would rise again when the stars were right. Then came out of the earth the black spirits of earth, mouldy and shadowy, and full of dim rumours picked up in caverns beneath forgotten sea-bottoms. But of them old Castro dared not speak much. He cut himself off hurriedly, and no amount of persuasion or subtlety could elicit more in this direction. The *size* of the Old Ones, too, he curiously declined to mention. Of the cult, he said that he thought the centre lay amid the pathless desert of Arabia, where Irem, the City of Pillars, dreams hidden and untouched. It was not allied to the European witch-cult, and was virtually unknown beyond its members. No book had ever really hinted of it, though the deathless Chinamen said that there were double meanings in the *Necronomicon* of the mad Arab Abdul Alhazred which the initiated might read as they chose, especially the much-discussed couplet:

> That is not dead which can eternal lie,
> And with strange aeons even death may die.

Legrasse, deeply impressed and not a little bewildered, had inquired in vain concerning the historic affiliations of the cult. Castro, apparently, had told the truth when he said that it was wholly secret. The authorities at Tulane University could shed no light upon either cult or image, and now the detective had come to the highest authorities in the country and met with no more than the Greenland tale of Professor Webb.

The feverish interest aroused at the meeting by Legrasse's tale, corroborated as it was by the statuette, is echoed in the subsequent correspondence of those who attended; although scant mention occurs in the formal publications of the society. Caution is the first care of those accustomed to face occasional charlatanry and imposture. Legrasse for some time lent the image to Professor Webb, but at the latter's death it was returned to him and remains in his possession, where I viewed it not long ago. It is truly a terrible thing, and unmistakably akin to the dream-sculpture of young Wilcox.

That my uncle was excited by the tale of the sculptor I did not wonder, for what thoughts must arise upon hearing, after a knowledge of what Legrasse had learned of the cult, of a sensitive young man who had *dreamed* not only the figure and exact hieroglyphics of the swamp-found image and the Greenland devil tablet, but had come *in his dreams* upon at least three of the precise words of the formula uttered alike by Esquimau diabolists and mongrel Louisianans? Professor Angell's instant start on an investigation of the utmost thoroughness was eminently natural; though privately I suspected young Wilcox of having heard of the cult in some indirect way, and of having invented a series of dreams to heighten and continue the mystery at my uncle's expense. The dream-narratives and cuttings collected by the professor were, of course, strong corroboration; but the rationalism of my mind and the extravagance of the whole subject led me to adopt what I thought the most sensible conclusions. So, after thoroughly studying the manuscript again and correlating the theosophical and anthropological notes with the cult narrative of Legrasse, I made a trip to Providence to see the sculptor and give him the rebuke I thought proper for so boldly imposing upon a learned and aged man.

Wilcox still lived alone in the Fleur-de-Lys Building in Thomas Street, a hideous Victorian imitation of seventeenth-century Breton architecture which flaunts its stuccoed front amidst the lovely colonial houses on the ancient hill, and under the very shadow of the finest Georgian steeple in America, I found him at work in his rooms, and at once conceded from the specimens scattered about that his genius is indeed profound and authentic. He will, I believe, some time be heard from as one of the great decadents; for he has crystallised in clay and will one day mirror in marble those nightmares and phantasies which Arthur Machen evokes in prose, and Clark Ashton Smith makes visible in verse and in painting.

Dark, frail, and somewhat unkempt in aspect, he turned languidly at my knock and asked me my business without rising. When I told him who I was, he displayed some interest; for my uncle had excited his curiosity in probing his strange dreams, yet had never explained the reason for the study. I did not enlarge his knowledge in this regard, but sought with some subtlety to draw him out. In a short time I became convinced of his absolute sincerity, for he spoke of the dreams in a manner none could mistake. They and their subconscious residuum had influenced his art profoundly, and he shewed me a morbid statue whose contours almost made me

shake with the potency of its black suggestion. He could not recall
having seen the original of this thing except in his own dream
bas-relief, but the outlines had formed themselves insensibly under
his hands. It was, no doubt, the giant shape he had raved of in
delirium. That he really knew nothing of the hidden cult, save from
what my uncle's relentless catechism had let fall, he soon made clear;
and again I strove to think of some way in which he could possibly
have received the weird impressions.

He talked of his dreams in a strangely poetic fashion; making me
see with terrible vividness the damp Cyclopean city of slimy green
stone—whose *geometry*, he oddly said, was *all wrong*—and hear with
frightened expectancy the ceaseless, half-mental calling from underground: *"Cthulhu fhtagn"*, *"Cthulhu fhtagn."* These words had
formed part of that dread ritual which told of dead Cthulhu's
dream-vigil in his stone vault at R'lyeh, and I felt deeply moved
despite my rational beliefs. Wilcox, I was sure, had heard of the cult
in some casual way, and had soon forgotten it amidst the mass of
his equally weird reading and imagining. Later, by virtue of its sheer
impressiveness, it had found subconscious expression in dreams, in
the bas-relief, and in the terrible statue I now beheld; so that his
imposture upon my uncle had been a very innocent one. The youth
was of a type, at once slightly affected and slightly ill-mannered,
which I could never like, but I was willing enough now to admit
both his genius and his honesty. I took leave of him amicably, and
wish him all the success his talent promises.

The matter of the cult still remained to fascinate me, and at times
I had visions of personal fame from researches into its origin and
connexions. I visited New Orleans, talked with Legrasse and others
of that old-time raiding-party, saw the frightful image, and even
questioned such of the mongrel prisoners as still survived. Old
Castro, unfortunately, had been dead for some years. What I now
heard so graphically at first-hand, though it was really no more than
a detailed confirmation of what my uncle had written, excited me
afresh; for I felt sure that I was on the track of a very real, very secret,
and very ancient religion whose discovery would make me an
anthropologist of note. My attitude was still one of absolute mate-
rialism, *as I wish it still were*, and I discounted with almost
inexplicable perversity the coincidence of the dream notes and odd
cuttings collected by Professor Angell.

One thing I began to suspect, and which I now fear I *know*, is that
my uncle's death was far from natural. He fell on a narrow hill street

leading up from an ancient waterfront swarming with foreign mongrels, after a careless push from a Negro sailor. I did not forget the mixed blood and marine pursuits of the cult-members in Louisiana, and would not be surprised to learn of secret methods and rites and beliefs. Legrasse and his men, it is true, have been let alone; but in Norway a certain seaman who saw things is dead. Might not the deeper inquiries of my uncle after encountering the sculptor's data have come to sinister ears? I think Professor Angell died because he knew too much, or because he was likely to learn too much. Whether I shall go as he did remains to be seen, for I have learned much now.

III. The Madness from the Sea

If heaven ever wishes to grant me a boon, it will be a total effacing of the results of a mere chance which fixed my eye on a certain stray piece of shelf-paper. It was nothing on which I would naturally have stumbled in the course of my daily round, for it was an old number of an Australian journal, the *Sydney Bulletin* for April 18, 1925. It had escaped even the cutting bureau which had at the time of its issuance been avidly collecting material for my uncle's research.

I had largely given over my inquiries into what Professor Angell called the "Cthulhu Cult", and was visiting a learned friend in Paterson, New Jersey; the curator of a local museum and a mineralogist of note. Examining one day the reserve specimens roughly set on the storage shelves in a rear room of the museum, my eye was caught by an odd picture in one of the old papers spread beneath the stones. It was the *Sydney Bulletin* I have mentioned, for my friend had wide affiliations in all conceivable foreign parts; and the picture was a half-tone cut of a hideous stone image almost identical with that which Legrasse had found in the swamp.

Eagerly clearing the sheet of its precious contents, I scanned the item in detail; and was disappointed to find it of only moderate length. What it suggested, however, was of portentous significance to my flagging quest; and I carefully tore it out for immediate action. It read as follows:

MYSTERY DERELICT FOUND AT SEA

Vigilant Arrives With Helpless Armed New Zealand Yacht in Tow.

One Survivor and Dead Man Found Aboard. Tale of Desperate
Battle and Deaths at Sea.

Rescued Seaman Refuses Particulars of Strange Experience.

Odd Idol Found in His Possession. Inquiry to Follow.

The Morrison Co.'s freighter *Vigilant*, bound from Valparaiso, arrived
this morning at its wharf in Darling Harbour, having in tow the battled and
disabled but heavily armed steam yacht *Alert* of Dunedin, N.Z., which was
sighted April 12th in S. Latitude 34°21′, W. Longitude 152°17′ with one
living and one dead man aboard.

The *Vigilant* left Valparaiso March 25th, and on April 2nd was driven
considerably south of her course by exceptionally heavy storms and monster
waves. On April 12th the derelict was sighted; and though apparently deserted, was found upon boarding to contain one survivor in a half-delirious
condition and one man who had evidently been dead for more than a week.
The living man was clutching a horrible stone idol of unknown origin, about a
foot in height, regarding whose nature authorities at Sydney University, the
Royal Society, and the Museum in College Street all profess complete bafflement, and which the survivor says he found in the cabin of the yacht, in a
small carved shrine of common pattern.

This man, after recovering his senses, told an exceedingly strange story of
piracy and slaughter. He is Gustaf Johansen, a Norwegian of some intelligence,
and had been second mate of the two-masted schooner *Emma* of Auckland,
which sailed for Callao February 20th with a complement of eleven men. The
Emma, he says, was delayed and thrown widely south of her course by the great
storm of March 1st, and on March 22nd, in S. Latitude 49°51′, W. Longitude
128°34′, encountered the *Alert*, manned by a queer and evil-looking crew of
Kanakas and half-castes. Being ordered peremptorily to turn back, Capt. Collins refused; whereupon the strange crew began to fire savagely and without
warning upon the schooner with a peculiarly heavy battery of brass cannon
forming part of the yacht's equipment. The *Emma*'s men shewed fight, says the
survivor, and though the schooner began to sink from shots beneath the waterline they managed to heave alongside their enemy and board her, grappling
with the savage crew on the yacht's deck, and being forced to kill them all, the
number being slightly superior, because of their particularly abhorrent and desperate though rather clumsy mode of fighting.

Three of the *Emma*'s men, including Capt. Collins and First Mate Green,
were killed; and the remaining eight under Second Mate Johansen proceeded
to navigate the captured yacht, going ahead in their original direction to see if
any reason for their ordering back had existed. The next day, it appears, they
raised and landed on a small island, although none is known to exist in that
part of the ocean; and six of the men somehow died ashore, though Johansen is
queerly reticent about this part of his story, and speaks only of their falling into
a rock chasm. Later, it seems, he and one companion boarded the yacht and

tried to manage her, but were beaten about by the storm of April 2nd. From that time till his rescue on the 12th the man remembers little, and he does not even recall when William Briden, his companion, died. Briden's death reveals no apparent cause, and was probably due to excitement or exposure. Cable advices from Dunedin report that the *Alert* was well known there as an island trader, and bore an evil reputation along the waterfront. It was owned by a curious group of half-castes whose frequent meetings and night trips to the woods attracted no little curiosity; and it had set sail in great haste just after the storm and earth tremors of March 1st. Our Auckland correspondent gives the *Emma* and her crew an excellent reputation, and Johansen is described as a sober and worthy man. The admiralty will institute an inquiry on the whole matter beginning tomorrow, at which every effort will be made to induce Johansen to speak more freely than he has done hitherto.

This was all, together with the picture of the hellish image; but what a train of ideas it started in my mind! Here were new treasuries of data on the Cthulhu Cult, and evidence that it had strange interests at sea as well as on land. What motive prompted the hybrid crew to order back the *Emma* as they sailed about with their hideous idol? What was the unknown island on which six of the *Emma's* crew had died, and about which the mate Johansen was so secretive? What had the vice-admiralty's investigation brought out, and what was known of the noxious cult in Dunedin? And most marvellous of all, what deep and more than natural linkage of dates was this which gave a malign and now undeniable significance to the various turns of events so carefully noted by my uncle?

March 1st—our February 28th according to the International Date Line—the earthquake and storm had come. From Dunedin the *Alert* and her noisome crew had darted eagerly forth as if imperiously summoned, and on the other side of the earth poets and artists had begun to dream of a strange, dank Cyclopean city whilst a young sculptor had moulded in his sleep the form of the dreaded Cthulhu. March 23rd the crew of the *Emma* landed on an unknown island and left six men dead; and on that date the dreams of sensitive men assumed a heightened vividness and darkened with dread of a giant monster's malign pursuit, whilst an architect had gone mad and a sculptor had lapsed suddenly into delirium! And what of this storm of April 2nd—the date on which all dreams of the dank city ceased, and Wilcox emerged unharmed from the bondage of strange fever? What of all this—and of those hints of old Castro about the sunken, star-born Old Ones and their coming reign; their faithful cult *and their mastery of dreams*? Was I tottering on the brink of cosmic horrors beyond man's power to bear? If so, they must be horrors of the mind alone, for in some way the second of April had put a stop to whatever monstrous menace had begun its siege of mankind's soul.

That evening, after a day of hurried cabling and arranging, I bade my host adieu and took a train for San Francisco. In less than a month I was in Dunedin; where, however, I found that little was known of the strange cult-members who had lingered in the old sea-taverns. Waterfront scum was far too common for special mention; though there was vague talk about one inland trip these mongrels had made, during which faint drumming and red flame were noted on the distant hills. In Auckland I learned that Johansen had returned *with yellow hair turned white* after a perfunctory and inconclusive questioning at Sydney, and had thereafter sold his cottage in West Street and sailed with his wife to his old home in Oslo. Of his stirring experience he would tell his friends no more than he had told the admiralty officials, and all they could do was to give me his Oslo address.

After that I went to Sydney and talked profitlessly with seamen and members of the vice-admiralty court. I saw the *Alert*, now sold and in commercial use, at Circular Quay in Sydney Cove, but gained nothing from its non-committal bulk. The crouching image with its cuttlefish head, dragon body, scaly wings, and hieroglyphed pedestal, was preserved in the Museum at Hyde Park; and I studied it long and well, finding it a thing of balefully exquisite workmanship, and with the same utter mystery, terrible antiquity, and unearthly strangeness of material which I had noted in Legrasse's smaller specimen. Geologists, the curator told me, had found it a monstrous puzzle; for they vowed that the world held no rock like it. Then I thought with a shudder of what Old Castro had told Legrasse about the Great Ones; "They had come from the stars, and had brought Their images with Them."

Shaken with such a mental revolution as I had never before known, I now resolved to visit Mate Johansen in Oslo. Sailing for London, I reembarked at once for the Norwegian capital; and one autumn day landed at the trim wharves in the shadow of the Egeberg. Johansen's address, I discovered, lay in the Old Town of King Harold Haardrada, which kept alive the name of Oslo during all the centuries that the greater city masqueraded as "Christiana." I made the brief trip by taxicab, and knocked with palpitant heart at the door of a neat and ancient building with plastered front. A sad-faced woman in black answered my summons, and I was stung with disappointment when she told me in halting English that Gustaf Johansen was no more.

He had not long survived his return, said his wife, for the doings at sea in 1925 had broken him. He had told her no more than he had told the public, but had left a long manuscript—of "technical matters" as he said—written in English, evidently in order to safeguard her from the peril of casual perusal. During a walk through a narrow lane near the Gothenburg dock, a bundle of papers falling from an attic window had knocked him down. Two Lascar sailors at once helped him to his feet, but before the ambulance could reach him he was dead. Physicians found no adequate cause for the end, and laid it to heart trouble and a weakened constitution.

I now felt gnawing at my vitals that dark terror which will never leave me till I, too, am at rest; "accidentally" or otherwise. Persuading the widow that my connexion with her husband's "technical matters" was sufficient to entitle me to his manuscript, I bore the document away and began to read it on the London boat. It was a simple, rambling thing—a naive sailor's effort at a post-facto diary—and strove to recall day by day that last awful voyage. I cannot attempt to transcribe it verbatim in all its cloudiness and redundance, but I will tell its gist enough to shew why the sound of the water against the vessel's sides became so unendurable to me that I stopped my ears with cotton.

Johansen, thank God, did not know quite all, even though he saw the city and the Thing, but I shall never sleep calmly again when I think of the horrors that lurk ceaselessly behind life in time and in space, and of those unhallowed blasphemies from elder stars which dream beneath the sea, known and favoured by a nightmare cult ready and eager to loose them on the world whenever another earthquake shall heave their monstrous stone city again to the sun and air.

Johansen's voyage had begun just as he told it to the vice-admiralty. The *Emma*, in ballast, had cleared Auckland on February 20th, and had felt the full force of that earthquake-born tempest which must have heaved up from the sea-bottom the horrors that filled men's dreams. Once more under control, the ship was making good progress when held up by the *Alert* on March 22nd, and I could feel the mate's regret as he wrote of her bombardment and sinking. Of the swarthy cult-fiends on the *Alert* he speaks with significant horror. There was some peculiarly abominable quality about them which made their destruction seem almost a duty, and Johansen shews ingenuous wonder at the charge of ruthlessness brought against his party during the proceedings of the court of inquiry. Then, driven ahead by curiosity in their captured yacht under Johansen's command, the men sight a great stone pillar sticking out of the sea, and in S. Latitude 47°9′, W. Longitude 126°43′ come upon a coast-line of mingled mud, ooze, and weedy Cyclopean masonry which can be nothing less than the tangible substance of earth's supreme terror—the nightmare corpse-city of R'lyeh, that was built in measureless aeons behind history by the vast, loathsome shapes that seeped down from the dark stars. There lay great Cthulhu and his hordes, hidden in green slimy vaults and sending out at last, after cycles incalculable, the thoughts that spread fear to the dreams of the sensitive and called imperiously to the faithful to come on a pilgrimage of liberation and restoration. All this Johansen did not suspect, but God knows he soon saw enough!

I suppose that only a single mountain-top, the hideous mono-lith-crowned citadel whereon great Cthulhu was buried, actually emerged from the waters. When I think of the *extent* of all that may be brooding down there I almost wish to kill myself forthwith. Johansen and his men were awed by the cosmetic majesty of this dripping Babylon of elder daemons, and must have guessed without guidance that it was nothing of this or of any sane planet. Awe at the unbelievable size of the greenish stone blocks, at the dizzying height of the great carven monolith, and at the stupefying identity of the colossal statues and bas-reliefs with the queer image found in the shrine on the *Alert*, is poignantly visible in every line of the mate's frightened description.

Without knowing what futurism is like, Johansen achieved something very close to it when he spoke of the city; for instead of describing any definite structure or building, he dwells only on broad impressions of vast angles and stone surfaces—surfaces too great to belong to any thing right or proper for this earth, and impious with horrible images and hieroglyphs. I mention his talk about *angles* because it suggests something Wilcox had told me of his awful dreams. He said that the *geometry* of the dream-place he saw was abnormal, non-Euclidean, and loathsomely redolent of spheres and dimensions apart from ours. Now an unlettered seaman felt the same thing whilst gazing at the terrible reality.

Johansen and his men landed at a sloping mud-bank on this monstrous Acropolis, and clambered slipperily up over titan oozy blocks which could have been no mortal staircase. The very sun of heaven seemed distorted when viewed through the polarising miasma welling out from this sea-soaked perversion, and twisted menace and suspense lurked leeringly in those crazily elusive angles of carven rock where a second glance shewed concavity after the first shewed convexity.

Something very like fright had come over all the explorers before anything more definite than rock and ooze and weed was seen. Each would have fled had he not feared the scorn of the others, and it was only half-heartedly that they searched—vainly, as it proved—for some portable souvenir to bear away.

It was Rodriguez the Portuguese who climbed up the foot of the monolith and shouted of what he had found. The rest followed him, and looked curiously at the immense carved door with the now familiar squid-dragon bas-relief. It was, Johansen said, like a great barn-door; and they all felt that it was a door because of the ornate lintel, threshold, and jambs around it, though they could not decide whether it lay flat like a trap-door or slantwise like an outside cellar-door. As Wilcox would have said, the geometry of the place was all wrong. One could not be sure that the sea and the ground were horizontal, hence the relative position of everything else seemed phantasmally variable.

Briden pushed at the stone in several places without result. Then Donovan felt over it delicately around the edge, pressing each point separately as he went. He climbed interminably along the grotesque stone moulding—that is, one would call it climbing if the thing was not after all horizontal—and the men wondered how any door in the universe could be so vast. Then, very softly and slowly, the acre-great panel began to give inward at the top; and they saw that it was balanced. Donovan slid or somehow propelled himself down or along the jamb and rejoined his fellows, and everyone watched the queer recession of the monstrously carven portal. In this phantasy of prismatic distortion it moved anomalously in a diagonal way, so that all the rules of matter and perspective seemed upset.

The aperture was black with a darkness almost material. That tenebrousness was indeed a *positive quality*; for it obscured such parts of the inner walls as ought to have been revealed, and actually burst forth like smoke from its aeon-long imprisonment, visibly darkening the sun as it slunk away into the shrunken and gibbous sky on flapping membraneous wings. The odour rising from the newly opened depths was intolerable, and at length the quick-eared Hawkins thought he heard a nasty, slopping sound down there.

Everyone listened, and everyone was listening still when It lumbered slobberingly into sight and gropingly squeezed Its gelatinous green immensity through the black doorway into the tainted outside air of that poison city of madness.

Poor Johansen's handwriting almost gave out when he wrote of this. Of the six men who never reached the ship, he thinks two perished of pure fright in that accursed instant. The Thing cannot be described—there is no language for such abysms of shrieking and immemorial lunacy, such eldritch contradictions of all matter, force, and cosmic order. A mountain walked or stumbled. God! What wonder that across the earth a great architect went mad, and poor Wilcox raved with fever in that telepathic instant? The Thing of the idols, the green, sticky spawn of the stars, had awaked to claim his own. The stars were right again, and what an age-old cult had failed to do by design, a band of innocent sailors had done by accident. After vigintillions of years great Cthulhu was loose again, and ravening for delight.

Three men were swept up by the flabby claws before anybody turned. God rest them, if there be any rest in the universe. They were Donovan, Guerrera, and Angstrom. Parker slipped as the other three were plunging frenziedly over endless vistas of green-crusted rock to the boat, and Johansen swears he was swallowed up by an angle of masonry which shouldn't have been there; an angle which was acute, but behaved as if it were obtuse. So only Briden and Johansen reached the boat, and pulled desperately for the *Alert* as the mountainous monstrosity flopped down the slimy stones and hesitated floundering at the edge of the water.

Steam had not been suffered to go down entirely, despite the departure of all hands for the shore; and it was the work of only a few moments of feverish rushing up and down between wheel and engines to get the *Alert* under way. Slowly, amidst the distorted horrors of that indescribable scene, she began to churn the lethal waters; whilst on the masonry of that charnel shore that was not of earth the titan Thing from the stars slavered and gibbered like Polypheme cursing the fleeing ship of Odysseus. Then, bolder than the storied Cyclops, great Cthulhu slid greasily into the water and began to pursue with vast wave-raising strokes of cosmic potency. Briden looked back and went mad, laughing shrilly as he kept on laughing at intervals till death found him one night in the cabin whilst Johansen was wandering deliriously.

But Johansen had not given out yet. Knowing that the Thing could surely overtake the *Alert* until steam was fully up, he resolved on a desperate chance; and, setting the engine for full speed, ran lightning-like on deck and reversed the wheel. There was a mighty eddying and foaming in the noisome brine, and as the steam mounted higher and higher the brave Norwegian drove his vessel head on against the pursuing jelly which rose above the unclean froth like the stern of a daemon galleon. The awful squid-head with writhing feelers came nearly up to the bowsprit of the sturdy yacht, but Johansen drove on relentlessly. There was a bursting as of an exploding bladder, a slushy nastiness as of a cloven sunfish, a stench as of a thousand opened graves, and a sound that the chronicler could not put on paper. For an instant the ship was befouled by an acrid and blinding green cloud, and then there was only a venomous seething astern; where—God in heaven!—the scattered plasticity of that nameless sky-spawn was nebulously *recombining* in its hateful original form, whilst its distance widened every second as the *Alert* gained impetus from its mounting steam.

That was all. After that Johansen only brooded over the idol in the cabin and attended to a few matters of food for himself and the laughing maniac by his side. He did not try to navigate after the first bold flight, for the reaction had taken something out of his soul. Then came the storm of April 2nd, and a gathering of the clouds about his consciousness. There is a sense of spectral whirling through liquid gulfs of infinity, of dizzying rides through reeling universes on a comet's tail, and of hysterical plunges from the pit to the moon and from the moon back again to the pit, all livened by a cachinnating chorus of the distorted, hilarious elder gods and the green, bat-winged mocking imps of Tartarus.

Out of that dream came rescue—the *Vigilant*, the vice-admiralty court, the streets of Dunedin, and the long voyage back home to the old house by the Egeberg. He could not tell—they would think him mad. He would write of what he knew before death came, but his wife must not guess. Death would be a boon if only it could blot out the memories.

That was the document I read, and now I have placed it in the tin box beside the bas-relief and the papers of Professor Angell. With it shall go this record of mine—this test of my own sanity, wherein is pieced together that which I hope may never be pieced together again. I have looked upon all that the universe has to hold of horror, and even the skies of spring and the flowers of summer must ever afterward be poison to me. But I do not think my life will be long. As my uncle went, as poor Johansen went, so I shall go. I know too much, and the cult still lives.

Cthulhu still lives, too, I suppose, again in that chasm of stone which has shielded him since the sun was young. His accursed city is sunken once more, for the *Vigilant* sailed over the spot after the April storm; but his ministers on earth still bellow and prance and slay around idol-capped monoliths in lonely places. He must have been trapped by the sinking whilst within his black abyss, or else the world would by now be screaming with fright and frenzy. Who knows the end? What has risen may sink, and what has sunk may rise. Loathsomeness waits and dreams in the deep, and decay spreads over the tottering cities of men. A time will come—but I must not and cannot think! Let me pray that, if I do not survive this manuscript, my executors may put caution before audacity and see that it meets no other eye.

LOVECRAFT'S DEVOTEE, August Derleth, just could not get enough of Lovecraft's fiction or his mythology. He was the archetypal Lovecraft fan. His Lovecraftian fiction is archetypal fan pastiche. It is not that young fans unwittingly ape Derleth instead of Lovecraft in their teeth-cutting efforts at fiction, as has been suggested. It is simply that there is an embryonic stage of pastiche writing we all go through, and the products of this period, like gilled fetuses in the womb, are inevitably the same. It doesn't much matter whether you are reading the young Derleth, Campbell, Searight, Hasse, etc. The stories sound much the same. And this is because only certain elements of the mythology, the names, the books, etc., strike the youthful fancy, while lessons of plot structure, mood, atmosphere, etc., remain unlearned and unsuspected.

The stories making up *The Trail of Cthulhu* bear some of these traits, an Innsmouth look of sorts shared by fan pastiches. But they are quite enjoyable, once one gets over the disappointment that he is not reading more Lovecraft (itself a fannish reaction!).

Derleth's occult detective Dr. Laban Shrewsbury is, like Derleth's Solar Pons, a clone of Sherlock Holmes. It has been remarked that Derleth did a much better job pastiching Arthur Conan Doyle than he did Lovecraft. But in fact Shrewsbury's "amazing crew" of young anti-Cthulhuvians reminds one of nothing so much as Doc Savage and his aides!

"The Black Island" originally appeared in *Weird Tales* in January 1952.

The Black Island

by August W. Derleth

1.

THAT SOME RECORD OF THE EVENTS leading up to the so-called "top secret experiment" conducted at an uncharted South Pacific island on a September day in 1947 ought to be made, I have no question. That it would be wise is a moot point. There are some things against which the human race, which has in any event but a brief moment to remain on this planet to add to the brief moment of its previous existence, can be only inadequately forewarned and fore-armed; and, this being so, it is conceivable that it would be better to remain silent and let one's fellow men wait upon events.

In final analysis, however, there are judges far better qualified than I, and the progression of events both before and since that "experiment" has been so disturbing and so suggestive of incredibly ancient evil almost beyond man's grasp that I am compelled to make this record before time dims these events—if ever it could—or before my obliteration, which is inevitable, and may, indeed, be nearer than I think.

The episode began prosaically enough in the most famous bar in the world, in Singapore ....

I saw the five gentlemen sitting together when first I came into the bar and sat down. I was not far from them, and alone, and I looked at them casually, thinking that someone I knew might be among them. An elderly man with dark glasses and a strangely impressive countenance, and four young men, in late twenties or early thirties, intent upon some discussion conducted with considerable animation. I recognized no one; so I looked away. I had sat there perhaps ten minutes, perhaps a little less; Henry Caravel had come up and spoken to me in passing, and we had taken note of the time together; he had just gone when I heard my name spoken.

"Perhaps Mr. Blayne could enlighten us?"

The voice was cordial, well-modulated, with a peculiar carrying power.

Looking up, I saw the five gentlemen at their table gazing toward me expectantly. At that instant, the old man stood.

"Our discussion is archaeological in a sense, Mr. Blayne," he said directly. "If I may presume—I am Professor Laban Shrewsbury, a fellow American. Will you join us?"

I thanked him and, moved by a lively curiosity, went over to his table.

He introduced his companions—Andrew Phelan, Abel Keane, Claiborne Boyd, and Nayland Colum—and turned once more to me.

"Of course, we all know Horvath Blayne. We have been following with keen interest your papers on Angkor-Vat and the Khmer civilization, and, with even more interest, your studies among the ruins of Ponape. It is no coincidence that we are at the moment discussing the pantheon of Polynesian deities. Tell us, in your opinion, does the Polynesian sea-god, Tangaroa, have the same origin as Neptune?"

"Probably Hindu or Indo-Chinese in origin," I guessed.

"Those people are not primarily sea-farers," said the professor promptly. "There is a concept older than those civilizations, even if we concede at once that the Polynesian civilization is much younger than those of the Asiatic continent which gave rise to them. No, we are not interested so much in their relation to other figures in the pantheon, as to the conceit which gave them being in the first place. And to its relation to so many batrachian or ichthyic figures and motifs which occur and recur in the art work, ancient and modern, to be found in the South Pacific islands."

I protested that I was not primarily an artist, and certainly could not presume to be a critic of art.

The professor brushed this aside with courteous detachment. "But you are familiar with art. And I wonder whether you can explain why the primitives of the South Pacific should emphasize the batrachian or ichthyic in their artifacts and arts, while the primitives of the North Pacific, for example, emphasize characteristics which are clearly avian. There are exceptions, of course; you will recognize them. The lizard figures of Easter Island and the batrachian pieces from Melanesia and Micronesia are common to these areas; the avian masks and headdresses of the North Pacific Indian tribes are common to the Canadian coast. But we find on occasion among those coastal Indian tribes disturbingly familiar motifs; consider, for instance, the markedly batrachian aspects of

the shaman's headdress of the Haida tribe common to Prince of
Wales Island and the ceremonial shark headdress of the Tlingit of
Ketchikan, Alaska. The totems of the North Pacific Indians are
primarily avian in concept, whereas such things as the ancestor
figures carved into the tree-ferns of the New Hebrides quite clearly
suggest aquatic dwellers."

I remarked that ancestor-worship was common to the Asiatic continent.

But this was not his principal thesis, which I recognized in the
expectance with which his companions attended to him. He came
to it presently. Apropos the sea-deities of primitive peoples, had I
ever encountered in my archaeological inquiries any of the legends
pertaining to the mythological being, Cthulhu, whom he regarded
as the progenitor of all sea-gods and the lesser deities connected
with water as an element?

The comments he had made now fell into a distinct and well-knit
pattern. Cthulhu, as the ancient god of water, the seas, a water
elemental in a sense, must be considered as the primal deity of the
South Pacific, while the avian motifs expressed in the artifacts and
works of art common to the North Pacific derived from a worship
of an air elemental rather than one of the sea. I was indeed familiar
with the Cthulhu Mythos, with its remarkable lore in essence so
similar to the Christian Mythos of the expulsion of Sathanus and
his followers and their ever-ceaseless attempts to reconquer heaven.

The mythos, as I recalled it while listening to the professor speak
engagingly of Cthulhu, turned on a conflict between beings known
as the Elder Gods, who presumably inhabited the cosmos many
light-years away, and lesser beings called the Ancient Ones or the
Great Old Ones, who were presumably the motive forces of evil as
opposed to those representing good, who were the benevolent Elder
Gods. All had apparently existed in harmony at one time, but then
a revolt on the part of the Ancient Ones—who were Cthulhu,
master of the waters; Hastur, who roamed the interplanetary spaces
before his imprisonment in the dark Lake of Hali; Yog-Sothoth,
most powerful of the Ancient Ones; Ithaqua, the god of the winds;
Tsathoggua and Shub-Niggurath, gods of the earth and of fecun-
dity; Nyarlathotep, their dread messenger; and others—resulted in
their vanquishment and banishment to various places in the universe, from which they hoped to rise once more against the Elder
Gods, and where they were served by their minions, cults of men
and animals reared in their service. There were, additionally, per-

taining to Cthulhu, supposedly inhabiting a secret place on Earth, rather shockingly suggestive legends that certain of his batrachian followers, known as the Deep Ones, had mated with men and produced a horrible travesty of mankind known to be habitants of certain coastal Massachusetts towns.

Moreover, the Cthulhu Mythos had sprung from a collection of incredibly old manuscripts and similar sources purporting to be factual accounts, though nothing was adduced to prove them anything other than fiction of a highly skilled order; these manuscripts and books—the *Necronomicon* of the mad Arab, Abdul Alhazred; the *Cultes des Goules*, the work of an eccentric French nobleman, the Count d'Erlette; the *Unaussprechlichen Kulten* of von Junzt, a known aberrant who had roamed Europe and Asia in search of the remnants of old cults; the *Celaeno Fragments*; the *R'lyeh Text*; the *Pnakotic Manuscript*; and the like—had been seized upon by writers of contemporary fiction and freely used as the source for incredible tales of fantasy and the macabre, and these had given a kind of aura of authenticity to what, at best, was a collection of lore and legends perhaps unique in the annals of mankind but surely little more.

"But you are skeptical, Mr. Blayne," observed the professor.

"I'm afraid I have the scientific mind," I answered.

"I rather think all of us here think similarly of ourselves," he said.

"Am I to understand that you believe in this volume of lore?"

He gazed at me disconcertingly from behind his dark spectacles.

"Mr. Blayne, for more than three decades I have been on the trail of Cthulhu. Time after time I have believed that I have closed his avenues of ingress into our time; time after time I have been misled in thinking so."

"Then if you believe one aspect of the pantheon, you must believe all the rest," I countered.

"That is not necessarily so," he replied. "But there are wide areas of belief. I have seen and I know."

"I, too," said Phelan, and his supporting cry was echoed by the others.

The truly scientific mind is as hesitant to deprecate as it is to lend support. "Let us begin with the primal struggle between the Elder Gods and the Great Old Ones," I said cautiously. "What is the nature of your evidence?"

"The sources are almost infinite. Consider almost all the ancient writings which speak of a great catastrophe which involved the earth. Look to the Old Testament, to the Battle of Beth-Horon, led by Joshua. 'And he said in the sight of Israel, Sun, stand thou still upon Gibeon; and thou, Moon, in the valley of Ajalon. And the sun stood still, and the moon stayed ....' Look to the *Annals of Cuauhtitlan* of the lore of the Nahua Indians of Mexico, which speak of an endless night, a tale verified by the Spanish priest, Fra. Bernardino de Sahagun, who, coming to the New World a generation after Columbus, told of the great catastrophe in which the sun rose but a little way over the horizon and then stood still, a catastrophe witnessed by the American Indians. And the Bible again: 'As they fled from before Israel ... the Lord cast down great stones upon them in Azekah, and they died ....' There are parallel accounts in other ancient manuscripts—the *Popul Vuh* of the Mayas, the Egyptian *Papyrus Ipuwer*, the Buddhist *Visuddhi-Magga*, the Persian *Zend-Avesta*, the Hindu *Vedas*, many another. There are curiously coincidental records left in ancient art—the Venus tablets of Babylon, found in the ruins of the library of Ashurbanipal at Nineveh, certain of the panoplies at Angkor-Vat, which you must know—and there are the strangely altered clocks of ancient times— the water clock of the Temple of Amon at Karnak, now inaccurate for day and night; the shadow clock of Fayum, Egypt, inaccurate too; the astronomical panel in the tomb of Senmut, in which the stars are shown in an order they do not have, but which may presumably have been correct for Senmut's time. And these stars, I submit, are not just accidentally those of the Orion-Taurus group, held to be the seat of both the Elder Gods—who are believed to exist at or near Betelgueze—and at least one of the Ancient Ones, Hastur; and were presumably home to all the Ancient Ones. So that the catastrophe duly recorded in the old documents may very well have been evidence of the titanic battle which was waged between the Elder Gods and the rebellious Ancient Ones."

I pointed out that there was a current theory concerning erratic conduct on the part of the planet now called Venus.

Professor Shrewsbury shrugged this away almost with impatience. "Entertaining, but pure nonsense. The concept of Venus as a one-time comet can be disproved scientifically; the concept of the conflict between the Elder Gods and the Ancient Ones cannot. I submit, Mr. Blayne, that your actual conviction of disbelief is not as strong as your words."

In this he was eminently correct. What this strange old man had said had aroused and awakened a thousand latent memories, all of which now coalesced in the events of the moment. An archaeologist cannot have seen the weird grotesques of Easter Island without a sense

of an impending past; he cannot have looked upon Angkor-Vat or
the shunned ruins of certain of the Marquesas Islands without a dim
awareness of the terror that lurked in ancient places; he cannot have
studied the legends of ancient peoples without recognizing that the
lore of mankind, however exaggerated, takes root in some remote
reality. Moreover, there was about my newly found companions an
air of gravity which was plain behind their good nature, and was
almost sinister without being malevolent. I could not doubt that
these gentlemen were deadly serious, for each of them testified mutely
that he had been on this quest for more than just a short time.

"You see," continued Professor Shrewsbury, "it would be folly to
pretend that this meeting was an accident. Your movements had
been studied enough to make it occur. It is just possible that in your
studies of ancient ruins and the drawings, hieroglyphics, and other
remains found among them, you may have happened upon something which might afford us a clue to the place we seek."

"And what is that?" I asked.

"An island." So saying, he unfolded before me a crudely drawn map.

I examined the map with interest which was quickened appre-
ciably when it dawned upon me that this was no ordinary map done
by the hand of an ill-informed person, but rather a map drawn by
someone who clearly believed in the objects he drew; that these
objects were not placed as he had placed them suggested an artist
of centuries ago.

"Java and Borneo," I said, identifying them. "These islands are
apparently the Carolines and the marked place is northward, but
the directions are not very clear."

"Yes, that is its drawback," agreed Professor Shrewsbury dryly.

I looked at him sharply. "Where did you get this, Professor?"

"From a very old man."

"He must have been very old indeed," I agreed.

"Almost fifteen centuries," he answered, without a smile. "But,
come, do you recognize this place beyond the Carolines?"

I shook my head.

"Then we fall back upon your own research, Mr. Blayne. You have
been in the South Pacific ever since the end of the Second World
War. You have gone from island to island, and you will have seen
certainly that in some areas there is a marked emphasis on the
batrachian motif, or the ichthyic motif—it matters little, save that
we have reason to believe one island at least to be either the focal

point or near the focal point of the occurrence of artifacts and works of art stressing the batrachian."

"Ponape," I said.

He nodded, and the others waited expectantly.

"You see," he went on, "I have been to the Black Island which has no name and is uncharted because it is not always visible and rises to the surface only at rare intervals. But my means of travel was somewhat unorthodox, my attempt to blast the island and its horrible ruins was ineffective; we must find it again, and we shall find it most readily by picking up the trail of the batrachian motif in Polynesian art."

"There are certain legends," I put in, "which speak of a vanishing land. It would presumably be stationary?"

"Yes, making its appearance only when upheavals of the ocean's bed thrust it up. And then evidently not for long. I need not remind you that there have been recent tremblors recorded by seismographs for the region of the South Pacific; conditions are thus ideal for our quest. We are at liberty to suppose it to be part of a larger, submerged land area, quite possibly one of the legendary continents."

"Mu," said Phelan.

"If Mu existed," countered the professor gravely.

"There is ample evidence to believe it did," I said, "together with Atlantis. If you were to fall back upon your own kind of evidence, there is plenty of legendry to give the belief body—the Bible's story of the Deluge, for instance; the ancient books' accounts of catastrophes, the submerging of vast land areas depicted in the drawings found at the sites of so much archaeological discovery."

One of the professor's companions grinned and said, "You're entering into the spirit of it, Mr. Blayne."

The professor, however, gazed at me without smiling. "You believe in the existence of Mu, Mr. Blayne?"

"I'm afraid I do."

"And presumably also in the ancient civilizations said to have inhabited Mu and Atlantis," he went on. "There are certain legends attributable to some such lost civilizations, Mr. Blayne—particularly in relation to their sea deities—and there are survivals of ancient worship in the Balearics, in the islands of the Carolines, at Innsmouth, Massachusetts, and in a few other widely separated areas. If Atlantis lay off the coast of Spain, and Mu near the Marshalls, presumably there might have been yet another land area at one time lying off the coast of Massachusetts. And the Black

Island might be part of yet another land area; we cannot know. But it is certain that the Bible's Deluge and other similar legendary catastrophes might well have resulted in the banishment of Cthulhu to one of the lost continents of this planet."

I nodded, aware for what seemed the first time of the intense scrutiny of the others.

"The Black Island is thus far the only known avenue directly to Cthulhu; all others are primarily in the possession of the Deep Ones. We must therefore search for it by every means at our disposal."

It was at this point of our conversation that I became aware of a subtle force vying with my interest, which was far keener than I had permitted myself to show; it was a blind feeling of hostility, and awareness, as it were, of something malign, in the very atmosphere. I looked from one to another of them, but there was nothing in their eyes save only an interest similar to my own. Yet the aura of fear, of enmity, was unmistakable, perhaps made all the more so by its very tenuousness. I looked past my companions, allowing my glance to travel along the bar, among the tables; I saw no one who was even aware of us, though the bar, as always, was crowded with people of all nationalities in all walks of life. The conviction of hostility, the aura of fear, persisted, lying against my consciousness as were it a tangible thing.

I gave my attention again to Professor Shrewsbury. He talked now of the trail of Cthulhu through the arts and crafts of primitive peoples, and his words conjured up from my own memories a thousand corroborating details—of the curious figures found in the Sepik River valley of New Guinea; of the tapa cloth designs of the Tonga islanders; of the hideously suggestive Fisherman's God of the Cook Islanders, with its misshapen torso and its substitution of tentacles for legs and arms; of the stone tiki of the Marquesas, markedly batrachian in aspect; of the carvings of the New Zealand Maori, which depict creatures neither man nor octopus, neither fish nor frog, but something of all four; of the revolting war-shield design used by Queenslanders, a design of a labyrinth under water with a tortuously malefic figure at the end of it, tentacles extended as if for prey; and the similar shell pendants of the Papuans; of the ceremonial music of the Indonesians, particularly the Batak dream music, and the Wayang shadow-play of leather puppets on the ancient themes dramatizing a legend of sea-beings. All these pointed unmistakably to Ponape from one direction, while the ceremonial figures used in some parts of the Hawaiian Islands and the great heads of Rano-raraku on Easter Island made a similar indication from the other.

Ponape, with its shunned ruins, its abandoned port in which the carvings are of unmistakable significance, carvings of brooding terror, of fish-men, of frog-men, of octopoids, all speaking mutely of a strange and terrible way of life led by inhabitants who were half-bestial, half-human. And from Ponape, where?

"You are thinking of Ponape," said Professor Shrewsbury quietly.

"Yes—and of what might lie beyond. If the Black Island is not between Ponape and Singapore, it must lie between that island and Easter Island."

"The only direction we have is that of the Johansen narrative, discovered in Lovecraft, and subsequently repeated in the story of the disappearance of the H.M.S. *Advocate*. S. Latitude 47°53′, W. Longitude 127°37′. That would be in the general area. But the latitude and longitude may not be correct; according to the Greenbie account, that is the place at which the *Advocate* ran into a storm 'blowing something terrible.' There is thus a possibility of some error, since we have no way of knowing how far off course the ship may have been blown, nor how long a time elapsed since Greenbie last ascertained longitude and latitude. He makes note that they were steering 'a course straight for the Admiralties or New Guinea ... but we saw by the stars that we were off course by west.'

"The Johansen narrative ...."

I interrupted him. "Forgive me, I am not familiar with these accounts."

"My apologies. Of course, you could not be. They are not vital to your knowledge, but exist only as curiously corroborative statements. Or rather, as statements which are extremely suggestive in the light of what we know. If one has no belief in Cthulhu and the pantheon of Elder Gods and Ancient Ones, such accounts are meaningless, and all too readily dismissed as hysteria; if one keeps an open mind, however, such accounts become damnably suggestive. One cannot dismiss them."

"These accounts apart, and all else, too," I said, "what do you expect of me?"

"I submit that you are perhaps more qualified to speak with authority on the arts and artifacts of the South Pacific than anyone else within the entire region. We are satisfied that the primitive drawings and sculptures of these people will point unmistakably to the approximate location of the Black Island. Specifically, we are interested in the occurrence of any work similar to the Fisherman's

God of Cook Island, which, we have reason to believe, is a representation, as seen by the primitive mind, of Cthulhu himself. By
narrowing the circle of its incidence, it is logical to suppose that we
can box in the site of the island."

I nodded thoughtfully, certain that I could almost effortlessly
construct the ring that Professor Shrewsbury visualized.

"Can we count on you, Mr. Blayne?"

"More than that. If you have room for me, I'll join your party."

Professor Shrewsbury favored me with a long silent glance which
I found somewhat disconcerting, but at last he said, "We have a
place for you, Mr. Blayne. We hope to leave Singapore in two days."
He gave me his card, writing rapidly on the back of it. "You will
find me at this address if you need me."

2.

I took leave of Professor Shrewsbury's party with curious misgivings. My offer to accompany them had been made almost involuntarily; I had had no intention of doing more than the professor had
asked, but some impulse stronger than my own wish had impelled
me instead to propose that I go with them to seek their goal. Once
outside the bar, I asked myself why I had not doubted the professor's
strange story; the evidence he had offered was purely circumstantial,
and I could not have said that I had in fact ever come upon anything
more to justify belief; and yet I found myself believing readily not
only in the existence of the Black Island, but also in the vast
mythology so sketchily outlined for me, in all that pantheon of
Elder Gods and Ancient Ones of which that oddly persuasive and
yet curiously repellent old man in the black glasses had spoken.
Moreover, I recognized that my belief stemmed from something
more than Professor Shrewsbury's words; it arose from a deep inner
conviction, as if I had known all this long before but had either
refused to acknowledge it or had failed to become aware of it because
the proper opportunity for recognition had never arisen.

And yet I had always been strangely stirred at sight of just such
art as Professor Shrewsbury had hinted at, and most of all, at the
Cook Islanders' horribly suggestive Fisherman's God. What Profes-

sor Shrewsbury had plainly intimated was that this work had had a living model; and of this I, despite my archaeological training, had never entertained the shadow of a doubt. I could ask myself now to discover the reasons for my belief in the face of the previous record of dubiety I had established in my field; I could not answer, save to point to an inner conviction far stronger than any amount of cold rationalization. For it could not be denied that Professor Shrewsbury's analysis was not in itself factual, that the explanation for the various events and the nature of the evidence he projected were alike hypothetical in the extreme, that other solutions presented themselves as well, for the annals of primitive peoples are replete with many weird symbols and customs utterly unrelated to the living-patterns of contemporary man. But no challenge caused any wavering in my conviction. I knew, as if I had been there, that there was indeed an uncharted island near Ponape, that it was part of a sunken kingdom which might indeed have been R'lyeh and part of Mu, that it was the source of an incredible power, and no rationalization could explain either my conviction or my complete refusal to consider any other explanation of the tentative outline Professor Shrewsbury had offered. He, too, knew; the facts he had adduced were but the tiniest fraction of the adducible evidence.

And what impulse was it that sent me into the shadows to wait upon the emergence of Professor Shrewsbury and his companions? I could not say; yet I remained in a place of concealment until the five men left the bar, watching them come out. I had no impulse to follow, but I knew as by intuition that they would not be unattended, and they were not. Their followers walked at a respectable distance behind them—one, a second, yet another, at widely separated intervals.

I stepped out and faced one of them. He met my eyes questioningly for a moment, held my gaze, and looked away. A lascar, I judged him, but oddly deformed, with a curiously suggestive head, foreshortened, with little brow, and repellently wide-mouthed, with scarcely a chin at all, but a sloping fold of skin that vanished into his neck. And his skin, too, was rough, warty. I felt no horror, looking at him. Perhaps Professor Shrewsbury's hints had prepared me for such an apparition, for I had known someone would be there. I was equally certain, however, that, for the present at least, my newly found friends were in no danger.

I took myself off to my quarters presently, very thoughtful and preoccupied, for there was manifestly something more than Professor Shrewsbury's story and the quest of the five for the mythological

Cthulhu to stir me. Once at my rooms, I found myself drawn to the packet of papers which had come down to me from my grandfather Waite—for my name had not always been Blayne, having undergone a change in the home of my foster-parents in Boston—my grandfather Asaph Waite, whom I had never consciously seen, and who perished with my grandmother, my father, and my mother in a disaster which had struck their town when I was yet only a babe in arms, and while I was on a visit with cousins who had forthwith adopted me after a loss which, to any other older child, would have been shockingly tragic.

My grandfather's papers were wrapped in oilskin—he had been a seafaring man out of Massachusetts, at one time an agent of the famous Marsh family, which for generations had been seafaring men, ranging far and wide over the face of the earth—and I had had them with me for years. I had examined the small packet from time to time, with curious stirrings and misgivings; tonight something Professor Shrewsbury had said had brought the papers back into my memory, and I wanted to look at them once more, without delay.

They consisted of fragments of an old diary—some pages had been torn out here and there; of fragmentary letters; a few documents, and some of what purported to be my grandfather's own writings entitled simply: *Invocations*, though down in one corner someone had added: *to Dagon*. The *Invocations* came to hand first. These were evidently intended as at least semi-poetry, and were written in a manner at times coherent, at others apparently incoherent—unless, as I was now prepared to admit, I lacked the proper key to understanding. I read but one of them, with considerably more care, however, than I had previously given it.

> "By all the depths of Y'ha-nthlei—and the dwellers thereof, for the One Over All;
>
> "By the Sign of Kish—and all who obey it, for its Author;
>
> "By the Door to Yhe—and all who use it, who have gone before and who shall come after, for Him to Whom It Leadeth;
>
> "By Him Who Is to Come ...
>
> "*Ph'nglui mglw-nafh Cthulhu R'lyeh wgah-nagl fhtagn.*"

I recognized in the final incomprehensible line, two of the names Dr. Shrewsbury had used, and I was even more disquieted than ever to discover them here in my possession, even if I had come by them in so casual a fashion.

I turned next to the diary, which was evidently, judging by notes pertinent to events of the day in the United States, for 1928. The entries were not frequent, but it was noteworthy that, after a beginning in which my grandfather had chronicled, journal-fashion, comments on the political and historical events of his time, his attention turned ever more and more to something mysterious and personal, to which the diary afforded no key. The entries pertinent to something which troubled my grandfather exceedingly began in late April of that year.

April 23. Out to D.R. again last night, where saw what M. affirms is Him. Amorphous, tentacled, inhuman. Could I have expected other? M. extremely excited. Cannot say that I shared his excitement except that I found myself vacillating between M.'s extreme on the one hand and an equal extremity of aversion on the other. A stormy night. Do not know where all this will lead.

April 24. Took note of many boat losses in last night's storm. But none from here, though many were to D.R. So evidently we have been protected for another purpose which will be made plain in good time. Met M. on the street today; he took no notice of me, as if he did not know who I was. I understand now why he constantly wears black gloves. If those who do not understand should see!

April 27. A stranger in town, questioning old Zadok. The word has gone around that Z. will have to be dealt with. A pity. He seemed always such a harmless, garrulous old tosspot. Too garrulous, perhaps. But no one has heard him say anything. The stranger, they say, plied him with liquor.

There were similar entries, and other accounts of strange journeys to the place given only as D.R., evidently to be reached only by water—the Atlantic—but not far from the settlement, for there was no account of lengthy traveling over water to reach the goal from the town. These entries varied in intensity, but became steadily more and more chaotic; evidently the town had been seriously disturbed by the prying questions of a strange visitor to that clannish community. By late May, he was writing:

May 21. Word passed around that a 'Federal Man' was asking questions in town today. Visited M.'s Refining Company. I have not seen him myself, but Obed mentioned seeing him. A short wiry man, very dark-skinned. A Southerner, perhaps. He supposedly comes directly from Washington. M. has cancelled the meeting tonight, and also a trip to D.R. Leopold was to have gone as the s. tonight. Now he will be passed over and the next one will be chosen.

May 22. The sea very turbulent last night. Anger at D.R.? The trip should not have been postponed.

May 23. Rumors grow. Gilman reported seeing a destroyer in the vicinity of D.R. last evening, but no one else saw it. Gilman entirely too imaginative. Should be disciplined for adding to the growing discontent.

May 27. Something wrong. More strangers in town. Also ships off the coast, apparently armed. The docks being examined by these tightlipped outsiders. Are they in reality Federal Men, or are they others—from H., for instance? How could we know? I have suggested it to M. but he says, no, they cannot be, he would "feel" it if so. M. does not appear to be disturbed, but he is not entirely at his ease. Everyone is running to him.

June. Z. has been taken care of, right under the noses of the Federal Men. What can they want? I am prevailing on J. to send the child off to Martha.

It was to this period of the diary to which one of the letters belonged; recognizing it, I had placed the letter to my foster-mother between the pages of the diary at this point; and I now opened it and read it once more.

7th June 1928

Dear Martha,

I write in considerable haste because we have had to make decisions in a hurry here these past few days. Events have turned up so that it would be best to send Horvath to you for safekeeping. John and Abigail have agreed, however reluctantly; so I send him with Amos. It might be best to keep Amos with him for a week or two, until he can accustom himself to you and your way of existence there in Boston. Then Amos may come home again, though I do not need him at present, and if you have use for him, by all means retain him until it is convenient for you to send him back to us.

Ever affectionately,

Asaph Waite.

Comparatively few entries remained in the diary, and all were undated, appearing simply under "June." They were increasingly disturbed, betraying what must have been my grandfather's extreme agitation.

June. M. reports questions very upsetting. Bear directly on D.R. and
the "goings-on" there. Someone must have talked to the Federal
Men. But who? If M. only knew, he would follow Z. There is no
room here for traitors, and whoever it is will be hunted down and destroyed. And not only him alone, but all who are with him or who
support him, including, if he is married, his wife and family.

June. Questions about the "rites" at Dagon Hall. Whoever talked knows.

June. Large-scale operations at docks. A destroyer out at D.R. Wild
talk of government taking control of situation.

June. It is true. Blasting begun, and fires have started to spread up
from the docks. They will go out of control. Some have taken to the
water, but the fire is cutting others off unless they go out of town
and around it ....

Reading these entries again, I found myself more disturbed than
ever. The nature of the catastrophe which overtook my progenitors
was still not clear. They might have been caught in the fires which
followed the inexplicable "blasting"; they might have become
involved in the blastings themselves. Whatever happened, the
events which took place in that Massachusetts town had occurred
in 1928; in that same year my parents and my grandparents had
been killed in an unnamed catastrophe; it was not unwarranted to
presume that these events were connected. The entries in my
grandfather's diary actually revealed nothing save that some enterprise with which he was connected, evidently led by the man M.,
had attracted the attention of Federal agents who had invaded the
town and taken corrective measures. There was no hint as to the
nature of the enterprise, but presumably it was illegal, for nothing
was set down in my grandfather's papers to identify it.

The remaining letters—there were but two others—were written
also in June, 1928. One was to my foster-parents.

10th June 1928.

Dear Martha and Arnold,

I have forwarded by mail out of Arkham a copy of my last will and
testament, should anything happen to me, putting you down as executors and administrators of the trust fund I shall leave to Horvath.
Apart from such fees as are set forth for you in the nature of a be-
quest, I have left all my property to my son and daughter-in-law,
but in the event of their death, to Horvath. I hope I am not too pes-

simistic, but I do not believe in being inexcusably sanguine. The
events of the past few days are not encouraging.

As always,

Asaph.

The second letter was undated, but by its nature it must have
been written in June also; it was not an original, as were those to my
foster-parents, but a copy my grandfather had evidently retained.

Dear W.,

A hasty note to let you know M. thinks all is lost for the present. He
does not think damage can be done to Y'ha., but none of us knows.
The place swarms with Federal Men. We think now it is all Zadok's
doing, but Z. has been taken care of. We do not know who it was he
talked to, but have reason to believe it was one of us. He will not escape. Though he was pursued up the tracks out of town and got
away, he will be forever haunted by what he had done. Of course,
you may say, as some have said, it would never have happened if the
Marshes had kept away from those strange creatures at P., but the
South Pacific is a long way from Massachusetts, and who would
guess that they could make their way here to the reef. I am afraid
now we are all getting what people call "the Marsh look." It is not
attractive. I shall write no more, but I adjure you, if anything happens to us, and that may be, for this thing has so impressed the Federal Men that there is no semblance of a trial here for anyone or any
place they elect to destroy—do what you can for my grandson, Horvath Waite, whom you will find in the care of Mr. and Mrs. Arnold
W. Blayne, in Boston.

Asaph.

These were the reactions of my grandfather Waite attendant upon
the catastrophe which struck at his town and at him and his family
in that summer of 1928. I had read these papers before, but never
with such fascination. Perhaps it was the knowledge of these, which
lay in memory, which accounted for my interest in the project which
occupied Professor Shrewsbury. And yet I could not wholly believe
that it was. Together with the conviction that within the boundaries
of Professor Shrewsbury's quest lay the solution to the mystery
which dogged my grandfather was a haunting memory which
loomed forever just on the perimeter of recognition, and it was this,
however nameless and faceless, which motivated my deeper and
more troubled concern with the trail of Cthulhu, for which I was
about to surrender for the time being at least all my archaeological

research, my hopes and ambitions for my future in the field I had chosen for my own. The compulsion was stronger than my wish.

I put my grandfather's papers away once more, wrapping them in the oilskin in which they had come to my foster-parents, and then, far from tired, I set about to track down, even as Professor Shrewsbury had asked, the occurrence of certain hideously suggestive motifs in the art patterns of the South Pacific islanders, particularly the Fisherman's God of Cook Island. At this I worked steadily for more than two hours, consulting not only such references as I owned, but also my own voluminous notes and sketches. At the end of that time I realized that the Fisherman's God had made its appearance in one form or another as far to the south as Australia, as far to the north as the Kuriles, and between, in Cambodia, Indo-China, Siam, and the Malay States; but I had affirmed also, as I had already foreseen, that the incidence of its occurrence was immeasurably greater in the vicinity of Ponape. However the circle were drawn, its center would be at or near Ponape; that the object of Professor Shrewsbury's quest lay in the immediate vicinity I had not a shred of doubt.

And that something inconceivably malign lay there in that hidden place, I had also no doubt. For it was from Ponape that the M. of my grandfather Waite's papers had come home, bringing in his aftermath the events which were to culminate in the tragedy of 1928. The recurrence of the island in the legends and corroborative accounts pertinent thereto was not an accident or chance; Ponape was the outpost of mankind's civilization, the outpost nearest the gate into the weird and terrible world of the Ancient Ones, of whom great Cthulhu alone lay forever sleeping, waiting upon the events which would some day rouse him from his centuries-old torpor and send him forth once more upon the unsuspecting peoples of the earth, forth to conquer and bring all the planet under his dominion.

3.

We shipped for Ponape on the second day, traveling by one of the regular steamers plying the islands. I had thought we were to have possession of a ship of our own, but Professor Shrewsbury offered in explanation that other arrangements had been made out of Ponape. We gathered together on the deck soon after leaving the docks, primarily for the purpose of comparing notes, and I discovered that all of them spoke most matter-of-factly of being under surveillance in Singapore.

"And you," Professor Shrewsbury turned to me. "Were you aware of being followed, Mr. Blayne?"

I shook my head. "But I had thought someone trailed after you," I admitted. "Who were they?"

"The Deep Ones," offered Phelan. "They are everywhere, but we've had other followers far more dangerous. The star protects us from them; they cannot harm us as long as we carry it."

"I have one for you, Mr. Blayne," said Professor Shrewsbury.

"Who are the Deep Ones?" I asked.

Professor Shrewsbury offered an immediate explanation. The Deep Ones, he said, were minions of Cthulhu. Originally they had been aquatic only—hideously suggestive of human beings, but essentially batrachian or ichthyic; but over a century ago certain American traders had come into the South Pacific and had formed alliances with the Deep Ones, mating with them and thus producing a hybrid breed which could exist equally well on land or in the sea; it was this hybrid breed which was to be found in most of the port cities of the world, never very far from water. That they were directed by some sort of super-intelligence from the sea seemed unquestionable, since they were never long in discovering any member of Professor Shrewsbury's party, all of whom had had previous encounters with the followers of Cthulhu—and, indeed, with certain minions of others of the Ancient Ones. Their purpose was clearly menacing, but the power of the five-pointed star, which was sealed with the seal of the Elder Gods, rendered them impotent. Should anyone of them fail to carry the star, however, he might fall victim to the Deep Ones, or to the Abominable Mi-Go, or to the Tcho-Tcho people, the Shoggoths, the Shantaks, or any among a score or more of those human and semi-human creatures dedicated to the service of the Ancient Ones.

Professor Shrewsbury excused himself to go to his cabin and bring to me the star of which he had spoken. It was a rough-surfaced stone, grey in color, with a barely distinguishable seal representing a pillar of light, as closely as I could approximate it. It was not large; it scarcely covered my palm, but it had a most peculiar effect on me, for it felt as if it burned my flesh, and I found it curiously repellent. I put it into my pocket, and there it seemed incredibly heavy; there, too, it left a burning sensation on my skin, despite the clothing between; it did not appear to have a similar effect on the others, as far as I could ascertain. Indeed, it became so heavy, presently, and afflicted me so sorely with the sensation of heat, that I found it necessary to excuse myself and hasten to my cabin so that I could remove the stone from my person and leave it among my possessions.

Only then did I feel free to rejoin my companions, where I took a listener's part in their discussion of events beyond my ken—not alone of Cthulhu and Hastur, and their minions, or of the others, not alone of the Elder Gods and that titanic battle which must have taken place aeons ago and involved countless universes, but of certain adventures these five had shared together, for they made countless references to ancient tablets, to books which, to judge by the dates which occurred in their conversation, had been made long before mankind had learned to write even on papyrus. They spoke repeatedly, too, of a "library" on "Celaeno", which was beyond my ken. I was loath to ask, but I gathered that they had undergone a period of exile at what must have been certainly an archaeologically priceless retreat, a city or library at a place called "Celaeno", of which I knew nothing and was reluctant to admit ignorance of a site so archaeologically ancient under a name I had hitherto associated only with the stars.

Their references to the Ancient Ones intimated too of feuds among these beings, between Hastur and Cthugha on the one hand, and Cthulhu and Ithaqua on the other; evidently these beings were united only against the Elder Gods, but vied with one another for the worship of their minions and the destruction or seduction of such inhabitants of their regions as came within their orbits. I gathered, too, that Professor Shrewsbury and his companions had been drawn together often by mere chance, that all had been exposed to similar dangers, and all had eventually sought the haven which the professor had discovered many years before. It was somewhat disquieting, too, to reflect upon certain casual references made by the Professor to events in which he had a part but which had taken place much longer ago than could have been possible, considering his age; but I concluded, finally, that I must have been in error and misunderstood.

That night I had the first of the curiously disturbing dreams which haunted our voyage. Though I slept soundly enough, I was never free of dreams. I dreamed that night that I found myself in a great city deep in the sea. My subaqueous existence did not trouble me; I was able to breathe, move about as I pleased, and carry on a normal existence in the ocean's depths. The city, however, was not a modern city; it was ancient—quite possibly such a city as might have been visualized by an archaeologist—far more ancient than any city I had ever known before, with vast, monolithic buildings, on the walls of many of which had been emblazoned representations of the sun, the moon, the stars, and certain grotesquely horrible figments of the artist's imagination, some of them amazingly similar to the Fisherman's God of the Cook Islanders. Moreover, some of the buildings featured doorways of an unusual size, both in width and height, as were they constructed for beings beyond the conception of mankind.

I moved about among the city's streets and lanes unmolested, but I was not alone. Other human or semi-human beings became visible from time to time, most of them strangely batrachian in their aspects and movements, and my own locomotion was rather more batrachian than human. I saw presently that all the inhabitants were moving in one general direction, and I followed in their wake, joining the stream. Thus I came presently to a rise in the sea-bottom, at the top of which stood a ruined building which was clearly a temple. The building was of black stone, of pieces suggesting the Egyptian pyramids; it was no longer intact, but had fallen away, disclosing beyond the great doorway a passage which struck downward, into the sea-bottom. Around this doorway, in a semi-circle, clustered the denizens of that ocean depth, I among them, waiting upon some event which was foreordained.

I grew aware of a chanting ululation rising from among them, but I could distinguish no words, for the language was not one I knew. Yet I had the conviction that I should know it, and several of the strange beings near me stared at me in a peculiarly revolting way, accusingly, as if I were guilty of some breach of conduct. But their attention was soon drawn away from me to that ruined doorway. Even while others were still joining the throng from the city below, a kind of glow began to come into being in the doorway, an oddly diffused light, not white or yellow, but pale green, lambent, like the movement of the curtain auroras, deepening in intensity as the moments passed. Then, deep in the heart of the passage, rising out of the light, came a great amorphous mass of flesh, preceded by incredibly long, lashing tentacles, a thing with

the head of what might have been a gigantic human being in its
upper half, and an octopoid creature below.

I caught but a single, horrified glimpse of it; then I screamed
aloud and woke.

I lay for some time trying to ascertain the reason for being of the
dream I had had. That it grew from my knowledge of the ancient
legends, I could not doubt; but how could I account for my
perspective in the dream? I was not an interloper, as I was in fact
on my way to discover the point of egress for Cthulhu. Moreover, I
was a witness to something more than was set down in any of the
references or sources I had read, and nothing of what I had dreamed
had been envisioned in anything Professor Shrewsbury had said.

But I puzzled over this problem in vain. The only explanation I
could credit lay in the work of a perfervid imagination, which might
conceivably have conjured up the substance of my dream. Lulled by
the smooth movement of the ship, I drifted off into sleep once more,
and again into dream.

This time, however, the setting was far different. I dreamed that
I was a spectator at cataclysmic events far out among the constellations and galaxies. There a great battle was joined between beings
far beyond the conceptions of a mere human being. They were great,
constantly changing, masses of what appeared to be pure light—
sometimes in the form of pillars, sometimes as great globes,
sometimes as clouds; these masses struggled titanically with other
masses likewise constantly changing not only in intensity and
shape, but also in color. Their size was monstrous; compared to
them, I had the size of an ant to a dinosaur. The battle raged in
space, and from time to time one of the opponents of the pillars of
light would be caught up and flung far outward, dwindling to the
sight, and altering hideously in shape, taking on the aspect of a
solid, fleshly form, yet undergoing unceasing metamorphosis.

Suddenly, in the midst of this interstellar engagement, it was as
if a curtain had been drawn across the scene; it faded away abruptly,
and slowly another took its place, or, rather, a succession of scenes—
a strange, black-watered lake, lost among crags in an utterly alien
landscape, certainly not terrestrial, with a boiling, churning disturbance in the water and the rising of a thing too hideous to be named;
a bleak, dark, windswept landscape with snow-covered crags ring-
ing in a great plateau, in the center of which rose a black structure
suggesting a many-turretted castle, within which sat enthroned a
quartet of sombre beings in the guise of men, attended by huge

bat-winged birds; a sea-kingdom, a far cry from Carcassone, similar to that of which I had previously dreamed; a snowy landscape, suggestive of Canadian regions, with a great shape striding across it, as on the wind, blotting out the stars, showing in their place great shining eyes, a grotesque caricature on mankind in the Arctic wastes.

These scenes passed before my eyes in dream with ever-increasing rapidity, and only one was remotely recognizable; a sea-coast town which, I was confident, was in Massachusetts or at least somewhere along the New England coast, and there I saw, moving about in its streets, people I remembered having seen far back in memory—particularly the always heavily veiled figure of the woman who had been my mother.

The dream ended at last. I woke again, far from sleep now, filled with a thousand perplexing questions, unable to know the meaning and significance of what I had seen in dream, the kaleidoscope of events utterly beyond my ken. I lay trying to thread them together, to evoke or create a common link; I could find none save the nebulous mythology of which Professor Shrewsbury had spoken in only the most superficial way.

I rose presently and went out on deck. The night was calm, a moon shone, the ship moved steadily through the South Pacific toward our goal. The hour was late, past midnight, and I stood at the rail watching the passing scene—the stars, wondering where, if any place, life such as mankind knew it existed; the sea, with the moonlight glinting and gleaming on the gently swelling water, wondering whether, indeed, there had ever existed the legendary sunken continents, whether cities had sunk beneath the sea's surface in ages gone by, and what denizens of the deep lurked in those depths as yet unknown to man.

Presently, however, the sound of our passage began to have a peculiarly illusory effect, and at the same time I was given to imagining that dark shapes swam with the ship, alongside, shapes in the guise, however distorted, of human beings; it seemed to my already overwrought mind that the very water seemed to whisper my name: *Horvath Blayne! Horvath Blayne!* over and over, and it was then as if a dozen voices whispered back: *Horvath Waite! Horvath Waite!*, until at last I was overcome by the conviction that I should turn back, go away, return to my ancestral home, as if I did not know that it had been destroyed in the holocaust of 1928. So overpoweringly suggestive did this illusion become, that I turned at last and sought the comparative peace of my cabin, where I took once again to my berth, hoping this time for sleep undisturbed by any dream.

Then at last I slept.

4.

On our arrival at Ponape, our party was met by a grim-visaged American naval official in white uniform, who drew Professor Shrewsbury to one side and spoke briefly with him, while we waited, together with a shabby-looking seaman who seemed also to desire some words with the professor. This seaman presently caught the professor's eye; certainly Professor Shrewsbury did not resent the seaman's familiarity, and within a few moments he was walking at the professor's side, talking animatedly in a dialect I did not clearly understand.

The professor listened to him but a short while. Then he halted our party and abruptly altered our immediate plans.

"Phelan and Blayne, come along with me. The rest of you go to our quarters. Keane, send for Brigadier-General Holberg, and ask him to see me."

Phelan and I therefore accompanied Professor Shrewsbury and his rough companion, who led the way through devious streets and lanes to a building which was assuredly little more than a hovel. Lying on a pallet there, another seaman awaited us. Both men had evidently had foreknowledge of our arrival, for the professor had sent ahead months ago for any lore of a mysterious island which rose on occasion and vanished as strangely. It was manifestly such knowledge as the ailing seaman wished now to impart.

His name was Satsume Sereke; he was of Japanese extraction, but clearly of mixed blood, and of more than usual education. He was approaching middle age, but looked older. He had been a hand on a tramp steamer, the *Yokohama*, out of Hong Kong; the steamer had been wrecked and he had been one of the men in a life-boat. Before permitting him to go farther, Professor Shrewsbury now asked us to take careful note of what Sereke said. The account I set down differed in no detail from Phelan's. We made no attempt, of course, to reproduce the exact language of the ailing man.

"Our course was for Ponape. Bailey had a compass, and so we knew about where we were going. The first night after the storm we were moving along all right—Henderson and Melik were at the oars, with Spolito and Yohira—it was clear, we had enough food and water, nobody dreaming anything, I mean—we saw something in the water. We thought it was sharks or porpoises, maybe marlins, we couldn't see well enough. It was dark, and they stayed away from the boat, just followed us and went along with us. Along about my watch, they came closer. They had a funny look, like they had arms and legs instead of fins and a tail, but they were up and down so much you couldn't be sure. Then, quicker than a cat, something reached over into the boat and got Spolito—just pulled him out; he screamed, and Melik reached out for him, but he was gone before Melik could get to him. Melik said he saw something like a webbed hand; he was near crazy with fear afterward; Spolito just went down and never came up again. All our followers were gone quick; then they came back, an hour later, and that time they got Yohira the same way. After that nothing more, and when morning came we saw the island.

"It was an island, where none was before. There was nothing growing on it, and it was black with muck, I think. But there were remains of buildings on it, buildings like I never saw before, with big, odd-shaped blocks of stone. There was an open door, very large, partly broken away. Henderson had the glasses, and he got a good look. Then he passed them around. Henderson wanted to go to the place, but I didn't. Well, he talked, and Mason, Melik, and Gunders decided to go ashore; Benton and I held back, and the way we settled it was we rowed over, and Benton and I stayed in the boat with the glasses to watch the others.

"They got out and sloshed through the muck and seaweed to the stones, and then they went on to that doorway. All four of them were there, and I was looking at them through the glasses. I don't know how it happened, but something big and black just puffed out of that doorway and fell on the four of them. It pulled back with a horrible sucking noise, but Henderson and Mason and the others were gone. Benton had seen it, too, but not as clear. I didn't go to look, I didn't want to see any more. We rowed as fast as we could and got away from there. We never stopped rowing until the freighter *Rhineland* picked us up."

"Did you set down the latitude and longitude of the island?" asked Professor Shrewsbury.

"No. But we lost the ship at about South Latitude 49°51', West Longitude 128°34'. It is toward Ponape from there, but not close to Ponape."

"You saw this thing in the morning, by daylight?"

"Yes, but there were fogs—green fogs; it was not clear."

"How far out of Ponape?"

"Perhaps a day."

Professor Shrewsbury succeeded in establishing no more. Nevertheless, he appeared pleased; he paused only long enough to ascertain that Sereke would recover from the shock and exhaustion which gripped him; then he returned to the quarters he had arranged for us.

There we found Brigadier-General Holberg, a grim, grey-haired man of approximately sixty, waiting for us. Immediately after introductions had been exchanged, he came to the subject of his presence and his reason for it.

"I have been told to place myself at your disposal, Professor Shrewsbury, by an authority I cannot very well disregard." He smiled frostily. "Operation Ponape is apparently your personal project, sir."

"You have been given some of the documents to read, surely?"

"I have read the documents, yes. I have no comment to make. This is your field, not mine. I have a destroyer ready for your use as soon as you wish to come aboard. A carrier is within call, and the weapon is in readiness, subject to my order. I understand you will attempt destruction with other weapons first?"

"That is the plan, yes."

"When do you expect to leave Ponape, sir?"

"Within a week, General."

"Very good. We shall be at your disposal."

The events of that week on Ponape were essentially trivial, concerning primarily the amassing of powerful explosive weapons for use on the Black Island, if indeed we could find that uncharted land area. But behind these superficial tasks loomed something profoundly disturbing. It was not alone the undeniable fact that we were under surveillance; we had come to expect that. It was not only that we were constantly aware of an impending task of singular magnitude; this too was to be expected. No, it was something more, it was the consciousness of the proximity of a vast and primeval power, which gave off a malignance almost tangible. All of us felt this; I alone felt something more.

Yet I could not define the tangible fear under which I labored. It was far more than fear of the evil that lurked in the sea off Ponape; it was something that reached to the very well-springs of my being, something integral in my essential self, something that was omnipresent like a pulsing undercurrent in my very blood and bone. Try as I might, I could not rid myself of it; I regretted a thousand times having yielded to Professor Shrewsbury's invitation that evening in Singapore, which already seemed incredibly far away. This cloud hung over me without alleviation day after day until the day of our departure from Ponape.

That day dawned sultry and hot—and, for me, filled with foreboding. We set out early on the destroyer *Hamilton*, with General Holberg aboard. Professor Shrewsbury had worked out a course; he had had further discussions with the seaman, Sereke, and he had arrived at an approximate location. Nor, I gathered, had the General been idle; aeroplanes had been scouting the sea in the vicinity of the place where the *Yokohama* had gone down, and one pilot had reported seeing a curiously fog-shrouded area in the sea; no land had been visible, but the occurrence of an unmoving mass of fog was in itself strange enough to command attention. The latitude and longitude had been sent in, and it was for this spot that the *Hamilton* set out.

Despite my forebodings, however, our journey was singularly uneventful. The clouds which had obscured the sun at dawn drew away by mid-day; the sultriness, too, vanished and gave way to a clear, less humid atmosphere. An air of excitement prevailed, a kind of tension which we all shared, except for the General, whose manner was that of a military man obeying an order without quite believing in its necessity. He and the professor held some colloquy on the destructiveness of modern warfare. And what, Professor Shrewsbury wanted to know, was likely to happen to so small a land area as the Black Island?

"Wiped out," said the General laconically.

"I wonder," answered the professor. "We shall see."

I do not know whether I actually expected the destroyer to reach the Black Island; certainly I did not share the General's calm confidence. But in late afternoon of that day we sighted an uncharted island, and within a short time we were lowering a boat containing Professor Shrewsbury, Phelan, Keane, and myself; a second boat carried paraphernalia together with Boyd and Colum, and two men from the destroyer. Significantly, the ship's guns were trained on the structure just visible on the island.

It did not surprise me to find the Black Island to be the temple peak of my dream. Here it was, exactly as I had seen it, with the carven door open and the mouth of that great portal yawning to the sun despite an aura of mist which lay greenly over everything. The ruins were breathtaking, though plainly ravaged by quakes and, quite clearly, by explosives, whose ineffectual damage differed from that greater damage of earthquake, which had burst asunder many of the angles of the colossal stone building. The stones, like the soil, were black, and forbidding; and their surfaces were covered with terrible hieroglyphs and shocking images. The building was composed of angles and planes which were non-Euclidean, hinting horribly of alien dimensions and spheres, as if this building and what remained of the sunken city beyond it had been constructed by non-terrestrials.

Professor Shrewsbury cautioned us before we landed.

"I believe Sereke's story to be substantially true," he said, "and I have no hope that this attack will seal the opening or destroy its guardians. We must therefore be prepared to flee at the slightest suggestion that something is rising from below. We need not fear anything other which might appear; the stones will protect us from them; but if He who waits dreaming below rises, we dare not linger. Let us therefore lose no time in mining the portal."

The surface of the island was cloying. The muck had not yet been exposed sufficiently to the sun to be dried; moreover, the pale green mists which continued to hang about the island were humid and faintly malodorous, not alone of the exposed surfaces of something long under water, but of something more, an animal-like smell which was neither a musk nor a pungence, but a cloying, almost charnel smell. The atmosphere of the island differed sharply from that of the surrounding sea; perhaps it was the cloying smell, perhaps the humidity, perhaps the exhalation of the ancient stones. And over all hung an aura of dread, all the more inexplicable for the still brightly shining sun, and the protective presence of the *Hamilton*, lying not far off shore.

We worked rapidly. Nevertheless, none of us could escape the growing sense of malevolence which was manifest. The aura of dread which clung to the island heightened steadily, apprehension of some impending horror increased; there was a mounting tension among us, despite the fact that Professor Shrewsbury maintained a ceaseless vigilance at the very threshold of the yawning cavern, ingress to which was afforded by the broken doorway; it was plain to see that he expected danger from this source, if no other, though the very waters around the island were fraught with peril, if Sereke's story were uncolored by his imagination.

At the same time I was agonizingly aware of inimical forces which seemed almost personal; I felt them physically, quite apart from the chaotic confusion of my thoughts. In truth, the island affected me profoundly, and its effect was cumulative, not only fear but a deep depression of my spirits, not only apprehension but a basic disorder of such a nature as to stir up within me a conflict, of the significance of which I was not cognizant, but a conflict which was alarmingly disorganizing, so that I found myself at one and the same time eager to help and anxious to impede or destroy the work being done by my companions.

It was almost with relief that I heard the professor's abrupt cry, "He is coming!"

I looked up. There was a faint green luminosity showing far down the well of dark within the portal, just such a luminosity as I had seen in my dream. I knew, beyond the shadow of a doubt, that what would emerge from that maw would be akin to the being seen in my dream, also, a terrifyingly horrible caricature of an octopoid creature with the grotesquely gigantic half-head of a human being. And for one instant I was moved, not to follow the others, who were already on their way down to the boats, carrying the detonator for the explosives which had been laid all about the portal, but to hurl myself down into that pit of darkness, down the monolithic steps, to that nether place in accursed R'lyeh where Great Cthulhu lay dreaming, waiting his time to rise once more and seize the waters and the land of Earth.

The moment broke. I turned at Professor Shrewsbury's sharp call, and followed, with the malevolence of that charnel place rising behind me like a cloud, and with the horrible conviction that I was marked as the especial victim of that ghastly being making its way out of the depths below that eldrich temple. I was the last of them to reach the boats, and at once we pushed off for the destroyer.

It was still light, though the day was now far gone. The sun had not yet gone down, so that what took place on that awe-inspiring island was plainly visible to all of us. We had moved as far out into the sea as the wires to the explosives permitted. There we waited upon Professor Shrewsbury's order to detonate the explosives, and we were accordingly given the opportunity to see the emergence of the ghastly being from the depths.

The first movement was of tentacles, which came oozing forth from the opening, slithering over the great rocks, accompanied by a horrible sloshing, sucking sound, as of great footsteps in the bowls of earth. Then abruptly there loomed within the portal, preceded by an emanation of green light, a thing which was little more than a protoplasmic mass, from the body of which a thousand tentacles of every length and thickness flailed forth, from the head of which, constantly altering in shape from an amorphous bulge to a simulacrum of a man's head, a single malevolent eye peered. A shocking sound as of retching, accompanied by ululations and a fluted whistling, came to us across the water.

I closed my eyes; I could not bear to see in reality the horror I had seen in dream so short a time ago.

At that instant, Professor Shrewsbury gave the signal.

The explosives burst with a tremendous concussion. What had survived that earlier explosion, including now the portal itself, burst upward and outward. The thing in the doorway, too, was torn open, and in a few moments, portions of the stone blocks fell upon it, further shattering it. But, chillingly, when the sound of the explosion had died away, there came to our ears still, without change, the ululations and the whistling and the retching sounds we had heard. And there, before our eyes, the shattered mass of the thing from the depths was flowing together like water, *reforming*, shaping itself anew once more!

Professor Shrewsbury's face was grim, but he did not hesitate. He ordered the boats returned to the destroyer at once; what we had seen lent strength and purpose to our arms, and we reached the *Hamilton* within a very short time.

General Holberg, glasses in hand, faced us on the top deck. "A shocking thing, Professor Shrewsbury. Must it be the weapon?"

Professor Shrewsbury nodded silently.

General Holberg raised one arm aloft.

"Now let us watch," he said.

The thing on the island was still growing. It towered now above the ruins, expanding into the heavens, beginning to flow down to the water's edge.

"Horrible, horrible," murmured General Holberg. "What in God's name is it?"

"Perhaps something from an alien dimension," replied the professor wearily. "No one knows. It may be that even the weapon is powerless against it."

"Nothing can resist that, sir."

"The military mind," murmured the professor.

The *Hamilton* was moving away, gathering speed.

"How long will it take, General?"

"The carrier will have had our signal by this time; the 'plane was loaded. It should not take longer than it takes us to reach the limit of safety."

On the island a great black mass stood out against the setting sun, diminishing now only because we were moving so rapidly away from it. Presently the island itself was lost, and only the suggestive black mass remained, dark upon the heavens.

Overhead roared an aeroplane, making for the island.

"There it goes," cried General Holberg. "Please look away. Even at this distance the light will be blinding."

We turned obediently.

In a few moments the sound came, shockingly. In another few seconds the force of the explosion struck us like a physical blow. It seemed a long time before the General spoke again.

"Look now, if you like."

We turned.

Over the place where the Black Island had been loomed now a gigantic cloud, mushrooming and billowing skyward, a cloud greater than the size of the island itself, of white and grey and tan colors, beautiful in itself to see. And I knew what the "Weapon" had been, remembering Hiroshima and the Bikini experiment. I knew what a titanic force had fallen upon that hideously menacing island risen from the Pacific for the last time only to be blown asunder with all that it contained, forever.

"I rather think it cannot have survived that," said General Holberg calmly.

"I pray Heaven you are right," said Professor Shrewsbury firmly.

I remember now, after all these months, how sober and grave Professor Shrewsbury was at our parting. I remember how he said something in sympathy, and I did not then understand it, but since then I have come to know that somehow, despite the fact that behind those black glasses he always wore, that strange and wise man had no eyes with which to see, and yet saw, he saw more than I myself knew about myself.

I think this now often. We parted where we had met, at Singapore. From Singapore I went back to Cambodia, then to Calcutta, then to Tibet and back to the coast, from which I took ship for America, driven now by more than curiosity about archaeology, by an insistence upon knowing more of myself, of my father and mother, of my grandparents. We parted as friends, united by a common bond. Professor Shrewsbury's words had been hopeful, yet faintly prophetic. Perhaps, he had said, *He* had died in the atomic blast; but we must recognize, he had insisted, that something from an alien dimension, something from another planet, might not be subject to our natural laws; one could only hope. His work was either done or had gone as far as it could go, short of ceaseless vigilance to stop up temporarily every avenue to the open that might be attempted by Cthulhu or those who followed him, who worshipped him and did the bidding of the Ancient Ones.

Because I alone, of the six of us, had no doubt. Not of the death and disintegration of the thing on the Black Island, but of its survival. I knew by an intuition I could not then explain that R'lyeh still stood in its depths, wounded but not destroyed, that the dweller in those subaqueous depths still existed in whatever form he chose to assume, that his worshippers still bowed in submission to him from every sea and port in the world.

I went home to find out why I had had what I recognized as a feeling of kinship for the Deep Ones, for the thing that lived in the sunken realm of R'lyeh, for Cthulhu, of whom it was once said and is still said, and will be said until the coming again, *"Ph'nglui mglw'nafh Cthulhu R'lyeh wgah-nagl fhtagn."* I went home to Massachusetts to discover why my mother went veiled for most of her life, to learn what it meant to be one of the Waites of Innsmouth, destroyed by the Federals in 1928 to wipe out the accursed plague which had come upon the inhabitants, including the Waites who were my grandparents and my parents.

For their blood flows in my veins, the blood of the Deep Ones, the spawn of that black mating in the South Pacific. And I know that I have earned their especial hatred as a traitor to that blood, for even now, I feel the longing to descend into the depths, to make my way to the glory of Y'ha-nthlei where it lies in the Atlantic off Devil's Reef beyond Innsmouth, to the splendor of R'lyeh in the waters near Ponape, and even now I know the fear of going to them with the taste of treachery in my mouth.

At night I hear them, calling, "Horvath Waite! Horvath Waite!"

And I wonder how long it will be before they seek me out and find me.

For it was vain to hope, as Professor Shrewsbury did, that Cthulhu could have been vanquished so easily. The battle of the Elder Gods had been far greater, far more titanic than even that impressive bomb which had erased the Black Island from the face of the Pacific that memorable day. And that interstellar battle had lasted long before victory was won by the Elder Gods, who were all-powerful, who were great above all others and banished the Ancient Ones to outer darkness forever.

For weeks after my shocking discovery, I asked myself which one of us would be the first to be discovered. I asked myself how it would be brought about—certainly by no crude means, no alarming crime which might startle into renewed activity Professor Shrewsbury and Andrew Phelan and the others.

And today the papers brought me an answer.

"Gloucester, Mass.—The Rev. Abel Keane, a newly ordained clergyman, was drowned today while swimming near Gloucester. He had been accounted an excellent swimmer, but went down within sight of many other bathers. His body has not yet been recovered ...."

Now I ask myself who will be next?

And how long will it be in the endless progression of days before those who serve Him will summon me to atonement in those black depths where Great Cthulhu lies dreaming, waiting upon his time to rise again and take possession of the lands and the seas and all that lives within them, once more as before, once more and forever?

THIS TALE OF Great Cthulhu first appeared in *The Arkham Collector* in 1971 (number 10, Summer). Only the previous day had its author discovered Lovecraft and his mad universe. He was so taken with it all (rather like young Wilcox, one supposes) that he sat right down and penned the following as a gag letter to August Derleth, who knew a good thing when he saw it and wrote Foster back pronto, accepting it as a story submission even though it hadn't been intended as one! In fact, it was Foster's first professional sale.

This is not Alan Dean Foster's only piece of Cthulhu Midrash. You may consult another such, "The Horror of the Beach", in my anthology *The New Lovecraft Circle* (Fedogan & Bremer, 1996).

Some Notes Concerning a Green Box

by Alan Dean Foster

S IRS: I DID NOT KNOW what to do with these notes until a friend of mine suggested that I send them along to you, assuming, I suppose, that you might find them of some interest. They form an exceedingly odd story, one with which I am now not so sure I wish to be connected. I report them here as they occurred.

I do not as a rule frequent the facilities of the anthropology department, but an occasion made it necessary. Being a graduate student, I was able to obtain access to files which are kept from the eyes of careless undergraduates and casual visitors. It was in a far corner of the old manuscript storage room that I first came across the box.

It caught my eye because it was clearly the only new thing in the ancient place. Curious, I made a seat for myself on a stack of old papers and examined the thing more closely. It was quite an ordinary-looking green box, except for the rather formidable-seeming lock on its cover and what I imagined (falsely, of course) to be some faint lingering phosphorescence around the edges. I tried the lid idly and discovered that the lock had not been fastened. More out of boredom than anything else, I then reached in and brought out the enclosed sheaf of papers. Most of these seemed quite new, but there were also a few scraps of some thick, coarse vellum which gave some indication that they had been treated with some chemical preservative, for when I first opened the box, an odor issued forth which was noxious in the extreme. It dissipated very rapidly, however, and I thought no more on it.

The contents of the box included typed letters on which were inscribed in longhand various notes, charts, and a sketch, in addition to the yellowed bits of vellum. As the letters seemed to bear somewhat on my area of study, I carried the box and its contents to the main room and began to Xerox the material for later, more leisurely study.

Presently an elderly librarian chanced to pass. Espying the box, she became unaccountably agitated, and quite vigorously insisted that I make a halt to what I was doing. The poor woman was in such a state that I agreed to pause while she went to fetch the librarian-in-charge. At the sight of the box and its revealed contents, that portly gentleman became quite as incensed as the old lady, and the very first thing he did was to return every scrap of paper to the container in question and lock it securely. Containing his obvious anger, he took the old woman off to one side, carefully keeping the box tucked tightly under one arm. Puzzled, I strained to hear their conversation, but I could make out only a few disjointed phrases, for they were careful to speak very softly. The man said, "... who is he? ... not permitted ... should have been *locked* ... delicate situation."

And the woman, "... didn't see! ... no reason to suspect ... ask him ... safe ...."

At this point they halted and the man returned to stare down at me intently. "Did you copy any of the material in this box, son?" I replied that I had not, at which words he seemed unaccountably relieved. When I ventured to inquire as to why I could not copy them, he replied that the manuscripts were as yet unpublished, and therefore not covered by copyright. He smiled for the first time since I had laid eyes on him and said, "No harm done, then!" and shook my hand. Continuing to play out the role, I replied that the material did not seem to offer me much aid anyway, so I was perfectly willing to forget the entire incident.

By a fortuitous coincidence, I had stopped earlier at the post office, having had need to refresh my stock of envelopes and stamps. Now it so happens that I have a friend who is also desirous of obtaining a position on our departmental expedition, and so I had placed my first copies in an envelope and sent them off to him by way of the library mail chute. As things turned out, it was unnecessary for me to write him and request the return of these copies, as the original envelope was returned to my apartment the next day, unopened, stamped "insufficient postage." Despite all my efforts to relocate that mysterious green box, I could not find a trace of it in its former cubbyhole, and deemed it injudicious to make inquiries.

The few copies I *had* succeeded in making consisted of the hand-marked letters and the scraps of yellowed paper. A quick survey of the materials convinced me that I was fortunate to obtain what little I had, as there was apparently a considerable defect in the copying machine. The old scraps, which had been printed in a dark black ink and covered with faded red stains, had failed entirely to be reproduced. It is most curious, as the stains themselves had been reprinted with perfect clarity. I have written to complain to the company, and in typically evasive manner, they replied that they never heard of such a thing.

The letters were apparently the work of two UCLA professors, and I was able to obtain some little information concerning them, which I here include:

"Jonathan Turner, Professor of Anthropology and Linguistics. Born, Providence, R.I. 1920. B.A., University of Maine, 1931. Worked way through college at height of Depression performing heavy manual labor. M.A., Yale, 1932, Ph.D., Yale, 1935, doctoral dissertation, *Some Inquiries into the Nature of Minor Religions of Southern Louisiana and Alabama, with Emphasis on the Cajun Peoples.* (This work, I found, is still available to the interested scholar from the Yale University Research Library, upon presentation of the proper credentials.) Member of American Anthropological Society, Académie Française, etc., etc. ... Married Emaline Henry of Boston, 1937. Following her tragic death in 1960, moved to California and accepted full professorship with UCLA. ... Author of numerous books on a wide range of subjects, including a famous essay on the Atlantis-Lemurian myths.

"Robert Nolan, Assistant Professor of Archeology. Born, Beverly Hills, Calif., 1944. B.A., M.A., University of California, Berkeley. Ph.D. thesis in preparation. Winner of numerous prizes for originality of theory on the archaeology of the Pacific area. Son of a wealthy Los Angeles lawyer."

As to more personal details regarding the two scholars, I was able to gain some insight from certain of their former students. This line of research was made necessary because the erudite colleagues of the two men displayed a marked hostility toward any questions. Turner was a tall, leonine individual equipped with a full spade beard and an unkempt shock of equally white hair. In contrast, the much younger Nolan was squat and almost entirely bald. Built from the innocuous base of a common interest in skindiving, the friendship of the two men grew rapidly despite the difference in their respective ages.

In 1966, both men took their sabbatical leaves together. With the money Turner had saved and Nolan's not inconsiderable resources of prize monies and family accounts, they purchased and outfitted a small, powered schooner and announced their intention to sail to Easter Island and the South American coasts. Turner had always wanted to visit the area, and Nolan was desirous of carrying out some field work of an unspecified nature.

At this juncture information on the professors begins to grow sketchy and unreliable. It is known that they returned to Los Angeles in September 1966, in excellent health and high good spirits. Surprisingly, both men proceeded to resign their positions with the University. This, to the great consternation of their respective department heads, who were understandably depressed at the prospect of losing two such brilliant members of their faculties, one old and venerable, the other a youngster of exceptional promise. But neither man could be dissuaded, and following the setting in order of certain personal affairs, they announced their intention to return once again to the area of their former travels. It is also known that they brought back a number of well preserved and extremely eccentric specimens of carved hieroglyphs and statuettes. These, Nolan maintained, had been found not on Isla de la Pascua (Easter Island), but on its smaller and little-visited neighbor to the west, Sala-y-Gomez. It is also reported that they consulted with a number of supposed specialists in matters occult, among them a rather notorious and disreputable old bookseller in the downtown section of San Diego. The man's shop is no longer there, the structure it was located in having since been torn down and replaced by a multilevel parking lot, one section of which I am able to report sags at the oddest angle, despite repeated attempts to correct it.

Due to the obvious sincerity with which his department deplored his resignation, Professor Nolan agreed to keep in touch with his old friends by means of occasional letters which he would forward whenever the opportunity presented itself. These are the missives which I was able to copy so hurriedly at the anthropology library. On some, the postmark was stamped into the envelope with sufficient force to leave an impression on the letter within, and by judicious use of fingerprinting materials, I have been able to bring them to a legible state. These dates vary from February 3 to May 18, 1967. All are postmarked from Valparaiso, Chile, and one of them confides that the expedition was forced to remain there for such an extended period of time so as to permit the repair of storm damage to their craft.

A letter to the man mentioned in that missive as the repairman, a Señor Juan María y Florez, brought as a reply a note scrawled in an awkward hand, as though the wielder of the pen were unfamiliar with its use. Of the professors it had little to say, except that he, Florez, had always thought of professors as being very composed individuals, and that these two Americans seemed both nervous and jumpy. Instead he dwelt on the damage to their schooner, which was totally alien to him, a man who had worked on ships for over forty years. For example, he mentions that he did not feel Professor Turner's explanation of an "unexpected heavy swell" entirely accounted for the odd twisting of the four-inch steel bar of the schooner's left drive shaft, nor for how three of the four blades came to be broken off the screw. A local shipman in Long Beach assures me that Mr. Florez, despite his forty years, is here doubtless indulging a natural penchant for native exaggeration.

The first of these letters, dated February 11, includes in longhand the note "40 degrees, 9 ' S, still on 110. Nothing visible on horiz. but Bob still conf."

This seemingly innocuous bit of information reveals on inspection a number of oddities. It would seem to indicate that although the letters to home were mailed from February to the middle of May, they were written not in Valparaiso, but while the professors were still at sea! Why the two men should do this and then wait to mail the letters *at staggered intervals* extending over three and a half months from the date of their arrival in Chile is beyond me. And the latitude given is 40 degrees S. It is quite clear. The "110" can only be the longitude. Thus, it must be inferred from this information that the ship was proceeding almost due south from Easter Island. But the most peculiar part of the phrase is the section which states "nothing visible on the horiz.", since this would seem to imply that perhaps the two men expected that there might *be* something on the horizon. This is blatant nonsense, since a quick glance at any map of the Pacific will suffice to show even the casual observer that there is nothing present in that section of ocean for hundreds of miles in *any* direction, let alone due south! It is interesting to note, though, that this course was taking them almost directly down the center of the subsurface mountain mass known as the Easter Island Cordillera.

The next letter carries in its margin the words, "Turned east, following Cook instruc." Once again consulting the Research Library files, I found that Captain James Cook had indeed passed this same section of sea in 1773 on his return voyage to England. What is *more* interesting is the fact that the following year the captain, usually a dead-accurate navigator, spent some considerable time wandering about in the area between 40 and 50 degrees latitude, and 120 and 130 degrees longitude. Certainly he could not have been there searching for something, as the area is as desolate a stretch of ocean as exists on this world.

The next legible note reads, "129 W. Bob discouraged, turning back w. current." This can only mean that Professor Nolan did indeed expect to find *something* in this empty piece of sea and, as one would anticipate, he had not. Also, the reverse side of the letter contains the admonition, "coord wrong? check Sydney Bulletin." At the time, this reference held no meaning for me.

There remained only one last notation of any consequence, and I have come to regard that one as the key to the entire baffling matter. It is at once the clearest and most mystifying of them all, and consists of three parts. The words, "check Lvcrft ref", some cryptic symbols in Professor Turner's hand, and one word, written underneath: "CTHULHU."

The reference to a "Lvcrft" puzzled me utterly, until I chanced to mention it to a fellow student. He informed me that my "Lvcrft" was possibly H. P. Lovecraft, a writer of the 20's and 30's who wrote weird fantastic stories. Searching out an index of the man's work, I was both surprised and pleased to encounter a tale containing mention of the odd word "Cthulhu", entitled "The Call of Cthulhu." Procuring a book containing the indicated story, I read it with what was at first avid interest. My interest quickly flagged. I was disappointed! Here I had thought I had unearthed some potentially great scientific discovery which for some unknown reason certain parties were trying to suppress, when in actuality all I was doing was wasting my time with the childish fantasies of two grown scholars who presumably should know better!

Still ...

Further along in the story I found references not only to that same *Sydney Bulletin*, but also to a certain mythical island or coastline that supposedly was found at "latitude 47 d, 9 ', and longitude 126 d, 43 '!" If only as a source of some little humor, these coincidences piqued my lagging interest considerably. I subsequently wrote to a newspaper friend of mine in Melbourne, who promised to locate for me a copy of the *Bulletin* for the date indicated in the story (April 18, 1925). Several weeks later I received a letter from my friend apologizing, in which he informed me that the only known complete file of the *Sydney Bulletin* had perished in the Sydney University fire of 1929. I found this an especial curiosity since Lovecraft's story had been written in 1928.

Additional research turned up more disturbing facts. I must add that I continued to pursue these tiresome researches because I have to date been unable to uncover any information whatsoever regarding the whereabouts of Professor Turner or Professor Nolan, who apparently dropped out of sight after departing Valparaiso on May 21 of '67. I would greatly appreciate any information concerning same. As a last resort I attempted to get in contact with the only surviving relative of either man, but Professor Nolan's father retired from his law practice last year and moved to Europe.

A recent chat with the Chilean consul in Los Angeles produced as a by-product a kind and gracious letter from one Carlos Malpelo, the Valparaiso Chief of Police. He writes that after the date mentioned, 21 May '67, there is no additional information on the two American professors, but that there are two items of related interest which he thought I might find interesting. The first is that the professors spent much time at the Santiago University, and in particular with an old friend of Professor Turner's, the renowned Chilean linguist P. C. Fernandez. It is also noted that the professor was much pleased upon receiving from the two Americans a gift consisting of a sealed box containing a peculiarly formed statuette of unusually repugnant design.

Unfortunately there appears to be no way to confirm any of this, because Professor Fernandez was one of the many casualties of the recent great Chilean earthquake. The few Indian porters in his party who survived the quake were too shaken to do more than report the death of the professor and of their fellows. These men were found in the mountains in the night after the quake, shivering and frightened. They were given food and clothing by the government rescue team and permitted to return to their families, except for one oldster who adamantly maintained in spite of the most determined expostulations that the professor was responsible for the quake. According to this patriarch, the professor had been performing some incomprehensible ritual with burning herbs and an odd little idol when the tremors had begun. At this point the old man's testimony lapses into insane drivel, as when he claims that the mountain across the valley from them got up on gigantic stone feet and stepped on the professor, killing most of the party with him. The poor man was placed in the public sanitarium for the poor at Rancagua, but apparently escaped last year from that well known institution.

The other "item of interest" which the good Senor Malpelo forwarded to me was much shorter, but of no less import. It was a bit from a small Valparaiso newspaper stating that one Juan María y Gomez, given occupation, shipwright, was missing and presumed lost at sea during the night of a storm on June 6, 1967. A trawling fishing boat came upon the shattered wreckage of Señor Gomez's boat the next day. It is mentioned that the ship must have passed through an exceptionally violent part of the storm, because what pieces of the ship's fittings were found were battered beyond all recognition, even to the shaft of one of the ship's screws, which was twisted quite completely out of shape.

Lately, I have been showing the cryptic symbols which appeared in Professor Turner's hand above the word Cthulhu around the University. The reaction I get is peculiar in the extreme. Most professors who see it take it in good humor as an unusual student prank. Those few who do not find it funny exhibit an odd trembling of the hands when they first set eyes upon it, but cover up very quickly thereafter and pronounce the symbol an insulting hoax. They are quire forceful about this, and wish to have no more to do with it. I am much puzzled, as this seems to occur almost always with the older professors.

The first of the charts I copied shows the general area of the South Pacific. It has drawn in Easter Island, a rough duplication of Cook's courses for his voyages of 1773-75, and a number of other notations and markings, most of which are unintelligible. Most peculiar of these is an "X" at approximately 167 degrees east longitude, and 77 degrees south latitude. Under these coordinates are the notes "Halley's, '86", which doubtless refers to the next reappearance of the famous Halley comet, due back in our solar vicinity in 1986. A check of a National Geographic map of this area reveals that the above coordinates intersect on or very near Mt. Erebus, the 15,000-foot-high active volcano on McMurdo Sound in Antarctica. What this has to do with the next appearance of Halley's comet is no doubt known only to Professors Turner and Nolan.

The second sketch is simply a crude map of the world with two lines drawn in on it. Although laughable in its simplicity, I was rather intrigued by this, as the two lines ran thusly: one went in a straight line from that "X" (Mt. Erebus?) to Easter Island. The other line runs from Easter Island, through the center of its neighbor,

Salay-y-Gomez, to a spot in the Andes of Northern Chile. This, again coincidentally, happens to be the area Professor Fernandez was exploring when he was killed by the earthquake. Straight as an arrow, it continues onward with three other "X's" marked along its length. One is somewhere in the jungle of the Matto Grosso (memo: write the Brazilian Land Survey), another in the Brazilian Basin, the deepest part of the Atlantic Ocean, to end finally near Addis Ababa, in Ethiopia.

The last item was neither note nor chart, but rather a sketch-drawing of what seemed to be some enormous pyramidlike structure of ridiculous shape, with accompanying notes in Turner's hand. This was the sole item I managed to smuggle from the library intact. I regret that soon afterward I was offered a really ridiculous sum of money for it, no questions asked, from a wealthy professor I was consulting, and so sold it to him. He has since moved.

That completes what I have found to be an exceedingly odd collection of facts, and until Professors Turner and Nolan return (from wherever they are) I am afraid much of this material must remain as puzzling as ever. I hope you find it of some little interest. Besides, I have come to think it wise to have the facts in the hands of an unadvertised party. Lately I have had the feeling of being followed, especially at night. I was also forced to move from my former apartment after experiencing a spell of severe nightmares unique in their prismatic horror. The doctor at the University assured me that these are the natural results of overwork at school. This may be, but the series of twelve grooves, six to a side, that I found etched into the glass of one of my windows one morning after a particularly vivid phantasm of terror have made me cautious. One thing I know, and that is that they were not the result of overwork at school.

That is all I have to say about my work with the green box and its odd contents. I am quite happy in my new lodgings, and I am no longer troubled by nightmares. Also, I have been selected to go on the University expedition to the South Seas! My associate and companion will be a brilliant and eccentric cinematographer named Pickman. Only one last thing bothers me unreasonably. My new landlord has the most peculiarly colored yellow eyes.

IN THE INTRODUCTION to this book, I windily discussed the possibility that some of the Commonplace Book plot germs that Lovecraft wound up using in "The Call of Cthulhu" seem to have been first intended for a rather different story, one set in the bayou country and centered on a decadent cult thriving there. HPL never actually wrote the original implied tale.

We got to wondering just what might have happened in that stillborn tale. Here's a strong possibility. C. J. Henderson, master of supernatural detective stories, seemed the ideal man for the job. As you will see, the story is set as a sequel to "The Call of Cthulhu", but it does sneak back and take a second look at the story Lovecraft swallowed whole. It is sometimes forgotten that Lovecraft maintained an interest in detective mysteries, ever since he organized his own sleuthing agency as a boy in Providence. He used the detective/police report form (from both sides of the interrogation table) in stories such as "The Haunter of the Dark", *The Case of Charles Dexter Ward*, and "The Statement of Randolph Carter." "The Lurking Fear" and "The Horror at Red Hook" actually have as their protagonists occult detectives. So it seems entirely in harmony with Lovecraft's intent to make the burly, rough-and-ready Inspector Legrasse the hero of what is essentially a "posthumous collaboration."

Patiently Waiting

A Tale of Inspector Legrasse

by C. J. Henderson

> The universe is full of magical things, patiently waiting for our
> wits to grow sharper.
>
> — Eden Phillpotts

"WELL, WELL," smirked the grinning lieutenant, his feet up on his desk, "look who's back." Throwing himself out of his chair, he stood quickly and then bent low to make a sweeping, near-comical bow to the man in the doorway, ushering him inside.

"Sooooooo very good to have you back, el Grande."

Inspector John Raymond Legrasse scowled at the bowing figure. The tall, thick-boned man was weary from both his long train journey and then the carriage ride from the station, delayed as it was by the monsoon-like storm pelting the city. Cold, tired, and wet, the inspector was not quite in the mood for the shenanigans of his second-in-command. Dropping his rain-soaked travel bag, but not the package under his other arm, Legrasse stepped aside to allow the older man behind him entrance.

"Professor William Channing Webb," he said, stripping off his water-logged hat and gloves, "Lieutenant Joseph D. Galvez."

Recognizing the elderly professor's name from a wire his superior had sent ahead before leaving Missouri, Galvez brought his clowning to an immediate end. He snapped to attention, his voice losing its comedic edge as he offered, "Quite good to meet you, sir. May I take your wrap, get you a hot beverage? Tea? Chicory coffee?"

"Oh, my," answered Webb, gratefully shucking off his drenched overcoat, "I've heard tell of your powerful Louisiana blends—that they simply grab a man's throat, pull it out of his body, and then do a dance on it with pointed shoes before they put it back—usually wrong end first."

"Tea, then?"

"Oh, no," answered Webb, a twinkle in his eye confirming that he might be something of a jokester himself, "I've waited some twenty years since I first had the effects of chicory described to me. At my age I don't believe it good to wait much longer. Please, sir, a large one. Black, with two generous dollops of sweetening, if you could."

Galvez smiled. He liked the tall older man immediately. He did not know who the professor was beyond his title, but the inspector's wire had hinted at *why* the man had returned with Legrasse. And, if he was there for *that*, then taking care of his wrap and fetching him some coffee was short payment. Short payment, indeed.

As Galvez bustled off with the professor's coat, Webb asked, "No coffee for you, Inspector?"

Legrasse did not look up from his immediate chore. Still unwrapping the package that had been under his arm, he answered, "Galvez? Fetch coffee for his inspector?" Switching his voice to a fair approximation of the short Spaniard's, he said indignantly, "I, sir, am a lieutenant. Not a waiter. What a suggestion—"

"Let him get his own coffee."

The interruption had come from a returning Galvez. His bit of a joke raised the corners of Legrasse's mouth into something that actually resembled a smile. It was the first such moment the inspector had experienced in nearly six months. The muscles of his face, so unused to such treatment, stabbed him with mild discomfort as if to show their resentment. Legrasse merely rubbed at his cheeks, massaging the surprised muscles. An actual smile was too precious a thing to abandon merely because of an unexpected bit of discomfort.

The lieutenant handed Professor Webb his requested coffee. Deep, murky steam pushed its way through the rancid humidity hanging in the chilly air of the station house. The old man blew on the near-boiling brew in his cup, then threw back a healthy slug. When the professor did not come away retching from the brew's thickly pungent taste or crying from the scalding temperature, Galvez expressed his admiration for a novice who could down his thick blend so easily.

"My boy," answered Webb, "I've drunk brews made from tree bark moss, crushed wood grubs, and corn husks mixed with animal dung, to name only a few of the less revolting. In my field, you meet a lot of different people tucked away in all sorts of the world's far corners. Why, to some of them, this little delight of yours would be considered nothing more than a cherry frappé."

"Speaking of revolting," interrupted Legrasse, finally done un-binding the package he had so gingerly carried from Louisiana to Missouri and then back to New Orleans, "why don't we get down to business, eh?"

All eyes turned toward the inspector. There was not a person in the room who did not know what was in the package, who had not seen it before, who did not want to avoid seeing it again—and yet, they looked. They could not help themselves.

Pushing back the slick oil paper wrapping, Legrasse discarded the box's thin wooden top, drawing forth the wads of protective stuffing between him and the "revolting business" within. When finally the box's contents were laid bare the inspector pulled on one of his drenched travel gloves once more. Then, with only the slightest hesitation, he reached in and extracted the thing which had sent him to Missouri in the first place—which had pulled Professor Webb back to New Orleans with him.

It was a statue, a diminutive figure between seven and eight inches in height. It was a piece of exquisitely artistic workmanship. It was also a thing whose utter strangeness and air of genuinely abysmal antiquity had sent the collective world of archaeology into an unbelieving tailspin when the inspector had shown it days earlier at the annual meeting of the American Archaeological Society in St. Louis. Indeed, Webb had followed him back for the chance to examine the site of its discovery, forsaking all on his already overcrowded schedule. Legrasse was happy to have him.

Setting the figurine on the desktop before him, the horror of the familiar piece assaulted him again—a blow he simply could not grow used to no matter how many times it was struck. Of course, as a mere piece of art, the statuette was not so fearsome on its own.

It represented a monster of vaguely anthropoid outline, but with an octopus-like head whose face was a mask of feelers, a scaly, rubbery-looking body, prodigious claws on hind and fore feet, and long, narrow wings behind. At least three eyes, clustered randomly, recalled the ocular chaos of certain spiders. The thing, whatever it might be, was designed with a somewhat bloated corpulence. It perched evilly on a rectangular block or pedestal covered with undecipherable characters. The tips of its wings touched the back edge of the block, its seat occupied the center, whilst the long, curved claws of its doubled-up, crouching hind legs gripped the front edge and extended a quarter of the way down toward the bottom of the pedestal. The figure's cephalopod head was bent forward so that the ends of its facial feelers brushed the backs of the huge forepaws which clasped the croucher's elevated knees.

But it was not the unnatural design of the beast or any particular skill on the part of the artist toward the bizarre that gave the bit of stone its repellent aspect. It, itself—either the very stone of it, or some mark left upon it by some foul previous contact, like the breath of a drunk pulled up out of the gutter, or the hand prints of a muddy child on the linen suit of its father—it was simply a malignant *thing*. A sketch of it, or a photograph—even one of the Lumière brother's moving pictures—would never be able to convey the monstrous horror one discovered through simple proximity. Merely staying in the same room with it for any amount of time was to invite nightmare. Handling it flirted with damnation.

"Didn't get any prettier," whispered Galvez, "did it?"

"No," responded the inspector absently, "but then, neither did you."

Galvez grinned sourly. Several of the other men in the vicinity chuckled. For anyone else the excitable young Spaniard would have had a ready response. But, rank having its privileges, the lieutenant allowed the crack to stand, knowing he would get his chance at Legrasse later. In the meantime, Professor Webb moved forward, more fascinated than repelled. He asked for the use of the inspector's chair. When it was granted the older man sat and then leaned forward, taking up once more the study of the figurine which he had begun in Missouri.

"What's with the genius, J. R.?" asked Galvez under his breath. "He know something about this thing?"

"Maybe," answered Legrasse. "It seems the professor came across something like our bunch of lunatics before. He won't really know for certain until we take him out to the swamp to inspect the site where we found the statue."

Galvez crossed himself involuntarily. On the first of November the previous year, he, Legrasse, and eighteen other officers had filled two carriages and an automobile and headed down into the usually quiet lagoon country to the south of New Orleans to answer a frantic summons for help. On the surface, it had appeared the squad had easily handled the crime they had rushed off to investigate.

The swamp squatters who had begged their assistance were of a breed that usually wished as little contact with the outside world as possible. But their people had been disappearing in a mysterious and bloody fashion and all that were left found themselves in the grip of an unknown malevolence.

The police had gone in, pressing off into the swamp when their local guides refused to take them any further, finding the source of the disturbance on their own. A group of naked men had taken over a grassy island in the middle of a natural glade. There they—or some unknown group before them—had erected a great granite monolith. Using it as their central focus, the savage troupe had built a monstrous ring-shaped bonfire around its base, which they themselves circled, dancing wildly. Around them stood a wider ring, one made up of ten scaffolds set out at regular intervals. From these hung, head down, the oddly marred bodies of the missing squatters.

Legrasse and his forces had routed the near hundred celebrants without any losses to their own numbers. Although those captured did not—indeed, could not—give the police any useful information, the operation had been considered an unequivocal success by the inspector's superiors. Legrasse and his men had solved the disappearances, captured scores of those responsible, and all with no loss of life except for that of five cultists slain during the melee. The officers had returned with forty-seven prisoners, the statue which was discovered atop the monolith, and an unsteady feeling that they had gotten off far luckier than they deserved.

As the months went on, however, the supposed "open-and-shut case" proved to be an incredible bafflement to Legrasse in particular and to the law enforcement agencies of New Orleans in general. First, their prisoners turned out to be worse than useless. The men all proved to be of a low, mixed blood and mentally aberrant. Most were seamen, but there were enough Negroes and mulattoes— mostly West Indians or Brava Portuguese—to give a coloring of voodooism to the heterogeneous cult.

Before many questions could be asked, it became manifest that something far deeper and older than mere African fetishism was involved. Degraded and ignorant as they were, the prisoners held with surprising consistency to the central idea of their loathsome faith.

They worshiped, so they said, the Great Old Ones who lived ages before there were any men, and who came to the young world out of the sky. Those Old Ones were gone now, inside the Earth and under the sea, but their dead bodies had told secrets in dreams to the first men, who had formed a cult which had never died. The cult had remained constant, and always would, its practitioners said, hidden in the distant wastes and dark places all over the world until the time when the great priest Cthulhu, from his dark house in the mighty city of R'lyeh under the waters, should rise and again bring the planet under his sway. Some day he would call, when the stars were ready, and the secret cult would be waiting to liberate him.

And that had been all the inspector, his men, or anyone else who made the attempt could wring out of the prisoners. Most of the miscreants had already been dealt with by the courts, routed on to the appropriate mental institutions or to the hangman, whichever had been deemed the more appropriate. If the horrific crime had been in any way even one step closer to a mundane atrocity, that might have been the end to it. But too much of the strange had continued on since that night in the swamp for the police simply to mark the case satisfactorily closed.

Although Legrasse's superiors considered it a job well done, the inspector himself had not been able to close the books on the incident in the swamp. He had made note of too many odd occurrences since the bayou raid simply to drop his investigation. The most striking of his observations had been the fact that none of the prisoners sentenced to execution protested the judgment. In truth, they almost seemed relieved at the prospect.

Legrasse and Galvez had attended the first, prompted more by empty curiosity than anything else. Sitting in the back courtyard where the sentence was to be executed, they watched as the condemned was led to the scaffold. Polite and acquiescent in his brutish way, he climbed the stairs eagerly, his eyes gleaming with the fierce triumph of a boxer who had just taken a great world prize, or an early Christian awaiting the release of the lions.

Having refused a last meal, and then a smoke or a blindfold as well, the swarthy individual asked only to be permitted a few last words. Because of his genuinely calm exterior, which those in charge of the proceedings mistook for some form of repentance, the request was granted. His hands still tied behind his back, the noose around his neck, the man stood over the trap, smiling, nodding his gratitude. Then, throwing back his head, his wild hair whipping with sweat, he bellowed in a clacking tongue, "*Ph'nglui mglw'nafh Cthulhu R'lyeh wgah'nagl fhtagn!*"

There may have been more to his speech, but the small crowd was not to hear it. The hangman, a godly man of a stern order of harsh Protestantism, released the trap pin, sending the jabbering prisoner on to the next realm. He did it on his own initiative, without orders to do so. No one saw fit to reprimand the usurpation of authority, however.

Legrasse and Galvez had left a bit disturbed, as had most of the crowd. More than simple curiosity drew the two officers to the next execution. That time they waited with dread holding a constricting hand across their breath. Once more, a model prisoner was brought forth who had but one request, a few last words. Smiling, he went to his end spewing the same incomprehensible bilge. When a third and fourth execution brought exactly the same results, Galvez suddenly decided he had seen enough executions for one year.

But Legrasse had not. He went to them all, adding another layer to the horror building within him with each one. Why he thought of the cultists as horrific merely because they went cheerfully to their deaths, all shrieking the same line of nonsense, he could not explain. But horrify him it did. What he later found in the asylums was worse.

Deciding to check the state of those prisoners found too unstable to stand trial, the inspector visited both of the hospitals in New Orleans to which the various cultists had been relegated by the courts. In the first, a bleak, cold series of buildings which confined its inmates to singular rooms of tiny, claustrophobic dimensions, he found that the new patients had taken to the asylum routine quite gracefully once they had been assured that they were merely being held for execution. None of them had anything new to tell Legrasse. They simply thanked him for his visit, several asking if there were not some way he might speed up the process so that they might be taken to the gallows faster.

In the second hospital, however, the inspector found a different situation. It was a far more modern facility than the first—the methods used within its walls quite progressive and experimental. It was a sunnier, healthier environment than practically any mental hospital in the country at that time. The progressive administrators, along with the doctors and nurses at that institution, had assured their new charges repeatedly that no one meant them any harm— that they were in no danger of execution there, and that they would be well cared for. Thus the staff were at a loss to understand why the patients had persisted in a state of dread and obsessive terror since their arrival—a state that only grew more shrill and violent with each new battery of assurances.

Several of the cultists managed to commit suicide. One in particular stood out from the rest. The danger of his possible self-destruction visibly obvious to all in attendance, the man was kept in a straightjacket to thwart his desires. One morning he was found dead, smothered in a manner the staff would have thought impossible previous to his success.

The man had chewed through the mattress covering his floor, straight down to the hardwood slats beneath. Then he had continued onward, chewing away at the boards below until finally he had reached a state where he could hook his teeth into the wood, anchoring himself against the floor. After that, he had induced vomiting and choked himself to death in a pool of his own liquefying dinner. It was after seeing the hole chewed into the old oak boards that Legrasse finally began to feel the same despair which had so shaken his lieutenant earlier. Indeed, at that point the inspector began his search for anything or anyone outside the usual sphere of police influence that might shed some light on what had motivated the events in the swamps outside his city.

Finding nothing for several weeks, Legrasse's last hope had been the conference to which he had taken the idol. Meeting Professor Webb had given the inspector a bit of hope. The elder academic had found the same cult, even the same type of graven image as Legrasse had, across the world in the frozen mountains of Greenland. His eagerness to explore the site of another branch of the same lost religion inspired Legrasse to the point where he thought he might finally be able to close the books on the monstrous case once and for all. As he continued to stare at the idol on his desk, the inspector ordered in a soft voice, "Galvez, gather all the men who were with us in the swamp into the announcements room, would you?"

The lieutenant went off to do what Legrasse had requested. As he did, the inspector and Professor Webb merely continued to stare at the statue on the desk. Neither man touched the dark stone—the dreams resultant from previous contact had taught them better—but stare they did.

For the moment, they could do nothing else.

*****

"And that, gentlemen," concluded Legrasse, "is all the background history any of us needs." The inspector had taken nearly an hour's time to retell the entire story to Webb, Galvez, and the eighteen other officers who had gone into the swamp, making sure each man in the room was as aware of every detail as everyone else present.

"So now, let us begin to outline what must be done next."

Throughout the room, his officers shuffled uneasily. Knowing what was in their minds, and knowing also that none of the men of lesser rank would dare speak, Galvez asked for them: "Sir, is there anything that says all the men from the first raid need go on the second?"

The quiet in the room stirred like the dust of an ancient tomb at the feet of the first to uncover it. The dry silence shifted soundlessly, moving against its will and then finally settling back to the ground. Feeling its weight, Legrasse answered, "I never ask any man to set foot where he knows he can't walk. I ...." His voice faltered for a moment, his mind deciding how much truth was good for his men. He continued after a moment, admitting, "I understand what hesitations there might be in a man's mind over all of this."

"Ain't no man here what's scaret too bad to follow *you*, Inspector," answered a street officer, Joel Carrinelle. He was a tall but thin man, with the bony hands and protruding Adam's apple common in those of lanky frame. Unconsciously brushing back his cropped hair, he swore, "God's oath, sir, if your gun's in hand, mine's at your back and you're covered right up to Satan's front door if need be. You strike the knocker, Inspector, I'll keep the neighbors busy."

"Thank you, Carrinelle. I'll keep that in mind should we need to venture so far south." As some of the men chuckled, Legrasse invited Professor Webb to the front of the room. Loud enough for his men to hear him, the inspector said, "I want these men to know just what I plan to drag them into. Please, Professor, tell them what you told me in Missouri." As Legrasse took a seat, the professor began to address the assembled police officers before him.

"You are brave men," he said sincerely, "all of you. Of that there can be no question. You have looked upon the cult of Cthulhu and not only kept your sanity, but apparently kept your wits as well. From what I know, *that*, gentlemen, takes a brave heart indeed." Coming from behind the lectern Legrasse had used, Webb moved out in front of it, spreading his hands as he continued.

"These cultists are, I am certain, the most odious, faithless, monstrous representatives of humanity there are to be found. They claim to be everywhere, hidden from the eyes of mankind. I believe them. Those that I discovered years ago, those you have found— curious and degenerate? Unquestionably. They are a deliberately bloodthirsty and repulsive pack of things. The mere mention of them to peoples from outside their number who might still have knowledge of their cult causes even the most degraded to shudder and turn away."

The officers listened intently. Webb told them what science could of the human sacrifice and queer rites practiced by those they were opposing. When he ran through his short bit of exact knowledge of the Cthulhu cult, he went on to tell of other, lesser sects he had studied. He told the officers of men who ate the hearts of their enemies to possess their souls, of slavers and exotic tortures and the secret prophecies of a score of religions, all twisted and foul, each more loathsome than the last. Finally, he told them, "For all we know, these sectarians you have stumbled upon could be capable of any of these cruelties, or things far worse that none of us could even imagine. But gentlemen, that is why it is precisely you and only you twenty in all of New Orleans—perhaps in all the Americas— that can stand against these beasts."

"Beggin' your pardon, Professor," ventured a flush-faced sergeant named Muller, "but what's so special about us?"

"A good question, Officer," answered Webb. "And I shall answer it. You men have all faced these maniacs once. I am told that several of you froze for a moment, that one of you fainted. You won't again. I'll tell you why. When first you see ... oh, what? A yapping dog, perhaps. It barks and howls and you pull back, not so much because it is so fierce, but because its presence came unexpectedly. Once you see what it is and gauge its ability to do you injury, your fear disappears. These things are no different."

Walking back toward the front of the room slowly, Webb threw his words over his shoulder.

"They are merely *men*. Nothing more. They might commit brutish, horrific crimes, but they are not more than flesh and blood. You proved that once. And that time they had the cloak of mystery and the unknown. You have stolen that wrap from their shoulders. They can not wear it to fool you again."

"But what about—"

Webb turned. One of the officers had blurted the few words only to be hushed by his fellows. When the professor could not draw the man out further, Legrasse demanded the officer finish his question. Reluctantly, surrounded by a sea of curious but embarrassed faces, all listened as he asked, "Professor, what if these bunch *be* more than just men? We ain't been eager to say much about little, but it could be you maybe don't know everything about this. I ain't meanin' no disrespect to you nor your learnin', sir, but we ....." The man hesitated again, flustered and uncomfortable. His pause evaporated, however, forcing him to blurt, "We, we saw things out there, *heard* things. Plenty of us saw those eyes—glowing eyes, off in the distance—and that mound, the white mound. It was alive. Alive! And that wasn't but all. There was giant things around us—flyin' things! *Flyin'!*"

"That's *enough*," snarled Legrasse. He understood his men's fears. He had been in the swamp with them, had felt the cold stare of unseen eyes following them throughout their raid. In truth, he had felt those eyes more than once since that night. Even in Missouri. But he would not have officers in his command breaking into frightened shrieks.

As the man sat back down, Webb took over, telling everyone, "There are many things in this world that none of us understands, my boy. I won't bother debating with you whether or not there was something else unseen out there in the swamp with you. In all honesty, from some of the blasted texts and unpublished works I have read over the years, I feared there might have been even before your mention. But, I will ask, if there was, who else is there to stop it but yourselves?"

As the officers looked from one to another, the professor told them, "Every religion awaits some sort of final outcome. Catholics, Jews, Protestants, Hindus, et cetera, all look toward the return of their messiah. Gentlemen, this cult of ours is no different. Each of the executed cultists, as your inspector discovered during his investigations, shrieked strange words before his death. The words mean 'In his house at R'lyeh dead Cthulhu waits dreaming.'" Staring into the eyes of the officer who had been brave enough to give voice to his comrades' fears, Webb said, "This Cthulhu is their messiah, and they await his return as you do that of yours. If the sound of great wings here means otherworldly presences, all I can say is if the angels of some devil-worshiping cult's messiah have arrived on the scene, then it is all the more important for you to prepare for battle."

Legrasse was glad no one was present save the men who had actually been in the swamp. What they were saying would have seemed madness, perhaps even unintelligible, to anyone who had not stood in the fetid air of the swamp that night, listening to the ominous snap of giant wings, feeling the cold taste of hungry eyes rubbing against their backs. As the inspector pushed the unnerving memories back to a safer compartment within his brain, Webb moved closer to the officer he had picked out from the others, telling him, "Whereas others would be venturing into the unknown, *you* have been there. As frightening as the thought of returning might be, imagine what it would do to others. *You* men, you have a better chance than any force in the world."

"A better chance of what?" asked Galvez, the words popping out of his mouth before he could stop them.

"Of surviving, of course," answered Webb, matter-of-factly. When asked, "Surviving what?", he answered, "I won't know that until I've inspected the site of the melee."

"And what if you *don't* survive?" asked yet another officer.

"Then I would suggest you kill all the cultists in your custody and every other one you can find, before they succeed in returning their god to this plane, which ... if my calculations are correct, they will be attempting to do again—" The professor reached into his jacket pocket and pulled forth a small note pad. Flipping it back a dozen or so leaves, he finally found the page he had been looking for. He scanned it for a moment, then answered, "Some time next month."

*****

Luckily for the quartet of boaters, the torrential storms had stopped during the night. The next morning, despite the danger presented by the swamp's treacherous bogs, Webb, Galvez, Carrinelle, and Legrasse set off for Monolith Island, the colorful name given the site of the November 1st foray by the lieutenant. Unlike the first trip, however, this time some of the locals accompanied the investigators the entire way. Having the use of the swamp-dwellers' crafts along with that of their owners' services in getting them to the island made the trip a far easier thing to accomplish than if they had been on their own.

Thanking their guides both with words and a pair of silver dollars, Legrasse instructed the boatmen to return for them in four hours—far into the late April afternoon, but still enough in advance of sundown to keep everyone happy. The pair of squatters agreed, departing in one boat, leaving the other behind in case their passengers had some then-unforeseen need for it. By the time their sleek, hand-carved bottom dragger had disappeared back into the moss-hung reeds, the inspector turned to find Webb hard at work, struggling to reach the top of the monolith.

With Carrinelle boosting him, the professor attained the platform of the great stone, a smooth surface of some five to six square feet. Legrasse ordered Carrinelle to remain with Webb while he and Galvez scouted about. The officer acknowledged his orders, taking up his post at the foot of the monolith while the professor busied himself atop it. At the same time, Legrasse and his lieutenant moved off to the other side of the island. As they walked, Galvez asked, "Inspector, what do you make of his talk yesterday, all that stuff about the things we thought we heard and saw? About heathen religions having their own gods and all?"

"Joseph," answered Legrasse, "what do you want from me? Should I say I think he's crazy and not be prepared? Should I say I think he's right and that we're surrounded by monsters from some savage's idea of Hell? I don't know what to think. None of us do. Maybe we were all letting things get to us last year. But then, maybe not. You have to remember, he needs facts just as much as we do. The more wild suppositions we supply him with, the more wild the answers he has to give us back."

The inspector stopped for a second, staring out over the vast mud flat the relentless rains had made of the island. The unnatural chill of the past few days still hung in the air, made to seem all the more damp by the oppressive cover of hard gray clouds teeming from horizon to horizon. Legrasse fought the urge to snap at his lieutenant. The breakdown of his self-control had been inching forward for months, each new bizarre occurrence shaking him along just another small fraction toward the comforting embrace of madness and fear. Resisting their inviting lure, however, the inspector turned to Galvez and said, "We're policemen. We have a job to do. No one ever said anything about winged monsters when we signed up— that's true. But then no one ever made you any assurances about anything. You swore to uphold the laws of the city of New Orleans and to act in good faith to protect its citizens." Legrasse shuddered slightly as a strange thought passed through his mind. Instantly he seized upon it as a way to make his point.

"Twenty-two years ago when I joined the force, no one said anything to me about monsters either. But two years later, we all read the papers out of London as they rattled on about the ghoul there carving up women. Twenty years now and that one's never been captured. Flesh stripped from the bodies of the victims, organs removed, breasts cut away, hints of perverted sexual mutilation ... who's to say *that* monster didn't have wings?"

Galvez tilted his head as if he had been slapped. His nostrils flared with distaste. It was not that the lieutenant did not like cases that made him think. He was a man of rare intelligence, skilled in reasoning down clear, deductive paths. But this case was beyond his ken. Galvez had long been known as a man who could anchor himself firmly and pull the facts of a situation to him, no matter how deeply he might have to dredge the various mires in which they might be hidden.

This time, however, he found he could not position himself. The case seemed too much like the swamp that had borne it. The lieutenant could find no ground solid enough to plant his feet so that he could begin dragging for the clues to its solution. Every other moment, instead of helping to clear his vision, each new fact seemed only to obscure things further—leaving him groping for the shore of his consciousness, drowning in the darkness. Abandoning the front lines, he acquiesced to Legrasse instead, asking, "So, what do we do then?"

"Whatever Professor Webb needs us to do. The pair of us aren't going to get anywhere with this on our own. We've been over this island twice by daylight now and not found anything that meant much to us. Our only hope now is that somehow—" And then, before Legrasse could continue, Professor Webb's voice interrupted his line of reason.

"Inspector! I say ... have you made note of that clearing over there?"

Legrasse and Galvez both looked off in the directionWebb was pointing. From their poorer vantage point, neither man could even make out that a clearing existed behind the bank of intervening rushes and overhung festoons of Spanish moss. So eager to investigate that which only he could see, the older man nearly fell from his high perch. The inspector ordered Carrinelle to assist the professor's descent while sending Galvez back to bring the squatter's flat-bottomer around so they might all be able to move across the swamp to whatever it was that Webb might have discovered. The lieutenant turned to head back for the boat, but just before he did so, he reminded Legrasse, "Inspector, over there—that grove— that's where, I mean, the men who saw the eyes ... and the big white shape ...."

"Get the boat," the inspector said quietly. Staring over at the remote ring of trees, he thought to himself that he needed no reminder as to where they were heading.

It took some time longer than Legrasse had anticipated for the quartet to make their way to the hidden clearing. Although the recent rains had brought up the water level of the swamp, allowing them to navigate past many of the bog's hidden traps—old logs, hidden sand shelves, grasping quick muds, and the like—that little-traveled part of the swamp was dreadfully overgrown, forcing Galvez to hack their way clear several times.

Even climbing the bank leading to the clearing proved nearly fatal when Professor Webb slipped, slamming into Carrinelle, sending him sliding backward down into the bog. Galvez managed to catch hold of his sinking fellow officer and pull him back to safety. Webb, of course, offered his profoundest apologies, which the policeman accepted with extreme good grace, commenting that if the worst thing that happened to him there was a dirty uniform then he would be well pleased.

Finally, however, the four men reached the clearing. What they found there gave them far more questions than they would have thought possible. Descending down the bank, the quartet moved cautiously, watching their step as best they could as they moved through the surrounding ring of trees and out into the open—the strange and unnatural opening that should not have existed.

"I don't get this, Inspector," offered Carrinelle. "What could do something like this?"

Not having an answer for the officer, Legrasse deferred to Webb. The professor took a moment, then finally managed, "I, I think maybe ... yes, maybe ...?"

Bending down, Webb knelt on the ground, examining the strange matting beneath all their feet. The clearing was a circular space roughly thirty yards wide at its diameter. The longer the inspector stared at its circumferential edge, the more convinced he became that it was a true circle, geometrically perfect.

Bending down, he studied the flooring of the area with an interest to match the professor's. He found the reeds and moss and other vegetation woven together into a type of matted carpeting. The sight stupefied the four, dragging all of them to their knees for a closer look. Legrasse did not know what to think. He poked vigorously against the pattern but could not force through so much as a single finger. Common horsetail and scouring rushes were webbed together with club moss and marsh ferns, all of it tightly interworked until it was solid as plate iron.

"Professor," asked Legrasse in a puzzled voice, "what could have done this? The storm, maybe?"

"This is simply fascinating," answered Webb, almost unaware he was doing so. Not looking up, crawling along the ground as if intent on inspecting every square inch of the puzzling phenomenon, he continued, saying, "Look at the workmanship. Not a stem broken, not a leaf or shoot torn away from its mother stem. No storm did this. This is even beyond the work of human hands. Look—look, will you? This isn't recent. You can see this was done some time ago. Note how the new growth is all above the lines of intersection."

Standing, the professor told the others, "I'm no botanist, but I'd be comfortable guessing that we are seeing four to five months of winter growth here since this circle was woven."

"You're saying the cultists did it?" asked Galvez.

"No," answered Webb noncommittally. "I'm merely inferring that it was most likely done at the same time as their ritual."

"Well," asked Legrasse, disturbed to have discovered a completely new mystery instead of any new answers, "if the cult didn't do it—and I wouldn't suspect any of that lot of being of a very artistic bent—who or what did?"

"I appreciate your curiosity, Inspector," answered the professor. "And I will tell you the only guess I have, although I'm afraid none of you will want to hear it."

The men around Webb all hesitated to varying degrees. Each had been wishing to turn the bizarre puzzle of the swamp into something easily processed and stored within the human mind. The professor's offer did not sound as if he would be providing such an answer. Having none of their own, however, each of the three nodded their willingness to hear what Webb had to say.

Understanding their apprehension—actually feeling some of it himself—the professor told them, "Again, gentlemen, I am not trying to mock you, nor am I saying that what I have to offer is the only answer. I am merely going to relate to you several stories I have heard." All three policemen remained quiet, their eyes riveted to Webb. Nodding his head in tight-lipped acceptance of their attitude, the professor swallowed a breath of the gray swamp air, and then launched into his tale.

"Back a few years, what was it ... '83, I believe. A Mexican astronomer named José Bonilla photographed over one hundred circular objects that moved across the solar disc. Before the end of that same decade, a Texan farmer saw a large circular object flying overhead. He called it a saucer. Now, mayhap none of you heard of either of those cases, but I'm certain that you've all heard of the scores of sightings of like objects over the past ten years." The professor paused to swat at a large, blood-seeking insect. Sending the buzzing annoyance on its way, he wiped at his brow and continued.

"All across the country, people have been seeing giant ... what would one call them? Airships, I suppose. Traveling much faster than any dirigible, capable of changing course at what appear to be frightfully high speeds, many have described them as seeming more alive than man-made."

"Very well and fine, Professor," interrupted Legrasse. Pointing downward with both hands, he spread them apart to indicate the entire clearing while he asked, "But what exactly does any of that have to do with *this?*"

Nodding with the understanding that he had failed to come to the point, Webb answered, "Wherever in the world these 'saucers' have been seen in the sky, sooner or later, on the ground below, circles such as these have appeared ... almost without fail."

*****

Legrasse raised his glass to his lips, downing another healthy slug of bourbon. He was not usually one to drink with his men. In fact, he was not usually one to drink at all. "Usually" no longer applied, however.

After exiting from the swamp, Legrasse, Galvez, and Carrinelle had taken Professor Webb to Jim Dandy's, a tavern of little repute on one of the darker back streets of the Quarter. Once properly hidden from public view in a dark, practically moldering corner, the four had set to work on a bottle of the local bourbon. When that one was finished, they promptly started a second. Older than the others, Webb found the opening of the second bottle his cue to remove himself to the toilet for a moment's relief. On the way back from the swamp he had reached a state of nervous agitation, the edge of which hard drinking had not yet been able to remove. As the elder academic tottered off, Carrinelle announced with a thickening tongue, "Sir, I don't know what to think."

"About what, Joel?" answered Legrasse. The liquor bending him to a more familiar tone than usual, he explained, "I mean, I know 'what about', but what about in particular?"

"Oh, hell, sir," admitted the more than slightly drunken officer. "Anything. Everything. I mean, I mean ... I ... I mean ... what? What was that? That professor ... sayin' he wasn't certain anymore about, about ... what was that again?"

"About 'the timetable of arrival,'" quoted Galvez.

"Yeah! Lookin' in his little book, climbin' all over that damn hunka stone. What was he talkin' about? And the way he's been gettin' since we left—spooky, crazy. I don't know. I don't know." Carrinelle raised his glass to knock back another powerful slug. Suddenly, however, he simply set the glass back down and asked quietly, "What? What're we doin', sir? What?"

"I don't know, either, Joel," answered the inspector honestly. Staring over the rim of his glass, his eyes leveling off in a straight line made up of heavy hoods and scarlet eyes, he said slowly, "Who could know? Do you know, Joe?" When the lieutenant merely waggled his head back and forth, blowing a few foamy bubbles through his moist lips, Legrasse pointed toward the lieutenant as drunken proof of some sort, saying, "See?"

The inspector drained a third of his glass as if in triumph. Then, instead of refilling it immediately, as had been the quartet's wont throughout the evening, he set the tumbler back down. Closing his eyes, Legrasse held his neck rigid, then shook his head several times. He could feel the bones at the top of his spine crack, could trace a sluggish pain within his head—the beginning screams of mild alcohol poisoning. Ignoring them both, realizing Carrinelle deserved a better answer, he took a deep breath and then tried to find one.

"What are we supposed to do? I don't know. We put an end to some swamp voodoo. Kill a few of the sect, capture some, run the rest off. That's it—usually. But, no, not for us." The inspector waved his hands in frustration.

"No, we can't just have a group of entrail readers painting each others' faces in chicken blood," he started again. "Oh, no ... not us. We're special. We have to have ... have to have ... what? Some kind of monumentally evil devil-worshiping secret society from the beginning of time. Human-sacrificing illuminati that hides in frozen mountains and swamps and every other out-of-the-way place in the world."

"It's our luck," said Galvez thickly, lifting his glass. Both the other officers lifted their own glasses as well. The trio brought their tumblers together, clinking them softly.

"Our luck," they all slurred, taking large sips immediately after. Then, as Carrinelle topped off all their glasses, Legrasse pushed his spine against the back of his chair, its rattan-covered top curve pressing into his shoulders.

"It's all so odd," the inspector announced, more to himself than to the others. "These cultists ... murdering swamp squatters. Why? Monsters watching us, flying monsters, cultists happy to die. Why? And Webb's saucers in the sky, that clearing ... that horrible little statue ... I wonder ... I mean to say—"

Legrasse froze. The words he was trying to utter hung suspended in his throat, trapped behind the weight of the connections his brain had started to make. In a blinding moment of clarity, the inspector had suddenly made a jump in reason too frightening for him to accept without further consideration. Next to him, Galvez began to raise his glass once more. Legrasse stuck out his hand, though, grasping at the lieutenant's wrist.

"No," he ordered, pushing at the fogging clouds settling within his brain. "No more for now."

Understanding the tone in his superior's voice, Galvez asked, "What is it, sir?"

"Webb ... he treats this all so, so ... serious. He's the only one who doesn't act as if he thinks we were children who scared ourselves out in the swamp. You tell me, Joe—*did* you see something out there last year or didn't you?"

"Well, I—"

"Dammit, Lieutenant. Did you or didn't you?!"

"Yes, sir," answered the excitable Spaniard. Propelled by the liquid courage of many a potent sip, he pushed aside the cautious responses he had given months before and finally admitted, "Yes, I did. You can throw me off the force for saying it, but I swear on my grandmother's grave ... where we stood today, where the reeds and all were wove together like some damned devil basket ... I saw a pair of demon eyes, watching us through the trees ... shining yellow slits carved in a mountainous white bulk ... it was there. I swear it, Inspector."

"Don't worry, Joseph," said Legrasse reassuringly. "I believe you." Before the inspector could say more, however, the owner of Jim

Dandy's came to their table. Bending low, he whispered to Legrasse, who merely nodded an assurance to the visibly disturbed man. As the owner left the table, the inspector told his men, "It seems the professor is having some difficulty in the toilet. Joel, see to him."

The officer rose without speaking, heading straight off to see what the matter was and to deal with it as quietly as possible. Legrasse and Galvez did not speak while he was gone. It somehow did not seem proper to either of them to discuss what was happening to them all with one of them absent. Finally, after some ten long minutes, Carrinelle returned to the table with Webb in tow. As they took their seats again, Legrasse gave the newly returned officer a look which asked what the problem had been. Carrinelle, knowing Legrasse did not want him to embarrass the professor, merely rolled his eyes and gave a shrug of his shoulders, moving his mouth in a manner that indicated Webb was losing his grip.

The inspector took the hint and decided to ignore whatever troubles there had been, having a feeling he already understood anyway. Thus, instead of wasting time worrying about the professor's nerves, Legrasse grabbed up their bottle and topped off Webb's glass, asking him directly, "So, is this all real or isn't it?"

When the professor protested the unsubstantiated theoretical position the inspector's question would force him to take, Legrasse brushed aside his complaints, adding, "Listen to me, Professor, you've been pushing us as if you want us to believe all this ... well, fine. Maybe we do. The question is—do *you* ... or don't you?"

"Inspector Legrasse, I don't want to argue with you now. You've had a great deal to drink and I—"

"Goddammit," roared Legrasse, "*do you or don't you?*" Lowering his voice, the inspector continued. "You said their cult was a religion, that it had a god and angels. You said people have been seeing saucers in the skies and that wherever they see these saucers, circles appear on the ground ... just like that one out in the swamp."

"Well, yes, but what I—"

"Listen—maybe the world's just changed too much for me. Maybe I can't keep up with it. When I was a boy men couldn't fly. Now they can. We have submarines, paint that comes out of guns, air conditioning, those, those ... vacuum tubes, and freeze-dried blood." Legrasse jammed his teeth together, stopping the flow of words spilling out of him. Shaking his head again, trying to drive away some of the alcohol blurring his vision, he snapped, "What I mean is, the cultists murdered the squatters. You said they were blood sacrifices. What if those sacrifices brought that thing my men saw—called to it? Or that damned statue—maybe that's their beacon."

Not looking at any of the others at the table, the inspector found himself shaking his head, not so much consciously, but merely allowing it to twitch. Forcing the motion to stop, he slapped the table again, snarling, "Who knows? *Who cares?!* What does it matter, how and why? *Where!* That's all that matters. If round things are flying down out of the sky and making those vegetation circles all around the world—why not here? You said this Cthulhu cult was hidden in all the dark corners of the world. There's plenty that call New Orleans a dark corner. So, tell me, Professor ... why not here?"

Legrasse grabbed hold of the edge of the table to calm himself. Instead, the shaking agitation raging through him caused him to set the table to bouncing nervously, startling both Webb and his own men. A terrible excitement pelted the inspector's consciousness with information, linking connections faster than he could vocalize them. Licking at the inside of his mouth, driving back the bourbon taste, he let go the table but continued on, asking, "The cultists being executed—each one said the same thing at the moment of his death. The same thing they were shouting when we broke up their ceremony. Is it a prayer? Are they priests?"

The professor turned away from Legrasse, his own hands trembling. Reaching across the table suddenly, the inspector captured Webb's lapels in his hands. Dragging the professor half across the table toward him, knocking over several of the glasses in the way as well as their new bottle, he shouted, "Their god, whatever he is, this Cthulhu ... you said he was sleeping. Well, what if they've decided it's time to wake him up?! What if these flying things everyone's seen are the same things *we* saw, heard ... what if—"

And then, Legrasse went calm. The building madness fled his eyes in an explosive moment of acceptance, replaced by a singularity of purpose. No longer questioning his beliefs, he asked Webb, "When you examined the monolith, you said your calculations had been off. That you had been mistaken about when this god of theirs is supposed to arise. So tell me, if it's not to be in the next month, when *is* it to be?"

With a shudder, the shaking professor answered, "I didn't know then. It all seemed ... seemed so, so academic. So orderly. It was a great mystery to set into place. The pieces were fitting so nicely ... I never thought—"

"When, Professor?" asked the inspector again, giving Webb a harsh shake.

Terrified, the old man yelped, "Tonight!"

Legrasse released the man, letting him fall back into his own chair. His eyes toward the table, hands clutching for his glass, the older man moaned, "I never thought ... of course, it *could* have been real, but who knew? *Who knew?* The concept of it ... all so, really, when you think of it—so, so ... outlandish, so terrifying, so, so ...."

Grasping at his overturned tumbler, the professor righted it and the bottle at the same time. Splashing the unspilled dregs into his glass, he let the bottle fall from his hands and then sucked down the several inches of bourbon he had been able to salvage.

At the same time, Legrasse ordered, "Carrinelle, get back to the station house. Get all of our original investigation force together. Get anyone else you can. Break out all the weapons we have, and send someone around to that construction in the north district up past Jordan Street, where they're taking down all those row houses. Commandeer all the explosives you can."

"Yes, sir," answered the officer. Getting to his feet as best he could, he asked, "Where shall I take them, sir?"

"You take them wherever you like, Joel. I'll be headed out to the swamp."

A huge smile cracked open the lanky officer's face. Heading to the door, he answered, "Stay long enough to have another drink, sir, and I'll have 'em there before you."

As Carrinelle made his way to the door, Webb let out a moaning wail. He had drained his glass and had no more liquor. Seeing that his jacket sleeve was soaked with bourbon, he shoved it into his mouth and sucked hard, pulling a thin drizzle of linty alcohol down his throat. Paying him no mind, Legrasse turned to his lieutenant. "Galvez," he said, "you're a dirty Spanish bastard and you can drink more than any man on the force and still come across as a bishop, agreed?"

"An old family talent," admitted the lieutenant with a sharp, clear-eyed smile that belied the amount of bourbon he had consumed that evening. "It is at your disposal, el Grande."

"Good. Is that old Navy destroyer still in dock?" When his man assured him it was, the inspector continued, ordering, "Then you get yourself down to the waterfront, find her captain, and put on a demeanor that will convince him to put to sea. Tell him we've got pirates, tell him anything you have to, but get him out there lined up with the swamps."

"Yes, sir," answered Galvez, pulling himself to his feet. Turning to head for the door, he suddenly stopped and turned back, asking, "Why?"

"Why? So if any Goddamned monster falls out of the sky at us he can blow it to smithereens."

The two officers rose from the table at the same time, smiling. Taking each others' hands, the two policemen stared for a moment into each others' eyes, both looking for the right words. Finally deciding that there were none, they let go their grip and then headed for the door. Behind them, Webb bent his head to the bourbon-soaked table, tears streaming down his face as he licked at the wet boards.

$$*****$$

This was much easier when someone else was doing all the work, decided Legrasse. Making his way through the growing breeze and the dark swamp night in a borrowed squatter's boat, he allowed himself a grim chuckle, thinking, *You'd better be right about this, Legrasse.*

The inspector had been quieting the cautious voices in his brain ever since he left Jim Dandy's. He knew how things would look if he were wrong. Drunk, dragging a score of officers out into the swamp at night, confiscating explosives, commandeering a U.S. Navy warship ... and why? Oh, because some devil monster was about to descend on New Orleans.

If I have this one wrong, he thought, *there won't be enough of my career left to feed a dog that's already had dinner. And yet—*

Legrasse's mind turned to take stock of what he thought he knew. If he *were* right—a world filled with blood-sacrificing covens, monsters that flew down out of the sky—huge, barn-sized things—angels of some demon religion that sent its congregations out to find it blood and treasure—

"Oh, shut up," he whispered to himself. "After all, maybe the world will be lucky. Maybe I *am* the crazy one. Maybe this is all in my head, and the world is safe after all."

The paddle in his hand came up in a cool, slow rhythm. As he passed it over the front of his skiff, drops fell in an arcing line, the

natural flow of their descent giving the world enough normalcy for
Legrasse to wish, "Maybe."

Cutting across the muddy green water of the swamp, the keening
sound of a thin, reedy piping broke through the whipping trill of
the hot, dry wind. Small and distant, it slammed against the
inspector's ears, making him shudder.

"And then again," he whispered, "maybe not."

He remembered the fluting noise from his first trip to the swamp.
At almost the moment he and his men had become convinced they
had lost their way, the distant sound of pipes and drums had drawn
them to the monolith and the heathen insanity capering around it.
Pulling his paddle inside his borrowed craft, Legrasse stopped all
movement, sending his senses out into the marsh. Listening, he
strained all his internal apparati, searching for any presence that
might know he was about. Feeling that he was still secure, the
inspector then pulled his pistol from beneath his jacket.

It was not common for officers, even high-ranking ones, to carry
firearms. Legrasse had fallen into the habit after being caught in an
alleyway by a trio of rumrunners with a particular aversion to
returning to prison. If not for the luck of a pair of passing beat
prowlers, the inspector's career might have been ended far earlier.

Yes, he thought. *What a pity if that had happened. I'd have missed
all the joy of this evening.*

The weapon was cold in his hand—cold and small and suddenly
seeming far too light to be an engine of destruction. Legrasse's mind
remembered the whispers of his men, of the gigantic white bulk so
many of them had seen. Stroking the German-made automatic, he
whispered to it, "Could you stop something so big, girl? Can
anything we do stop these things?"

Legrasse suddenly jammed the gun back into his waistband.
His cheeks burning, he wondered when he had become such a
child. Whining, filled with self-pity ... pushing on into the
unknown and yet sitting tight-kneed like some school girl. What
was next, he wondered—the vapors? Was it the liquor? Was it
Webb and his highbrow notions? Legrasse had known other men
of science, confident and filled with advice and theories. Until
something went wrong.

Then it was always hand-wringing and frayed nerves and tears.
Arrogance or hopeless fright—that's all you got from academics.
Sliding his paddle into the water once more, the inspector pushed
off toward the sound of the growing music. As his flat-bottomer

slid through the rushes, pushing aside those it could not crush over completely, Legrasse thought about Professor Webb.

He was grateful for Webb's assistance. Indeed, if the older man's theory about the cult was correct—and the crude tune filtering through the night was a strong indicator that he was—then his help would most likely prove invaluable. But clues and suggestions and ideas, that's all his type—professors and scientists—were good for. If Webb were there in the boat with him, he knew the man's horror would have already destroyed them.

Whereas, to be honest with himself, Legrasse was finding his true, inner self almost eager to reach the monolith. As a trace of light slashed through the cattails whipping back and forth in the mounting breeze before his boat, coaxing him on, he felt his pulse quickening. He was getting close.

"Good."

The single word was a whisper, barely louder than his breath, and yet it filled the inspector with a snaking thrill that heated his blood and made the juice run in his mouth.

He had been away from the thick of things for too long. When promotion had raised him above the honest life of a patrolman, Legrasse had become a puppet of formality, an observer of human nature, a seeker of clues, a judge or some other form of civil marionette. Still within him ached the heart of a man, one waiting for its moment—waiting for something worthy of his own self image against which he could test himself.

One silent stroke after another pushed the flat-bottomer along, Legrasse having almost forcefully to hold himself in check. He wanted to charge forward, to take on the whole lot of them ... he could feel their bones breaking beneath his fists, taste their blood in his mouth, smell their fear as he tore at their eyes, hear the sounds of their tears mingled with his laughter ....

Stroke after stroke, the silent swamp boat glided through the marsh, Legrasse growing hotter for the moment of reckoning. His pulse racing, lungs filling to bursting, he knew he was as ready as a normal man could be for whatever lay ahead.

"Yes ...," he breathed, his nostrils flaring, eyes narrowing, smile growing cold and grim. And then, instinctively, the inspector stopped his bottom-dragger. Reaching forward, he parted the rushes in front of the boat a fraction of an inch. There was no further to go. Legrasse had returned to Monolith Island.

Once again, the bonfire had been built, naked dancers braying and writhing about its base ... and also, once again, the scaffolds had been erected. A score of bodies hung from the rough poles, each with at least one corpse swinging from it, most with two, all of them running red from their feet to their heads. The inspector jammed his teeth together at the sight.

For a brief moment, he thought he had failed the squatters of the area. Then Legrasse realized that the cultists had not made victims of the swamp dwellers again. This time, they had used their own brethren. From his vantage point, the inspector studied the area ahead, mapping his strategy. As the dancers rounded the monolith over and over, he counted in excess of a good forty foes. The numbers made sense. The inspector knew he and his men had swept up less than half the cultists during their previous raid. Counting the bodies hanging before him, he knew all of them had returned that night to partake—one way or the other—in their final ceremony. Which was to be ... what?

No matter which way he looked at his scant collection of facts, he could not put the puzzle straight. If the last sacrifice had been used to call a flying monster down out of the sky, then what had become of it? Where was it? And where had it been for nearly half a year?

As he watched the cavorting worshipers, trying to puzzle out his next move, Legrasse was forced to duck down as the heated wind, which had been nothing more than an annoyance so far that evening, now bent his cover back, nearly exposing him. The inspector was forced to lie in the flat of his boat, watching the reeds before him whip back and forth in the mounting gale. Suddenly, as he watched the marsh weeds tangling with each other, Legrasse exclaimed, "Bloody God! That's it!"

Grabbing at his paddle, the inspector forced himself erect through the growing wind. He had been thinking of the monster as something substantial—a physical presence such as a dog or an alligator. But Webb had hinted at godhood for the white mound. What if he had been right? What if they both had been right? What if the normal rules of science did not apply to this horror from beyond?

If the sacrifices were *to summon their god,* Legrasse reasoned, *what if the cultists simply hadn't spilled* enough *blood by the time we arrived? Perhaps it had just* begun *to appear when we arrived. Cutting off the flow of blood to it might have broken its link with this world ... and that was why only some of us saw it. It was here, but when we cut off the sacrifices, it disappeared back to the wherever from which it came.*

Legrasse bent to work with his paddle. No longer concerned with stealth, he aimed his boat straight for the island, tacking against the fiercely growing wind as he thought, *What if they've been killing themselves all along to finish the job? Overjoyed to die one at a time, bit by bit ... using their lives as starvation rations for their god. Webb made noises about certain gravities needing to be right, stars positioned just so ... maybe, maybe these deaths since the raid have just been, been ...* snacks *for this thing of theirs. And now, as Webb said, if tonight* is *the night when they can bring their god back—fully back—to our world ... that would explain the abundance of death here tonight.*

Then a figure on shore pointed directly at Legrasse. For a moment, none of the cultist's fellows heard him over their own feverish musicians and the growling sounds of the ever-increasing wind. Soon, drawn by his gestures if not his voice, others broke off from their dance, spotting the approaching inspector. Realizing he had no other choice, Legrasse pulled his Luger and pointed it, saying, "Very well, you want to meet the devil tonight, you bastards ... let me help you."

The inspector squeezed his trigger. The gesturing cultist's head burst open in a scarlet explosion. Before the dead man's knees could buckle, Legrasse fired again. The motion of his boat on the wind-churned swamp waters throwing off his aim, the inspector hit a second man in the chest instead of the head which had been his target. Falling to the ground, the severely wounded cultist croaked, *"Ph'nglui mglw'nafh Cthulhu R'lyeh wgah'nagl fhtagn."*

A cheer went up from the dancers. Suddenly the force of the swirling winds cutting through the swamp doubled in speed and strength. Although the pipers and drummers kept up their sinister beat, the other cultists all rushed into the water toward Legrasse, chanting and laughing. The inspector used his bullets wisely, shooting down his best target each time, missing completely only once.

As the cultists worked their way through the bog and the fierce winds, Legrasse emptied his automatic. At the first "click" he coolly dropped out the magazine, pocketing the empty clip while fishing a new one out of his jacket pocket. The nearest cultist was but ten feet from the inspector's boat when the policeman finished reloading and began firing once more.

His first shot tore through the head of the closest worshiper, blinding the man behind him with a spray of blood and gray matter.

Legrasse paid neither cultist any heed. Shifting his aim over to the left, he fired again, dropping another.

By the time the jabbering pack reached his boat, the inspector had dispatched nearly a score of them, wounding several others. Bodies floated face down across the marsh, signaling to the carnivores that lived throughout the swamp. Expending his last few shots recklessly, Legrasse dropped his weapon into the bottom of his boat and grabbed up his oar.

The first of the worshipers to reach the flat-bottomer took the full force of the hard wood slat across his face. The blow spun the man around, sending him crashing into one of his fellows. The second to reach the boat, coming up on Legrasse's opposite side, received a slamming even harder than the first man—a blow so hard it shattered the paddle up the center.

Before the inspector could react to the destruction of his weapon, however, one of his attackers threw himself forward, hitting Legrasse in the legs, swamping his boat. The inspector disappeared beneath the dark, oily waters of the marsh, his gun lost, boat overturned. He resurfaced a moment later, coughing and gagging. As three of the cultists splashed forward toward him, Legrasse spat out the last of the foul water he had swallowed and balled his fists.

The inspector sent a driving blow into the face of the first cultist to reach him, knocking the man off his feet. A second swing buried his left fist inches deep in one worshiper's abdomen. Sadly, his third swing missed, allowing two of the cultists to tackle him. The three men splashed about in the thin mud, crushing the centuries-old stands of vegetation, tangling themselves in floating swamp creepers. Legrasse managed to knock one of the cultists away, but the triumph was a small one.

Two more men took their fallen brother's place, dragging the inspector to his feet with the help of the other man with whom Legrasse had first gone down. Then, the howling wind buffeting them mercilessly, the worshipers dragged the inspector to Monolith Island.

Legrasse struggled as best he could, but to no avail. He had swallowed too much swamp water, exerted himself too greatly to resist the dozen rough hands pulling him along. Dragging him up to the great block of granite in the center of the island, through the ring of bloodied corpses, the gibbering cultists shoved the inspector up against the massive slab. Lashing his left wrist tightly, they ran the stout ship's rope completely about the monolith and then lashed his right as well. Then, stepping back from their captive, their leader, a large, glowering Negro with skin blacker than the surrounding night, told Legrasse, "You one lucky white worm, piece shit boy, dat you be."

While the dancing began again, one sweating body after another passing before the inspector's eyes, the high priest came forward and caught Legrasse's chin with his hand. Holding the inspector's face firmly, he laughed and said, "You been try stop mighty Tulu. Foolish little white worm thing. You slide across the ground, you think you be the grand king of all, but you just a bag of air with no eyes. Blind and sad and fit for the grave."

Behind the high priest, Legrasse could see that the musicians had joined the dance, jumping and leaping with the rest of the worshipers as they circled the monolith again and again. Completing the circle, the wind joined them, revolving around the granite block in step with the capering cultists. The inspector could see the whole picture. Blood and spells—whatever intricate pattern they wove—that called the wind. Twisting itself faster and faster, spinning the air around the monolith, the wind was what the cultists used to break the barriers of time and space to drag their foul gods to Earth.

"Yes!" answered the high priest as if he had read Legrasse's mind merely by looking into his eyes. "The worm *understands*! It *understands*!!"

The storm was what wove the strange design in the plants they had found earlier, and it was what called forth the monsters from the sky. The high priest, delighted at the mad understanding he found in the inspector's eyes, unhitched the lead-weighted club dangling from the girdle he wore, the only piece of clothing to be found on any of the cultists. Holding his club on high, an insane gleam in his eye, the black-skinned man shouted to be heard over the howling pain of wind and screams.

"You know—dat good. Good and good. Now you know why die must, to bring down de priests dat will rise up great R'lyeh, and thus free almighty Tulu!"

As a piercing whoop went up from the worshipers, the high priest aimed his club for Legrasse's head and intoned, "*Ph'nglui mglw'nafh Cthulhu R'lyeh—*"

The first bullet ripped through the side of the Negro's head, exploding out the other side, sending an arc of blood out into the growing wind. The second and third hit his body at different levels a split second apart, spinning his shattered frame first one way, then the other. Then, before Legrasse's brain could form the slightest prayer of thanks, suddenly two lines of police broke clear of the distant foliage where the inspector's boat had been swamped, streaming toward the island.

The cultists raced to the water's edge to greet their attackers. None of them possessed weapons outside of teeth and nails, but they seemed oblivious to such concerns. Charging through the ever-tightening circle of wind surrounding the island, they drove forward to the edge of the swamp and then off into its foaming waters, straight on at the attacking line of police.

Legrasse's men allowed them to gain no further vantage than he had. As soon as targets were clear, the officers opened fire, dropping one naked corpse after another into the churning marsh. The wind howling, spinning madly, the constant gunfire, and the shrieks of those it cut down all conspired to fill the air with a masking cacophony, hiding what was really transpiring. Still lashed to the monolith, however, Legrasse was not deceived.

"For our dear Lord's sake, *don't kill them!*"

But none could hear the inspector as he struggled against his bonds. One after another, he watched the cultists die, saw their smiling lips repeat the damning words—

"*Ph'nglui mglw'nafh Cthulhu R'lyeh wgah'nagl fhtagn.*"

Carrinelle reached Legrasse's side just as the inspector had almost freed his left hand. Long strips of skin hung from his wrist and thumb, blood flowing freely, but Legrasse cared not. As his man cut through the last of the restraints, the inspector shouted, "They can't kill them! That's what they want. Every death brings it a bit closer."

"What, inspector?" asked Carrinelle. "Brings *what* closer?"

A sudden dreadful knowledge gripping him, Legrasse looked upward through the horrible storm and pointed, screaming, "*That!*"

Carrinelle looked up along the line of the inspector's arm. Shielding his eyes from the sand and other debris whipping through the cyclonic winds, the officer stared up into the sky. What he saw made him gasp. Descending slowly toward the island, some staggering distance overhead, a white shape spun wildly, hanging suspended due to the gale currents and its own great wings. Carrinelle jammed the fingers of one hand into his mouth. Words sputtered out around his drool-slicked fingers, meaningless and stupid.

Grabbing him, Legrasse demanded, "Get hold of yourself, man— that's an order!" When the officer continued to stare blankly, his pupils contracting to the merest pin points, the inspector slapped him, leaving a bloody outline on Carrinelle's cheek from his own dripping wound. The man blinked, then began to beg Legrasse's pardon. The inspector silenced him, saying, "No time, Joel. I understand. Forget it. Right now we've got to deal with that ... that *thing*!"

"But *how*, inspector? What can we *do*?"

"Did you get the explosives?" When Carrinelle shakenly indicated that they had brought an entire boatload, Legrasse ordered, "Then get them up here—now!"

While the officer made his way to the beach, Legrasse turned to the monolith behind him. Heedless of his torn hand or his exhaustion, the inspector threw himself against the great granite slab, grappling for the crude hand and foot holds that would take him to the top. The violently swirling winds threatened to knock him free several times, but he managed to hang on, leaving a smearing trail of blood behind him until finally he reached the top.

Looking over the edge, there in the center of the small platform atop the monolith, Legrasse found another statue, exactly as he had the first time. His eye caught by the smooth dark carving, he fell into the spell of the hideous statue, lost to time until, after he knew not how long, Carrinelle's voice came to him.

"Inspector! We've got the explosives!"

Grateful for the distraction, Legrasse grabbed the new statue with his unprotected hand and then released his hold on the monolith, sliding down its side until he slammed against the ground. As he staggered to his feet, he found that only some four of his men had managed to keep their wits besides Carrinelle. Where the rest had run off to, he did not know or care. He could not blame any man for cracking under what they had seen that night; he could only thank God for those that had not. Gathering those few together, the inspector pulled them close so as to be heard over the roar of the building storm.

"How you kept your wits, gentlemen," he bellowed, "I won't ask. We can all make thanks on Sunday come—"

"If we live that long," interrupted one officer, a wild, terrified look in his eye.

Understanding, wishing he could give in to the madness eating at him, Legrasse nodded, saying, "We'll live." Pointing upward, seeing that the ghastly white shape was half again closer than before, the inspector swore, "It's *that* thing that's going to Hell tonight. It's drawn by prayers and blood. Well, this is where the prayers were, and this is where the blood is, so let's fix it a dinner it will remember."

Understanding Legrasse's meaning, the men tore open the crates of explosives they had brought with them so gingerly through the marsh. As they worked to rig all the different boxes together to form one large bomb around the monolith, the inspector looked upward once more and whispered, "So you and yours ruled the Earth a million years ago, eh? Well, we've got a few tricks now the cavemen didn't." Pulling one of the flaking tan sticks from the crate closest to him, Legrasse shook it at the sky. "This is one of them," he bellowed. "It's a German invention. They call it *dynamite!*"

"Sir," said Carrinelle, "we're ready."

"Then light the fuse," answered the inspector. Throwing the damnable figurine he had grabbed from atop the monolith into one of the explosives boxes, he spat, hitting its tentacled face. Sneering, he added, "And let's get out of here."

The strike of a match and the smell of burning gunpowder sent the last six human beings in the area charging through the massing tornado off into the swamp. Throwing themselves into the water, each man swam back to the general area of the boats. Above them, over the pitching howl of the storm, the grotesque sound of monstrous wings penetrated the shattering din, calling to each of them. It was a plaintive, seductive sound, a buzzing song that promised all, a magnetic allure near impossible to resist.

Legrasse and Carrinelle reached one of the large flat-bottomed skiffs. Dragging themselves inside, they looked about, trying to see how their fellow officers had managed. Two of the men they saw pulling themselves into one of the other boats. The other two, however, had not been so lucky.

Unable to fight the siren call of the monstrous thing descending from the sky, the pair had turned and begun staggering back toward the island. Carrinelle made to leave the boat to try and restrain them, but Legrasse caught his arm and whispered, "It's too late."

As if in response to the inspector's prediction, suddenly two polypous appendages flew forward from the center of the grotesque bulk hovering over the swamp. One wrapped around each of the mesmerized officers, jerking them up out of the swamp, dragging them through the air and into the body of the nightmare in the sky.

"Damn you!" screamed Carrinelle. "Damn you to a thousand hells!"

Then flame touched powder, and the night seemed as dawn.

*****

"Ah, look who's finally back amongst us."

Legrasse fought hard to stay awake—putting everything he had into opening his eyes completely. Turning his head slightly, he caught sight of the Chief of Police out of the corner of his eye. The man rose from his seat, admonishing the inspector.

"No, no, Legrasse. Don't try to move. The doctors don't advise it. Rest. You rest and let me take a look at our hero of the hour."

It all came back to him. The explosion that tore apart Monolith Island, the shrieking of the horror in the sky as it was rocked by shock waves, pelted by massive chunks of granite. Its glimmering wings had caught fire, turning it into a torch seen, the reports would eventually confirm, in the skies of four different states.

"So, tell me ... whatever am I to do with you, Legrasse, eh?"

"I, I ...." The inspector was dismayed to hear how raw his voice was, to feel the weakness that had him so firmly in its grasp. "I don't know what you mean, sir."

"No, actually," acknowledged the Chief, "I'm certain you don't."

Legrasse could still see the burning horror, hanging in the sky, righting itself, healing before his very eyes. The inspector had stood in his boat, staring, pointing, laughing. Despite his best efforts, he had not beaten the monster. A simple explosion powerful enough to obliterate an island had not been enough to stop the cultists' god. Not nearly enough.

"But don't worry," the Chief of Police assured Legrasse. "I'll explain it all to you." Coming closer to the inspector's bed, the older man told him, "You are in a hospital, Legrasse. Your friend the professor has disappeared, back to his college I'd imagine. Most of your men survived. Thirteen of you made it back from the swamp. Word is six, perhaps seven of you will be fit for duty after a while. The question is, what kind of duty?"

"'Kind', sir?"

As the winds grew even stronger, the thing had turned its attention to Legrasse and the others. Although they had not surrendered themselves to it as had the two officers drawn into its bulk, it did not seem to matter. The inspector could feel inside his soul that the hovering white mass was coming for him. It was moving slowly, making certain of its energies. His plan had wounded it, slowed it down, but ....

No good, he had thought, *not enough. Not enough!*

Then the shelling had begun.

"Yes, what kind of duty can I give you now? I'll be frank, Legrasse. We've managed to keep a lid on this wild business, but ... well, this is New Orleans. The word of what went on out in the marshlands has run from one end of town to the other and back again—twice. And, of course, your legend grows with each new version."

Somehow, he had forgotten about Galvez. He had jumped up and down in the flat-bottomer, laughing, shrieking. Two hundred pound shells rained down out of the night, splashing against the horror in the sky, crashing it down against the Earth. The force of the constant pounding flipped the already unstable boat, sending the inspector and his subordinate into the swamp just as its wind-dried surface was set ablaze. Legrasse and Carrinelle had surfaced and begun running for their lives.

That was the last thing the inspector remembered.

"That cyclone that started out there, after the Navy started their shelling ... damn, how'd you live through that ... it jumped up out of the swamp. Came back down upstate and dug a two and a half mile swath out of Louisiana and on into Mississippi. They say it killed over three hundred people."

Legrasse wondered at that. Perhaps the death of the flying thing, whatever it had been, had broken the spell the cultists had called forth. With that energy released, maybe the storm could not simply be dissipated, and thus had come to ground far away, burning itself out in the simpler kind of mindless destruction people could take for granted. Before the inspector could dwell on the topic, though, the Chief of Police added, "You know, there are people talking about running you for governor."

Legrasse's attention finally snapped to, focusing on the older man. Suddenly, a thousand different futures intersected within his brain, showing him the play of his destiny depending on what course he set himself upon in the next few seconds.

While part of his mind reviewed the events of the past months over in his head, another more immediate section weighed the worlds he had so recently discovered against the ones he had known all his life. Hero of the masses, chained to their petty antics by the cheap trinkets of cash and adoration, or a forgotten face, poking into all the dark corners of the world, searching for more of the reality he had only just begun to understand.

Signaling the Chief to bend closer, working his sore throat as best he could, the inspector whispered in a painfully thin voice, "I think it best we downplay this story, sir."

"Really?" asked the Chief, equal portions of disbelief and relief obvious in his voice.

Giving the older man no time to debate, Legrasse croaked, "Yes, sir. I'm not much a one for public life. Besides, I would think one needs more credentials to run for office than the title of 'monster hunter.' Even in New Orleans."

The Chief of Police laughed. Just the reaction Legrasse had hoped for. The inspector was no fool. He knew how the world worked. It was no sense of noble duty that had moved the Chief to visit an injured officer, waiting by his bed to be the first to see him when he awoke. He had been sent by his political superiors to check out the threat of the city's new "hero" to their tiny, jaded futures. As if after what he had seen, after what he now understood, he could actually be interested in mere temporal gratification.

Picking up his hat, the obviously relieved Chief of Police said, "You're a good man, Legrasse … a good man. Don't you worry, we'll downplay this ridiculous monster nonsense."

"Thank you," lied the inspector, suddenly impatient for the political stooge to leave. As the Chief closed the door on his way out, Legrasse turned toward the window. The sun was out, shining brightly. Was it the sun of the next morning, he wondered, or two days later—three?

Who knows? he thought. *Who cares?*

Smiling, he closed his eyes. Fate had reached down and given him a chance to die foolishly side by side with an equal chance to rise above the snare of ordinary life. He had seen a slice of the world few men could observe and keep their sanity.

Of course, he thought, *who's to say you're still sane?*

Legrasse chuckled, perhaps a bit too loudly. Insane or not, what did it matter? He knew what he would do next, regardless. Professor Webb had hinted that the world was filled with horrors and those men mad enough to keep truck with them.

He would not be able to set out immediately. He would have to regain his strength, put his affairs in order, and then one day just quietly slip away. He would put the idea to Galvez and Carrinelle. They deserved the chance to go with him. They had earned it.

Where they would go, what they might find, Legrasse had no way of knowing. Nor did he care to speculate.

One thing at a time, he told himself. *One thing at a time. Whatever other horrors there be in this world, don't worry. They're out there. Patiently waiting. And we'll find them all.*

Legrasse drifted toward sleep. His eyes heavy, tired, he blinked them several times, then closed them again. In seconds he was snoring lightly, a pleased, untroubled look settling over him.

From the window, the sun continued to flood his room, its rays warming the inspector, protecting him from harm.

D AVID C. SMITH is well known as the author of a number of sword and sorcery novels, including the Oron the Barbarian series from Zebra Books and, along with collaborator Richard L. Tierney, the Red Sonja series from Ace Books. The latter set of six novels, while based on Roy Thomas' adaptation of Robert E. Howard's Red Sonya character (see "The Shadow of the Vulture" in Howard's collection *The Sowers of the Thunder*, Zebra Books, 1975), also contains elements of the Lovecraft Mythos. In "The Sign of Kutullu", Smith turns directly to matters Lovecraftian, in a brief tale that first appeared in his fanzine *Abaddon* (a supplement to issue #1, 1974), which he contributed quarterly to the Esoteric Order of Dagon Amateur Press Association.

Following in the footsteps of HPL himself, Smith did not hesitate to build the tale around a set of in-jokes: If you happen to notice some vague resemblance between one character's name and that of Dirk Mosig, Lovecraft scholar, you probably won't be far wrong. "Dean Morris?" My guess is that his first name is Harry, editor/publisher of the premier Lovecraftian periodical *Nyctalops*. And just as "Kutullu" is supposed to be a Sumerian version of "Cthulhu", so is "Dawoud" Arabic for "David", as in Smith.

The Sign of Kutullu

by David C. Smith

T HE FACTS IN THE CASE of the untimely death of Dr. Derrik Mossik last month need no further elucidation here. A recognized scholar of national repute, and distinguished bearer of the Professor Emeritus Award of Honor at his own North Central University, his grim and terrible murder was a genuine blow to his every associate and correspondent. But the daily press has well recorded the events of his end on that night of September 16. What the press did not reveal—and what has only recently come to light—are startling new antecedents to the crime, which tend to shed an even more unpalatable aura upon the entire episode.

Two months prior to his demise, Dr. Mossik had made public, within the social context of his closer university acquaintances, his discovery of certain ancient Sumerian Babylonian cuneiform inscriptions which, he stated, would abolish all heretofore accepted theories of antique theology. He was not ridiculed for these suppositions; a man of Dr. Mossik's accomplishments deserved a respect due his station and reputation. Some felt, however, that his inordinant predisposition toward the outré had taken a dangerous turn, and that his latest researches might prove disastrous to an otherwise illustrious academic career. But Dr. Mossik was not to be gainsaid. During the course of the month, however, his university circle of comrades noted an increasing tension in his demeanor; he repeatedly appeared at his daily lectures ten, fifteen, even twenty minutes tardy. Dean Morris of the Archaeological Department courteously advanced the possibility of a leave of absence, but Dr. Mossik steadfastly refused any interruption to his work, even on so congenial a ground.

At the end of August, however, two events occurred which put a more somber atmosphere upon Dr. Mossik's studies. The first was his obtaining the copy of that dreaded text of Abdul Alhazred—the *Necronomicon*—from the Miskatonic University Library at Arkham, Massachusetts; the second was a visit from an Egyptian scholar of antiquities named Mr. Dawoud.

There are witnesses to that first cordial meeting between Dr. Mossik and Mr. Dawoud: Both Dean Morris and Dr. Mossik's secretary, Ellen Bowser, were present. Although they decline any specific authorization of their acknowledgement of the fact—this in light of later occurrences—both will, in private, admit to being present at that first meeting.

Dr. Mossik and Mr. Dawoud received one another amicably, and soon enough fell into an animated discourse specifically bearing upon their mutual field of attainment. The particulars were noted (rather sketchily) by Dr. Mossik in his journal, which he assiduously kept up to date during this time:

August 31. Dawoud arrived today. He is a queer fellow of mixed background, won't talk much about himself. *He is on the track of the same thing I am.* I confided to him my discovery of the "kutullu" cuneiform. He has told me that during the past two years he has followed—through hearsay testimony—what he understood to be the very route Alhazred traveled twelve hundred years ago—from his own Cairo to the great desert Raba el-Khaliyeh to the ruins of old Babylon. He says that at a certain unnamed site he discovered a cylinder seal which speaks of "kutullu." I doubt him; he does not have the seal with him, claiming to have deposited it in his private vault at the Cairo Museum. I do not trust him.

Sept'r 2. Second talk with Dawoud. He says he *must* see the *Necronomicon*—that we are both after the same thing—that each of us can verify the other's hypotheses. I relented, showed him the copy of Alhazred's book.

September 6. Dawoud's and my studies continue. I have no choice but to trust him. His cylinder story is not fiction! He reproduced for me the essential design, although he cannot himself read the ancient cuneiform symbols. "Kutullu" is mentioned five or six times; it seems definitely to be some sort of prayer. I translate it tomorrow.

Sept'r 7. A prayer to "Kutullu"—four thousand years old! And mention of other "old ones" from the stars above the plains of the lower Euphrates Valley!

Sept'r 9. Dawoud and I had a lengthy discussion tonight. He dwelt at length upon his own speculations, saying: "I have traveled the ancient routes of the East. I have the old blood in my veins, Dr. Mossik. I have looked upon the ancient things. Listen to me. Let me ask you this—and put aside your conventional mythology. What was the Tower of Babel? Why was it built? Can you tell me? What was the purpose of the Great Pyramid at Gizeh? What was the purpose of those step-pyramids in the jungles of Mexico? And the blocked stones of Stonehenge in Britain? Eh? Can you tell me? I can tell you!

For I found this cylinder seal *not three kilometers* from the site of the ziggurat of King Ur-Nammu in Sumeria!"

September 11. Hypothesis confirmed! A passage in the *Necronomicon* is a *direct translation* of Dawoud's cylinder seal cuneiforms! "Kutullu" is Cthulhu! Iä! ha! ha!

September 13. I conceded to Dawoud tonight my intention of publishing our mutual findings. He is against it. We had an unpleasant argument.

Sept'r 15. Dawoud again. I agreed that our findings are blasphemous, but said that the rule of science is to forward blasphemy and banish hypocrisy. Dawoud ranted. I stated unequivocally that the interest of science *demanded* the publication of my paper, and that despite his manifold assistance, he could not deter me. I had to bodily force him from my office.

Dr. Mossik's journal entries conclude here. His corpse was discovered late the following night in his office in the Chalmers Building on the NCU campus. The testimony of the night watchman, Mr. Cyrus Griffin, yields further particulars than were made public in the *Daily Standard* and other newspapers. Despite Mr. Griffin's confessed penchant for drink at late hours, his word is the only one which allows for the final pertinent details to fill in the gaps of the narrative.

According to Mr. Griffin, then, he reports that at approximately 11:15 on the night of September 16 he heard sounds of violent quarrel issuing from Dr. Mossik's third-floor office. Mr. Griffin decided to investigate. Before reaching the office, however, he heard two distinctly different sorts of screams or yells: one certainly in the voice of Dr. Mossik, the other thick and muffled, "like a farriner, talkin' some damn' langwich er other." These were followed by a sharp series of high-pitched wails and shrieks and loud crashing and smashing sounds.

Just as Mr. Griffin attempted to force open the door of Dr. Mossik's office, the lights inside were extinguished. Mr. Griffin flicked on his flashlight and forced open the door against some dead resisting weight on the other side. It was Dr. Mossik's britally mutilated corpse. His flashlight showed Mr. Griffin a scattered pile of books and loose papers surrounding the body; then he heard a scruffling noise from the window ledge which caused him to direct his light there. Someone Mr. Griffin could not recognize—apparently Dr. Mossik's murderer—climbed out the window and dropped three stories to the ground below and effectively made his escape. But Mr. Griffin has not been able to disclose the identity of the suspect, for—whether the cause of drink or his shock or cumulative other effects—he stoutly maintains to this day that the face of the form at the window that night was *not a human face*—that what he saw looking into the beam of his flashlight had *webbed hands—yellow staring eyes*—and a head covered by a mass of *squirming, writhing tentacles*!

LEONARD CARPENTER is well known as the author of some dozen Conan novels, but his real love is the short story. And it is a requited love, if the story you read here is any example. Carpenter, like T. E. D. Klein, is able to rehabilitate, really to reincarnate, traditional Lovecraft notions in the flesh of more modern-sounding prose.

One note about the cult appearing in this story, really a thought about the "nameless cults" that crop up through the whole Mythos canon. Each seems to be modeled on an actual genre of eccentric cults in the writer's own day, as is only natural. Lovecraft's Starry Wisdom Church in "The Haunter of the Dark" seems to me pretty obviously to reflect the genteel yet wacky Theosophical Society (also the source of the Cthulhu cult's "deathless leaders" in the mountains of China in "The Call of Cthulhu"). They had become too stale to use again by the time James Wade wrote "The Deep Ones" in 1969, so he modeled his League for Spiritual Discovery, led by one Alonzo Waite, after Timothy Leary and the hippies of the 60's. Carpenter's Paleozoic League, whom you will meet in this story, are fictional transmogrifications of various radical ecology groups in the present generation. Are we being told that these eccentric groups are more insidious than they seem? Or, more likely, is it that each Mythos cult is like a wolf masquerading in sheep's clothing?

"Recrudescence" was originally published in *Amazing Stories*, January 1988.

Recrudescence

by Leonard Carpenter

re-cru-desce (re' kroo-des') *intransitive verb*. To break out afresh after a period of latency or relative inactivity; to become active again, as a disease.

MY INVOLVEMENT WITH Lease Tract 102 began after exploratory drilling had already commenced. I was just finishing final grades when I got a phone call from Jean Hinchcliffe, a former student of mine employed aboard the pilot platform. She wanted a university paleontologist's opinion; her scientific curiosity was aroused by what the drill string had brought up from eighteen thousand feet below the ocean floor.

"You really have to see the fossils yourself, Olin," she told me. "I'd be afraid to try and describe them over the phone, or tell you what I think." A hiss of static on the land-sea line made her sound much more distant than a few dozen miles up the California coast and out a dozen more across the choppy blue expanse of Pismo Bay. "Can you come up?"

"I really don't think so, right now ...." I hadn't been feeling very ambitious lately, so I groped for an excuse. But in fact it was the end of spring quarter, and my calendar was empty. "Couldn't you just mail me a sample?"

"You aren't put off by my job, are you? I haven't abandoned life sciences for good, you know."

"Really? I'm glad to hear it." Frankly, it had irked me to learn that one of my best students was working as an assistant geologist on an Exoco offshore rig.

"Just come on out. I could arrange a 'copter shuttle. Or else you could ride the crew boat from Port San Luis."

"Well ... let's make it by boat. I like seasickness better than airsickness. Wednesday and Thursday, you said?"

"Oh, yes. That would be terrific! I'll have the office phone you back to confirm it." She said a hurried good-bye, and the line went dead, leaving me listening to rushing white noise that conjured visions in my mind of spreading sea foam on tossing waves.

I put down the phone, feeling a new flicker of interest in Jean Hinchcliffe. Even more tantalizing to me were her hints of a new fossil life form dredged up from the unexplored strata of the earth's crust. I knew that my skills as a fossil-reading expert might be valuable to the oil company in its search for black gold, and I was wary of somehow being used to promote something I didn't agree with. Still, Jean's motive clearly wasn't profit, just scientific inquiry and friendship.

As I sat in my faculty office gazing out across the U.C. Santa Barbara campus at a small, priceless patch of shining Pacific framed by eucalyptus trees, I thought myself mature and world-weary. I imagined that I knew nearly all there was to know about the sea, the earth's past, and the evolution of its life forms.

But soon I'd be learning just how pettily, pathetically ignorant I was. I'll never experience that smug, dangerous peace of mind again.

At sunrise on Wednesday I left Goleta and drove north on 101. At first the ocean scenery was obscured by cottony fog; it disappeared on the inland stretch of road, but still clung to the coast when I rejoined it at Pismo. It was just burning off, the sky shredding to a bright, wispy blue overhead, as I rolled into Avila Beach.

The tiny resort town, always fragile-looking and overshadowed by the tank farm on the hill, was suffering even more of an identity crisis with the arrival of the offshore industry. It had borne increased road and port traffic, but not yet the full impact on its beaches and air quality; the town's atmosphere still managed to seem rural and recreational. I drove around the small harbor to the company jetty where the crew boat was loading.

The cabin at the steel vessel's bow was already crowded with riggers, and more were loitering on the open deck among drums and pallets. The robust, weather-beaten men chatted and joked together with the gruff familiarity of members of an athletic team or a military unit.

I identified myself to the skipper, stowed my single bag in the rusted rack, and found a seat next to an amiable coffee-colored man who moved his gear aside for me. "I ought to hold this baby in my lap anyhow." He winked up at me, opening a flannel-wrapped bundle to reveal a massive new Penn deep-sea reel.

As the craft got underway, its powerful diesels thrusting us out past the pier and the anchored pleasure boats, we carried on a disjointed conversation. His name was Lem, and his pet enthusiasm was fishing from the rigs.

"The company doesn't mind?" I asked.

"Not if it's on my own time." He had an air of country ease about him. "Not many of the fellas do it—but there's nothin' like the fishin' out there. All kinds of fish, tuna, rock cod, bottom fishes, lots I don't know."

"I suppose the fish are drawn to the platform," I said, putting facts together in my mind. Even in tidal waters the open ocean can be more barren of life than a landlocked desert, and yet human activity can create an oasis there. The presence of fixed structures at tidal level for plants and animals to take root on, combined with the release of waste nutrients, can attract a variety of organisms. That is, until the human activity that created it just as casually devastates it.

"Yes indeed, we got fishes out there like you never seen."

That had been part of my interest in the rig all along; I wanted to look at the ocean from that unique vantage and get an idea of the biological relationships that might be developing. Though drilling had begun only recently, the platform had been in place for several months during construction and fitting out.

"We must be getting near it now?" I asked.

All I could see, through the curtain of spray kicked up before the cabin ports, were different shades of blue-gray. As Lem and I talked, we were jolting across the dark-toned sea, flying in the teeth of wind and waves, hurtling toward a rampart of fog that appeared to the eye as solid as ancient granite.

But the fog bank must already have been receding; Lem nudged me and pointed as, over the passing of a few moments, the skeletal form of the *Daffodil* platform materialized out of the grayness: a cluster of large, bulky modular boxes perched atop ungainly jacket-legs, with derricks and cranes sprouting up crazily against the sky. The yellow-painted steel emphasized the odd resemblance of the structure to a giant robot flower in the midst of that desolate, blustery seascape.

As we drew near the platform, I began to grasp its true size, towering two hundred feet above the waves, and who knew how many more hundreds below. It was a guyed-tower type platform, mounted on a slender framework held tense and vertical by cables radiating from an invisible point underwater. Structurally a new concept, it was also the first rig in the recently opened Santa Maria exploration basin. Its nearest neighboring rig was almost a hundred miles outward, by treacherous seas, in the relatively calm channel off Santa Barbara.

The crew boat's diesels soon slowed, and we cruised into the shadow of the platform. Between its tubular legs, which were now incredibly massive-looking, I could see only a maze of structural underpinnings and pipes. The boat passengers began to stir and go out on deck in the spray-laden wind. The sea was blustery but not rough, rolling underfoot with long, stately swells. We disembarked by means of a slender gangway that flexed with the pitch of the crew boat. Beyond was a steep, railed stairway; an underslung group of commuters made the climb silently and stoically, but Lem stayed with me to offer reassurance and answer my questions. He left me with a wave on the sheltered entry deck, where I found Jean waiting.

"Olin, hello! I'm so glad you're here." She skipped forward and squeezed my fingers in her two warm hands. Years had lent a comfortable fullness to her form, which I remembered as being athletic and boyish. She was dressed in slacks and a lab smock. The deep-sea tanned face, under the blondish curls that fringed her safety helmet, made her eyes seem brighter and livelier than ever as they sought out mine. "You're looking as ... professorly as ever! How's your family?"

"All right, I guess ... I don't really know. They divorced me." I blushed. "That is ... my daughter is married now, living on the East Coast, and my wife just remarried. So I'm ... footloose."

"Oh, I hadn't heard." Her eyes flicked back to mine with genuine, pained sympathy. Abruptly, she gestured toward the older man at her side. "Olin, this is Blair Vincent, my lab supervisor. Blair— Professor Olin Simonsen."

Blair was a tall, slightly stout, curly-haired administrator type wearing black-framed glasses and a vinyl penholder stuck in the pocket of his white shirt. He clasped my hand officiously. "Glad you could make it, Prof! I think we can both learn a lot from what we've turned up. Here, see if this fits." He handed me a yellow hard hat identical to his own, right down to the black-on-red logo reading EXOCO and a plasticized security card clipped to the brim.

"How was your shuttle trip? Did you run into much fog?" Jean's chatty questions were answered gradually along the way while we deposited my bag in the tiny guest room and went on a quick tour of the platform.

From a windblown outer terrace we viewed one of the derricks, where grimy-gloved roustabouts wrestled enormous lengths of drill pipe into position on the mud-slimed floor. Beyond them, seen over the taut windscreens, the sea surface and atmospheric haze were blindingly bright. Inside the factory-like expanses of the rig, we walked through the production areas, forests and galleries of yellow-painted pipes and valves still pristine and unused. It was quieter there, but I began to feel like an insect crawling through a vast, vibrating machine—an impression that stayed with me as long as I was on the rig.

We passed by the vats and pumps that dispensed the drill mud, a viscous sludge forced into the well to maintain pressure and circulate debris back to the surface. Nearby was Jean's work area, where the drill cuttings were sifted, washed, and analyzed to get information about the subocean strata the drill bit was invading.

"It's all fascinating. How soon do you expect to strike oil?" My question was addressed to Jean, but, in his officious way, Blair fielded it instead.

"In producible quantities, you mean? At five hundred feet per day ... in three or four days, if we're lucky." He tugged at the bill of his hard hat. "Our first hole was dry, in spite of the drill ship's findings, but we've learned enough to be sure it's down there. Just a matter of sniffing it out."

Jean added, "The first well was where we found ... what I told you about on the phone. Can we show him now?" She looked up at Blair, whose smile seemed slightly indulgent. Then she took my arm and led me toward a door in one of the modular compartments.

The lab was windowless, but brightly lit; a little cramped, but well organized. Troughs and trays in its center contained rock samples, most of them labeled and arranged in sequence. More counters at the sides of the room held microscopes and other testing equipment. A blackboard on one wall displayed an unfinished chart showing earth stratum lines and depth measurements. Jean walked to it and pointed.

"The strata are sheared and folded back on themselves here, you see. Consequently, we ran into similar deposits at different levels." She reached into a tray. "But I'm sure these were originally deposited in a single layer. Here, what do you think?"

She handed me a small, hard flake of rock. It wasn't more than three inches in length, and flat, a quarter-inch thick. It was formed or fractured in a distinctive, indented parallelogram or hexate shape that might be pictured like this:

I examined it, a little nonplussed. "Well, it's not articulated, just a shape. If it's an organic fossil, I should think it would be a fragment of a larger animal or plant." I shrugged. "Most likely, it's just shale. You said there were others?"

Blair slid the tray toward me. "If you can explain it, you're sharper than I am."

The other stone chips in the tray were strange in only one way: They were exactly the same as the first—except for a few that appeared to have been cut or shattered by the drill tool. Bemusedly, I picked up two and matched them side by side.

"Uniform shape, uniform size. All relatively flat. Smooth, but they have a fine texture that could be organic." I looked up at Jean and nodded. "I can see why you believe they're part of a life form. Ordinary rocks wouldn't be so regular."

"Not unless they were crystalline—which these aren't. Or formed from cooling cracks, like a lava postpile." She leaned forward over the table. "But you haven't seen the most interesting thing." Working deftly, she arranged the stone pieces on the tray. When she'd finished, the angled corners were roughly meshed to form a mosaic pattern, thus:

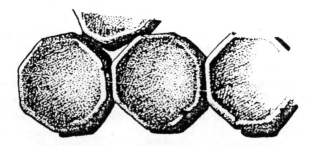

"Why, that's remarkable," I told her. "Cooling or drying cracks would be hexagonal—but there's a unique, infinitely repeatable shape, and very regular. I can't imagine what conditions would produce it mechanically, can you? It looks almost man-made."

Jean flushed with enthusiasm that mirrored my own. "They must be either bark plates or scales of animal armor, don't you think?"

"Possibly," I admitted. "What depth did you say they came from?"

"Between fifteen and twenty-two thousand feet." She moved to the blackboard and pointed to an area of chalk cross-hatching. "We're fairly sure they'd be from the late Mississippian period."

"Hmm. Probably vegetable," I said. It seemed to me that animal remnants would have been too rare to be turned up by random drilling —at least the remnants of such large animals. "If these were bony plates from one of the Mississippian armored fishes, the creature would have been longer than this room."

"That would be such a find!" Jean glowed. "But unlikely, I guess." She ran her hand wistfully over the contents of the tray.

"Have any other fossils been turned up in these fields?" I asked.

"Oh yes, these." She indicated a tray containing mottled fragments of stone with seashell imprints, and a few trilobites. "Nothing unusual." She looked up at Blair. "Still, we hope to get a better picture from the second hole. When we get near the same strata, we plan to take a series of core samples that will preserve all the layers intact. Don't we, Blair?"

"Yes ... well, I think we could do that," he said, hovering a little more closely over his assistant. "Of course, our work here is oil production. We can't always follow up on these biological sidelines, you understand." He glanced at me, then turned back to the sample tray. "But these little scales, widespread as they seem to be, could turn out to be valuable as an index fossil, to lead us to the oil."

I nodded; here it came, harnessed greed in action. "Have they been closely associated with oil pools?"

"Yes, they have. They were right on top of the trace deposits we tapped in our first hole." He gestured to some flasks of viscous black goo along the wall. "High-grade hydrocarbons, but not enough of it yet." He sighed. "I'd hoped, Professor, that you'd be able to identify them right off the bat for us, and maybe tell us more about what kind of geological formations we're dealing with."

"Sorry. I'm afraid they're new to me." I smiled at Jean. "But I can try to research them back at U.C. and I'd definitely like to get a look at any new specimens."

After a good deal more technical discussion, Blair entrusted a couple of samples to me for study. Then he and Jean went off to catch up on their day's work, most of which was to be done in a large and bustling room down the hall. I spent part of the day trying to examine the samples with the equipment in the small lab, without any further success, checking in with Jean occasionally. Later I strolled about the platform as far as I could—though I was restricted largely to uninteresting areas by safety- and security-conscious personnel.

Finally, I sat in the employee canteen, sipping coffee and reading a magazine. I was joined there by Jean at the end of her shift. Blair strolled in soon afterward.

The three of us talked.

To call the evening a disappointment would be to admit the foolish extravagance of the hopes I'd started to build up. Jean and I had never been more than teacher and student, and I had no reason to expect her suddenly to fall madly in love with me.

We chatted interminably over beers, she and I reminiscing about the university, she and he about their shorter mutual experience in the Exoco corporation. We stayed up late—remarkably so, in view of their twelve-hour shifts; nevertheless, I was the first to yield to fatigue and ennui. I insisted on retiring alone to my room; I left them talking together.

Once in bed, my weariness vanished. I lay there, brooding for hours before going to sleep. The perpetual noises of the drilling seemed much louder in the darkness, and I discovered that, in spite of their massive size, the great offshore platforms do stir and sway in the rolling night sea.

Next morning I cut my misery short and arose early. I dressed and went to the canteen to toy with some scrambled eggs—no sign of Jean or Blair. Then I packed, leaving my hard hat on the bed, and took my suitcase outside through the empty vestibule and down the hanging stair toward the boat platform. I still hoped to get a close look at what sea life I could, and I knew that the tide was low.

The fog was wet and dense, and the steel grids of the stairway were slick beneath my rubber-soled shoes. At each landing, the flights above and below me seemed to funnel off into oblivion. The sound of the sea and the loom of the rig's superstructure made me feel that I was in a vast, dark sea grotto. On the sloping stair, amid drifting fog, it seemed almost possible to forget from moment to moment which way was up and which down.

Finally, the dock materialized beneath me, and beyond it the rolling waves. I stepped off the stairs gratefully, though not to much greater security.

The platform was a rigid steel-mesh structure supported by cables, made to be raised and lowered with the tide on clanking vertical rails. Its sway wasn't that of the sea, but rather that of the platform above, and the effect was still disorienting. I had to stand there motionless a while to settle my stomach.

I could see one other human figure nearby in the fog—wearing a slicker, seated on a box, holding a fishing pole propped against the railing. When his head turned, I recognized Lem.

"Another early riser!" I called as I walked over.

"Early bird catches the worm," he told me sagely. "'Cept I'm usin' shrimps."

"Are they biting?" It was a rhetorical question, judging from the way the oversized gunnysack hung empty at his side.

"Always bitin' out here. Won't be long." He flicked a lever on his gleaming high-tech reel and let out more line. "You get to see your fossils?"

"Yes, indeed. Interesting ones." I told him a little about what I'd seen, trying not to launch into professional detail.

"Hnnh." He gazed into the fog. "Y'know, a couple fellas quit the platform yesterday on account of those fossils. Two British fellas." He glanced sidelong at me. "Said they saw the same thing once at an onshore rig in Kenya."

"Really? Why should that make them quit?"

"Who knows?" He made a noncommittal motion of his head. "Could be there was some gas in that other well, caused a fire. Bad memories." He began to reel in his line. "Riggers got plenty o' superstitions, just like any other trade." He cranked in silence until his half-pound lead weight and naked, evil-looking twelve-ought hook rose dripping out of the sea.

While he was replacing his stolen bait, I moved on. The dock was too high to afford a close view of the water, but at its end was a descending stair blocked by a chain, with a sign reading AUTHORIZED PERSONNEL ONLY. Elated at the chance to flout authority, I stepped over it and climbed down to the lower level.

The frail catwalk took me near the main vertical members of the platform. I saw a number of things I found interesting: snails, mussels, kelp, an anchovy school, and glimpses of larger fish moving far below in the clear deep-sea water.

But it was something else that drew my attention forcibly: a fist-sized, flitting shape tossed momentarily up to the surface of a wave. Its appearance was familiar, yet preposterously out of place here. I moved as near as I could, knelt on the slippery walk, and grabbed for it—in vain. The rise and fall of the sea made it hard to judge the object's motion. I hooked my arm around one of the railing supports and reached precariously out over the water to try again.

I knew I'd need tangible evidence if I was going to persuade anyone that I'd sighted a living, swimming trilobite.

With the size of the rolling swells and the swaying of the catwalk, I knew that I risked a wetting—but I wasn't prepared for the violent, clanging lurch of the metal structure that occurred then. It tore my grip almost loose, trailing me deep into water that, I later recalled, felt strangely warm. I was left clinging to slick metal by one hand and one leg. An instant later, a great splash somewhere nearby threw up a cascade that nearly dragged me under.

I struggled back onto the walkway and hauled myself upright—to find its entire length, and the railings of the boat loading platform ahead of me, were mangled. Nevertheless, it was surely a safer position than my current one. I worked my way toward it, dripping, with the waves washing over my ankles.

As I mounted the short stairway, I thought of Lem, and I began to call his name. There was no sign of him in the radius of vision the fog allowed. My voice sounded weak and muffled. There'd been some heavy impact here, as I could see the buckled floor grids and the damaged railings on two sides. A boat collision? If so, the vessel had appeared and sunk with impossible swiftness.

Near where Lem had been fishing, the rail was parted completely, its broken ends scraping the wave tops. I was drawn toward the breach by a humming sound I couldn't identify.

Then I saw the Penn reel lying on the edge of the platform, caught against an upright that now arched sharply back down. The spool of heavy fishline was still unwinding, shirring away patiently into the depths.

There was hardly any line left. Unthinkingly, I knelt, took hold of the reel, and pressed a catch on its stainless metal side. It stopped spinning. Instantaneously, the stout pole jerked out of my grasp, flicked overboard, and disappeared underwater.

My shocked, bemused mental state finally metamorphosed to fear. I gazed over my shoulder at the trail of devastation leading to where I stood, then I ran to the stairs and began to climb away from the sea—just as the first crewmen were nearing the bottom.

After careful and skeptical investigation, the Coast Guard's finding was the same one I'd reached: that Lemuel Jackson had been taken off the platform by the attack of some large shark or cetacean. Killer whales are capable of such a maneuver, launching themselves out of the water and over the top of an obstacle to carry off their prey. In this case, the creature had simply been huge and tough enough to do it by crashing through massive steel railings.

I was the only witness, though I'd seen little. The physical evidence told the story. But I'd been privy to certain details: the force of the strike, the immense splash as the creature reentered the water, the ease with which its departing speed whisked away Lem's fishing pole. Being in a more exposed place, I'd been lucky not to be the one killed. I could visualize it all; I even imagined I knew what Lem had been doing at the moment of the strike.

Baiting his hook.

Days after my return to Goleta, I was still unable to make any progress classifying Jean's fossil fragments. I threw myself into the task, partly to block out the anguish of Lem's death and my own near death. But all the university's vast repositories and archives didn't seem to hold the answer. At times, the object of the search seemed as illusory as my "trilobite" sighting—which by then I regarded as a mere embarrassing private mistake.

There were other emotions that turned my thoughts back to the rig. On the day of the tragedy, after my questioning, I'd spent a little more time with Jean Hinchcliffe. I realized that she might be open to a personal relationship after all. She was understanding and level-headed about my experience, and our talk hinted at the possibility of getting together socially later, ashore. Blair Vincent would be out of the picture, she intimated—in the company of his wife and three children.

I could see all too clearly the danger of placing my affections on one so much younger than myself, and I knew that some of what I felt must be energy rebounding from my divorce. Nevertheless, she was an attractive woman, and I was involved whether I wanted to be or not.

Her phone calls kept me informed of developments on the rig during the week: the repair and strengthening of the landing platform; the taking of the core samples, revealing more hexate fossil scales bedded together as she had predicted in a tight, mosaic layer; and the presence of a rich deposit of crude oil just under this "capping" formation. The rig was readied for oil production, and Jean broached the idea of my making a second visit to study the new samples.

The tiff that resulted wasn't serious. Two people just getting to know each other are prone to misunderstandings. It all stemmed from my unwillingness to admit to Jean my newborn fear—my surreal, surreptitious unease regarding the sea and the platform, stemming from my recent experiences there. Jean somehow took it for mere stubbornness and was annoyed when I refused to discuss it further. On reflection later, I decided that was as good a time as any to cut our relationship short.

Whether I would eventually have found the nerve to visit her on the platform again, I'm not sure. Other distractions soon became more urgent.

It was on Saturday night that I saw a TV news item about an anti-oil demonstration in Avila Beach. The coverage was brief, and the protest looked relatively small for the town that had recently witnessed huge demonstrations against the nearby Diablo Canyon nuclear power plant.

Still, I've learned to mistrust media coverage of protests, and this story struck a peculiar note.

As often happens at such affairs, a tiny, off-the-wall faction turned out as a sideshow to the main protest and received equal or greater TV coverage. A short visual showed a suntanned, puka-beaded spokesman fixing his gaze on the camera and rapping earnestly about "the sanctity of mineral deposits laid down in our planet's youth." He wasn't a bad public speaker, and I blamed choppy news editing for some of his incoherence. The piece ended with the mention of another rally to be held the following day, at the street entrance to the Santa Barbara harbor.

It was a strange echo of the concerns that had been keeping me busy the last few days. So it was more curiosity than chance that led my steps that way during my Sunday morning jog. The spot is a natural place for demonstrations, and it was a natural time to draw a crowd; the weather is balmy there most of the year, artists display their works along the palm-fringed sea front, and tourists, skaters, and cyclists promenade endlessly along the beach and pier.

Even so, the gathering, when I found it, wasn't large. It seemed to be only of passing interest to most of the strollers. Circulating in an orderly line were a few score concerned citizens armed with picket signs and leaflets. The turnout included some U.C. students and faculty, some older local residents. Some dedicated-looking ones had obviously paid their dues as vibram-soled eco-activists, cleaning tar out of the plumage of sea birds during the big '69 spill. Their sloganeering was aimed primarily at laxness and high-handedness in the government leasing policy, with the personalities of the president and certain cabinet members looming large. Some of their literature bore the imprint of GOO, the local "get oil out" lobby.

Standing to one side was a clutch of pro-offshore advocates, who appeared largely to be industry employees and their relatives. Their ranks were thinner, but their pamphlets glossier. No hostility was evident between the groups, but a pair of extremely laid-back uniformed cops leaned against a nearby planter keeping an eye on things. I didn't doubt that more were waiting in the wings.

Finally, I spotted a familiar, lanky form, that of my colleague Peter Magnusson, bending over an Arctic jug behind the loop of pickets. I edged my way through the line, apologizing to the picketers, and clapped him on the back.

"Well, Pete, I'm glad to see you down from the Ivory Tower, to take a stand on the Relevant Concerns of the Day. Which side are you on, by the way?"

Wincing, he looked around and offered me a styro cup of water. "You've got to be kidding. You think I'd sit around and let those S.O.B.'s auction off tide lands and fisheries to their financial backers without fighting it?"

I laughed. "I'd have to agree with you, I suppose." I sipped some water. "But are you against offshore drilling? Or just the administration's gung-ho approach?"

"Well, it's basically the broad energy policy—or the lack of a policy! Maybe the oil is going to be drilled eventually. But it should be done fairly, carefully, and slowly!" He examined his plastic cup critically. "This country's oil consumption has got to be slowed down."

"You mean, to conserve resources."

"More than that, to control pollution! Even if the oil were plentiful." He glanced toward Cabrillo Boulevard as a new tide of traffic surged forward from the stoplight. "Do you have any idea what it would do to the planet to release all the carbon that's been locked underground in the form of fossil fuel?"

I shrugged. "Most of it would eventually turn into carbon dioxide, or eventually living matter. Not exactly the worst pollutants."

"True. But the increased amounts of carbon gases in the atmosphere would alter Earth's climate. They tend to trap solar rays that now are reflected into space, you know. It could heat things up quite a bit."

"The so-called greenhouse effect." I drained my water cup. "It's not proven or even agreed on by authorities, Peter."

"Maybe not. But consider: During the Carboniferous period, when all the hydrocarbons were at the Earth's surface, the entire planet was hotter. The polar ice caps were small or nonexistent then, so sea levels were higher worldwide." His arms moved as if to conjure up a small tsunami wave from the harbor behind him. "Living matter was much denser in oceans and swamps—so profuse, really, that the processes of decay couldn't keep up with growth and death. The dead carbon was slowly deposited as soil and peat, and buried—and the world changed, by geologic processes, to the kind of habitat you and I evolved in." His gesture swept to include the palm-lined beach, the hazy sea, and the tangle of streets and houses climbing the base of the Santa Ynez Mountains. "Doesn't that sound like a natural cycle to you? Would you want to bring back the Carboniferous age, dinosaurs and all ? It might be interesting, but ...."

I shook my head. "You're out of your specialty; dinosaurs didn't evolve until after the Carboniferous. Anyway, it all sounds pretty fanciful to me."

Peter smiled. "Still, a lot of knowledgeable folks are worried about energy pollution. It even has its advocates—like the League over there." He wrinkled his forehead. "If weirdos like that are for it, it can't be all good."

I followed his gaze to the parking lot, where a number of youths were forming a new phalanx of pickets. "You mean they're pro-greenhousers?"

"I gather so. But if you can figure out what the Leaguers really stand for, you're ahead of most of us." Peter looked bemused. "I don't actually know why they bother to turn up at these demonstrations."

"Maybe I'll check them out." I started to move away. "So long, Pete. It was interesting."

He turned away with a good-natured shrug.

The new demonstrators were hard to place, comprising a third group that stood apart from the fairly well defined pro- and anti-oil factions. They had an aspect that marked them as members of a close-knit group: nothing as noticeable as the freak *chic* of groups like the Hare Krishnas or similar begging organizations, but a certain odd style nevertheless. Not students, I decided right away. But clearly local, judging from their tans and their preference for light cotton garb. They worked together with the ease of a shared creed. Their uniformly lettered picket signs bore slogans like RESPECT EARTH'S HERITAGE and DON'T DESPOIL OIL. They played to the onlookers who, at that side of the plaza, were primarily the scruffy nomads who frequent the relief missions around lower State Street.

Near the curb of the boulevard, where drivers gawked without slowing down, a small, lithe man who was clearly associated with the group had just finished talking to a photographer. He looked somewhat older and tanner than the others. Then I recognized him: He was none other than the spokesman I'd seen on the TV news clip the night before.

He turned and surveyed the scene, and his gaze settled on me as being, even in my jogging suit, one of the steadier-looking bystanders.

Then my attention was galvanized, and my sense of unreality welled up more dizzyingly than it ever had. For as he approached, I caught sight of the ornament hanging from his puka-shell necklace, which had been cut out of his TV picture by the camera's talking-head shot of him.

Dangling against his tan, downy chest—and identical, except for a perforation and a gold mounting ring, to those I'd recently seen—was one of the hexate fossil scales from deep beneath the Earth's surface.

While my thoughts raced, I got an excellent look at the object. Its wearer soon moved close to me, uncomfortably close. He was, I vaguely realized, using a common technique of religious cults to gain the attention of a targeted individual, by violating my personal "space." He smiled confidently up into my face with his polished teeth.

"Want to help protect Earth's heritage?" He radiated confidence. "Come join us! We've got more signs on the bus if you want to carry one." He pointed to a middle-aged, powder-blue vehicle that was taking up four parking spaces nearby.

I stepped back from him to gain a psychological buffer zone, although I'd resolved to get some information if I could. "Well, to do that, I'd have to know more about your group. What are you trying to accomplish?"

"We want to take political action to rationalize energy policy and promote human potential." He looked at me boldly in the face, with the air of a trained publicist. My move.

"In what way, exactly? Do you oppose offshore drilling? Or favor it?"

He kept smiling. "That depends on whether the drilling is done so that it preserves the full potentiality of Earth's hydrocarbon stock. Regardless of whether the drilling is offshore or onshore."

"You mean you oppose onshore wells, too?" My buffer zone was swiftly being reclaimed. "You're talking about regulated drilling? Or more efficient burning of fossil fuels?"

He glanced around us for an audience, but none had gathered, except some seedy loungers a dozen feet away. "Not fossil fuel, but fossil inheritance. Would you burn up books as fuel? Or human bodies?" The wrinkles that began to furrow his brow were quickly reabsorbed then, into an amiable expression. "There's more than mere fuel to be gained by tapping our fossil reserves."

I kept backing away. "I think I may have heard your argument before; correct me if I'm wrong. You say hydrocarbons are too valuable to become fuel, and that they ought to be saved for use in plastics and synthetics—as now is done only with the largest, most complex molecules. Right?"

He smiled tolerantly, gently. "Your concept of 'saving' is a strange one. It still assumes man has the right to seize precious resources and put them to gross uses—building materials and such. Remember, we're talking about the preserved essence, the vital potential, of whole epochs of Earth's youth." He rubbed his brow with the back of his hand, then flashed me a particularly winning smile. "By the way, my name's Zig Larkin. What's yours?"

To tell him my own name seemed as strangely imperative then as to shake the hand that he offered. When I admitted that I worked at the university, he seemed to warm up to me even more, though still refusing to do more than hint at the goals of his organization. Its name, I learned, was the Paleozoic League. Because of the peculiar way Larkin's interest in the remote past dovetailed with my own special area of knowledge, we struck some harmonious chords. But my attention was still fixed on one thing.

"What's that ornament you're wearing on your neck, if I may ask?"

"This? It's from Africa. The stone is an ancient relic." He held it forward in an oddly formalized way, thumb and forefinger each pressing one of the points. "Ever seen one like it?"

"No." I wasn't quite certain why I lied. "I wonder what its function would have been?"

"It's a ceramic tile from ... a prehistoric settlement." His eyes rested calmly on my face. "The shape had a ritual significance. We'll be discussing it this evening, at my group's intake session."

A curious thing had happened. In spite of my grounds for mistrust of Larkin, or because of them, I was hooked. Whether he guessed that my initial motivation was that of skeptic, or even spy, I don't know. Such was the attraction of the mysteries his remarks hinted at that—and I now find my actions hard to rationalize or excuse—I agreed to ride with him to his cult's headquarters on Painted Caves Road. I was to go immediately, just as I was, in my track suit, and leave my car parked downtown.

And so there commenced an episode of which my memories aren't too clear. Later, after the insane culmination, this lack of continuity was used by Federal agents to discredit my version of the events. Recently, more of it has come back to me, though I haven't necessarily welcomed it.

Perhaps Larkin's amulet really had the mystical or hypnotic powers he ascribed to it. Perhaps the cult's inane songs and chants were capable of evoking an unconscious, atavistic level of behavior and feelings. At some point in the evening, I'm convinced, a hallucinogen was administered to me, either in the cult's spicy vegetable curry dinner or in the watery wine that accompanied it. But my mental lapse had begun well before that.

I remember being jostled by all the bland youngsters as I boarded the sea-blue bus, after the demonstration dissipated. I saw that a couple of the weathered lower-State-Street people had also been recruited to the Paleozoic cause. One was an unshaven, soiled man in an army coat, from whose torn pocket a wine bottle protruded; the other was a thin, sunburned fellow whose steel-rimmed glasses were taped together above his nose. I can't remember feeling any dismay at being grouped with them, at the time.

Painted Caves Road meanders over the crest of the Santa Ynez range—overlooking the sea, though itself nightly set adrift in a sea of fog. Its recesses shelter a few homes and hovels of artists, mystics, and the wealthy. After negotiating its loop in the ungainly bus, I had a dim impression of a ranch house and outbuildings nestled in a brushy canyon.

Inside the house, as on the bus, there was a lot of close, embracing family feeling—gummy pink smiles, rolled eyes, and asexual cuddling by the female members of the cult. After dinner came a solemn, sermonlike talk by Larkin, but my capacity to make sense of it was badly impaired. I can only repeat the gist of what was told me during the two days that, by mental reconstruction, I must have spent there.

The cult's mastermind wasn't Larkin, but a mysterious personage named Emil Sturla. He was a recluse who claimed to receive enlightenment from a psychic source. During most of my visit, he remained shut up in a guest house on the sea-facing edge of the estate.

Larkin's role was that of lieutenant or mouthpiece of the cult, though much of the day-to-day authority seemed to rest with him —including the assignment of a spiritual mentor to follow me to the toilet and take the bunk below mine. That was Pence, a frizzy-haired youngster whose sort I'd flunked on countless midterm exams. Since Larkin was absent or aloof much of the time, my indoctrination in cult teachings was left largely to Pence.

Their beliefs centered around a remotely prehistoric race whom they referred to as the Shapers. I can't say how many invocations and explications of this ancient people I heard, before it dawned on me that they were supposed *not* to be people—a race superior to humans in countless ways, the cultists assured me, but predating our species on Earth by as much as 350 million years. And, it was implied, their extraterrestrial origins were far older.

No descriptions or depictions of the Shapers were part of the League's teachings. They had descended to Earth by unspecified means at the end of the Permian geological period, a time of Eden-like vigor and profusion among the planet's developing life forms. And they'd decided to stay.

Indeed, they found the Carboniferous regime so hospitable to their way of life that they roamed the youthful planet without reliance on roads or cities, living easily among the primeval jungles and swamps. What material monuments they may have erected are buried by the eons, but their technology was so advanced as not to depend on a human-style devastation and subjugation of their environment. For instance, as Larkin maintained, they had no use for fire, and no knowledge of it, except perhaps as a natural curiosity.

The sources and channels of their power were obscure to human understanding, possibly even magical, but tremendously potent. Reputedly, they possessed the ability to transform the face of the planet at will and to direct the development of its life forms to serve their needs. Their casual experimentation, as cult doctrine would have it, brought the first sea beasts crawling onto the land, hastening their evolution to amphibians. Hence their position of worship as the Shapers of earthly life.

It is at the height of the Shapers' benign million-year dominion that the Paleozoic League's creation myth takes a cataclysmic turn. It develops that the Shapers who came to our world were only refugees or fugitives from a parent culture, an empire that held sway elsewhere on a cosmic scale. Those other beings, although kindred to the beings that colonized Earth, were also their powerful and implacable enemies. Ultimately, they unleashed a holocaust on the Earth-dwellers.

There is in the cult's mythos the implication that the Shapers were somehow being punished for befriending or tampering with the flora and fauna of Earth—a twist of dogma similar to the Promethean myth of Greek tradition. Perhaps Earth had been placed off-limits. Perhaps, in mingling with local life forms, the visitors had violated some extraterrestrial taboo as potent as our own bans on incest and bestiality. That would help to explain the severity of the retribution that was visited on them.

The method of vengeance was an ingenious one that also offered me a chilling glimpse of alien thought. The gravity of Earth, by means of the off-worlders' arcane technology, was magnified a thousandfold. The effect, wherever the dreadful weapon was applied, was not merely to crush all living things, including the Shapers, but to render them practically liquid. Reduced to a viscous torrent, they ran to the lowest pockets of terrain, amid a cataclysm that rocked the planet, initiating many of the geologic forms that underlie the modern landscape. The native species were left to recover as best they could, but the Shapers' reign was ended.

And yet, in spite of what seems the utter extirpation of their erring brethren, the avengers weren't finished. According to a central doctrine of League teaching, there was a kind of immortality in these alien beings—an insidious vitality that would make them ever capable of reviving, even from such comprehensive destruction. So the last step in the Shapers' subjugation, before their righteous kin turned away from Earth and forgot it forever, was to pave over entirely the denatured masses of animal and vegetable matter in those areas of the planet where the Shapers had been destroyed.

The paving surface consisted of small, uniform ceramic tiles, that whether because of their interlocking shapes or other mystical properties, were thought immovable and impermeable to the alien life force beneath.

So here was the source of my intense fascination with the cult: that the antediluvian paving-tiles were none other than the small hexate fossil flake drilled up by the *Daffodil* rig—the fossils which had lately come to pattern my thoughts and dreams. They were the sole tangible, undeniable evidence that, time and again during my dazed sojourn with the League, set my imagination reeling across cosmic gulfs.

Needless to explain, the formless remains of the Shapers and their Carboniferous habitat had gone on in cult belief to become one with the immense fossil mineral deposits laid down all around them. The hexate tiles capping some of the deepest oil deposits remained the only clue to the weird alien origin. Impossibly, the Shapers' tenacious life spark was said to persist right up to the present day, but the only way it could reach outside its prison of primeval rock was in the form of psychic power, shaping the dreams and meditations of a few sensitive, sentient organisms on the earth above, and bringing them visions of the Shapers' vast premortal kingdom. Emil Sturla, the Paleozoic League's founder, claimed to be one so blessed. It had become his mission to perpetuate the memory and worship of the beings into modern centuries—and also, it was hinted, to prepare the way for their ultimate resurrection. The details of the Rising, as it was called, were known only to the inner circle of the cult, but the prayers and hopes of all the members were focused on it as ardently and as urgently as one might expect in any fanatical religious sect.

Such were the beliefs I was exposed to during long, brotherly chats with Pence, cloyingly confessional "faith sessions" with groups of earnest cultists, and glib suppertime sermons by Larkin. Yet these only skimmed the surface; I wasn't initiated to the deeper workings of the cult. There were many talks I was barred from, and often I noticed odd gestures and words being used whose meanings Pence couldn't or wouldn't explain.

The most tantalizing exclusion occurred the second night, when the majority of the membership followed Larkin out of the ranch house and up the brushy mountain slope, carrying flashlights and gas lanterns. It must have been an outdoor meeting, for its noises and diffused light occasionally found their way back down to us through the drifting fog. Pence, obviously assigned as a babysitter, sat restless beside me on the tattered sofa in the dayroom. He pretended to read and reread a mimeographed tract, but kept glancing out the grimy picture window. We were the only ones left behind; I even saw the two down-and-out vagabonds who had been recruited with me leaving with the others—though I don't recall seeing them return. I had dozed off by the time the celebrants came back, and I let myself be walked sleepily to my bunk.

Then, the very next day, came the event that roused me from what had become my passive, receptive stupor. Even before lunch I sensed a ferment of expectation among the cultists—but after the soupy meal we were told to remain seated at the long tables in the dining room. Feeling uneasy, I was able to spill my doped Kool-aid and make it look like an accident, without having more of it forced on me. Then we were hushed by none other than Sturla himself, our reclusive leader, for an announcement that was clearly to be of weighty importance.

He was an impressive figure—large and rawboned, old but not elderly, with a big, angular, ill-shaven face that now appeared slightly puffed and pink with excitement. His shock of white hair was uncared for, sticking up at odd angles here and there. He wore a rumpled white shirt, loose gray slacks held up by suspenders, and frayed house slippers. The pale hands that he rested on the sideboard ended in half-inch lengths of fingernail, untrimmed but unsoiled.

His eyes searched the room without focusing, and he began speaking in a voice that was deep but unmodulated. "Dear allies in the Paleozoic cause. I am ... that is ... I have waited so long for this moment ...."

He stopped and shook his shaggy head with an air that would have seemed theatric, if it had been planned.

"It's ... hard to put it into words. We've searched, and plotted, and dreamed ... the dreaming was the hardest, yes." During his pause, a murmur of standardized assent filled the room.

"My friends! All is to be as prophesied. And sooner, much sooner, than we hoped." He turned his face down to the smudged table, then up to the ceiling. "The fruits of last night's ceremony were propitious ... and the time of the Rising has been vouchsafed to me.

"It will be ... tonight!"

At his word, electricity passed through the room. Everyone stood, and a hubbub of exclamations and questions arose. Over it, Sturla's voice gradually reemerged.

"... and yes, there's much to be done. Our intercession tonight may be crucial. Now listen to friend Larkin for the details ...." Sturla's wraithlike form stooped and receded, though it still loomed over Larkin's as he pushed forward.

"Everyone, remember your jobs." The propagandist's manner had become brusque and authoritative. "Crew members, leave now and prepare the boat. The rest of you will attend a meeting in the briefing room immediately. Go!"

The group boiled away into activity. I was interested, though still a little out of it, and I drifted along with the crowd down an unfamiliar corridor. As I neared its end, a tan, blond-haired arm— Larkin's—shot in front of me and barred my way.

"Olin, sorry." He hardly smiled. "I'm afraid you're not ready for this phase. Our schedule's been pushed way ahead. Go with Pence— he'll find you something useful to do." He leaned toward the youth, who'd just come up behind me, and spoke quietly into his ear.

A moment later, I let my young guardian lead me away without protest. But my brain was no longer quiescent; it was busily sorting out what I'd glimpsed over the heads of the cultists as they filed into the assembly room. There'd been a large color photo cut from a recent issue of *Offshore Industries* magazine: an Exoco ad, picturing the *Daffodil* platform. And on the green chalkboard next to it were sketched some larger diagrams, clearly depicting the same structure.

How the bizarre linkages kept multiplying! There was suddenly no doubt in my mind; the rig was the target of the cult's imminent boat trip! As the realization settled home, I felt my dormant distaste for the cultists hardening into anger. Their planned excursion—presumably an attack on the platform—reminded me forcefully, for the first time in days, of Jean Hinchcliffe. My growing concern was more for her and other innocent victims than for any of Exoco's holdings.

Pence led me through the kitchen and down the exterior stairs, toward the carports under the end of the house. Outside the fog was just beginning to break up, with occasional apertures of dazzling blue illuminating the gray sky. The bus was parked in front of the carports, its wheels chocked against the steep slope of the drive, its side cargo hatches open. A pair of male cultists deposited two red cylinders into the luggage bays just as we came down; then they disappeared around the corner of the building.

"We can help with the loading," Pence announced, looking back at me resignedly. "We're supposed to get all the equipment from around the place—hey, where are you going?"

"Home," I said, turning my back to him.

"You can't leave now." As I moved away, I felt his presence close behind me, and his hand reached over my shoulder. Remembering my three weeks of aikido training, I clasped his hand flat against my chest and stepped into motion, twisting my body sharply away. This brought him up against one of the steel pipes that supported the house. His only sound was a muffled half-gasp, but the metal post made a deep thrumming noise as his skull struck it.

Ready for more of a struggle, I grasped his arm, but his body was already limp. I checked his pulse, then wrestled him over to the row of grimy garbage cans that stood along the house. I lowered him behind them with as little clatter as possible. He lay unmoving but breathing regularly, cushioned on a pile of soggy newsprint.

Rather than to go to the exposed western side of the house where the two men had gone moments before, I headed straight for the hillside. I had a vague idea of the direction of the San Marcos Pass highway, and wisps of blowing fog still screened me from the house moment by moment.

Dense chaparral made parts of the slope impassible. I was scratched painfully through my track suit, and I knew that the poison oak I brushed against would cause me misery in a week or two—but in my stay at the ranch I'd glimpsed the cult's discipline, and I expected pursuit momentarily. I worked my way up a ravine, found a well trodden path crossing it, and followed it away from the ranch. It ended in a clearing with grass recently trampled, brush cut back, and soil dug and churned.

It must, I realized, have been the site of the cult's nocturnal meeting. There was nothing to show the exact nature of the gathering, but I did see strange things in the dirt: drying, brine-whitened floats and leaves of still-pungent ocean kelp, and half a crushed steel eyeglass frame, its lens gone.

After prolonged, desperate struggles with manzanita and crumbling cliffs, I made it down to the highway. By that time the sun had banished the morning mists and commenced burning my skin and dehydrating me. I started walking down the steep road grade.

The dozenth car to pass slowed for my raised thumb, then stopped half-off the pavement on a blind curve. It was an open-topped Triumph occupied by two college girls in tennis outfits. I jumped in and perched wordlessly on the ledge behind the seats as the sports car spun its cliffside wheel on loose gravel. It caught with a jerk, and we took off down the hairpin road toward city and sea, spreading in silver vistas below us.

After a ride that was too hair-raising for conversation, the girls dropped me downtown, not far from the harbor and my car. My first and final question to my benefactors—whether or not they had change for a dollar—was the subject of noisy sophomore hilarity as they drove off.

I finally got change from a liquor store and found an open phone stall on traffic-laden Chorro Street. I spent the balance of the waning afternoon plugged into a buzzing network of wires and relays, calling law enforcement agencies.

Looking back, I guess it's not surprising that my efforts were in vain. One uncertainty is whether my thoughts and speech were by then quite lucid or still befuddled by my experiences with the cult. Another problem I ran into was the jurisdictional uncertainty regarding offshore rigs. The local police and sheriff's office were of little help, and when I finally reached the Coast Guard, the people there were unwilling to take my warnings seriously. Exoco's private security agency, on the other hand, heard me with ill-concealed suspicion, as if my message were a threat rather than a warning.

Their insistence on getting personal data on me caused me to hang up, in the belief that the call was being traced.

I tried to reach Peter Magnusson for backup or suggestions. He wasn't available at home or work.

The last call I made was to the platform, to warn Jean Hinchcliffe personally. I was told that Exoco's land-sea equipment was malfunctioning. Contact would probably be restored within a few hours, the operator said.

I found that my car hadn't been towed, though it had garnered two parking tickets. I got in and drove to my apartment for the sake of showering, changing clothes, and washing down some leftovers with stale orange juice from the fridge. All the while my thoughts were unreeling. I didn't believe it would do any good to renew my phone haggling, even if I could manage to get the cult's mountain retreat raided. Its new focus was obviously the sea.

So I took a warm coat and a watch cap and got back into my car. As the sun sank toward Point Concepcion, I drove straight into its glare, heading westward and northward toward Avila Beach.

By the time Route 101 edged into sight of the sea again, day had faded. It was now only a faint fringe of blue above the flat rim of ocean, which was featureless except for the pinprick lights of the *Daffodil* platform a long way out. After parking in the cramped lot near the public pier, I strolled past returning charter-boat patrons toward the water.

Marine field trips and expeditions, often undercrewed, have given me a good general knowledge of boats, as well as a good specific knowledge of where certain unguarded ones may be found. *Narwhal*, a small, muscular cabin cruiser belonging to California Polytechnic U., was moored year-round at Avila for field study use. It was no great trouble to walk out on the pier, clamber down a ladder to the water, and appropriate one of the sloshing rowboats moored there by yacht owners. I rowed out amid the anchored craft in the last dimness of dusk. My recollection of the harbor was accurate enough to lead me straight out to *Narwhal*. I moored the rowboat to the buoy and climbed aboard.

The vessel was maintained with an institutional sort of informality; I could tell that I wasn't the first casual user to hot-wire it. With ample fuel in the tank and the platform lights beckoning offshore, my course was clear.

I fired up the motor, cast off, and maneuvered the nimble craft out past the breakwater before switching on the running lights. When I saw the rotating beacon of Point San Luis to starboard, I pointed her and set the throttle at a chugging cruising speed. I had good visibility and very little chop, so there wasn't much else for me to do, except worry and wait.

In the broad sense I wasn't sure what I was doing there, and I wondered how much of my behavior could be attributed to drug aftereffects. Underneath the thrill of larceny, I experienced alternate pangs of urgency, anxiety, and embarrassment. I might not be allowed to land at the rig, and yet my appearance there could still ready them for a more dangerous invasion by cultists, if only I arrived in time. The puzzle of the cult's immediate goals I'd given up as insoluble—partly because it involved asking myself how much truth might lurk in their fantastic, fanatic beliefs. But the destination seemed certain.

So I sat at the wheel, wrestling my own pet demons. The cruise, in any event, promised to be an easy one—but then, it's easy to forget all the ways down the years the California coast has proven to be the most dangerous one in the world. For one thing, as I crawled across Pismo Bay, a fog began to rise.

Not that it's at all common, really, for a fog to rise at sea. Usually, it's blown in, by warm winds moving across the colder water. That hadn't seemed at all likely tonight, nor had it been forecast on the radio news I'd listened to while driving up. The mild, sage-scented land breeze I'd felt in the harbor certainly couldn't have produced a fog over cool summer seas.

Yet here was one being born all around me. I felt an oppressive density in the air, and visible vapors hung over the spray from *Narwhal*'s bow. The bright necklace of land lights behind me had already started to twinkle and dim.

I aimed the boat's bow carefully and noted my compass curve. Current and tide shouldn't prove to be important factors, I reasoned, in the hour or so of cruising ahead. Presumably, to prevent collisions, the platform would sound a foghorn, like the one on the point that was starting to moan dismally behind me.

I hoped at first that my steady progress would outrun the weather change, but on the dark sea ahead, the platform lights were soon obscured. In the course of a few minutes, wisps of fog lit by pale starlight seemed almost to boil up from the sea and engulf its still-distant outline. I recalled the tepid, tropical warmth of the water that had soaked me at the base of the platform, and it occurred to me that a local temperature anomaly might possibly give rise to a convection fog—swamp fog.

Then grayness sealed me in. I groped in a locker for the foghorn and commenced blowing at short intervals, listening in between. But I didn't reduce my speed.

I was insane, you say? I deny it. It's easy to feel insane when bounding through a gray nothingness backlit by beams of red, white, and green running lights, hurtling toward an unseen goal.

But I felt entirely rational—until certain physical impressions began to challenge my rationality.

A seaman can sense changes in wind, weather, and current by the feel of his vessel. Different motions of the ship are associated with varying tidal conditions, and a seasoned hand can detect them even while shut up below decks. Yet I, that foggy night, though not a skilled sailor, began to experience evolutions wildly unsuited to time, place, and weather.

First there was an odd feeling of acceleration, like voyaging downhill, if that were possible, in rising seas; Narwhal started to pitch with the giddy motion of a surfboat. When the first great wave broke over the bow, I wondered whether I was crossing the wake of some huge ship, perhaps a supertanker, but the swells continued with a jolting regularity that ruled out that possibility.

At one point a freakish cross-wave struck from the port side, and I almost imagined the loom of a huge sea beast surfacing off my beam. But it was only a thick shred of mist that drifted across the deck and scattered. A series of rollers broke over the bulwarks with almost seismic force, scouring the deck. The shocks threw me from side to side, dangling me from the wheel like a puppet, while bilge water splashed my knees. I held on, keeping the engine laboring for survival's sake, though it seemed the screw must be clear of the water most of the time.

After long minutes of fighting the wheel, tempest-tossed on an impossibly windless sea, there came sounds, too—sounds even stranger than the sea's spastic motions. There was the hissing crash of breakers against rocks, a dreaded noise I should only have heard leagues from my present position; but then, these were random, irregular crashes, not like any earthly breakers. Terrifyingly, they seemed to emanate from all sides.

Even more menacing was a vast resonance that my ears positively declined to believe: the deep thundering of a great cataract. Its size and distance were shrouded by the fog, which nevertheless seemed almost to roil with the force of it. I debated whether to cut my engine to keep from getting any nearer.

Then a current of riverine intensity caused the boat to yaw; I swear that she was making sternway, in spite of the laboring motor. Momentarily, the sea was transformed into the heaving maelstrom of a malevolent child's bathtub; then, with a horrid grating, *Narwhal* went aground. I was thrown over backward and knocked senseless.

I wasn't unconscious long, I can say in retrospect, judging by the
expanses and convolutions of that mad night which still lay ahead
of me. I awoke in the bilge, in the depressed stern of the boat, which
was dead aground and crazily askew. And I opened my eyes on stars:
bright, icy, unwinking stars that shone down with an airless clarity
one would expect only in desert latitudes or mountains.

As I lifted my throbbing head, the light of a late-risen moon
smote me from low in the sky. I remember thinking that the same
freakish weather which befogged the night must have preternatu-
rally cleared it. I fingered the back of my skull and found it painful
to touch, then I gathered my cold, cramped limbs under me and
stood upright against the sloping gunwale.

The lungfuls of air that accompanied my exertion had the briny
reek of low tide, so, strangely, the sight that awaited me wasn't a
surprise. Part of me expected it, yet that didn't stop the terror of it
from sweeping through my chest and numbing my fingers and toes.

On all sides the sea had flown; its rocky bed lay exposed. It had
bared to the stars a weird, asteroidal landscape. Miry, sodden
meadows spread between ragged hillocks crested with coral and
lank weed. Smooth tarns of trapped seawater gleamed everywhere
under the lurid moonlight.

The newborn terrain was rough and uneroded, but generally
even-trending, and my vision carried for miles in some directions.
In the east, however, the anguished contours of subseascape ended
abruptly in a snow-white fogbank. The damnable vapor now hung
solidly where the moon told me the view of natural coastline should
have been. I thought I could make out the ranked peaks of the Coast
Range along the indistinct upper edge of cloud, but the shoreline
itself was smothered.

To westward my vision was curtailed by the trend of slope—
which should have been falling away toward the brink of the Pacific
Trench, but now ascended to the level of some low crests or mesas
reared against the stars. Water ran down them in splattering
rivulets, combining two streams that flowed through deep shadows
near the boat. Their gurglings in invisible crevices gave the eerie
impression of human voices close at hand.

Where six hundred feet of living ocean had suddenly gone, I
couldn't conceive. Such a displacement in depth! But had the sea
sunk or the land risen, and over how great an area? Deep-sea life
would have been devastated by the loss of pressure, as the audible
flopping and splashing around me of dying fish with ruptured air

bladders confirmed. Dazedly, I tried to judge the magnitude of the ecological catastrophe, then I thought of the probable effect on the oil rig and the coastal cities.

Moving up the canted deck, I found that my body still functioned, though painfully. My mind, less resilient to a greater shock, was partly numbed, but it still worked smoothly on a subrational level. Thoughts circld in my mind like deep-swimming fish: my concern for Jean, my intent to help the other riggers, my awe of a vast natural phenomenon, the love of the sea, my survival instinct— all swam about in the cauldron of my brain, but none surfaced, as I prepared to leave the boat.

I knew that usually, in cases of freak tidal groundings, such an action is considered foolhardy. Yet in the weird urgency of my situation, it seemed the only possible choice. I threw a few items from the boat's equipment locker into a duffel bag: water bottle, first-aid kit, inflatable life vest. I exchanged my coat for a dry windbreaker, but my other damp clothes had to stay on. Squelching track shoes were as good a footwear as any for walking where no human had walked. With a feeling of Dantean adventure, I eased myself over the stern rail to set my feet in a weedy pool.

Walking the sea floor proved less difficult than I expected. The fury of the sea's retreat had done damage in the form of freshly eroded gullies and windrows of tumbled kelp. But the level places usually gave a firm, sandy footing, and the rocky surfaces were covered with slick but angular coral.

The land wasn't formed for drainage, hence the numerous pools, ranging in size from puddles to small lakes. Most that I found on the sloping terrain were narrow and shallow enough to cross.

If I'd had the leisure to study those pools and drained sea gardens, I would have learned much. Life was there in profusion, even if some of the species lay in helpless agony; other dark shapes could be seen flitting beneath the waters of the deeper pools, and stirrings and sputterings were audible around their margins. Some ponds were wet meadows of zostera and posidonia plants, alive with sheltering fish, shrimp, and gastropods, while elsewhere stood drooping specimens of coral-branching *Carophyllia* and polypous *Cerianthus*. Echinoderms and crinoids sparkled in bright pastels, spotlighted by the ascending moon.

Still, the very abundance of life in and around the pools made me cautious. I was reluctant to wade too deeply among the predatory sea creatures that might be starved or frenzied; some of the splashes and eddies looked powerful. Therefore, I skirted all but the shallowest sea puddles, staying watchful.

The steepest part of my climb was just above my grounded boat. After negotiating a box canyon heaped with raw sand, possibly the site of the cataract I'd heard roaring an eternity ago, I surveyed a new, glacial vista of pools and hillocks extending several hundred yards ahead. The next horizon, only slightly elevated, was eerily outlined by pale phosphorescence shining out of the west.

But the most unnerving new sight was an immense snakelike form twisting out of a tangle of weed at my feet. I'd already tensed to run from it when I saw that its bulging head was a set of concrete cylinders, and that its sinuous tail, winding out of sight underwater, was a steel cable as thick as my thigh. It was, presumably, one of the massive clump-weights stabilizing the half-mile hawsers that radiated from the *Daffodil* tower and supported it. The cable's slackness on the floor didn't bode well for the rig; I scanned the sky ahead for its lights and its angular shape, in vain.

For the first time in many minutes, Jean came back to my thoughts, bringing an aching clench of anxiety to my heart. Could she possibly be alive? For all I knew, my feelings for her were still pathetically one-sided. Yet now, suddenly, I craved the chance to find out, and win her over. I envisioned her reclining in the cafeteria chair that evening on the rig, when Blair Vincent had seemed such an obstacle. She'd treated both of us with warmth, and it was clear now that his patronage of her was just an arrogant pose. "Idiot!" I cursed myself for nursing petty jealousies while lives were at stake.

Talking to yourself is a sign of mental distraction, but hearing yourself answered can be alarming. I cast about nervously until I realized that the sounds I heard were the echoes of other human voices to the southward.

I felt a surge of hope, yet something made me refrain from crying out. I ran across a rippled sand expanse toward the sounds, scaled a low hummock, and peered around a jagged coral bush. I saw a party of walkers approaching on lower ground.

Leaguers. They formed a straggling line, heading toward a convergence with my own route ahead. I counted twenty-three, some carrying red cylinders slung over their shoulders: fire extinguishers, I now saw. At the front of the procession were a tall and a short figure whom I recognized as Emil Sturla and Zig Larkin.

There was no sign of their boat; presumably, it had grounded like my own. The pack plodded resolutely along, engaging in speech only to hurry the slowest members up. Sturla, his white shirt hanging untucked from the back of his soggy pants, forged ahead like an unkempt Moses, while Larkin gave his attention to those behind. Some of the followers, even the unburdened ones, were obviously weak or lacking agility for the trek; one slid down a mossy bank into a pool as I watched, and had to be dragged out by three tired companions amidst a flurry of splashes.

They, too, had to be seeking the platform. They seemed to have a firm idea of its location.

I hurried ahead on a parallel course, keeping pace with the party without being seen. The ground was broken enough to afford me cover, so I didn't have to give all my attention to the stalking cultists. As I pressed on, I began to notice disturbing changes.

One was the raw reek of hydrocarbons in the air. It told me, since the night remained windless, that I was drawing nearer the rig. The smell was becoming so intense that I feared it might make a close approach impossible, or that any survivors near the rig might have been asphyxiated. Crude oil fumes have made my head swim before, but this odor had a particularly rank, pungent quality, fortified by the sewage fragrance of butane gas. It was almost putrescent, with undertones of marsh or zoo. Strangely, as it worsened, the night itself seemed to grow balmier and warmer.

A more subtle transformation was in the appearance of life forms around me. I'd become almost accustomed to mounds and drooping shrubs of variously shaped and tinted corals. Discreet constellations of starfish and slumped tapestries of glossy-green weed had been present all along, where the moon struck or reflected up from a pond surface. But now I began to discern plant outlines that were more erect and vaguely fernlike or reedlike. A stand of thin-bladed plants at a pool's edge waved with surprising resilience when stirred by water currents, while small, frog-sized splashes began to mark my approach to new ponds.

In all, the ecology gradually seemed hardier and less stricken by the sea's passing. A quick, scuttering disappearance into a black recess of rock, though only half glimpsed, somehow bespoke scorpion more than crab.

I knew that I might be seeing a natural transition to a deeper level of ocean floor, or at least formerly deeper. Yet I had an eerie impression that many of the life forms were terrestrial rather than marine, and primitive rather than modern. Most incongruous was a recurring squat, thick-based growth with frondlike branches projecting upward and outward, resembling a long-extinct cycad. I even shifted my course, after gauging the steady progress of the cultists, to pass near one of the treelike things, but I couldn't walk close because its vicinity was heavily polluted by thick, reeking oil.

Looking around, I saw other traces of bunker oil. It seemed to be carried mainly on the water, spreading in black rainbows or clotted like floating sewage. Most of the dry ground was free of it, though I did begin to feel sticky clumps adhering to the soles of my shoes. I tried to trace its flow, with little success, but it clearly originated from the general direction of the plateau that rose before me. I began to interpret the radiance in the air as a spreading miasma of oil-born gases refracting the moonlight.

And yet that explanation wasn't quite adequate, for there were strange flickers and pulses of overlying luminescence, resembling an aurora borealis in their effect. They were caused, I decided, by the spontaneous combustion of highly volatile gases mixing with night air, as occurs in some dense swamps. A peculiar situation, and in this case possibly a hazardous one.

While I tried to find more patterns in the insane jumble of my surroundings, the cultists had drawn ahead of me. Their party was spread along a defile angling up toward the now-bright plateau crest. As I hurried to follow their course, I saw enough to convince me that the flora and fauna really were changing. I felt like a hiker crossing vegetation zones as he ascends a mountain, but that metaphor is deficient. Rather I felt that I was descending, and not in elevation but in time.

For the species I was seeing were definitely prehistoric. It was the oil that spawned them; wherever it lapped against rock, there stood primitive plants rooted in its congealed slime. Lycopods, calamites, seed-ferns—they were thick enough now to give the impression of a primeval marsh superimposed over the drained sea floor. Mental calculations led me to date the vegetation as late Mississippian, the very age of the fossiliferous oil strata the offshore rig had tapped. I couldn't guess how long this regeneration of ancient life had been going on, or how far it might spread. But its association with the flow of freshly leaked oil made its growth seem alarmingly swift.

And the furtive movements in and about the pools made it clear that the strange recrudescence wasn't limited to the plant kingdom. A look into a clear, moonlit pond revealed trilobites and small, lobe-finned fishes darting and creeping along its bottom. Hurried as I was, every professional instinct urged me to stay and observe. But as I tried to peer closer, I was startled by a loud, cracking buzz in the air near my head. Something hurtled past, grotesquely resembling a dragonfly—except that its wingspan easily exceeded two feet! It was enough to start me moving again. Moments later, while skirting a deep tarn, I clearly saw a squat, four-legged, fin-tailed shape slide beneath the surface of the water and disappear. The thing was as large as a collie, and clamped in its jaws had been a wriggling salmon.

With my faculty of amazement long since overtaxed, the only emotion left to me was dread. What I was seeing tallied all too closely with the cult's insane prediction of a Paleozoic Rising. Though they awaited it with zealous anticipation, to me it could mean only evil. As a paleontologist I couldn't regard the strange creatures springing up around me as repellent or monstrous, of course. Rather they were of intense scientific interest; there wasn't one of them I wouldn't have delighted in studying. But there was something distinctly unwholesome about the notion of an ancient regime superimposing itself on a modern, healthy ecosystem—feeding on it, and blotting it out, all with super-natural speed and vitality. The implied menace to Earth and humanity was tremendous.

Consequently, I became even more cautious. The bizarre logic of the situation indicated that any life I encountered wouldn't have evolved much past the amphibian stage; still, that included some nasty customers, and I took care to avoid surprising any large or aggressive species. The local vegetation was becoming dense enough to obstruct my way—and when I pushed through it, clouds of clacking insects swarmed up in my face. It took me long minutes to reach the next eminence, forced as I was to skirt the cultists' route. Then I had to stop to take in the view that dawned.

Before me lay the Carboniferous swamp in all its lush, primeval menace. It spread away in thickets and watery reaches that rippled silver under the moon. Its interior was well grown up compared to the fringe that I'd crossed; groves of supple, jagged-fronded trees formed weirdly evocative skylines against mists drifting upward from bogs. Foliage seemed to grow and multiply at almost a visible rate; the largest palm trunks were thicker than a man's body, with dense fern jungles making their bases invisible.

Extending an unguessable distance, the swamp provided an eerie backdrop; in its foreground lay the vast wreckage of the *Daffodil* rig. A hundred feet of the supporting central tower still stood above the marsh at a crippled angle, twisted off cruelly at the top. Below, more ironwork lay in a colossal jumble of half-submerged struts and cables, doubled back on themselves by the shearing forces of the ocean's subsidence.

The concrete base of the tower, with its drill template and steel-pipe Christmas trees, had ruptured; that was inevitable, ripped as it was half out of the sea floor. That provided the copious fountain of oil that fed the life teeming all around. From the gaping wreckage, viscous blackness poured into a pool that seemed to flow and eddy with a life of its own, before streaming away to nourish the swamp. From both fount and pool sputtered the gases that flickered and burned away in strange-hued foxfires overhead.

Washed by their fitful light, at the very brink of the oil pool, was the most heart-wrenching part of the scene: the demolished super-structure of the platform. All of it—machinery, production areas, and crew quarters—appeared to have been dashed on one side to the sea floor, or else staved in by tumultuous seas. With no built-in flotation, it may have sunk before the final flight of the waters, but in any event, there seemed little hope of finding survivors inside. The massive structure was buckled and rent, its cranes and derricks sprawled in the weeds, its ruptured oil storage tanks oozing tangled swamp verdure out over the wreckage.

I felt numbing despair at the sight, for Jean. The fate of the others was a grave concern, but it wouldn't have made me feel the same plummeting emotion. Still, I knew it would be premature to rule out the hope of survivors in or near the wreck. I needed to be sure.

The coral-topped rise where I stood was still fairly clean of swamp growth, and the cultists were in plain view down its slope. They loitered on the reedy marge of an oil-scummed lake that spread between us and the platform ruins. The leaders had stopped to reform the party, and the stragglers were just catching up. Sturla seemed impatient to go on; he stood, swiveling between his follow- ers and the wilderness prospect ahead, gesturing with both his arms, and inveighing in words I couldn't make out. Meanwhile, Larkin moved among the troops, laying hands on shoulders and urging them forward. Soon, though the last arrivals had scarcely been given time to rest, they were moving on again in a narrow file, thigh-deep along the lake's edge.

Just then the water seemed to explode in the midst of the group. Where spray scattered, I saw a gleaming, shingled back raised a yard out of the water, twisting and arching in currents churned by powerful fins. Screams drifted up to me from the scattering pilgrims, and flailing limbs attested that one or more of their number were dragged down.

Water jetted to alternate sides as their assailant, a great armored fish, backed itself out of the shallows. Then its supple tail flicked once, driving it out of sight into the murky depths of the lake.

The aftermath of the terror was strangely anticlimactic. Larkin was already shouting as he marshaled the group once more. He picked up discarded fire extinguishers and thrust them at cultists, who took them quietly. Sturla forged far ahead through the swamp, as if he hadn't even noticed the incident.

As they resumed their march, I found myself descending toward the lake to follow them. Their course seemed to lie near the wreckage, where I wanted to go. But I wasn't ready to throw my life away; I took a wider detour through the lake shallows to avoid its largest denizens.

Partly because of this, shadowing the cultists proved toilsome. My rucksack was heavy with dampness, and my wet trousers chafed. The marsh reeds had rough edges that caught at my clothing and abraded my hands. With each step my feet sank deep into oily muck, and from time to time I felt live things writhing hurriedly from under my probing shoe soles. My vision was clouded by giant, blundering gnats and the clacking dragonflies that hunted them. Worst of all were the oil fumes: Almost tangible in the tropic heat, they filled my battered head with a low, steady pain.

The surroundings grew more menacing as I moved into a zone of palmlike trees that arched high overhead. The ground there was firmer, but also brushier, and I felt sure that the shadowy thickets harbored new and unguessed dangers.

Yet the shadows served to shelter me when I heard low voices nearby. I pushed stealthily forward through a fern-choked glade and found the cult assembled on the high bank of a pitchy, gleaming lagoon. The cultists had drawn close under the angled ruin of the steel tower; a few dozen yards further along the shore, the oil rig's superstructure loomed like a toppled office block.

The morass in front of us seemed to mark the very heart of the swamp. The wavelets lapping at the cultists' feet were driven by the gush of oil from forbidden strata far beneath. The coarse liquid could be heard sputtering and bubbling thickly somewhere nearby. Viewed this closely, the lagoon's aspect was utterly unearthly.

As I'd noted, the waters at its center seemed to swirl with a crude animism of their own. Now, by the wavering light of the swamp-gas auroras, I thought I could see vague shapes rearing up and subsiding in the flow: amphibian and plant forms, trunks and extremities, striving of their own will to accrue and combine into rudimentary creatures, then falling back to oil liquescence, even as their substance gushed raw out of the warm bowels of the earth.

While hiding in the ferns, I closed my eyes and shook my head, thinking the bad air might be making me hallucinate. But when I turned my gaze back to the near edge of the maelstrom, my mad perception was confirmed. There, on a slimy beach amid weed-crawling wreckage, I watched a cow-sized batrachian creature—the uneasy mating of fish and frog—hauling itself forth as if to bask in moon rays. But an instant before, I had seen it, not surface from the pond, but rather coalesce in it, raising itself like an Escher nightmare from the very substance of the pool's shallowest edge, writhing and heaving even while its half-formed limbs still grossly extruded themselves.

That was my clearest glimpse of how the jungle around me had come to exist, miraculously, in the few short hours since the sea drained away: through the virulent life-energy of the hydrocarbons the *Daffodil* rig had tapped. For once, oil and water could mix —instantly, to reconstitute an extinct world, speeded by strange, massive physiographic and climatic changes.

Of all the questions raised in my mind, the foremost were: What force impelled and guided this phenomenon? Was it intelligent? Was it benign, or at least natural? If the cult's beliefs were valid, as they now seemed, then an ancient power was reestablishing itself on Earth. And if the League's own inhuman practices and the feral aspect of the world springing up around me were any indication, then the guiding power scarcely seemed to need human adoration and worship. Whatever it was, it was powerful, clearly—but benevolent?

The best evidence to the contrary lay before me: the shattered wreckage of the rig. As with the pond, close inspection revealed unpleasant sights. The blossoming prehistoric life, denser and more vital near its source, seemed to be hugging the ruin with a special obscene intimacy. Thick-bellied palms clustered in shattered windows and doorways, while fronds and creepers caressed the skewed catwalks. I scanned in vain for any sign of human survival; no lights or systematic movements showed. But to my horror, on the sloping surface of the helicopter pad, two of the squat amphibian creatures tugged and worried with tooth-fringed jaws at something—a tattered morsel whose shape suggested that it might once have been human. Stomach clenching, I stared in horror.

My grim reconnaissance had been made over the shoulders of the waiting cult members. Now I looked up as their low, nervous talk was hushed by Larkin. He moved through the group and urged them forward to the water's edge, there to kneel. When they were down, he fell to his own knees beside them.

In their midst only Sturla remained erect, facing the water with arms folded. When his disciples were stilled, he cupped his hands to his mouth, drew a deep breath of the miasmic air, and issued a weird, shrieking cry: "Hriak-ak-ak!" It echoed across the lagoon and faded to silence. He raised his pale hands, repeating it once, then again. "Hriak-ak-ak!" Silence.

Then his third cry was answered from the swamp.

Not that the response was the same sound. Though vaguely similar, it had more the quality of air being forced, against immense resistance, out of a huge, wet bladder. There was in that cry a croaking resonance no human throat could ever fully imitate.

The sound was repeated, louder this time, and nearer. Waves slapped the lagoon shore, indicating the approach through the water of something large.

If I fail adequately to describe what then waded out of a tree-girt reach of swamp—well, call it the first instance of my newfound squeamishness. When I boasted that I'd never seen a natural biological form that repelled me, much less one so loathsome as to make me avert my eyes, it was because my experience had been limited to the flora and fauna of Earth. I had seen nothing before that night that could truly be labeled a demon, an unholy abomination.

Of course, the thing was at least half-submerged. And given its bulk, it's doubtful that it ever could have lifted its nether part entirely out of the water. Hence, perhaps, its fondness for the primordial swamp as home.

Intelligent? Perhaps not in a human sense. But then, its immense powers may have placed it forever beyond the need of puny human intellect. That the Shaper was an astute, discriminating being was evident: from the way its dinner-plate eyes pivoted as it surveyed the waiting humans; from the ample size of the brain lobes it displayed as its barnlike body heaved up, sluicing off sheets of water and oil; and from the careful, discrimi-

nating way its mouth-feelers reached down and seized three of its
awed worshipers, among them Zig Larkin, to be drawn up shrieking
into its vast, amorphous maw.

By the time the others began to stagger and crawl back from their
kneeling places, I was groping blindly inside my waterlogged duffel
bag. Only one possible weapon was at hand: the flare pistol in its
watertight plastic case. I fumbled it open, twisted a cartridge into
the gun grip, and stepped clear of the undergrowth.

Of course, I wasn't blind to the danger of using an incendiary
weapon. With oil flowing from the earth nearby and volatile gases
steaming lazily off the swamp, the risk was extreme and obvious.

Yet by then I'd written off the chance of there being any survivors,
including myself. My own life and those of the remaining cultists
seemed somehow unimportant at that moment, in view of the
enormous, absolute menace of the Rising and the intense hateful-
ness of the thing whose face, or facelike appendage, was looming
each moment horribly nearer.

I fired.

Light flared and, forgetting all, I turned to run. But I'd barely
spun away when, instantaneously, a blast wave sped me along into
a tangle of ferns, scorching my ears and the back of my neck. As I
was picking myself up, with the vast detonation still throbbing in
my pain-ridden head, I risked looking back.

The Shaper was a quivering mass of flame. It belched and bleated
thunderously, dragging itself back toward the lagoon's center. But
a sheet of living fire was flying across the foul water, engulfing other
bulky forms that had been rising from its depths. Gases were
igniting in flares that streamed high overhead. Trees at the water's
edge began exploding into flame.

None of the cultists were visible on the beach except Sturla, who
stood fast at the shore. He had been transfigured into a tall torch—
one that sagged slowly, limply to earth as I watched.

The mingled exultation and disgust I felt were both soon over-
ruled by panic, and I flung myself away, running blindly—against
a cool breeze that flowed toward the heart of the fire storm blossoming behind me. From time to time new shocks and flashes
overtook me, while the sounds emitted by the burning Shapers fell
to hoarse, monotonous bellows and subsided. My memories of the
flight are few, but blindingly bright: the explosions; the spectacle
of escaping cultists caught in lake shallows, in a day-blaze of orange
firelight, beset by lunging, snapping sea beasts attacking frenziedly

even as the marsh all around them blazed up; and a glance back at the ruined tower, reduced to a wilting steel candle in a jet of flame that roared skyward from the center of a Hades of dancing fire.

After that, the holocaust receded to a towering glow in the dark sky. Memory doesn't supply me any other details. My senses were scorched and overloaded, my reactions merely automatic; they led me, semiconscious, in a painful, infinitely prolonged descent that ended in oblivion.

When the mental curtain lifted, it was morning. I saw that I was in the cabin of the *Narwhal*, slumped in the pilot's chair. Sea motion was trying to toss me out, but more insistent was the sloshing of brine against my calves, for the vessel was almost awash.

I rose unsteadily, found my way to the rail, and surveyed a glinting, unbounded expanse of ocean.

I stood there, reeling more from weakness and confusion than from the roll of the light seas. My mind had to reach and grope first, tamely, to recall my acquisition of the boat. Then the night's events began to tumble forth like sinister toys from a high closet shelf; I glimpsed each one with a mounting sense of disbelief. Finally, my thoughts grounded abruptly, jarringly, on the realization of having lost Jean. Totally and irrevocably. The intensity of that feeling made it impossible for me to doubt all the rest.

Physical exhaustion made the weight of despair all the more crushing. My regard for her must have been deeply felt. When I turned my face into the breeze, I knew that my eyes were wet with more than seawater.

Yet plenty of distraction, both from sorrow and wonder, lay in my surroundings. It was a fair, calm day with visibility limited by a silver-gray haze. No land, either freakish or natural, was in sight. Even the sea looked normal, except for some floating oil smears on the waves. *Narwhal*, back in her element, was pitching sluggishly; the water inboard, that helped stabilize her motion, also told of damage to the hull. I switched on the bilge pump and found that it still worked.

As to what had happened, I had to conclude that the fugitive sea had flooded back during my unconsciousness. Whether its return had left any land intact—or indeed, any earthly human artifacts besides my boat—was for the time being imponderable. Of course, I began to entertain doubts of my own memories, and of my sanity, but it all remained vivid to me. My shoes were so caked with tar that I threw them overboard, and my eyes and skin were still scorched by the world-cleansing fire I'd kindled. Although others later attributed my physical depletion and my burns to a day of exposure in a drifting boat, I see their dismissals as cynical maneuvers, or as facile props to their own sanity.

During the hours I labored to get the engine back into operation, I needn't have worried about the fate of mankind. Before nightfall, a Coast Guard cutter hove into view. It closed quickly with my wallowing craft and took me aboard. She was returning from an otherwise fruitless search for *Daffodil* survivors. The swamped *Narwhal* was abandoned, and I was taken to Morro Bay and the busy emergency facility that had been set up there.

In the absence of any other witnesses to prove confirmation, my account must indeed have sounded like ravings to the guardsmen and medics. When we put into port, they gave me prompt access to higher personnel, but my debriefings by Coast Guard officers, police, and Exoco staff were conducted with what was either maddening ignorance or artful skepticism. Some of the questions they asked, and some of the flickers of their eyes, showed me that they had an inkling of the truth. But they chose to hush it up. Perhaps their "high deniability profile" will be adequate to guard us against another Rising. I pray so.

By the time I was released to face the press, I knew the score. My public testimony conformed to the scant information that was officially acknowledged: a low-intensity but amazingly prolonged seismic episode, associated with record low tides and freakishly dense fog; the complete absence of one night's high tide, followed by the vicious little locally generated tidal wave that swept the area clear of shipping and that battered coastal towns. While the wave did damage to San Luis and Morro harbors, it was mild compared to the tsunami that later struck the Hawaiian Islands.

Of course, the worst disaster in human terms was the sinking of the *Daffodil* platform with all hands. The burning oil leak that resulted was brought under control weeks later by the injection of concrete into deep subocean strata. That reportedly licked the problem—although it's been hard in the months since then to get a trustworthy estimate of the rate of continuing oil seepage from the ocean floor.

My own silence continues. If I hadn't said what I was expected to say, the legal problems arising from my theft of the boat could have been worse, and my standing at the university would be laughable. Of course, my instinct was to put up a fight, even in my weakened state, until I finally realized the situation. No one was going to believe me.

Admittedly, it's been made easier, and my recovery has been speeded, by my closeness to Jean Hinchcliffe. That she was ashore, on sick leave, at the time of the disaster was blessed good luck for us; rather the opposite for Blair Vincent, who was working in her place. I found my feelings for her shared and requited, and her love has erased much of the horror. But not all.

Our life is tranquil, except for my little preoccupations and mental aftershocks. She comforts me after the dreams, tolerates my obsessive monitoring of offshore sightings of sharks and other sea life, and carries more of the burden of my college job than I like to admit. I think she will stay.

Yet it's not the same as if she'd heard the full story—or worse, believed it. The knowledge exacts a toll, and I wouldn't want to inflict it on her. The innocent pleasure she still takes in walking on the beach, for instance—would it continue if she saw, as I do, the strange properties of the bunker oil that now washes southward from Pismo Bay? I've seen others notice it and recoil, but none so much as I—repelled by its clinging texture, its rank smell, and the way that, when scraped from your skin, it always seems to leave a smear vaguely resembling the form of a fern leaf, or fish, or claw.

No, it's too hateful. I'll keep silent.

WILL MURRAY'S NAME will be well known to you as the leading authority in the field of pulp fiction studies. (There ought to be such a department at Miskatonic U., don't you think?) His *Duende History of the Shadow Magazine* is a classic, and his archaeological spadework unearthing all sorts of early Doc Savage drafts, radio scripts, comic books, and manuscripts is worthy of Heinrich Schliemann or Indiana Jones. But for all this, Will's name should be even better known than it is, namely as the writer of the current series both of Doc Savage and The Destroyer novels. In the present story, Will brings to bear his omniscient knowledge of just about anything a story's background requires of him. In so doing, as you will see, he factors in two important Lovecraftian elements: the careful simulation of the mundane as a setup for the numinous revelation, and the pivotal role of random chance in determining the fate of human history.

Rude Awakening

by Will Murray

WHERE THE WARM BLUE CURRENTS of the Pacific meet the deep green tides of its colder reaches, a long line of whitecaps broke and squirmed. They had squirmed for millennia. They would squirm for untold ages to come. Long after man, whose time as Lord and Master of his dry-land domain neared its final stage, the clash of the opposing tides of the mightiest ocean on the planet would go on.

On that line, the oceanographic research vessel *Lemuria* came to a dead stop and, with a harsh rattle of chain, dropped anchor.

Carl Blackshear, Team Leader of Operation Deep Sound, pounded down a companionway shouting, "Hop to it! Get the submersible ready to go overboard. I mean *now*!"

The crew fell to undoing the clamps that held the bright yellow underwater explorer fastened to aft deck chocks. Blackshear extended the aerial of his satellite uplink phone, furiously punching out a long distance number.

The phone at the other end rang immediately. There was going to be one hell of a bill, but radio transmissions can be overheard.

"This is Big Sur Sending Station. Odom speaking."

"Odom, we're at the line, and about to drop *Challenger* over the side."

"What's your rush, man?"

"Two hard years fighting all the way to the U.S. Supreme Court for the right to undertake a perfectly reasonable and eminently safe undersea experiment is my damn rush," Blackshear bit out. "Are you ready to send the first wave?"

"All systems on line. The emitters are in the water."

"Fine. Stand by." Tapping the disconnect button, Blackshear punched out a New Zealand number.

"Great Barrier Island Receiving," a voice said. "Go ahead."

"Blackshear. Big Sur is ready to send. Are you ready to receive?"

"We are, *Lemuria*. You are on station, I presume?"

"Right on the line. We have whitecaps breaking in a line as far as the eye can see."

"That puts you right in the shout path."

"You got it." Abruptly, Blackshear looked up. "Damn."

"What's the problem?" Great Barrier asked.

Blackshear shouted up to the bridge. "Approaching craft! Make them out?"

The word came back flat and disgusted. "Greenpeace."

"Damn them. They lost in the courts. Why don't they just roll over and die?"

"Are we aborting?" Great Barrier asked.

Blackshear popped the receiver to his glowering face. "We are *not* aborting. We are going. Stand by. The next voice you hear will be Storesund giving the three-minute warning. Blackshear out."

"Understood. Great Barrier out."

Blackshear strode over to the *Challenger*. They had thrown open the main hatch of the squat yellow saucer of a craft to air it out, preparatory to operations.

"She about ready to go over?" he demanded.

"Yes, sir."

"Then do it."

The T-bar crane toiled upward, lifting *Challenger* off the sun-drenched steel deck. It swung like a big primary-colored gimbal as the crane shifted it jerkily out over the water.

Blackshear watched it with his knuckles whitening to bone.

Three years preparing for this moment. Two additional years fending off environmentalist groups, getting international permits and tap-dancing with and around lawyers. He wasn't going to let anything stop them now. Mankind's future depended on it.

The *Challenger* splashed into the warm green side of the whitecap seam and began bobbing. Its circular hydraulic thrusters swung idly like maimed flippers.

Blackshear stripped off his windbreaker and, shooting hail to the bridge, stepped onto the Jacob's ladder and rattled down to a Boston Whaler bumping under the stern.

A seaman sat at the engine, gripping the throttle.

"Take me over," Blackshear said, casting off the lines himself.

The Whaler muttered away from the tossing ship. It was a short distance to the *Challenger*, but too far to jump or swim safely.

To port, the big rustbucket Greenpeace tub was putting Zodiac boats into the water. The lead boat was already skimming toward them and some idiot in the bow was trying to hold a Greenpeace flag high as the warm Pacific trades fought him strenuously.

"Morons," Blackshear muttered. "What do they think they're going to accomplish this late in the game?"

The pilot said nothing. He cut the engine and the Whaler glided in a shallow arc to the *Challenger*'s stern.

When the rubber bumpers thumped the yellow hull, Blackshear stood up and grabbed for the aluminum handholds.

"Wish me luck," he muttered, and began climbing.

Reaching the dorsal hull he squirmed into the open hatch with practiced ease and dropped into the cramped womb of the deep-sea submersible. Closing the hatch, he dogged it tight, got down in the control bucket, and began warming up the electronics.

Over the radio came the captain's terse voice.

"The Greenpeace ship is trying to raise us."

"Ignore them."

"They sound pretty frantic."

"Losers always do," said Blackshear.

"Tell me when you want the umbilical lines lowered, *Challenger*."

"Give me a few minutes," Blackshear grunted, checking the digital readouts and performing other safety checks.

The captain's tight voice came on again.

"Those Zodiacs are circling *Lemuria* like sharks. They're hailing us with bullhorns."

"Bullhorns," Blackshear grunted. "Now that's appropriate."

A rude rush of sound filled the tiny space, where equatorial sunlight poured in through bulbous portholes.

"What's that?" Blackshear snapped.

"Static."

"I know. Why are we getting static out here?"

"Unknown. Try channel 3."

Blackshear switched over. "How's that?"

The captain's voice came again, busy with pops and crackles.

"*Crackle* ... not so hot ... *pop* ... peace hear."

"Say again, *Lemuria*."

"I said *crackle* Greenpeace is ... on ... *crackle* channel *spit*."

"Go back to channel 2, *Lemuria*. You're breaking up."

"Carl, I said Greenpeace has switched to channel 3."

"So what?"

"They're probably going to 2 right now."

"Damn."

And under a steady buzz of static, an anxiously polite voice said, "Attention, *Lemuria*. Call off your experiment. You cannot comprehend the harm you could cause."

"Screw you," Blackshear shot back. "This is a lawful scientific experiment sanctioned by the National Oceanic and Atmospheric Administration, and approved by the National Marine Fisheries Service. Our environmental impact statement is on file. Go read it."

"It's never been done before."

"Neither had radio before Marconi. Now kindly get off our communications frequency."

"Sir, I implore you to consider the consequences of your present course of action. Deep sea marine life is the most isolated population of the face of the earth. There is no predicting what effect these horrific sounds will have on the cephalopod population—"

"Octopi? I thought you people were worried about whales!"

"We're worried about every form of deep-sea denizen, but there's one in particular that you should know about—"

Blackshear switched the channel and began chanting, "*Challenger* to *Lemuria*. I have switched to channel 4. *Challenger* to *Lemuria*, if you're as smart as I am, you'll have done the same." And as he finished his pre-dive checklist, Blackshear fell to whistling angrily into his filament mike so the frequency remained active.

Over the loudspeaker came a rush of static and the *Lemuria* captain's voice saying, "*Challenger* ... *spit* ... copy."

"Good man, Stan. We can live with bursts of static if it gives us a little peace."

"Roger ... *pop* ... go."

"If you just asked me if I were set to go, the answer is a rousing affirmative. Do you read, *Lemuria*? Go for dive, I am ready to dive dive dive dive."

"Roger, *Challenger*."

And with a bouncing *thunk*, the cables holding *Challenger* high in the swells began paying out. The submersible dropped deeper into the water. Through the lower ports, Blackshear could see the soapy heaving waterline rise.

"I'm initiating dive sequence," he said, throwing switches.

Intake tanks engorged themselves and the wallowing yellow deep sea craft began to sink. The waterline rose past the lower bubble ports to engulf the upper ones, devouring the pure blue sky over the Pacific.

The first five minutes of the dive were the most tense. There was only the hissing and wheezing of the oxygen supply. The diatom-choked green water turned aquamarine, then cobalt, then slate, and gradually shaded to a rich black.

A green spike appeared on the spectrogram screen. Blackshear recognized the fingerprint of a passing dolphin, so when one arrowed past a port, he was not surprised.

"Going to lights," Blackshear said.

In response to a flipped switch, hull floodlights blazed into life, illuminating the swirling diatoms that gave the water its greenish hue.

"*Challenger* to *Lemuria*. Do you copy?"

"*Crackle* ... Copy, *Challenger*."

"Stan, listen carefully. When I give the signal, inform Great Barrier Island to get ready. Then and only then, have Big Sur initiate the first pulse. Got that? Great Barrier first. Big Sur only after Great Barrier is informed."

"Understood, *Challenger* ... *crackle*."

Exactly five hundred feet down by the digital depth gauge, Blackshear checked the analog backup. It read 498 feet. He waited until the needle crawled to 499 before calling up.

"All stop."

"All stop," came back the reply.

And the *Challenger* stopped descending so smoothly it hardly rocked. The analog dial read exactly 500 feet down.

Blackshear allowed himself a moment to take stock. All systems read shipshape. He picked up the hydro-earphones and set them on his head, keeping one ear free to talk to the mother ship.

"Deploying the ventral hydrophones," he said.

Nothing came back from *Lemuria* except angry static.

"Damn these whale kissers," Blackshear said.

A minute later, the captain's voice called down, "Carl, we have a *crackle* fishing trawler on site."

"A what?"

"Japanese fishing trawler *pop*."

"What do *they* want?"

"They want us to *crackle*."

"To what?"

"Stop. Stop. They want us to stop!"

"What's *their* problem?"

"Unknown. It's on channel 3, in broken English salted with Japanese."

Blackshear switched to channel 3. He listened as rapid words filled the submersible.

"*Lemuria*, switch back to 2," he asked. "Have Great Barrier listen in. Maybe they can make sense of that jabber."

After a few minutes, the captain came on again.

"According to Great Barrier, they're babbling about something they call Tako-ika."

"What the hell is Tako-ika?"

"Great Barrier says it's a compound word he never heard before. Translated literally, it means Devilfish-cuttlefish."

"Devilfish-cuttlefish?"

"Great Barrier's saying they're imploring us to call off the experiment before we arouse Devilfish-cuttlefish."

"That translation must be wrong."

"Great Barrier swears the word is Devilfish-cuttlefish."

"Anything else?"

"There is another word Great Barrier can't translate."

"What's that?"

"Rerahu, or something. It doesn't translate but Great Barrier thinks from the pronunciation it may have some L's in it. The Japanese have trouble with their L's. And if it's a one-syllable word, they probably added the vowel on the end too. They can't handle one-syllable words."

"So it might be Lelah."

"Might be. They're saying this Rerahu is the abode—exact translation there—of Devilfish-cuttlefish, and it's deep in these very waters."

"Sounds like superstitious fisher talk. Who are these clowns?"

"They're identifying themselves as representatives of some Japanese fishing guild I never heard of. Could be they're worried about their catches, and are trying to scare us off."

"Screw them too. We're in international waters. I want you to stand by. We're going soon."

"Roger, *Challenger*."

Steady static again filled the *Challenger* as Carl Blackshear finished modulating his receiving equipment.

"First, it was save the whales," he grumbled. "Now it's don't annoy Devilfish-cuttlefish. Whatever happened to the upward march of civilization through applied science?"

The captain came back. "Carl, we think you should know Greenpeace is running up and down the band, searching for our com frequency."

"Let's keep talk to a minimum then. We go in three minutes. Copy?"

The too-polite Greenpeace voice suddenly intruded.

"... what you do ... *pop* ... forces you cannot comprehend ... *crackle* ... until too ... late *spit.*"

"Turn green and die," Blackshear muttered, his eyes angrily checking the spectrogram readouts. Switching on the two tape decks, he let them run briefly, rewound, and played back the eerie sounds of the deep Pacific back through his earphones.

"Hydrophone mikes check. Tapes check. Backups green. Okay, it's time to shout across the wide Pacific." He brought the filament mike closer to his mouth. "*Lemuria*, initiate."

"What say?"

"I said initiate Deep Sound, damn it!"

"Roger."

Then the worst of it began. Blackshear, headphones over both ears, rolled tape and prayed Greenpeace would not find their frequency until it was all over.

He glanced at his watch: 2:44. By now, Stan had instructed Great Barrier to ready their receiving and recording equipment. He would be talking to Big Sur now. And over there, sophisticated sonic emitters would set in motion a wave of sound traveling from one end of the Pacific Ocean to the other, all underwater, all unheard, except by Great Barrier Island Receiving and *Challenger*.

Unless one counted maybe three billion assorted cetaceans, pinnipeds, marine mammals and cephalopods swimming in between.

Blackshear wasn't concerned about the fish. Fish could hear underwater. Everyone knew that. They might be startled; they might be spooked by the 200-decibel sound wave about to roar their way. Some would awaken from sleep. Maybe a few might suffer nightmares. Who cared? Sound didn't kill. The experiment was perfectly safe. NOAA had so certified it. And the mission—to chart global warming trends—was important to the survival of all life on earth.

The scientific principle was very simple. Sound waves travel fastest and furthest in warm water. By firing sonic shots at daily intervals for a month, and recording their velocity, the degree of global warming as it impacts upon the Pacific could be measured as a corollary of any increase in speed. Past tests had shown to the astonishment of the scientific community that sufficiently powerful bursts of sound could be sustained as far as there was water to propagate it with only modest decreases in decibel levels.

Blackshear waited. No one knew how long it would take the pulse to travel outward from the California coast. That was why he was at the midpoint. *Challenger* was the control. He would be the first to hear the pulse and Great Barrier would receive it at the other end, some six thousand nautical miles from the Sending Station. It was a very safe experiment. Perfectly within international environmental guidelines. Nothing could go wrong. Except—

The static rush warned of an incoming radio transmission. Blackshear's heart was in his throat. *Please let that be* Lemuria, he thought.

"Once again, we are *crackle* demanding you call off this—"

"Screw the whales!" Blackshear roared. "And get off this frequency!"

"We don't care about the whales," a frantic voice called back. "That's what we've been trying to tell you. "This isn't about whales. It's about ... *pop pop*."

"About what?"

The pulse reached *Challenger*. A low extended bass note, it rolled across the gently rocking sub to fill Blackshear's earphones. It was like having a magnetic current pass through your body, he thought. It seemed to vibrate right through his marrow. The amalgam fillings in his back teeth vibrated like tuning forks.

It passed as quickly as it came. Three seconds in duration by the digital clock—but it seemed like six times that long.

"I capture it, *Lemuria*," he barked. "It's strong and it's still traveling. Clocks in at 185 decibels."

There was no answer from the mother ship.

"*Lemuria*, did you copy my transmission?"

No answer.

Then a dull voice. "Blackshear. What's happening down there?"

"Nothing. Now."

"We have churning in the water."

Blackshear peered out the starboard ports, upper and lower. He saw nothing. Portside checked out fine as well.

"I have nothing down here but passing dolphin," he reported.

"Are they agitated?"

"Negative. I see no agitation," Blackshear said, letting the tape run.

"Well, something's caused that Japanese trawler to beat away like a gaffed tuna."

Then a gulp of sound as big as a bathtub came into his earphones.

"I have another sound," he informed *Lemuria*.

"A second pulse?"

"No. It's different." And past one window arose a wobbling air bubble big enough to have been expelled by a blue whale. It registered as a weird green smudge on the spectrogram monitor.

"It appears the pulse may have dislodged an air pocket on the sea floor," Blackshear reported. "Anything from Great Barrier yet?"

"Negative. We're still awaiting word."

Then Greenpeace intruded again.

"Oceanographic submersible *Challenger*. Cease all untested operations. Repeat. Cease all untested operations."

Over that came Stan's frantic voice.

"Carl. We have an emergency transmission from Washington."

"Washington?"

"They say they're with the National Reconnaissance Office."

"What's the National Reconnaissance want with us?"

"They want a patch through to you."

"Do it."

Blackshear waited impatiently. Right now the pulse should be approaching New Zealand if it retained its velocity. Of all the times for some Washington bureaucrat to intrude. Well, if they're calling it off, they're too late. It's begun.

"Carl Blackshear. Do you read me? This is Vincent of the National Reconnaissance Office. Reply if you copy."

"Blackshear here. Go ahead, Vincent."

"We have just received a satellite feed of your position. You must evacuate your position immediately. Do not initiate your experiment. Leave immediately. This is a direct order of the highest authority."

"Are you crazy? You have no jurisdiction over us."

"Blackshear, this is the Cryptic Events Evaluation section of NRO. According to our database, you are directly over ... *crackle* ...."

"Over what?"

"*Crackle.*"

"Say again, NRO. You are breaking up."

"R'lyeh. R'lyeh. R'lyeh. You are over R'lyeh. Your damned sonic pulse is going to pass through that infernal vault that has been down there since before Christ was a corporal. If you wake it, there's no putting the genie back in the bottle."

"Wake it? Wake what?"

"*Crackle pop pop spit.*"

"I am not copying."

"Cthulhu Cthulhu Cthulhu," the NRO voice shouted over and over again.

"Say again?"

"Cthulhu. You'll wake Cthulhu!"

"Please spell the word. I am not receiving, NRO."

"C as in Charlie. Tom. Harry. *pop* Harry. Upton."

"Again."

"Charlie. Tom. Harry. Upton. Linda. *crackle* Upton."

In his cramped station, Carl Blackshear tried to visualize the letters as they came over his headset. They made no sense. They spelled no word he had ever heard before.

"Did you say C as in Charlie Tom Harry Upton Linda Harry Upton?" Blackshear radioed back.

"Affirmative."

"That's what I thought. Well, you're too late. The pulse should be reaching New Zealand about now."

There came a long burst of static.

And in the hissing pause that followed, a tiny voice said a very weak, "Oh, shit."

"Sorry," Blackshear said, not really sorry at all.

Then Stan was saying, "The water is really roiling now, *Challenger*."

"Let it roil. Our job is done for today. Reel me back in."

And the umbilical cables began their slow upward toil.

As *Challenger* rose, the hissing radio headset began to pop and rush anew, and an excited voice erupted in some foreign tongue.

"Stan! I thought you said that Jap trawler took off."

"It did. This one's flying the flag of South Korea."

"They're a long way from home."

"I think they're speaking English now."

"Give me radio silence, *Lemuria*."

And over the headphones came the excited high-pitched voice again.

"Attention, please. Attention, please. You are in very dangerous waters. This is Korean vessel *Yong Wang*. These waters belong to Nagji-ojingo. You must not awaken Nagji-ojingo. There is great danger in awakening Nagji-ojingo."

"*Yong Wang*. This is the submersible *Challenger*. Please advise. Who or what is Nagji-ojingo? Over."

"Nagji-ojingo is evil. Nagji-ojingo is beyond evil. Do not disturb Nagji-ojingo's slumber, please. Scientific knowledge is not worth it."

"Oh, brother." Blackshear muttered. Into the mike, he chanted, "*Yong Wang*. I do not copy. Advise on nature of Nagji-ojingo."

"*Challenger*, Nagji-ojingo is our ancient name for this being. It means in English Great Octopus-squid."

"Octopus-squid?" Blackshear muttered. "*Yong Wang*, is your Nagji-ojingo any relation to Tako-ika?"

"Yes! Yes! Tako-ika is Japanese name for Nagji-ojingo. It mean the same thing. You understand now?"

"Yeah. I understand. Nice try but no sale. The experiment has begun. You and your whale-loving friends can all go cry in your saki—or whatever it is you drink."

From the *Yong Wang* came a very pained syllable Blackshear assumed was a Korean curse word.

As he climbed back to the *Lemuria*'s deck once more, Carl Blackshear saw the agitated state of the blue Pacific. The foam line that stitched the Pacific's face for some 500 miles in each direction had turned grotesque. It looked for all the world as if it were trying to tear itself apart.

Normally, it was busy with leaping dolphin and flying fish. No fish broke the surface now.

And everywhere he looked, Carl Blackshear saw the Pacific on both sides of the mighty whitecap seam was frightened. Very frightened.

Stan met him on deck.

"Great Barrier Receiving must be delirious with joy," Blackshear said.

"Let's hope it makes up for how upset they are in Washington," Stan said, thick-voiced.

"Screw Washington. This is no business of the NRO."

"They've been in touch, Carl. They're asking if we're still alive."

"Idiots."

"They're also asking if we've sighted the Kraken yet."

"Kraken?"

Stan's eyes were sick. "Yeah. That's what they're calling it now."

Blackshear frowned. "Wasn't the Kraken supposed to be a giant octopus that slept at the bottom of the sea until the world ended and it would awaken?"

The captain nodded. "Octopus. Or squid."

Blackshear frowned. "Greenpeace mentioned cephalopods, too ...."

They were looking out across the angry water now.

Stan said, "They say deep sea squid can grow to be as long as 100 feet. At least they've found sucker scars on big whales that suggest that size. No one's ever seen a 100-foot-long giant squid, though."

Blackshear looked out over the agitated water.

"I always figured the whales got those marks when they were young. As they grew, the sucker scars grew with them. Just like on a person. You cut your hand as a kid. And as your skin grows, the scars stretch."

"That doesn't explain why the Japanese, the Koreans, and the U.S. National Reconnaissance Office are all warning us about some kind of giant hybrid octopus-squid. Or devilfish-cuttlefish."

"Ah, I don't believe any of it."

"So what's agitating the water?"

"Fish. They heard the sonic pulse. It's made them a little weird. You know how the balance organ of most marine life is located in the ear, just as it is with humans. The pulse may have upset their equilibrium a little. It'll pass. Vertigo always does."

Then from the bridge the First Mate called down.

"Washington's back on the horn. Their satellites show the line is disappearing!"

"The line?" Blackshear said.

Far to the south, the foam line that had existed since before man first ventured across the oceans of the world threshed and hissed.

"Carl?"

"Yeah?"

"If it's only fish, why don't we see fins and tails beating on the surface?"

"I don't know," Carl Blackshear admitted uneasily.

"And why didn't you see activity down below?"

Carl Blackshear made no reply. His eyes were fixed on the frightened ocean and the angry clash of whitecaps and sea foam that, while it eternally changed, had been a constant since the continents first arose from the muddy sea bottoms.

And was now in the throes of a convulsion as vast as the mighty Pacific itself.

All at once, a dolphin leaped from the water. Arching, it fell back, only to leap up again. And again.

Others appeared. Leaping, straining, their behavior grew increasingly frantic. Flying fish showed themselves. But where flying fish skimmed the surface, these leaped in true vertical jumps. Suddenly, the sea was frantic with dolphins and flying fish mindlessly energetically fruitlessly propelling themselves into the blue sky, only to fall back in defeat.

"It can't be," Blackshear muttered.

"What?"

"The sound has passed. They can't be reacting to it. They didn't go crazy when it reached this area. Why should they start now?"

"Maybe it's not the wave."

The fish were straining wildly now. It was as if the water had become inimical to them. As if the alien atmosphere of oxygen and nitrogen and other unbreathable gasses was now preferable to their true watery home.

"Does it look to you like they're trying to beach themselves in the sky?" Stan said thickly.

"Yeah," Blackshear said. "It looks exactly like that."

And when a bottlenose dolphin landed flopping and gasping on the port side not six yards from where they stood, Carl Blackshear asked a hoarse, unanswerable question.

"What in God's name is down there that would frighten the fish from the only home they have?"

Squatting on his dais of slave starfish, Great Cthulhu roused. The corpse-gray sac of his immense cranium began pulsing as the gray warmed to blue and the blue turned a vivid green. Two superintelligent eyes peeled open. Coiled tentacles uncoiled, to grope up and about ropily.

From under one thick tentacle root, his great siphon quested about, gargantuan and thirsty. It pulsed tentatively. Sea water was drawn in, slowly at first, but with increasing velocity.

Fish, coral, plankton, sharks, even helpless whales were sucked into the voracious organ as if they were no more than current-borne flotsam.

Aabove, on the deck of the *Lemuria*, two men watched as the eternal line separating the warm green side of the Pacific from the cool blue side spun apart; a swirling vortex sucked it down to the deepest coldest unfathomed depths of the ocean as if a stopper the size of the moon had been dislodged.

Taking the *Lemuria* and themselves down to the place their screaming minds told them all life on earth would soon be consigned.

DON BURLESON DEMONSTRATES here that one can use tried-&-true Lovecraftian themes in new ways, so that what might not even be noticed for its familiarity (which breeds contempt, or at least boredom) strikes the readerly eye as disturbingly out of focus, requiring a second look, careful scrutiny—just like the old familiar thing did the first time we saw it.

At the same time, Burleson is no new-waver, not a writer of the kind of tale whose Cthulhoid references serve to accentuate how far removed from the Lovecraftian tradition the story really is. Don, along with a very few others, is able to invoke a sense of the classic mode of weird fiction narrative that we savor in Poe, LeFanu, HPL, Machen, and the other Old Ones.

A word anent the title. It represents the way HPL said the name ought to be pronounced, according to various passages in the epistles of the Apostle Lovecraft and various *hadith*, or traditions of his sayings. To Duane Rimel he wrote, "The actual sound—as nearly as human organs could imitate it or human letters record it—may be taken as something like Khlul-hloo, with the first syllable pronounced very gutturally and very thickly. The *u* is about like that in *full*; and the first syllable is not unlike *klul* in sound, since the *h* represents the guttural thickness. The second syllable is not very well rendered—the *l* being unrepresented." Well, if you say so, master. Keep in mind this is a name Lovecraft himself created! When asked why he didn't spell it the way he wanted it said, he facetiously protested that it wasn't *his* fault: The Old Ones had coined the name, not he!

In another letter he recommends the pronunciation "Cluh-Lhu", while in "Medusa's Coil" we read of "Clooloo" and in "Winged Death" of "Clulu." In "The Mound" it is "Tulu." Lovecraft's friend W. Paul Cook recalled him saying "Thulhu" with both "u's" long, but another Lovecraft pal, Robert Barlow, remembered, or thought he did, "Koot-u-lew." Don Wandrei recalled pronouncing "Thool-Hoo" only to be corrected by HPL, who demanded "K-Lutl-Lutl." Yeah, okay. Lovecraft be damned, I say: I think Wandrei was right the first time.

"The Eye of Hlu-Hlu" first appeared in *The Morgan and Rice Gazette*, vol. 10, no. 2, whole number 38, Lammas 1993.

The Eye of Hlu-Hlu

by Donald R. Burleson

I T IS TRUE THAT I have left my native New England forever for the desert highlands of New Mexico. But it is equally true that I cannot escape, even here, the maddening memory and the soul-shattering implications of what I have seen. If only I could live out whatever years remain to me in the blissful ignorance I once possessed! But I am cursed—cursed to know the truth of what those centuried woodlands of southern New Hampshire conceal.

My name is Charles Lloyd Hutchinson. Being, as circumstances evolved, the sole heir of my paternal grandfather, the late Mycroft Ward Hutchinson, Ph.D., I came into his whole estate some time ago, inheriting not only a vast sum of money but his house and lands as well. It was when I delved, foolishly, into the maze of papers left in his study that I began to learn of the horror that has come to infest my dreams.

My grandfather Dr. Hutchinson was a noted scholar whose professional accomplishments in several fields—archaeology, cultural anthropology, and linguistics among them—are well known. Independently wealthy from young adulthood, he declined to take a teaching position or research post at a university—although Harvard, Yale, and many other institutions had at one time or other offered him what would have been prestigious positions—preferring to pursue his researches independently. His scholarly articles in such areas as archaeolinguistics and folklore are familiar to readers of the professional journals. He traveled widely, piecing together fabrics of research that were astonishingly erudite even when they dwelt upon relatively traditional and mundane matters. Would that they had dwelt only upon such things, and not upon that darker matter that his inquiries gradually uncovered, or partially uncovered.

After his death at the age of ninety-four, and upon coming into the inheritance, I gave up my job at the small Connecticut college where I had been teaching history for over twenty years, and moved from New Haven up to the outskirts of Melham, New Hampshire to take up residence in my late grandfather's lonely country house, an ancient peaked-roof relic quite distant from any neighbors and abutted by dark and far-reaching woods, all part of his lands.

When I was fairly well settled in, I began to go through the mass of papers in my grandfather's study. I found evidence that he had started burning his papers, but only a small fraction of them were destroyed, for death had found him before he finished the job—death due not, I feel sure, to advanced age alone, for he had maintained remarkable health, but due rather to the drain upon his system imposed by the shock of what his researches had lately revealed to him. It was in examining his surviving papers, documents clearly not meant for other eyes, even mine, that in time I found my world changed forever.

My grandfather had long been pursuing a line of mythic tradition so obscure and scattered that, as his notebooks and diaries revealed, several years of research and travel had been required to piece the salient features together. This line of myth involved an ancient god or demon known, in various cultures, by variegated but obviously linguistically cognate names: by island peoples of the Pacific He was called Khulu, by the vanished Pennacook Indians He was known (according to historical archives handed down by generations of folklorists) as Hlu-Hlu, by the Navajos of Arizona and New Mexico (who were extremely disinclined to speak of Him, and who associated Him with certain obscure pictographs left by the ancient Anasazi people) He was called Chullao, in certain obscure strains of Norse myth He was named Khwul-Ulh, and in references found in the *Necronomicon* and other such grimoires He was known variously as Cthulhu, Tu-Lu, and Khlul-Hliu. Dr. Hutchinson seemed to favor the designation Hlu-Hlu handed down from the traditions of the Indians once inhabiting his very grounds. The entity in question, by whatever name, was clearly not a cheerful prospect.

Hlu-Hlu, tradition said, had come to Earth from the stars in unimaginably early times, before even the great saurian beasts prowled the land, and was a sort of high priest among His kind. Of His precise form and appearance, all accounts were strangely reticent—indeed, the bodies of folklore having anything to say of Him at all were inclined to treat Him as a sort of hushed obscurity, not a main feature in their healthier mythologies—and Dr. Hutchinson had learned, at the expense of much time and painstaking effort, that indeed there was some agreement that the primordial being *had* no particular physical form.

The learned doctor had traveled, at one point, to a mountain village in Roumania to talk with an aged scholar there named Vachescu, a wizened creature feared by the superstitious multitude and never approached by anyone but certain specialized scholars like my grandfather, and then only at long intervals. Vachescu had told Dr. Hutchinson, in a croaking and wheezing Roumanian and with eyes in which advanced age had not extinguished a certain cold light of mystery, that much of what was thought to be known of Hlu-Hlu, or Cthulhu or Tu-Lu, was metaphor erroneously assumed to be literal—but that the truth remaining was dreadful enough. The *Necronomicon*, Vachescu had said, offered oblique references to a high priest-god Cthulhu, supposedly a tentacled aquatic creature, who had been trapped in a watery tomb when the island bearing His stone fortress sank, in ancient times, into the Pacific Ocean; when the stars came around right, He would move again, reclaiming the world that was His. (My grandfather had several times used the privilege of his scholarly prestige to consult the volume in question at the Widener Library at Harvard, and knew of these accounts.)

But, Vachescu had explained, this story was allegorical, a figural account allegorizing the more literal story—that great Cthulhu, or Hlu-Hlu, was indeed "submerged", or occluded, but not by water: His incorporeal being was in the earth, everywhere present, undead, watchful, waiting only for His time to be right; He had seeped into the world, in unsubstantial but surviving essence, to watch and wait. And the suggestion of watching was the worst part, because—and here even the squinting lizard-faced Vachescu grew squeamish—it was not *entirely* the case that Hlu-Hlu had no physical form. There was one tangible aspect: an enormous eye, alert, quiet but unsleeping, that watched the world, the stars, with a sense that was not sight as we know it. Of the physical location of this eye, Vachescu could not—or, my grandfather suspected, would not—speak.

Dr. Hutchinson, whose linguistic attainments were virtually unparalleled and whose energies even at his age knew virtually no limits, had traveled to other parts of the world to extend his knowledge of the strange matter thus imparted to him. On a small island near Fiji, he questioned, this time haltingly and with the aid of an interpreter of the Melanesian dialect spoken there, a native holy man, and brought up the matter of the hidden eye of Hlu-Hlu, explaining that the holy man probably knew of the entity as Khulu. The reaction was immediate and alarming; the native priest was angry and afraid, and threatened to withdraw from my grandfather's contact altogether. But the aging scholar persisted, speaking gently but persuasively, and at length the rest of the apparently archetypal story was extracted: that indeed old legends did tell of a great World-Watching Eye, somewhere in a northern woodland, beneath an entrance into the earth surrounded by a ring of stones. The great Eye, it was said, was attended by a retinue of blind zombie servants—for to see the Eye oneself, with one's own eyes, was a blasphemy. And the Pacific legend agreed with that which he had uncovered in Roumania on the main feature that the great Eye was merely a local bodily manifestation of something more farflung and spiritlike, yet real, something that waited for its time to be proclaimed ready by the stars. When that happened, the world as we know it would end.

Shaken by this account but determined to corroborate it, Dr. Hutchinson traveled anew, speaking with shamen and wise men and witch doctors and medicine men in places as diverse as west coastal Africa, the mountain passes of Chile and Peru, the outback of western Australia, the bleak rural villages of Norway, the desert wastes of Iraq, and the frozen northlands of Canada. He found, everywhere, with local variation but with what was now coming to be a disturbing degree of underlying consistency, the same tale unfolding. Somewhere, somewhere on the earth in a "northern woodland", rested a circle of stones, surrounding an entrance to regions below, where waited—a thing almost not to be entertained even in fantasy or nightmare.

It was my grandfather's curse, and mine, that he found the place.

He had been living in western Massachusetts, and (being familiar with much dark and peculiar folklore about the region) had searched the woods there extensively, finding many fascinating stone structures but not the one he sought. He was aware, of course, that he might not even be looking on the right continent. But traveling about New England, talking to people, asking guarded questions, he cast his net farther out, and finally encountered a local story in the town of Melham, in southern New Hampshire, that seemed to promise some connection.

There was an old house outside of town, a seventeenth-century structure bordered in the back by thick woods; the house stood upon what had once been Pennacook Indian land, and within the woods there was a circle of six granite boulders about which opinions differed—some said the stones were irregularly arranged enough to be the result of glacial deposit or some other chance geological placement, while others maintained that the site looked contrived and deliberate, and might even be the work of the departed Indian peoples who had once known the land as their own—although some ethnologists claimed that the bygone Pennacooks had been deathly, morbidly afraid of the stones. Professional archaeological opinion, in any event, seemed to favor the notion that the stones were natural, not a sign of some ancient cultural activity; scientists, though invited to do so, had uniformly declined to do an archaeological dig on the site. Most of the local people, in fact, agreed that it would be a waste of time and money to investigate the spot.

But the linkage between this local tale on the one hand and, on the other, the scraps of folklore collected at remote points of the globe—particularly the Pennacook myths of Hlu-Hlu, given the earlier presence of that tribe on this very site—was one that did not escape Dr. Hutchinson's attention. In his fertile and imaginative mind there grew a conviction that this could well be the ring of stones of which legends spoke so darkly.

The house had sat vacant for many years, according to the townspeople. On something of a whim—for such urges are not uncommon in the wealthy—he purchased the house and its woodlands and moved in. Naturally, he hiked almost daily back into his woods to inspect the group of stones, a nearly perfect circle, some forty feet in diameter, of roundish granite boulders each roughly the size of a small automobile. The more he looked at them, there in the dappled shadow of the woods, the more he tended to suspect that they were in fact too symmetrical, too systematic to be a geological accident. He had bought the house in April, and it was in June of that year that he commenced an archaeological dig. He worked alone; no one of his acquaintance in the town would have been likely to be interested in helping, and in any case his thoughts on what he might find were so bizarre that he dared not share them with more prosaic minds.

It is at this point in the account that I found my grandfather's notes the most poignantly disturbing.

According to his diary, he dug at one particular spot just inside the circle of stones, delving down perhaps four feet in the mulchy sod of the forest floor, and found a flat stone surface appearing to be something like flagstones tightly and accurately joined. Expanding the uncovered surface a few feet on each side, he discovered that what he was looking at was in fact a section of a horizontal stone ring in the ground: two concentric circles of flagstone surface, the outer circle lying just inside the boulders themselves, the inner circle being some eight feet less in diameter than the outer circle and surrounding, apparently, a sort of dirt-choked but discernible well or chasm leading farther down. At this point, it would seem that the whole weight of implication garnered from his investigation into the pertinent folklore came crashing down on his mind. If indeed this flagstone surface lay within the circle of boulders, a flat, annular surface buried several feet under the ground and surrounding what could only be a cylindrical passage leading down into the earth—if what he was already seeing was true, then what unspeakable horror might lie beneath his very feet?

For an old man, tired and afraid, it was too much. He covered his dig back over and abandoned any thought of resuming his work on the site, but its emotional toll on his health had already been taken. He grew weaker daily, and his notes more and more took on a tone of morbid fear of what might lie festering beneath his very land. Gradually the notes became more distracted and incoherent. I knew the rest anyway; about a month after his attempt at digging within the circle of stone, Dr. Mycroft Ward Hutchinson passed away, having left a hurriedly scrawled but legally sound will giving everything to his grandson and only heir, myself.

And now I lived in the house, with its sinisterly suggestive border of woods, and with thoughts of all that I perused in my grandfather's notes clamoring like uncouth demons in my head.

I scarcely knew what to make of the whole affair. Was one to believe the scattered but oddly consistent scraps of folklore that Dr. Hutchinson had unearthed? Had not Carl Jung argued that widely separated races of people produce parallel mythologies, because of archetypal patterns programmed from the start into the human psyche? Somehow, in spite of my every attempt at being level-headed, I found this explanation unsatisfying. How could one simply dismiss a train of thought that had led my grandfather, an intelligent man, an accomplished scholar, to far ends of the earth? A train of thought that had broken him in the end?

When I finally consciously made the decision, I realized that I had already unconsciously made it days, perhaps weeks, before. I would, of course, dig within the circle of stones and search for whatever it was that might conceivably be down there, the mere thought of which had driven my grandfather to despair.

It was a crisp autumn morning in early October when, shoulder-
ing my spades, I hiked into the woods—not just to look at the stones
this time, as I had done on several occasions since reading my
grandfather's journals. This time I would see, I would make sure.
If nothing of importance was there, then I would know that a noble
old man had sadly seen his life destroyed without adequate cause.
If something *was* there—but I had no wish to dwell on that
possibility yet.

This particular morning I found the six stones as I had seen them
before: standing like solemn gray sentries in the woods, a little too
regular in appearance to impart a sense of comfort. Within the
circle, the ground was clear of trees, except for a few fugitive
saplings, and these looked oddly withered and unhealthy. But there
was no time for pointless reflections; I had come to dig. My methods
were scarcely those of the professionally trained archaeologist. I did
not mark off regions on the ground surface with posts and strings;
I did not measure, I did not record, I did not photograph. I simply
dug, beginning at a spot near one of the boulders where there
seemed to be a slight indentation in the ground already, a barely
perceptible hollow which I took to be the imperfectly effaced site
of my grandfather's own digging.

My efforts were not long in yielding results. I soon saw, scraping
dirt off it with a spade, that a few feet down there was indeed a flat
flagstone surface. It took the remainder of that day and the two days
that followed to uncover in its entirety the large flagstone ring that
lay within the circle of boulders. Upon some of the flagstones I half
thought that I could make out the faint remains of what might have
been symbolic or ceremonial inscriptions or carvings of some sort,
but I could not be sure. In the middle of this ring of flagstones,
though choked with dirt and fallen leaves, there indeed appeared
to be, as legend had suggested, the opening to a sort of large
cylindrical well, its sides formed of perfectly fitted flat stones,
leading down into the earth; I can scarcely describe the sense of dark
fascination, mingled with dread, that the sight afforded me.

I spent the fourth day clearing the soil out of the opening, finding
as I did so that the blockage extended only a few yards down; the
space yawning below was clear and apparently bottomless, and there
were handholds, somewhat like the rungs of a ladder, carved into
the very stone, leading downward—carved by whom and at what
remote period in time, I could not, nor can I now, give any specific
conjecture. Seeing this perversely beckoning chasm, I slept but

poorly that night, but went out on the fifth day to make what I must have known all along would inevitably be my descent into the earth beneath the circle of stones.

Equipped with coils of rope and a powerful flashlight, I walked into the woods that morning with a sense that I might not come back the same, or come back at all. But I had to see. With the flashlight lashed to my side in such a way that I could turn it on and aim it downward with minimal effort when necessary, I began the descent.

The handholds in the stone, some three feet or so apart, were damp and nitrous, and it was difficult to hang on. At first I had a pale, forest-filtered daylight to guide me, but by perhaps the twentieth rung this light no longer sufficed, and I switched on the flashlight to continue my way down.

I could never have imagined such a descent outside of the churning realms of nightmare. By perhaps the fiftieth rung—I had long since lost count—the fabricated stone siding of the well gave way to natural rock, with handholds continuing down as before; the play of my flashlight showed only more rungs leading down, and no suggestion of a bottom. Clutching the damp and slippery rungs, desperate not to fall into this silent, unthinkable pit, I slowly and carefully made my way down, down, incredibly far down into the earth beneath the woods. My senses were dulled and confused by the extent of the descent, but I would not exaggerate if I said that I had traversed many, many hundreds of rungs, seeing only more of the well gaping below me in the shaft of my light, hearing only the rocky echoes of my own breathing and my own scraping and grasping at the handholds. I felt, at intervals, as if I must be insane even to attempt such as this; but this feeling would invariably be followed by another: that having come this far, I might be even more insane to turn back without glimpsing what, if anything, lay below me.

Never in my life had I felt so wretchedly, frighteningly alone, a mere microbe in the sable bowels of the earth; I felt, looking down and beholding only more featureless depth, that the well might extend even to the center of the planet. But at great length—my wristwatch showed that I had been descending for over three hours—I saw, in the farthest reaches of the flashlight's beam, what appeared to be a level rock surface far below me. The well had a bottom after all, and I did not know whether to greet this discovery with joy or dread.

A few more minutes brought me to the bottommost rung. There had been one further rung below it, but it was broken off, showing only two rocky stumps protruding from the wall, with a drop of some ten feet from the last intact rung to the floor of the well. Fearing harm to myself in such a drop onto a rock surface, I fastened one of my ropes around the last whole rung, let the rest drop to the floor, and eased myself down the length of the rope, elated, in spite of my general sense of foreboding, to feel a solid surface beneath my feet. I unhooked my flashlight, from which the light was growing too dim for me to see much of my surroundings. I had brought spare batteries, but it required more courage than I thought I possessed to switch off the light and leave it off long enough to replace the batteries, fumbling and feeling with my fingers in a dark more profound than any I had ever known.

When I switched the light back on and played it around, I saw that the cylindrical wall rising from the rock floor was featureless here, with one exception: a low semicircular opening in the wall at one point, level with the floor and perhaps three feet in diameter, forming a sort of horizontal tunnel carved into the solid rock and leading off to some other region. Getting to my knees and directing the flashlight beam down this tunnel, I could see no end to it. I knew, of course, that I had to crawl through it, though the thought of such increased confinement, with countless millions of tons of rock above my head, filled me with an anticipatory sense of claustrophobia such as I had never experienced. Still, there was nothing to do but go on—and go on without further loss of time, for I had no desire to make my climb back up the well in total darkness if the new batteries died.

Training the beam of light ahead of me as best I could, I began my crawl through the tunnel. I had forgotten to look at my wristwatch before I left the bottom of the well, but after wriggling forward for what seemed a discouragingly long time I consulted the watch and estimated, as well as I could, that I had been crawling in the tunnel for somewhat over two hours. My muscles had been aching and tired already, from the descent, and I was now close to exhaustion, with no sign of an end ahead. The only thing I could reasonably do was persevere, and I did so. After another long period—I was by now too tired to think of looking at my watch again—I finally spied what seemed to be an opening-out, ahead, in the contours of the tunnel.

Another few minutes' crawling brought me to the spot, where indeed the tunnel came out into a larger space. I pulled myself through and stood up, tremendously relieved to be able to stand upright, and found myself in what could only be a cavern of indeterminate extent.

Flashing the light around, I could make out only a dim suggestion of a ceiling above, a faraway ceiling apparently as free of stalactites as the cavern floor was of stalagmites; the effect, in my mind, was to suggest that the cavern was not entirely natural. I sniffed; the air in here was clammy and somewhat nitrous, but quite breathable, more so than the close air of the tunnel through which I had come. Horizontally, I could see no end to the enormous space that yawned ahead of me. Drawing upon what little reserves of nerve and physical strength remained to me, I began my walk into the cavern.

Somehow this place was almost more disturbing to me, though in a different way, than the confines of the tunnel had been: a colossal empty space, black, silent, and immensely lonely. The floor beneath me was apparently natural rock, but very flat. It did not fail to occur to me, of course, that I might easily become lost, and I concentrated on walking an absolutely straight line from the point at which I had emerged from the tunnel.

After some time, my flashlight revealed the presence of something ahead. Something flat in the rock floor of the cavern. Something evidently quite large. As I drew closer to it, I saw that it appeared to be a sort of circular rimless pool, some eighty feet in diameter as well as I could judge, and apparently filled with some grayish liquid, the surface of which was slightly convex. When I stood within a few yards of its edge, playing the light over it, I could see that the surface of this liquid, which seemed thick and sluggish, was slightly undulating. I speculated that the pool was an incalculably old condensation of brackish water, thickened by rock dust and mineral deposits and stirred into slight animation by subtle drafts of air.

This naive reflection was perhaps my last moment of anything approaching peace of mind. For as I watched, the surface of the liquid began to shift. The far side of it rose up to form a huge glistening surface that slanted down toward me at an angle of perhaps forty-five degrees. It was like watching the motion of some enormous and obscene slug. And a change was taking place in the middle of the slanted semiliquid disc.

But I had, mercifully, only a moment to contemplate that change, for now a more tactile shock confronted me. A rough hand was placed on my shoulder.

Wheeling about with the flashlight, I saw standing, in the space immediately behind me, a figure whose presence was so devastating in its implications that I nearly reeled; that there could be anyone here at all, in this forsaken place perhaps miles beneath the earth, was shocking enough, but the physical appearance of the creature surpassed even that effect. I directed my light straight upon him. It was a large man, naked and gray-skinned, with only gaping black sockets where there should have been eyes. He carried about him an odor that was truly abominable, one putting me in mind of spoiled meat. His hand had released my shoulder in my whirling around to face him, but he now took a step toward me.

I turned to run, but had only the viscous, slanting surface behind me. Turning back around to face the figure standing there in the dark, I dodged around him. His tattered arms flailed, reaching for me, but I eluded him. Eluded him, only to notice that other such figures were emerging from the dark ahead of me, from all directions. Twenty, perhaps thirty of them, at spaces of only a few yards between.

Flashing my light around them, I saw in their decayed faces the same eyeless visages as in the first instance, and mouths that hung agape in endless expressionlessness. I must have walked through their midst, coming here; they had been lurking in shadow, only now aroused to action by impulses that I dared not ponder.

There was no time for thought in any event; I must get back to the tunnel. Twisting and dodging among the shambling, eyeless figures, I ran—screaming, I think, though I was not entirely aware of what I did. I had to run in as nearly a straight line as I could, for there to be any hope of finding the mouth of the tunnel at the cavern's edge, but I had to run so circuitously to avoid the shuffling, reaching shapes around me that I could not be sure if I was going in the right direction. Their blindness seemed to render the other senses of my pursuers all the more acute, for at every moment they turned toward me in their courses with dreadful accuracy. It was all I could do to keep myself beyond their foul reach. At one point a cold, gray hand found mine and hung on, and when I pulled my hand free I could feel lifeless flesh sloughing off into my palm.

Choking with terror and despair, I ran on, playing the flashlight beam ahead of me like some insane lantern-show of dream. At length, the shambling figures seemed all to be behind me, but a glance back with the light confirmed my fears: They were still coming for me. My lungs ached, my muscles begged for rest, and I came suddenly to feel that I could not go on—that I could only

stop, let them have me, let them dispense whatever loathsome fate
to me they might. But I could not succumb to this strange temp-
tation. I ran on, gasping for breath, searching for the rock wall that
would signal arrival at the edge of the cavern.

Finally I spotted it ahead, looming gray and indifferent in the
gloom. I ran to it, but nearly collapsed now with frustration. I had
miscalculated and hit the wrong spot; the opening to the tunnel
was not here.

Even as I realized this, I could hear shuffling feet in the dark
behind me, and the rasp of breath in unthinkable throats. The blind
zombies inhabiting this eldritch region, despite their shambling
gait, progressed across the stone floor with surprising speed. Sob-
bing now, I began to run along beside the wall of the cavern,
searching. Heaven does dispense some mercy, it would seem, for
after a few minutes I came upon the gaping aperture I sought, and
scrambled inside the tunnel.

I had wriggled forward only a few yards when it became clear
that my pursuers would not stop at the cavern's end, but would
follow me even here. Twisting about in the low passage, I flashed
my light backward to find the entrance blocked from view by
nodding gray faces, remorseless figures steadily advancing upon me.
Turning back around, I continued crawling, praying that the batteries would last. My prayers were in vain. After some considerable
time in the tunnel, pulling myself forward, away from the hideous
sniffing and scraping behind me, I saw the flashlight dim, then
flicker, then go out altogether. I would have to crawl forward in
total darkness.

Even as I formed this thought, I felt a dry, dead hand clutch my
left ankle. Shrieking, I pulled myself forward with desperate speed,
and heard the raspy breathing recede behind me. But the clutch on
my ankle remained, tight and unyielding, and it took me a terrible
moment to realize that the hand, that I was still dragging forward
with me, had come off. I scraped my leg against the side of the
tunnel as I went, and at length I felt the hand fall away.

From that point I recall only an interminable nightmare of
crawling, crawling, ever forward in the dark. After what seemed
like hours, I felt the tunnel give way to an open space that I knew
to be the bottom of the cylindrical well, and pulled myself through.
I banged the flashlight against the nearest rock wall I could find
and flicked the switch on and off, hoping to regain the light, but
in vain. Somewhere in the blackness behind me, I could hear

scraping sounds that could only mean the persistence of my pursuers; in a moment, the nearest of them would be out of the tunnel and upon me.

Shaking with fear, I felt around in the dark and finally closed my fingers upon the rope I had left dangling from the lowermost intact rung of the well. Even as I hauled myself up the rope, I heard a figure emerge from the tunnel and begin to thrash about for me, so that in the last moments before I reached the rung I had to coil my legs up under me for fear that a pair of grasping hands would close upon them. But my fingers did find the rung, and I pulled myself up and made a reach for the next rung up, which I found. Wheezing for breath, I began my ascent, which, I knew with a hopelessness more profound than any I had ever felt, would be a great deal more arduous than even the exhausting descent had been.

My mind records only a kaleidoscopic nightmare of climbing in the dark, climbing, reaching, pulling, climbing, up and up, rung after clammy rung—that, and the unmistakable fact that the eyeless monstrosities beneath me were climbing too. Time ceased to exist for me, or I ceased to be able to comprehend it. I could only pull myself up, clutch at each rung, try to catch some breath in my agonized lungs, and fumble for the next rung. There was no suggestion of daylight in the region above me, and with what little corner of my mind remained for analysis, I found myself at a loss to know whether the absence of light meant a still appalling distance to go, or meant that more time had elapsed than I thought and night had fallen in the outer world, or both.

Faint with exhaustion and horror, I continued to climb, sensing that the fumbling and rasping in the dark below me was gaining. At long last a wan play of light became visible above, and I knew that I had both approached the top and had arrived before nightfall. As in a nightmare, I scarcely seemed to be able to manage those last few dozen rungs, but finally did find myself, seen in my mind's eye as if watching the antics of a stranger, scrambling out of the well onto the level flagstone ring outside. The sun was just then beginning to set.

I lay on my side for some time, catching at my breath, until the pain in my lungs subsided somewhat. Peering back down into that yawning pit, I could hear furtive sounds, but they seemed to be receding, and I concluded, with an ineffable sense of gratitude and relief, that the blind and shambling figures from below would not follow me into the outer world. I stumbled back through the woods to the house, went inside, locked all the doors and windows, collapsed on my grandfather's sofa, and fell into a long and oddly dreamless sleep.

It was my last sleep in that house. The next day I nailed together a hasty but sturdy platform of boards and dragged it across the opening of the well and covered it with several feet of dirt and rock. And within the day I departed.

For, as I have said, I have forsaken my native New England for the desert highlands of New Mexico. I look out my sunbaked adobe doorway now, not at gnarled oaks and slate-gray skies, but at a mountain-rimmed desert vista of sand and cactus and sagebrush. But even here I know a truth that no man should have to know. I know what festering horror those placid-looking woodlands of New Hampshire really conceal. And I know, looking across the sands, that one day—perhaps tomorrow, perhaps in a thousand years—the very earth, the very chaparral, will breathe forth its lurking essence: The stars will one day come right, or wrong, and that diffuse and timeless spirit that is Hlu-Hlu will seep forth to stride the earth.

I began to understand this all too well in that moment down in the cavern, when I glimpsed the hideous change in the bleary and mucoid surface that slanted before me in the wavering light—when the center of the bulging surface swam together in a darkening mass that could only be the weirdly oblong *pupil* of that never-sleeping Eye, a dark and hideous pupil that looked at me, looked at the blasphemer who stood in Its presence with eyes of his own. It peered at me then, in the gloom of an unknown cavern deep in the New England earth, and it peers at me in the full clear light of day under a blue desert sky, seeing to the bottom of my shaken soul, even now.

MANY READERS OF an earlier volume in this august series, *The Shub-Niggurath Cycle*, much enjoyed Will Murray's tale of Yeb, son of Shub-Niggurath, "To Clear the Earth." The story matched like halves of the Tao with another one, "Black Fire." We alerted you to its upcoming appearance in another publisher's anthology. Many readers who took our bum steer made sure they ordered that book for one reason alone: to read "Black Fire"—and were taken aback to find it conspicuous by its absence. What happened? Seems that someone connected with that project found Murray's characterization of the Eskimos not to be politically correct! I am mystified, as you will be. At any rate, that book's loss is manifestly our gain.

Will Murray perhaps became interested in the "evil twins" Nug and Yeb (whose chief cosmic bane seems to be causing typists to misspell their names!) while doing some interesting research into the bits of eldritch lore sprinkled fulsomely by HPL in the datings, salutations, and closings of his epistles. These contain several references to the galaxy-wide religion of Nug and Yeb as practiced at oddly angled altars and blasphemous shrines all over the place. Murray observed that, despite Lovecraft's own later statement that he had coined the two names to have a "Thibetan-Tatar" sound, other factors suggested that Nug and Yeb were Lovecraftian counterparts to Nut and Geb, a pair of deities in ancient Egypt (or is that "Nighted Khem?"). Murray has made good use of these Lovecraftian tidbits, the most important of which is that Lovecraft made Nug none other than *the father of Great Cthulhu*! Thus his appearance in this collection.

Black Fire

by Will Murray

THE ICE CRACKED, as foretold.

Far, far north of Yellowknife, above the Arctic Circle, the northern wastes ran smooth and white. No footprints disturbed the sterile dusting of snow. Caribou did not venture here. So the Inuit did not follow.

Thus there were no eyes to observe the splitting of the ice, or to quail before the dull thunder crack as a dark protruberance resembling vitrified horn thrust up from under the separating crust of ice and snow that had refused the sun's softening rays since the Earth of Man last changed the tilt of its axis.

The thing that pushed a shattered star of ice up and aside had been laid there in the days when the Earth belonged not to man, but to the Old Ones.

It stopped, a great hump like a fire-blackened kettle set upside down with a finger of horn jutting up from its highest part. It smoked in the supercold air.

The ice chunks settled about the dark thing, which lay in wait for Man to discover it. As he surely would. How long it would take, did not matter. The Old Ones slept long and would sleep for far longer. The artifact they had set beneath the ice was new compared to the Old Ones. And it would attract human hands to it well before the Old Ones were fated to return.

And human hands were all that were required.

The ice had cracked, as foretold by the *Necronomicon*. But few read the *Necronomicon* anymore—or believed its warnings.

The dark season passed, and the long cool summer came. The snow melted, exposing a slick epidermis of ice. And for the first time in millennia the ice slipped slowly into the long-buried tundra. Warmed by the dark thing that looked like vitrified horn, tufts of grass sprouted from seeds long in hibernation.

In time, caribou came to tug at the grass with their teeth. Man, ever hungry, followed.

The first human eyes to fall upon the artifact of the Old Ones belonged to Kiyok the hunter. He beheld the dark thing and ran to tell others. They shivered under the excited lash of his words.

In the brightest, warmest part of the summer, the Inuits of Kiyok's clan sought out the dark thing that had pushed up through the Earth's cold crust to arouse their curiosity.

They gathered around it, pointing and prodding and questioning. But there were no answers. The Inuits were an unlettered people. They had never heard of the *Necronomicon*. Or of Nug, whose son is called Great Cthulhu.

So they prodded it with their harpoons of polished walrus ivory. The surface of the thing was black and striated, shiny in spots, dull in others. Thin-walled black bubbles of varied circumferences lay in eruptive patches on the dull surface.

Many had broken when the thing pushed upward, leaving pits and craters and sprinklings of obsidian-like shards in the renewed tundra about the object.

The Inuits knew nothing of obsidian or volcanos or lava. They only knew that when handled carelessly, these glassy shards cut the skin with a magical ease.

They gathered up as many of the shards as they could, and when they realized there was not enough for every hunter, they began breaking the intact bubbles with their soapstone tools and harvested fresh shards.

The bubbles released gases that had not mingled with the atmosphere of Earth since the time of the Old Ones' banishment. This, too, had been foretold.

They made new harpoon barbs with the black glass that was not of this Earth, only set in it, and Kiyok led them in search of the caribou which had come in plenty to the melted circle surrounding the thing like vitrified horn.

The caribou fell before the black spear points, and their carcasses were dragged back to the warming shadow of the thing from under the Earth to be dressed and cooked and consumed with gulping relish.

It was Kiyok, his belly hot and full, who stood up at the end of the feast and proclaimed the black thing that had given them wondrous new spear points to be the Good Warm Spirit of the Earth.

They were illiterate Inuits, so reality was whatever their imaginings conjured up. They knew nothing of the lower worlds of men and cities and universities, where the dark book called the *Necronomicon* could be found, in which a woodcut drawing printed in evil black ink was inscribed. A drawing that showed the thing they called the Good Warm Spirit of the Earth and which the *Necronomicon* called the Torch of Nug.

If some warning hand had shown them that page, they could not have read the dire prophecies, although they would have recognized the drawing as traced out in bold, portentous lines. That alone might have stayed their wind-burned hands. But these things did not happen. Instead, they brought their women and their children to the slush edge of the spongy tundra and laid down new laws.

Women and children were forbidden to step within the circle, Kiyok proclaimed. Only men had that privilege. Only men, because the Good Spirit of the Earth had long ago sanctified Man as master of the world. Somewhere in the cosmic vortex, the daemon-sultan Azathoth laughed at the supremely cosmic joke.

That night, they fashioned igloos out of square-cut blocks of ice and slept in a new-found sense of security and wonder, unsuspecting.

In the morning, the men crawled over the Torch of Nug, seeking other gifts. The air was now thick with the gases of long ago, but they knew it not. These gases had no taste or odor, nor in their free state have any effect on the human constitution.

They came upon the wheel. It was Avalak who saw it first.

The Inuits knew nothing of the wheel. They had their dogs and their sleds with which to travel the icepacks. No wheel ever cut or found traction on the permafrost, so it was a startling sight to behold.

The wheel was set high on one side of the Torch of Nug. It was as big around as the fishing holes the Inuits would cut into the coastal icepack during the long dark winter so as to fish with their cunning caribou antler hooks. The shape of the wheel reminded them of their fishing holes and made their caribou-satiated bellies yearn for trout.

Avalak set his hands to the wheel and tried to make it turn. Now the Old Ones who had fashioned the wheel knew the mind of Man—although man had not yet been created when they fashioned the wheel. They knew that man would attempt to move the wheel, just as a seal seeks the low-hanging frost smoke that means water or a dog digs into the pink-spattered camp snow for fresh bones.

The wheel was hard and horny and cold to the touch. It cut the fingers. Avalak's bloodied and smarting hands recoiled from the wheel and he cursed it volubly.

The other Inuits laughed and Etokana stepped up to pit his mortal muscles against the wheel. He too surrendered to the wheel's obdurate fixity.

Kiyok tried next. His hands were calloused and stronger than most, and so under the force of his exertions, the wheel turned with an ancient creak. But it was not enough.

No man's strength by itself was sufficient to turn the wheel. But because the wheel had defied these men, the supposed masters of their domain, they were determined to turn it all the more.

Many hands were laid on the wheel. Many sealskin boots dug into the springy tundra and the vitrified horn of Nug's torch to force the wheel to yield to the will of Man.

In reality, Man was following the genetic programming that impelled him to do the bidding of those Elder beings who strained his most primitive predecessors from the primordial ooze and set them on the hard path to walking upright and breathing the air.

It had all been foretold long ago. There was no turning back.

The wheel creaked anew. It had moved but an inch. Heartened, the men who sought to master their new-found god exerted themselves again. The wheel groaned in a slow quarter turn. The men laughed. They were conquering the stubborn thing that resisted them.

In reality, they were dooming the World of Man. But they were illiterate Inuits who knew nothing of the *Necronomicon* nor of Nug, offspring of Shub-Niggurath, and could not be blamed.

Long into the day foretold as the Last Day of Man, the Inuits strove to turn the wheel for which they had no name. It creaked and groaned and fought them, because the Old Ones who fashioned the wheel understood that Man was easily bored and would soon turn away from a task that was too difficult or too easy, leaving it undone. And the wheel must finish a full revolution to ignite the Torch of Nug.

So the wheel surrendered little by little with the creaking and groaning of a windlass turning. Each sound brought renewed efforts. The Inuits sweated and grunted in their sealskin furs and, bellies full of caribou sent by the Good Warm Spirit of the Earth, they were determined to succeed.

When the wheel had toiled one half revolution, there came a thunderclap detonation and the finger of horn cascaded down like a shattered icicle, setting the Inuits scurrying.

They withdrew to their igloos at the furthest rim of the circle of warmth, but no further because while fear clutched at their hearts, they were loath to abandon their new-found god—and the warmth it provided. This too the Old Ones had reckoned very long ago.

When no terrible events transpired, they returned to kick at the heavy ebony shards and, finding them harmless, the people of Kiyok cast them away with grunts of disdain.

Where the finger of horn had reared up at the summit of the artifact, a black-rimmed well was revealed. Kiyok hunkered over the hole and saw only darkness. He announced this to the others and all came to look. All saw darkness, too. They dropped a line into the impenetrable hole, but the hook came up empty time and again.

They returned to the wheel and labored anew.

The wheel turned more easily now and the Inuits redoubled their efforts. These exertions went on for many long hours. There was no night, and so no need to return to their igloos built just beyond the zone of warmth where they would not melt.

At last the wheel had been turned three quarters of its circumference. The Inuits paused to congratulate themselves and fortify their resolve with spit-roasted caribou.

When they set hands to it again, it surrendered completely. The wheel turned smoothly and without complaint. Upon completing one full revolution, it clicked into place with a flat finality.

Deep in the Torch of Nug, a roar began, dull and distinct as if from far within the Earth that was about to betray its supposed lords. The sound came from the black-rimmed well.

Avalak strode to the hole and looked down. He saw only blackness, as before.

With a sudden *whoof*, the blackness erupted skyward.

Avalak had no time to scream. The uprush caught him full in the face. He threw up his hands and turned. His face came into view. It was black, as if smeared with the campfire embers. His parka hood broke about his skull, falling in pieces to shatter at his feet. His eyelids opened—and cracked off like eggshells. His lips peeled back from teeth that were once white but were now coal.

Avalak stared fixedly through his lidless eyes. A groan rolled from between his welded teeth, and he began running.

Avalak ran past his friends, stumbled across the tundra in an unerring line directly toward the cluster of igloos. Once, he fell on his face. And when he struggled to his feet, he left pieces of his face behind in the wet tundra. Seeing him approach, the women and children retreated to their igloos.

Avalak seemed oblivious to them all—oblivious to everything except the smoldering campfire where the caribou lay with their viscera discoloring the ground and the red meat shining under the distant sun.

Avalak threw himself at the campfire. He plunged his face into it, like a man who cools his skin in a soothing pool of water.

His sealskin boots kicking in agony, Avalak lay face down in the fire until his body stopped twitching and his rounded muscles seemed to deflate.

The men saw this and shuddered. They turned away from the sight and their eyes returned to the thing that had caused a sane man to seek relief in searing fire.

Now, the Inuits knew fire. They used it to cook, and to warm themselves. They knew that it was sometimes red and sometimes yellow and sometimes orange, and frequently a blending of these comforting hues.

This flame was black. Moreover, no warmth or shadow came from it. It had a curiously liquid quality about it. Yet in all other respects it resembled a long column of flame.

Now they were Inuits and illiterate. And naturally superstitious. They knew fire and knew its healthy color. Black was not a good color for a flame and it chilled their souls to see such an uncanny sight.

The black flame that would ignite the atmosphere and clear the Earth of Man and make it welcome for the Old Ones' ultimate return wavered cold and evil. It was not evil. It was uncaring. But to Inuit eyes, it was a malevolent black spirit.

They fell on the wheel, desperate to quench the wickedly unnatural fire. But the wheel they had striven against so long had sapped their energies. And it had locked into place. It would not move back. It could not move back, by design.

Withdrawing, they threw caribou bones at the flowing black spirit. The bones passed through and when they gathered around on the other side, they saw the bones were now black and brittle to the touch. They were also cold. Very cold. The thick calloused skin of their recoiling fingertips came off where they touched it.

The Inuits knew nothing of atomic composition and so did not understand that the bones had not been burned but disintegrated by the black fire of Nug, spawn of Yog-Sothoth.

They only knew that they had unleashed something terrible upon their world and must defeat it.

And so they threw their weapons at the pillar of negative flame. Those tools that passed through the liquid-like plume shattered upon landing on the other side. Those that missed fell upon the base of the Torch of Nug. Almost every thrown object broke more of the black blisters that released the gas devised to saturate the atmosphere.

Beyond the zone of warmth, the women and children cried and pleaded for their men to retreat. Stubbornly, the Inuits kept on. Their ulus and axes soon ran out and they stood limp-fingered and impotent before the inexplicable demon they had aroused.

And as the minutes melted away, the cold radiance of the black flame of Nug chilled their hearts. The ground began to shine with frost, but they noticed it not. They only knew that the fire that neither consumed nor gave heat was as cold as the vast abyss of the interstellar night sky.

And all the while the gases that would render combustible the very atmosphere all warm-blooded things breathed spread and bonded with the free-floating molecules of oxygen.

Frightened, they began to retreat. They walked backward with careful, gingerly steps, their boots making the new frost squeak in timid complaint. It was as if they understood that once they turned their backs on the black fire it would send out leaping tongues to lick their souls out from their open mouths.

All but Kiyok the hunter. He remained. He would not run. He had never run from danger. He would not run now.

Kiyok studied the immense black flame which grew taller with each passing moment, trying to fathom its intent. It was not a living thing, but Kiyok saw it as malevolent and, to his ignorant eyes, that meant it lived.

And in his Inuit ignorance, Kiyok had seized upon a truth. He began dragging the carcasses of the caribou up to the flame. When he had them side by side, he lay on his belly and began pushing the loose-necked animals into the well from which sprang the dancing blackness that was like a lazy tongue of fire.

Kiyok found a spear that was still intact. He used this to urge one caribou carcass into the flame. The head went in and was lost from sight. He urged the rest of it after.

When the hind hooves were all he could make out, the weight of the carcass dragged it into the flame. The hind legs remained, broken off where the black fire had licked languidly.

After that, there came a hard rattle like a great stone striking the bottom of a cooking pot. The clattery sound reverberated up from the vitrified horn under Kiyok's flattened belly.

The black flame danced on.

Undaunted, Kiyok pushed the second carcass into the flame. Surely, he thought, two would be enough to smother this fire that should not be.

But it was not. The second carcass went in whole and the sound like a stone reaching the end of its fall came again.

Belling outward at the base, the black flame shrank. The wavering tip of fire grew thinner. Still, it burned cold and unquenchable.

Kiyok stood up, fists balled in frustration, his strong teeth in his sun-bronzed face bared and gleaming like those of an animal.

Behind him, the others shouted for Kiyok to run from the liquid black flame. Amid their exhortations, he heard the high wailing of Yua, his wife, and the crying of his only son, still unnamed.

Kiyok wavered in his resolve.

And the long black flame that was the pilot light for the clearing of all unimportant life from the Earth suddenly belled outward at its base.

The atmosphere was beginning to ignite from the black cleansing fire.

Kiyok did not know this. He saw only a terrible malevolence suddenly grow, and an intuition that had nothing to do with books, either good or bad, but which sprang from the most noble well inside a man's being, told him that unless he acted now, his wife would perish, his son would never become a man—and if these things came to pass it did not matter whether Kiyok the hunter lived or lived not.

So Kiyok stepped up to the Torch of Nug, shutting out the anguished wail of his wife, and plunged into the black fire.

It enwrapped him like ice. It was cold and liquid and in the first instant of contact, his clothes cracked off his skin, and his skin became like iron sheathing muscle. His muscles contracted over his bones, and his bones turned to anthracite. The fused black clinker that had been Kiyok the hunter floated upright in the black fire of Nug for two heartbeats. No more.

Then gravity exerted its inexorable attraction and his shrunken remains dropped into the well.

How far Kiyok fell no one of his clan ever knew. He was lost to their sight from the first moment he stepped into the black flame.

But they all heard the muffled but distinctive sound that came when he struck bottom. It was a sound dogs make when they gulp a too-large dollop of caribou meat thrown to them. Yua shrieked out in her pain and realization, and turned her wind-seamed face from the flame that had taken her mate forever.

She missed what transpired next. Everyone else saw it.

The black fire began hissing. It thinned, belled outward and thinned again, as if gasping for breath—or fuel. New sounds came from the Torch of Nug—interruptive sputterings and barks. Low frantic bangings followed, like a great metal portal caught by some gargantuanly angry wind. With a final crash, the portal seemed to drop shut.

The black column shrank, dwindled, and retreated with resentful stubbornness back into the well from which it had sprung forth. It did not die easily. Twice, it struggled to reignite, but deep within the Torch of Nug, it was blocked at the source by the calcified remains of what had once been a simple unschooled Inuit whom the lower world of civilization did not know and history would never record.

By morning, there was only the hump of vitrified horn, like the buried crown of a great fire-seared skull.

The clan of Kiyok abandoned their igloos and moved on. In time they would forget. But they would never understand. For they were only unimaginative Inuits whose knowledge was bounded by the shimmering horizons of snow and ice that comprised their narrow world of struggle and survival.

The Old Ones had forgotten that those who had created man had created him well. And even illiterate and superstitious Inuits possessed heart and courage and intelligence.

The Torch of Nug retracted into the Earth. By the next winter the tundra would turn again to frost as new snows fell. Over successive seasons, it would pile up and melt, pile up and melt, until the hard crust of ice was formed anew, leaving no sign that on this spot mankind had struggled with his own nature and with forces which thought him less than a dog.

And had triumphed.

The ice cracked, as foretold.

A broken star of cracked permafrost appeared on the south polar continent, lifted in the center and fell back in chunks as a crackle-skinned sphere of pitted brown metal reared into view.

The Furnace of Yeb, offspring of the hellish union of Yog-Sothoth and Shub-Niggurath, twin brother to Nug, lifted to the impossibly blue Antarctic sky.

In the vastness of snow and ice, it began to roar. The dull sound rippled outward in snow-disturbing waves. No human ears heard it, but that did not matter. If necessary, it would roar for generations to come, calling out to Man the programmed, who would not rest content until he had explored even the most forbidding and inhospitable regions of the Earth.

On and on it roared, calling for some unwitting Prometheus ....

I HAVE OFTEN PONDERED the Ligotti-like imagery in that New Testament saying "If the light that is within you is darkness, then how profound is that darkness!" (Matthew 6:23). *A light that is darkness!* The anti-light of the Black Hole Sun that *eliminates* as it *illuminates*. A darkness in which the Dark Mysteries can at last be seen. I suppose that is the strange brilliance in which the blind and hooded prophets of ancient myth, such as Tiresias and Balaam, saw the advance of Doom. Lovecraft uses this imagery effectively in that segment of "The Haunter of the Dark" in which he relates the eon-long journey of the avatar through the awful abysses of white light. Here is another tale from the black gulfs. From the land down under comes this yarn by Australian Steven Paulsen.

Paulsen is right up front in his admission that the story has been inspired by one of Lovecraft's sonnets from "The Fungi from Yuggoth", the same one from which August Derleth's "The Lamp of Alhazred" took its rise. This fact itself is symbolic. The two stories emerge from the same lamp in different eras, like cast shadows of terrible revelation from the black eons of the remote past. Who knows what will happen the *next* time some hapless fool dares rub the lamp of the mad Arab Aladdin!

"In the Light of the Lamp" originally appeared in Leigh Blackmore's collection *Terror Australis: The Best of Australian Horror* (Coronet Books, Hodder & Stoughton [Australia] Pty Ltd. 1993).

In the Light of the Lamp

by Steven Paulsen

It blazed—Great God! But the vast shapes we saw

In that mad flash have seared our lives with awe.

— H. P. Lovecraft, "The Lamp"

I.

PETER BRIGGS AND his girlfriend, Jocelyn Harris, stood shivering in the cobbled lane behind a small group of shops. "Back at two," read the scribble on the brown paper bag taped to the stairwell door.

"He's out, damn it!" said Jocelyn, pulling a crocheted shawl about her shoulders.

"Yeah," said Peter. "We needn't have rushed to catch that bloody train after all." He glanced at his watch and shrugged.

"Half an hour. We've got to score, so we'll just have to wait." He ran his fingers through his long, lank hair, freeing some of the knots the wind had tied in it.

"Well, it's too damn cold to hang around here, man. I'm freezing. And look at those clouds, there's rain on the way. Let's go and browse in the shops."

They left the lane—the cold wind pushing them out from it—and circled around to the front of the shops.

The buildings were old and dilapidated, superseded now by the all-in-one complex on the highway that had bypassed them twenty years ago. They seemed to huddle around the mostly quiet railway station as if it was their only hope, grimy, dull, and forlorn.

Peter and Jocelyn passed one uninviting doorway after another: An espresso bar—dark-eyed men playing cards, drinking thick black coffee from tiny cups; a derelict shop, its windows daubed in spray enamel with the words WAIT FOR WHEN THE STARS ARE RIGHT; the pizza shop, above which their dope dealer lived; a dingy book store displaying yellowed volumes of poetry by Justin Geoffrey; until finally they paused outside a cluttered bric-a-brac shop. Boxes, furniture, bolts of cloth, and all manner of other merchandise were precariously stacked up against the inside of its grimy window, hiding the interior.

"This'll do," Peter said, squinting, trying to peer into the shop through the maze of oddments. He opened the door and they stepped inside.

The shop was relatively warm, but the air seemed somehow tainted—damp, dusty, and aged. The only illumination came from a single fly-specked light bulb suspended from the ceiling. It was dim—so dim in fact that shadows obscured much of the stock, and parts of the shop were in darkness. The old, chipped glass sales counter, smudged with countless fingerprints, was deserted.

They peered into the gloom. Objects of unrecognizable shapes were hung and stacked all about. In one corner there seemed to be huge earthenware jars and amphorae, while from the walls trophy-mounted animal heads appeared to watch them with ominous and fiery lifelike eyes. Behind the glass counter they could see hundreds of tinted-glass apothecary phials stacked in a tall rack.

"Let's look around," suggested Jocelyn, not really caring what they did. She strolled over to the nearest table, examining the objects laid out on it. Peter moved to another table and began picking through a selection of brass ornaments, suppressing a sneeze as he stirred dust with his movements.

Something tickled Jocelyn's ankle and she shivered uncomfortably. Then, suddenly, as she tried to move away it grabbed her ankle. She screamed, kicking her foot free, and a loud staccato screech from under the table made her scream again and run to Peter's side.

"Peter ...," she managed between sobs, "there's something horrible under there."

He pried her grip from his arm and went to where she had been standing. Striking a match, he took a deep breath, bent over, and thrust the flame below the table.

"It's a monkey!" he cried. "It's cool, come and have a look. It's only a monkey."

He struck another match and they both peered under the table. There, in a bamboo cage, sat a large-eyed, scrawny monkey with its head tilted to one side. It seemed to be laughing at them, revealing a shiny gold front tooth.

"Ah, he's cute," Jocelyn said, placing her hand into the cage, patting its head. "Hello there, boy."

Peter laughed. "A minute ago you thought he was horrible."

Suddenly the monkey swiveled its head and lunged at Jocelyn's hand. She snatched it away as his jaw snapped shut. "He tried to bite me!" She stood up. "Let's go, I don't think I like him after all."

She followed Peter to another table, casting backward glances into the dark recess she knew contained the strange gold-toothed monkey. She felt uneasy about it and slightly suspicious about this place. Catching up to Peter, she noticed the counter was still unattended.

Peter stopped before a tall brass water-pipe. "Far out! Hey, Joss, get a load of this hookah, will you."

"Oh, *wow* ...," Jocelyn stared at Peter's find. "Isn't it great? I wonder how much they want for it?"

"*Salaam*, young *Effendi*, young Madam."

Peter and Jocelyn spun around. Jocelyn gasped. Peter took hold of her hand. Before them, as if from nowhere, stood a tall, swarthy hook-nosed man, dressed in flowing robes and a turban. He was smiling, but his eyes held an unnerving glint.

"In answer to your question, Madam, two hundred dollars is the price for the hubble-bubble. Hand tooled by Tso Tso craftsmen. A bargain, don't you think?" His words oozed politeness, but a mocking tone seemed to deny servility.

Jocelyn raised her eyebrows at Peter.

The man smiled, his top lip curling up in one corner.

"Can I show you something else? Some trinkets perhaps, or a talisman?"

"It's cool," said Peter. "Just looking, man."

"Just looking," repeated the shopkeeper. "Then please allow me to draw your attention to some very special merchandise." He strode to a table in the middle of the shop, easily avoiding the obstacles that cluttered the gloom. "These items are bargain priced, 'on special', I think you say. For a very short time, just for you, *Effendi*, everything on this table is priced at a mere five dollars." He gave his curled-lip smile, bowed, and moved quietly away to stand behind the counter.

"Junk," whispered Jocelyn, the urge to leave growing in her.

"You never know," Peter said as he began to sift through the unusual assortment of paraphernalia. "There could be something good in here."

Every so often he paused to examine one of the curios or trinkets as its presence caught his attention: an octagonal piece of thick red glass; a multi-faceted black-red sphere suspended in a lidless box; a rusty dagger with a serpentine blade; a sheaf of handwritten parchment fragments in Latin or some such; a cloudy jewel-like orb about the size of a tennis ball. Finally he paused a bit longer over one particular object—admiring it, looking at it from different angles.

"Hey, look at this, Joss."

Looking up from playing in the dust with her feet, Jocelyn said, "Come on, Pete, let's go. Dealer-Bob'll be back any time."

"Yeah, okay, just look at this first." He held out a tarnished metal object.

Jocelyn glanced at it, disinterested. "What is it, Peter? A teapot or something?"

"It's an old oil lamp, I think." Peter ran his fingers lightly over the surface of the metal body. "You know, like Aladdin's lamp. Yeah, listen"—he shook it—"you can hear the oil sloshing around inside."

Jocelyn smiled crookedly, then giggled, her heavy mood lifted briefly. "Maybe there's a *genie* in it—let's polish it and see."

"Maybe there is," said Peter pretending to be serious, "it looks really old. Look, it's even engraved with runes and hieroglyphics. I think I'll buy it."

"Don't be silly, we can't afford it. Besides, it was probably made in Taiwan last week."

"I don't care if it was, I'm still going to buy it."

"Well, just make sure you've still got enough to pay Dealer-Bob! And hurry up."

Digging into the pockets of his threadbare jeans, Peter counted five dollars in coins onto the counter. The shopkeeper nodded, verifying the amount, but Jocelyn was already leading Peter from the unusual shop. As she opened the door, a shaft of cold sunlight broke into the shop, revealing an empty bamboo cage under a nearby table. Peter closed the door without either of them noticing it.

When they had left the man laughed aloud, showing his teeth for the first time—his gold front tooth glinting, catching the light from the feeble light globe.

II

Sitting, polishing the lamp later that night in their small, bare living room, Peter Briggs marveled at the quality of the workmanship as the grime and tarnish came away. It looked just like he had always imagined Aladdin's lamp would look—like a squat, oblong teapot sort of thing stretched to a spout at one end with a handle on the other.

Jocelyn had knelt by him on the floor when he first began to clean it, but soon lost interest when her *genie* failed to appear. Now she was sitting cross-legged on the floor in front of his chair, preparing a joint on a Cheech and Chong record album cover with the marijuana they had bought from Dealer-Bob.

The lamp gleamed in Peter's hands as he gave it a final buff with a soft cloth, more the color of gold than brass—but for five dollars *that* was impossible.

"I think I'll light it," Peter said as he pulled the wick from the spout with a pair of tweezers.

"Do you have to, man? The damn thing'll probably smoke and stink out the room—or even worse, what if it blows up or catches fire or something?"

Peter laughed. "It won't blow up, and that's just the Brasso you can smell."

"You can't be sure—it mightn't be safe. Anyway, I just don't like it. It makes me uncomfortable. You can light it if you like, but I'm going to bed, *to sleep*, if you do."

"Aw, Joss, don't be like that." He put the lamp on the coffee table and got down on his hands and knees, nuzzling his face into her small breasts.

"Careful, you nearly spilled the dope." She squealed and pushed him away as he playfully took her nipple between his lips through her thin cotton caftan.

"*Peter*, I mean it!"

"Okay, already. I won't light it."

"Thank you."

Outside then, a flash of lightning suddenly flared brilliantly, starkly illuminating the entire room. Peter's head jerked up and Jocelyn gave a little gasp, gripping Peter's arm tightly. It was followed moments later by a violent peal of thunder that rattled the windows in their frames and seemed to shake the very foundation of the house.

"Wow!" exclaimed Jocelyn, putting her hands over her ears.

"Jeez, that was close." Peter got to his feet and returned to his armchair. "Looks like we're in for a doozy storm."

"I don't like storms." Jocelyn went to the windows and pulled the blinds down over them. Thunder rumbled deeply in the distance and the light in their room flickered off and on. She came back to Peter and sat on the arm of his chair. "I *really* don't like storms."

"Well, let's light this then. It will make you feel better."

Peter leaned over and picked up the reefer and a box of matches from where Jocelyn had left them. He sat back and lit the oversized cigarette, inhaling the smoke deeply before he passed it to Jocelyn.

"Anyway," Peter said as he exhaled the smoke, "there's nothing to worry about. The chances of actually being hit by lightning are billions to one. And even if—"

He was cut short by a flash of lightning so bright it illuminated the room through the blinds. Then the lights went out, plunging the house in darkness, and a mighty crack of thunder pounded against the windows.

"Peter!"

"It's all right, Joss; hang on a sec ...." A match flared. Peter cupped it in his hands. "There."

"Have we got any candles?"

"Not that I know of—no candles, no torch, no nothing. Ouch!" Peter shook out the match and blew on his burnt finger.

"Well, do something." There was a note of panic in her voice.

He struck another match. "I suppose I could light the lamp ...."

"Light the lamp, then."

"But you said—"

"I don't care what I said, just light it."

He leaned over and picked the lamp from the coffee table, putting the burning match to it. The flame sputtered for a moment, then stabilized. The light the lamp gave was surprisingly strong, illuminating the room with a warm, steady brilliance.

"There," Peter said smugly. "That's done the trick. See, it doesn't smoke and it hasn't blown up after all." He placed it back on the table. "Look, it's even better than a candle would've been."

But Jocelyn wasn't listening; instead she was engrossed in something across the room, her fear of the storm and the dark shocked from her mind.

"Peter," she said slowly, shakily, holding the joint up in front of her face, "what's in this stuff we're smoking? I think I'm hallucinating."

"It's just grass, what—"

Then they both stared dumbfounded, for now Peter too wondered if he was hallucinating. All around them the walls of the room had come to life. Everywhere the light from the lamp fell, images and scenes were forming before their very eyes. Except, that is, where shadows fell onto the walls from furniture and the like; there the scenes were empty, incomplete, like pieces missing from a nearly finished jigsaw puzzle.

Pictures formed and faded away before they could properly make them out. Peter stared incredulously, blinking every so often and rubbing his eyes.

Then the kaleidoscope sensation began to ease and a scene slowly began to come into focus. Before them now lay a wooded slope leading down to a flat riverbank. Around them stood dark green trees, tall, majestic. It was as though they were standing looking out from a glade on a forest hillside. Peter thought he could almost smell the freshness of pine, of dew, feel the subtle, ghostly sensation of a breeze brushing lightly against his face. The storm that had moments before thrilled him was now forgotten.

"Look!"

Jocelyn pointed as a figure, a boy, came into view by the dark river. He stopped, looking towards them, then slipped from sight behind some trees on the wooded riverbank.

Then the scene twisted out of focus, shifting, changing, and another began to appear.

Peter took Jocelyn's hand in his. "It's the lamp," he whispered huskily, "not the dope. I can feel it." He turned back to the images.

Before him now stretched a boundless white-blue landscape. Mighty mountains of ice and stone thrusting out from immense frozen plains. Peter felt drawn toward them, fascinated, enthralled. He imagined he could step into the scene as though it were just beyond a doorway. Holding his arm before him, fingers outstretched, he shuffled toward the icy panorama on the wall.

Jocelyn reached out and took his other hand in her own, subconsciously holding him back.

He reached the wall and placed his fingertips against it, holding them there for a second or two. Then all of a sudden he withdrew them with an audible sharp intake of breath.

"What's wrong?" hissed Jocelyn.

Peter removed his fingertips from his mouth and blew on them. "I thought they were burning ... but they're *cold*."

"This is *weird*, Peter! What's going on? What do you mean, 'It's the lamp', huh? I think I'm freaking out on this stuff!" She threw Peter's hand aside and covered her face with her own as she began to weep.

"Don't cry, Joss. I'll show you. Look ...."

Peter snuffed the lamp out with the side of the matchbox, throwing the room into a darkness that seemed to amplify the howling wind and driving rain pounding against the windows, cascading from the overflowing gutters. Peter lit another match and held it up: Now the images were gone from the walls with no sign of them ever having been there.

Jocelyn watched him as he relit the wick, and when she looked back at the walls in the light of the lamp, the familiar blank surfaces had been replaced by the shifting patterns of a new scene as it began to form. The sounds of the storm that moments before had reasserted their presence seemed to recede into the darkness outside like a dying echo.

A time-worn city jutting from the sands of a vast desert came into focus all of a sudden out of a misty blurred image. Some of the ancient buildings and walls were half buried in the ever-moving sand dunes, while others—at the whim of the wind—had their crumbling forms fully exposed.

But the image was fleeting, melting back into the swirling sand and mist before they could take in any details. And even as this nameless city disappeared, another scene was already beginning to form.

This time, a moonlit hillock appeared before them in the distance, and the scene seemed to grow as if they were falling into it. Closer and closer it came—until at last they saw movement on it, a tiny dancing creature, recognizing it as the gold-toothed monkey from the curio shop.

The animal raised its head, lifting its face to the moon, and began to grow before their very eyes. It grew with impossible speed, and as it did, its shape began to change. In a matter of seconds its size had doubled and its features were taking on human aspects. Then they recognized it as the swarthy shopkeeper—his hands on his hips, his laughing head thrown back, a contemptuous sneer on his face. And still he grew and changed, his arms elongating, his hands replaced by huge pincer-like claws.

"I don't like this at all," Jocelyn said timidly. "How can a lamp do this?" But then anything else she might have said remained stuck in her throat as she tried to comprehend the horror before her.

The creature's face—the thing now resembled neither monkey nor man—was stretching and changing color. Finally the shifting ceased and the fiendish horror raised the long blood-red tentacle that had once been its face toward the moon and howled. A howl that Peter and Jocelyn felt rather than heard, but a howl that clawed at their hearts with icy fingers.

Then the scene blurred. It was changing again.

"I can't take this, Peter!"

But Peter did not reply or acknowledge Jocelyn in any way. He stood motionless, transfixed, oblivious to anything other than the new scene now on the wall.

Steaming, mud-covered, and wet, a might Cyclopean city of spires and monoliths and confused geometry seemed to stretch interminably before him. Water poured from its black ramparts and queerly angled towers, and green slime oozed thickly down its prehuman edifices and walls, as though the city had suddenly burst into the sunlight after aeons at the bottom of the sea.

"R'lyeh," whispered Peter without knowing why, for the word had formed itself and issued from his lips of its own accord. He had the impression of many distant voices chanting monotonously. Then somehow he knew he had uttered the name of the dank, black city.

A movement high above the rest of the buildings caught his attention. He looked toward it. An immense gate or doorway had opened in the high citadel at the center of the city, revealing a mighty cavern so dark, Peter could only imagine what it contained.

But even though he could see nothing, Peter *knew* something was there. Something huge, something moving, something ancient—

Then they saw it.

Bloated and lumbering, it squeezed its rubbery mass through the immense gap and slopped itself into the sunlight. It was an obscene green scaly thing, sticky with ooze and slime. The tentacles around its kraken-like face writhed and whipped, and it lumbered forward on four clawed feet.

The chanting both Peter and Jocelyn had felt suddenly became ominously audible, and although the guttural words themselves meant nothing to either of them, in response the *Thing* seemed to increase its speed over the carven monoliths and masonry of the city. Then a hideous stench, not unlike putrid seaweed and decaying fish, permeated the room.

The guttural, monotonous chanting went on, louder and louder, a chant older than civilized man's collective memory.

a voice hardly louder than a whisper, Peter joined in the
merizing chorus.

"Dear God!" screamed Jocelyn. "What are you saying? What's
going on? Stop it, Peter. Put the lamp out!"

The gelatinous bloated monster stopped and fixed its malignant
gaze on Peter and Jocelyn. Leering, awful eyes pierced their very
beings, savoring their souls. Then it moved with uncanny speed,
slavering and groping toward them.

"Put it out, Peter!"

But Peter hesitated, turning back to look as the slobbering
rampant horror filled the wall with its unnatural bulk. And in that
instant, a monstrous, dripping, rubbery member lashed into the
room and plucked Peter from where he stood.

Screaming, spittle spraying from her lips, Jocelyn dove for the
lamp and clasped her hand over the flame. In the lamp's dying
flicker, a nauseating sucking sound came from beyond the wall and
she looked up in time to see Peter's limp form enveloped in a
writhing mass of slippery tentacles. Then the room went dark and
the sounds of the wind and the rain once again roared through the
house, but even then they could not blanket Jocelyn's shrieking.

III

The police patrol car cruised along the deserted street at little more
than walking pace. A flurry of rain filled the beam of its headlights.
Occasionally, the yellow glimmer of candle or lantern light shone
from one of the blacked-out houses.

Constable Rex Whatley stopped the patrol car and peered out
into the downpour at a narrow Victorian-style house. He pulled the
car over to the curb and switched the engine off. The windscreen
wipers clunked as they came to rest, and the heavy rain beat loudly
on the metal roof.

"This's the place, Sarge," he said. "It's difficult to see if anything's
going on from here."

"Yeah," said Sergeant David Finch. He picked up the heavy-duty
police flashlight from the seat beside him. "Grab your torch, Rex."

A disturbance had been reported by neighbors—it sounded like
a domestic violence—and the two officers had reluctantly left their
warm station house to check it out.

Splashing through the water in the flooded roadside gutters and the puddles along the footpath, they reached the front porch. Sergeant Finch knocked loudly on the door and it swung open a little, unlatched, but there was no reply from the darkened house. Finch motioned Whatley around to the rear, then knocked again, louder. Still no reply.

Cautiously, he let himself into the house, holding his breath while he listened. No sound. When he breathed again a fetid smell assaulted his nostrils. He switched on his torch and moved cautiously into the lounge room. He shone his light around, noting a plastic bag full of marijuana on the floor and other drug paraphernalia on the mantlepiece and coffee table.

Over by the wall he noticed a pool of slimy liquid splashed across the floor. As he approached it the offensive smell became stronger. He screwed up his nose in distaste.

Another light flashed across the room. Constable Whatley appeared.

"The house seems empty, Sarge. Phew! What stinks in here? It smells like someone's left a dead cat in the corner."

"Something rotten's been spilled on the floor over there," said Finch. "Dirty bloody druggies." He shone his torch on the illicit drugs. "Looks like they shot through in a hurry."

The portable radio on Finch's belt crackled to life with their call sign.

"Richmond-203 responding," he said.

"Roger, Richmond-203," replied a tinny voice. "Code 12 and 16 on the corner of Belrose Avenue and Center Road. Ambulance en route. Can you attend?"

"That's just around the corner," said Whatley.

"Affirmative, D24. We're on our way."

IV

Run! Escape! were the only coherent thoughts in Jocelyn's terror-seared mind. The other images and thoughts that jostled in confusion threatened to push her over the edge of sanity.

She fled from the house, vomit dribbling from her chin, oblivious to the rain, feeling no pain in her burnt right hand. Retching, gasping for air, she ran down the street, still clutching the lamp.

At the end of the street Jocelyn paused, confused, her breast heaving. Suddenly she realized she was still holding the lamp. Cold dread gripped her and she flung it away into the darkness. Somewhere in the back of her mind she heard a thud as it struck the ground, and she ran.

Jocelyn ran in fear for her very soul.

She ran blindly down the center of the road, into the middle of the intersection.

A horn blared. Brakes screeched. Headlights illuminated Jocelyn's wan, hollow-cheeked face. Her eyes wide, unseeing. There was a thud. Pain. Everything went black.

Somewhere in the distance Jocelyn could hear voices. She began to pray to herself. She had not said a prayer since she was a little girl. This one was for Peter, but somehow she knew he was beyond God's help.

She began to tremble, gibbering quietly to herself, unaware of the rain, the approaching siren, the flashing blue and red lights.

The two policemen made their way through the inevitable onlookers. Sergeant Finch went to the distressed driver and Constable Whatley went to attend to the injured girl lying on the road. He could hear an ambulance wending its way to the accident.

The girl was lying quiet, the side of her face grazed and bloody, her lips and chin flecked with spittle and vomit. It looked to Whatley as though her leg might be broken. He reached out to wipe the girl's face clean.

Jocelyn was wondering how God could possibly allow such a horribly evil creature to exist. But her contemplation was broken by the sight of a tentacle, its wet suckers pulsing, reaching for her face.

"Put it out!" she screamed. "Out!"

She struck out at Whatley, her nails drawing blood from his cheek as she lurched away from him, scrabbling on her hands and one good leg, gibbering and mumbling.

"The monkey's not a monkey ... it's a man, but it's not really a man, it's a, a ...." She began to sob. "Oh, help me. Dear God, help me. Got to destroy the lamp. Find the lamp."

Jocelyn reared up as they reached her, thrashing, screaming the words in their faces as they restrained her, her voice breaking.

"Find the lamp!"

All she could finally manage as they held her were gut-wrenching sobs. The last thing she said was, "The lamp is a door."

The two policemen exchanged glances.

Finch shrugged.

Whatley shook his head. "The things these stupid kids do to themselves with dope."

V

The next morning, eleven-year-old Jamie Bonnar wheeled his bicycle from the garage on his way to school. The storm had passed during the night, but it was cold, his breath coming out in visible clouds.

He scooted his bike down the drive, avoiding puddles of rainwater. But as he threw his leg over the saddle some burnished thing on the front lawn caught his eye and he stopped.

Jamie laid his bike on the ground and squelched across the lawn to retrieve the curious object. He recognized it immediately as a Middle Eastern-style oil lamp. What a find! It was made of brass, chased with obscure symbols and patterned scrolls. It even appeared still to have oil in it. And it was on his own front lawn!

He glanced about, wondering where it had come from, wondering if he had been seen. There was nobody in sight. Quickly, he took it around the back of the house to the cubby he and his mates had built behind the garage.

When his eyes adjusted to the dim light inside the ramshackle hut, he put the lamp in their secret compartment in the wall, behind the plywood where they kept their cigarettes and matches. It would be safe there for now.

Tonight, after school, they could try it out—light it and see if it worked.

HERE IS A TALE which may strike you as a bit out of the ordinary, not exactly an exercise in Lovecraftian mood or cosmic vision. It has a tradition behind it nonetheless. Conceived as something of a Brian Lumley homage, it takes its inspiration from such Lumley tales of undersea horror as "The Deep Sea Conch" and "The Cypress Shell", as well as from Robert Bloch stories including "He Waits beneath the Sea" and "Terror at Cut-Throat Cove."

Pierre Comtois is a writer and editor whose work has appeared in *Churchyard*, *Shudder Stories*, *Crypt of Cthulhu*, and other titles. He was also the founding editor of *Chronicles of the Cthulhu Codex*, a controversial small press publication featuring new Cthulhu Mythos fiction.

Zombies from R'lyeh

by Pierre Comtois

THE MONEY HAS FINALLY RUN OUT. It was the only thought that kept repeating itself in my tired brain. *The money has finally run out.* Crossing my arms on the bar planks in front of me, I brought my head down on them to rest, knocking over an empty glass as I did so. I heard it roll off as if from a million miles away, almost as far away as the Florida coast where I'd left behind all my dreams. As the harsh sounds of the crowded bar receded around me, my mind went back to those simpler days, days in which it was easier to imagine success as a treasure hunter scouring the Keys than it was to work toward a chemistry degree at MIT. I'd gotten a little money together and when I had had the opportunity to buy myself a boat while on spring break in Miami, I took it. I was already a good diver, and with the boat it was easy to abandon myself to the carefree life of a scavenger among the Florida Keys looking for sunken artifacts and treasure from the hundreds of wrecks littering the bottom of those clear waters. But those seas were too crowded with other, larger outfits, and the only treasure I ever found was Carol, who became my unofficial partner and lover.

I felt a tightness in my loins and thought I heard a groan from my throat as I thought back to our first meeting. I had had the boat anchored in shallow water off Bimini in the Ten Thousand Islands and was just getting set to squeeze into my wetsuit when I caught a glimpse of something dark moving through those crystal clear waters. At first I thought it was a shark, so graceful were its movements, but as it moved closer, I realized my mistake. At last, the figure reached the rope ladder that hung over the side of the boat and as the water poured from its visage, I saw just how wrong I'd been. It was a girl, and a mighty fine-looking one at that. Like a fool, instead of helping her up, I shaded my eyes and scanned the horizon and, as expected, reassured myself that my position was far from any landfall.

"Permission to come aboard?" The words dragged my attention back to the girl. I must have mumbled permission, because all I could remember afterward was stepping back in surprise as she hauled herself up, saying, "Help me with this, will you?" I grabbed hold of her tanks as she shrugged out of them and continued to marvel as she divested herself of the rest of her rig.

At last, seeing that she wasn't going to stop with her flippers, I finally managed to say, "Who are you? How'd you get here?" She smiled and said her name was Carol, that she was from California, but lately she'd been living in St. Pete. She'd spotted my boat from time to time in the last few weeks, noticed I was alone, and figured I might like a junior partner. By the time she'd finished speaking, she'd shed her black wetsuit like a second skin and stood unselfconsciously before me in one of the smallest bathing suits I'd ever seen. The next thing I knew, she had her arms around my neck and her lips were massaging mine. What could I say to an argument like that?

Like I said, as things turned out, she was the only thing of value I found the whole time we spent in those waters. At last I convinced myself that if we were going to strike it big, we had to move to less frequented waters. I sold the trinkets we had found and outfitted the boat for a long voyage and, together, Carol and I crossed the Atlantic to the west African shore. It took us three years to dive and trawl our way around the Cape and over to India, following the old Portuguese barges. I'd had the Philippines vaguely in mind as our ultimate destination when I'd first started out, but we had no better luck than we had had in the Caribbean and what money we had was running out. At last, we put in at Labuan in Brunei, and couldn't get out again. With only enough money left to buy a few drinks and some rice balls, and just shy of the Philippines, we were forced to go to ground in what must be the armpit of the world. Labuan, the capitol of Brunei, was bad enough, but the only place we could afford to flop was the lower waterfront district, a nightmare jumble of shanty bars, buildings made of driftwood and tarpaper, and rotting wharves with a sea mist that never seemed to lift, draping the whole area in a pall of moist, gray gloom.

Since then, I'd been supporting myself with a combination of begging and petty theft with my nights spent either in the clink or the gutter. But with Carol gone, I just couldn't work up the energy to do anything about my condition. Carol! She wasn't the sort of girl to be stopped by a run of bad luck. I'd also say she wasn't the type to take things lying down, but that wouldn't be exactly true. Soon after we arrived in Labuan, I was hauled off to jail by the local constabulary for not paying a harbor tax. I stayed there for two weeks, and when I got out, I found that Carol hadn't been idle. She'd been shacking up at the boat with a local bruiser the size of a small house and told me in no uncertain terms that if I wanted to stay around, I could have the engine hold. Well, the idea of living in a cramped, dirty, airless, rat-infested hold on my own boat while Carol lay in the arms of any sailor with a wad of money in our cabin two decks over my head was just too much to take. Ever since then, I'd been on the streets living on garbage and straight whiskey, taking a few bucks from Carol now and then when desperation drove me back to the boat. Just then, I wasn't quite drunk enough to forget my troubles on account of not having enough money to buy the requisite liquor. Maybe that was lucky, because I was able to notice when someone began shaking my shoulder. I looked up and when my eyes focused again, they showed me that Carol was standing over me.

"Vic, c'mon, I know you're still sober; you haven't the money for a good soaking." She was right, so I forced myself out of the stupor I'd wished myself into and asked her what she wanted. "I have something to show you, Vic; I think we're back in business." It took a few seconds for her words to sink in and in the end, I think it was the obvious sincerity in her voice that convinced me she wasn't kidding. She must've seen the same thing in my eyes, because she didn't wait for an answer. Grabbing me by the arm, she hauled me from the bar and didn't stop until we got to the boat. From there, she shoved me up the gangplank and into the cabin. I half expected one of her friends to be there and stiffened against it, but no one was there. For the first time since we had arrived in Labuan, Carol and I shared the cabin alone.

"Sit down, Vic," she said as she opened the secret trap beneath the bunk. I backed myself wearily into a bench at the fold-down table beneath the starboard porthole. While she was reaching beneath the bunk, I couldn't help noticing the dinginess of the cabin, the smell of stale food and sweat and the yellowed disarray of the bed sheets on the bunk. At last she straightened and came over to the table. Remaining on her feet, she placed a typed manuscript in front of me and from what I could see of its worn and rumpled title page, it seemed to be a diary by someone named Johansen.

"So?" I said.

"I found this in the belongings of Joe Mahmoud; you remember Joe, don't you?"

I wasn't sure, but I didn't want to admit it, so I took an almost sure bet. "One of your roommates, wasn't he?"

She didn't bat an eye. "Right. Anyway, Joe got himself arrested a few weeks ago. I was called to the police station yesterday to identify his body. It was in the yard out back. It was him all right. But since he was dead, I figured I had the right to his things. This was in them." She rested a finger on the dirty manuscript, but I wasn't terribly interested.

"What about money?" I asked, more to the point.

She took her hand back and rested her fists on her hips. "There was some, and since I'm the only one who's been able to earn some bread in this partnership, I'm deciding what to do with it, got it?" I admit it, I was just too darn tired after the years at sea and months at Labuan to argue. In effect, I capitulated control of our relationship into Carol's hands. She became the boss then, and knew it. I must have nodded, because she continued. "Joe had some money and together with the rest I've been able to save, we're going to reoutfit the boat and make one more scavenger hunt."

"Look, Carol, I'm tired. We're never going to find anything. Why don't we just haul up and try to make it back home?"

The stinging pain of a sharp slap across my face caught my attention but good, and, if that wasn't enough, Carol's hand got hold of a fistful of my hair and jerked my head back until her angry eyes were able to stare directly into my own. "Now listen up, and listen good," she said with repressed rage, "I don't have any intention of going back to the States empty-handed! We came out here to strike it rich, and we'll do it yet, even over your dead body, got it?" For the first time in our long relationship, I saw Carol's true nature: brave, resourceful, intelligent, ruthless, and utterly lacking in genuine sentiment. I'd been blinded by my own feelings for her when our relationship was merely one of convenience for her. But as her anger subsided and she let go her hold on my hair, she allowed the veneer of tenderness to return to her face and voice until, eerily, she was the woman I though I'd been in love with all this time. The woman, heaven help me, I still loved.

She stroked my cheek in a way that both aroused my old passion and chilled my blood, saying, "I can see you do understand, Vic darling. You see, I remember Joe saying that this manuscript was stolen from a man named Thurston over fifty years ago by a group Joe said his father had belonged to. It was a kind of cult and when his father left it years later, he took this manuscript with him. Joe seemed to think it might be worth something and after he died, I read it and Vic, I think it just might be our ticket home." I looked down at the manuscript with new interest and Carol noticed. "It seems that Johansen discovered an island that had recently risen up from the ocean floor somewhere in these waters and, from what I used to hear Joe saying in his sleep, there was treasure on that island that Johansen never took off." I started to thumb the pages. "There are coordinates listed in the manuscript that show exactly where we can find it, too."

She leaned onto the table. "I want to start getting this boat into shape again and take it out to that island, Vic, and I want to start tomorrow. I'll go ashore and do some shopping. Tonight, you can read the manuscript, after we've taken care of business." I looked up at her last words just as her lips met mine; pleasure like lightning coursed along my body. They lifted me from my seat as she steered me toward the bunk. My mind told me the fire of her passion cast no heat, but instinct and longing and the desire to please her were stronger, and, in the end, I never noticed the filth of the bedding.

The next few weeks were a blur of hard work as we prepared the boat for its long journey. As I busied myself with scrubbing, painting, and mechanical repair, Carol bought equipment, food, checked the diving gear, and generally kept an eagle eye on me. Finally, when the work was nearly finished, she came to me and said, "Why don't we take the afternoon off, and go for a walk?"

I knew by then about her singlemindedness and doubted a simple walk was all she intended, so I asked, "Where to?"

"Over to the Lanes to see someone." My eyes must've narrowed at that. I knew the Lanes to be the merchant district of the lower wharves area, mostly occupied by shady characters who dealt with illegal merchandise and smuggled goods. Not a healthy part of town, but one Carol seemed at home with.

An hour later, we were making our way down a crowded alley in the Lanes when Carol suddenly said, "Here it is." She slipped into a dark doorway I would've missed completely and we found ourselves in a crowded, dingy room obviously meant to be a store.

I looked around, wrinkling my nose at the smell of moldering paper, a smell I'd not encountered in years. I knew before my eyes had accustomed themselves to the gloom that we were in a bookstore. "Why'd you bring us here?"

"Because Kwan might have something that could make our voyage a little easier. You ought to know the worth of research, college boy." The words hurt and humiliated me, and Carol knew it. "Johansen's diary," she continued, "mentioned good directions to that island, but there's no harm in double checking against some old charts."

"He also mentioned a lot of other stuff that didn't sound too healthy—"

Carol laughed shortly. "Oh, c'mon, an educated guy like you falling for fairy tales about sea monsters, next you'll be telling me about the tooth fairy—"

"Cut it out, Carol. You're not funny." She smiled that mocking smile that made my blood boil. The smile that told me she knew I'd lost my nerve, or whatever it was that made me a man, and that that had enabled her to take charge. I decided to shut up rather than risk her reminding me again of our new relationship. Just then, a fat old Chinaman entered the room from behind a dirty curtain.

Carol surprised me by saying something to him in a mixture of English, Chinese, and Malay that the man actually understood. He nodded his head and began rummaging about the room until at last he'd brought over a small stack of dusty, insect-eaten tomes. Carol turned them around one by one, flipped open their covers to scan their headings, and tossed aside the ones not written in English. Some were oversize chart books that we looked through, trying to match Johansen's descriptions with their own, and some were just literary books covering various South Seas subjects such as anthropology, ichthyology, coral reefs, geography, and tides and currents. "What about this?" Carol suddenly asked, shoving an open book in front of me. I read the title: *Hydrophinnae.*

"Never heard of it." But I picked it up anyway and began thumbing through its pages, stopping here and there to scan the words. It was written in a hard-to-understand style, sort of a cross between formal English and scientific jargon. "Hey, this book is about the same stuff Johansen talks about in his diary."

"What do you mean?"

"I mean the stuff about sea monsters and ... yeah, this book calls it 'Cthulhut'—." Carol didn't give me time to continue as she clapped the book shut and, taking it from me, tossed it back onto the counter.

"Forget it," she said, "we don't need more fairy tales. What we're looking for is firm directions or descriptions of that island."

I was kind of disappointed, but I wasn't prepared to confront Carol on the issue of keeping the book. Then she handed me another one —*Unterzee Kulten* read the binding. "This one's in German," I said.

"Oh well, then we can forget—"

"No, wait a minute; I had to learn some German for chemistry back at MIT, maybe I can dope out something here."

"Well, what's it about?" As I flipped through the pages, the sections with reproductions of old woodcuts caught my attention. They were usually illustrations of strange forms of sea life I'd never heard of, until I came across one that looked like a cross between a squid and an impossible jelly fish. When I looked at the legend beneath the illustration, it read "Cthulhu." My heart skipped a beat then, and I got a flash of intuition that filled me with a vague dread. "What is it?" asked Carol, peering over the edge of the open book.

"Nothing," I said, "it's just that this book mentions that same creature that Johansen describes."

"Again?" I could tell she was really beginning to lose her patience.

"Carol, I'd like to keep this book—"

"Look, Vic, we can't go around wasting our money on useless stuff like monster books."

She took the book from me and threw it back on the counter, raising a small puff of dust. "These two chart books ought to come in a lot handier. How much are they, Kwan?" The Chinaman made signs indicating their value, but Carol wasn't having any of it. She made an offer and the Chinaman took it.

The night before we were to set off, my eyes wouldn't stay shut. Although I'd long since gotten used to sharing the narrow bunk with Carol, I found the nights uncomfortable and frequently sleepless. I sat up slowly so as not to wake Carol, who slept soundlessly, her face to the wall. In the dim starlight that came in through the two cabin portholes, I could make out enough detail to appreciate Carol's still impressive curves and featureless skin. The long months of questionable liaisons had hardly worn her down at all. Quietly, I left the bunk, took down one of the chart books we had bought, and made my way topside. Sitting beneath the bow light, I opened the book to the title page. It was written in French, but beneath it, someone had long ago written a translation: *Uncharted Waters.* I'd studied the book many times since we bought it and concluded that it was a collection of maps and charts drawn up by untutored hands, mostly castaways who'd attempted to describe their unintended voyages. They were difficult to follow, but some had accurate longitudinal and latitudinal markings that made it easier to guess at the designer's route. One in particular, that I'd pointed out to Carol, seemed to show the very island we were bound for. Of course, that was no guarantee that it existed, but it was some kind of independent corroboration of Johansen's story. The date affixed to the chart indicated that it was first drawn sometime near the beginning of the First World War by a drug addict who'd committed suicide by throwing himself out of a window. Sitting there under stars strange to someone born on the other side of the world, that same feeling of dread I'd experienced in the book shop came over me. Was it over these fairy tales, as Carol called them, or was it something deeper? Something to do with my very psyche, whatever it was that'd robbed me of my male pride? That was all the time I had before I heard Carol call me from the cabin doorway: "Vic, c'mon back to bed, I can't sleep." It wasn't a wish, it was a command, and, still trying to understand what made me do it, I got up and followed meekly after her.

I have to admit, even though I wasn't completely comfortable with our destination, the day we left Labuan lifted my spirits higher than they'd been since the early days along the African coast. The sea mist had suddenly lifted and a light breeze came off the ocean as I steered the boat out of the harbor into the sunlit open water. The hum of the engine sounded pretty and the sea breeze against my face was bracing, and Carol—man, Carol looked delicious as she scrambled over the deck doing the odd things that needed doing in khaki shorts and a bikini top. She was all bronzed skin and dark hair as she moved in easy, fluid motions handling the ropes and diving gear. I could almost forget the artificiality of her personality and the position she, and mostly I, kept me in. The next few weeks passed quickly with days negotiating the currents that allowed us to pass from among the islands of the Philippine Archipelago, through the southern regions of Micronesia, across the Gilberts and American Samoa, to the region where our mysterious island was supposed to rest. If all went well, we could take our treasure and head straight to Hawaii when we'd finished. Our nights were spent on calm seas and deserted lagoons in one another's arms, frolicking in the surf, or diving naked in the shallow waters looking for shells. Living that life, I could almost forget that the past few months had ever happened, but then, at the end of the day, I'd be reminded again of who called the shots as Carol would suddenly grow serious and declare fun time over, that we needed our sleep.

At last, after endless weeks at sea, and having been out of sight of land for days, we entered the area in which, according to our charts, our mysterious island ought to rest. Idling the engines, I descended from the wheel and joined Carol at the chart table on deck. She had Johansen's notes out and the sets of new charts and the one I had found in *Uncharted Waters* open alongside. "It should be around here somewhere," she said unnecessarily. "We'll begin a circular search pattern from this point," she added, indicating a spot on one of the charts. Since we'd refitted with all the supplies we'd need for a month at our last landfall, there was nothing much I could say and so I said nothing.

"Let me know when you get there, I'm going aft for some sun."

"Sure," I said, as I watched her balance herself along the edge of the boat toward the stern. By the time I was aloft at the wheel again, I could see that she'd already stripped and was lying on a towel looking up at the sun. A pair of sunglasses hid her expression as I found myself envying the apparent self assurance she still had and that I couldn't recapture.

It was two days later when I spotted it. "Land ho," I called out excitedly. "Carol! Carol! I think we got it!"

Carol was lying on her towel aft again. When she heard me cry out, she didn't bother getting dressed before she leapt for the ladder and scampered up beside me. By that time, she was as dark as brown sugar, and as trim and hard as a navy cruiser. "Where?" she said breathlessly when she reached me.

"Over there," I said, pointing to a smudge on the horizon.

She took the binoculars and had a look. "Well, it's in the right spot. There shouldn't be any other islands around here." She put the glasses down, unable to hide her glee. "Vic, this is it! This is where we hit the jackpot!" She threw her arms around me and hugged me for all she was worth, which was considerable, and I hugged back, lifting her feet from the deck and spinning us around.

When I put her down, I was relieved to see that she was still smiling as she headed for the ladder. "Head straight in and find anchorage, and I'll get the gear set," she said over her shoulder.

"No sweat, and don't forget the champagne," I replied and smacked her on the rump. She didn't mind at all as she slid down the ladder and disappeared below.

An hour later, the island loomed large in front of us and I guided the boat carefully parallel with its shore as Carol sat forward looking out for hidden reefs. In the excitement of arrival, she'd prepared all

the gear and pulled lookout duty without ever bothering to get
dressed, a fact I didn't have time to appreciate as I studied the island.
It was strange for a South Seas island in that it didn't seem to be
volcanic in origin. Instead, although it was covered in tropical
vegetation, its dark earth indicated that it'd been thrown up from
the ocean floor once years before. It wasn't a very large island either;
we made the circumference in fairly short order and it seemed
completely devoid of animal or bird life. At last, Carol shouted that
we'd come to a spot to weigh anchor, and I turned the bow in that
direction. As Carol used the plum rod to gauge the water's depth,
I eased up on the engine and then shut it down completely, allowing
it to drift into a final position. "Cast anchor," I said. I couldn't help
noticing the sun shine over Carol's bronzed flesh as she lifted the
anchor and tossed it overboard.

"Anchor aweigh," she called, as the heavy object splashed into
the sea. In another moment, Carol threw herself into the water and
began swimming to the beach of black sand that stretched only
a few dozen yards from the boat. When she stood up again,
streaming seawater, she motioned for me to follow. Shrugging, I
stripped and dove from the wheel loft and in another minute was
standing beside her.

"This is a funny beach for an island like this. The land just falls
away only yards from shore."

"It makes a perfect natural harbor," said Carol.

"I guess." I was still looking into the water when Carol called me
over to where she was standing looking at a jumble of boulders that
seemed to be the end of a mountain ridge that ran from higher up
inland down into the sea where we stood.

"See this? It almost looks like writing or hieroglyphics, doesn't
it?" I looked more closely at where she rested her hand, but couldn't
decide if it really was writing or just random cracks in the rocks.

"I don't know, it could be anything."

She took my arm and we walked a bit along the beach scanning
the rocks for a passage inland until Carol stopped short and gasped.
She freed my arm and stooped to the sand. I saw her digging for a
bit, but before I could say anything, she straightened and held out
an object that glittered in the setting sun. "Gold!" she cried. And
it was. Strangely worked jewelry, but definitely gold.

"This is it, Vic! Johansen's island. C'mon, let's see what else we
can find—"

"Wait a minute," I said, with unaccustomed vigor, "we can't just go charging inland like we are."

For the first time since spotting the island, Carol seemed to notice that she was naked and laughed. "Am I a nut! Let's get back to the boat ...." She looked up at the sky. "No, let's wait until first light tomorrow, it's too late now. In the meantime, we'll celebrate with that champagne and a little lovemaking ...."

It was early the next morning when we again left the boat, this time in the dinghy, and a light sea mist clung along the shore of the island. As Carol leaned eagerly forward in the bow, I could already see wisps of fog breaking loose farther inland, slowly revealing the rest of the island. "Careful for the drop-off," I warned, as Carol prepared to jump ship.

"Right," she said as she leapt overboard and waited while I beached the boat. A few minutes later, we'd hauled it farther up the beach, hoisted our day packs, and checked the pistols on our web belts. I wore a shirt, shorts, and hiking boots, while Carol was in her usual khaki shorts and bikini top with her hair tied back in a ponytail. Marching over to the spot where we had found the jewelry the day before, Carol scanned the rubble that lined the inner shore.

"I think we can make it through up there," she said pointing, and took the lead scrambling over the smaller boulders. I followed, content to be an Indian to her chief and vaguely wondering over the shape of the boulders we were climbing over. Not that there was anything really strange about them, it was just that they seemed so regular, like the rubble you'd see from a blasted building worn down after years of exposure to the elements. On the other side there was a short field of more rubble, as if a small mountain had shattered into pieces that lay scattered about, and then the green of the jungle on the other side. Carol didn't hesitate as she leapt from boulder to boulder toward the inviting greenery. When I finally caught up with her, she was breathing hard and already sweating profusely in the tropical heat.

"What do you make of this?" I asked as we caught our breath there beneath the shade of the trees.

"Make of what?"

"You don't find the layout of this island kind of funny? Unlike any other island we've visited?"

Suddenly her expression clouded. "You're not going to bring up that stuff about monsters again, are you? Because if you are—"

I held up my hands in protest, fearing her anger, "No, no. I just think this island is made kind of funny, that's all."

She visibly relaxed, and said, "All right then, stop fretting and follow me." She turned and began making her way up the slight incline beneath the trees. As the land began to rise gently I noticed that the terrain beneath the trees wasn't smooth. Here and there amid the foliage, which was in no way thick or heavy, more like a lightly wooded forest glade, I spied huge boulders, one might even call them blocks, resting haphazardly all about us. Soon I realized that not only were there hundreds of them within sight, but that the very ground we walked on was composed of the same rubble we had encountered on the beach. The only difference was that because it was farther inland, silt that had settled about it while the island had presumably rested on the bottom of the ocean had not been eroded away by the action of the surf. As we continued to climb, and the way became steeper and steeper, the boulders became more plentiful and the trees gave way to mere undergrowth. The walk became a climb and soon we were obliged to help each other up over the rocks that increased in size until finally, resting atop one, we took the time to look back at the way we'd come.

The morning mist had fully lifted by that time, revealing the island in its entirety. Carol and I found ourselves on an outcropping of rocks that formed a fractured ledge overlooking the portion of the island we'd just traversed. I could see the boat resting along the shore and the black beach from which we'd started our hike. From where we stood, we could see a good portion of the island and it became more apparent to me than ever that there was something not quite right about it. Except for patches of greenery here and there in its lower reaches, its entire surface was a single, vast pile of shattered stone that seemed to tumble down to the sea. As a matter of fact, from where I stood, I could see that whole ridges of boulders simply wound down the face of the high ground and disappeared beneath the sea. At last, I turned to face the upper reaches of the island, on part of which I stood. Although it didn't tower too much further than where we rested, it seemed much larger than it must've been. It had a huge escarpment of sorts, now more obviously segmented into gargantuan blocks that rested together without need of mortar and, as my eyes trailed downward from those heights to the sea, I became convinced that the formation, whatever it was, wasn't natural. Even as I looked, I could guess that the whole island was merely the tip of some colossal structure that had been shattered in the cataclysmic force that hurled the sea floor upon which it rested to the surface.

"Look, Vic," said Carol, breaking into my thoughts, "here are those funny marks again." I looked at where she was pointing, and again saw the strange cracks in the rocks that we'd seen the day before on the beach. They weren't hieroglyphics or writing of any kind, I was sure of that. They seemed to be more in the nature of stress lines, as if a gigantic weight had settled over the whole island. As if, ridiculous as it sounds, part of the island had existed in an environment with different laws than that of the earth and maybe when it was forcibly thrown upward, it was torn from those forces that held it together. But I was saved from wasting more time thinking over such fantasies by Carol's latest exclamation.

"Vic, look!" She was holding another piece of golden jewelry. "We're on the right track," she said, putting the piece in my hand. I was still looking at it when she exclaimed again. "Hey, what was that?"

"What was what?" I said, looking up.

"I saw something move up there," she said, pointing up toward the truncated high ground of the island.

"Are you sure? We haven't seen a living thing all day." As a matter of fact, we hadn't seen a living thing outside of plants since we had spotted the island. The thought of finding something now, instead of reassuring me, only gave me the chills.

"I'm sure of it. Let's go check it out." So saying, she began to negotiate the last expanse of rock to the top. With no choice but to follow, I did likewise.

"Check this out," Carol suddenly called back over her shoulder. Looking up past her legs and rear end, I saw her holding out more of the golden jewelry. She tucked it into her back pocket, where I saw it dangle against her buttocks as she made it the rest of the way to the top. In another minute I joined her. "The main cache must be around here somewhere," she was saying as she scanned the cracked and fissured surface before her.

"What about that movement you said you saw?" I asked nervously.

She sensed my unease and dismissed it with, "Forget about that, it was probably just a bird. Start looking around for more treasure. Why don't you start over there?" Not liking the idea of separating, I did as instructed anyway and began to wander over to a short outcropping of rock. Carol grew smaller and smaller in the distance as she searched in the opposite direction. Then I heard her cry out and spun around. I caught a glimpse of her just as she disappeared over the edge of the escarpment. Fearing for her safety, I dashed across the intervening space in minutes and when I arrived at the spot from which she'd vanished, I saw her, gun in hand, peeking cautiously into a darkened fissure in the side of the mountain.

"Is there anything wrong?" I asked.

"No," she said, without looking up, "... I don't know. I saw something down here that looked like gold, and when I jumped down, I thought I saw something move in here."

"Well, c'mon back up."

"No way; you come on down and back me up." I hesitated until she looked back at me, her eyes flashing, and said, "Let's go, Vic!"

Gulping, I crouched down and jumped the eight feet or so to the ledge. When I straightened, Carol said, "Get your gun out, just in case; stay here and watch my back. I'm gonna take a look just inside the opening and look for some sign of treasure; it sure looks like the perfect hideout for it."

I took out my pistol and nodded, not trusting my voice. For some reason I couldn't explain, the island was straining my already weakened nerves. "Be careful, Carol," was all I could say.

"Just don't chicken out on me, Vic."

Then she slipped out of sight. I moved over to where she'd been standing, glancing nervously around the ledge and holding my gun up. Carefully, I inched closer to the opening and peeked inside. I could see Carol moving about, stooping here and there as she checked for more jewelry. "See anything?" I asked.

"Nothing," she replied testily. "C'mon over and help me look." Swallowing, I rounded the corner and stepped into the cool interior.

"Put that thing away, and start sifting through some of this sand." I had just holstered my gun when there was a slight rustling sound from the darkened rear of the fissure and suddenly Carol's scream filled the tiny space like a physical thing. I instinctively stepped back in surprise and tripped over a rock. With Carol's screams still in my ears, I felt rough hands try to get hold of me, but I wriggled out of them and regained my feet. For an instant I thought of running, but there was just enough of my manly pride to think of Carol, so instead I shoved my way the few feet to where I could see her struggling against whomever it was that had tried to grab me. The weight of my body must have taken them by surprise, because I managed to wrench Carol free and drag her toward the entrance. Her bikini top had vanished in the struggle and her gun was gone.

"Let's get out of here," I yelled, but Carol, unbelievably, still hesitated.

She swung her angry face in my direction and said through gritted teeth and wisps of undone hair that hung before her eyes, "And leave the treasure? You've still got your gun, use it!"

I hesitated, and in that hesitation she took the gun from my holster herself and swung it in the direction of our assailants, whom I'd imagined simply to be island natives. But as the first few advanced into the light near the entrance of the fissure, their true nature was revealed. Dressed in what seemed a combination of various seaweeds, dried kelp, and sea shells, it was their faces that revealed the fact that they were no mere natives but white men. I froze as the first flashes of Carol's pistol shots showed the chamber crowded with the forlorn figures and, though it was impossible for her to miss under such circumstances, I thought she must have, until I saw her last shot pass through the forehead of the man closest to us without effect.

After that, they were on us again, Carol kicking and shouting defiant curses and I ... I reeled back outside and scrambled down the face of the mountain. Blind panic had eroded the last vestiges of my pride and sheer fright propelled me downward over that landscape made harsher in the dying light of the day. By the time I reached the treeline, I was exhausted and my clothes were in ribbons; I stumbled to a breathless halt on my hands and knees as my ears finally began to register the pitiful screams still dimly emanating from the cavern mouth. I scrambled to my feet, not returning to my right mind until long after I had climbed aboard ship, a ragged, bleeding mess.

When the clouds finally began to lift from my brain, I found myself perched on the edge of the boat's bunk with an empty bottle of Scotch rolling back and forth on the deck. There'd only been a few fingers left to it, but it was all the liquor we'd had left. Unfortunately, it hadn't been enough to erase the memory of the events of a few hours before. But was it the memories I'd been trying to wipe out, or the shame of my being driven to this kind of mental paralysis? Over and over again, I rationalized it all in my mind: years of failed effort scavenging the seas of the world, months of degradation in Labuan and having gotten used to Carol doing the thinking for the both of us had made me a different man. There were too many of those ... things, up there. And Carol, I knew she didn't love me, she only tolerated me because she needed me. How many times had we made love without passion or feeling? How often had she treated me with thoughtless, even cruel, abandon? She'd been an opportunist from that first day she swam up to the boat in Florida, and like a sap I'd fallen for her like a ton of bricks. I'd been a sap all right, and still was one, because even then, I couldn't help feeling something for her. Whether she or I liked it or not, she'd become a part of my life and I couldn't imagine it without her. I guess I loved her, despite it all. Suddenly, as if to punctuate that last difficult admission, I heard, or thought I heard, a distant scream come over the water; like a siren, it seemed to pull me from the darkened confines of the cabin out onto the open deck of the boat. I think I must've been irrational then; how else to explain the fact that I just dove into the water and swam to shore without even bothering to supply myself with fresh clothes or a gun? I hardly remember following our trail back up the escarpment, the way lit only by the light of the full moon. At last, I found myself back at the entrance to the fissure from which Carol had been taken. All was quiet then, so I slipped inside, stopped, and listened. I didn't hear anything, so I found a wall and followed it to the rear of the chamber.

With my heart pounding like mad, I discovered the opening those things had boiled out from and stepped through and continued on down the passage in the same manner I'd used in the fissure.

As my hand ran along the walls, I could feel irregularities that seemed to cover every inch of them, irregularities that felt too regular to be more of the cracks that we'd seen on the outside. Although I couldn't see them, as I concentrated on the markings, they began to impress on my fevered mind certain suggestions that, as they became clearer, began to repulse me. At last it reached a point where I had to jerk my hand back as if I'd received an electric shock. I shrank back from the wall as the loathsome images in my brain began to fade, only to be replaced by other, as yet vague, intrusions. Somewhere in the back of my mind I was surprised at myself as, instead of turning back and running, I faced forward, and continued on; as I did so, I found what fears I had had melted away. At last I seemed to come upon a slight decline that soon began to slope definitely steeply downward. I walked along that narrow tunnel for what seemed hours until suddenly I could see a dim glow of light ahead. Going forward cautiously, I seemed to hear a jumble of voices all speaking or maybe chanting together that grew stronger the more closely I approached the light. Then I came to a wide opening and, peeking around the edge, saw that it gave onto a vast, sunken chamber. The opening at which I stood led out onto a narrow ledge that lined one side of the chamber. At regular intervals, blazing torches were stuck into the walls, which were oddly carved with vile imagery. Strangely, feeling no apprehension, I stepped out onto the ledge, upon which also stood the creatures who'd taken Carol. They were still dressed in their robes of seaweed, but now they were festooned, incongruously, with the same strange, pale gold jewelry they must have placed like breadcrumbs on a trail to lead us here. There was our treasure: tiaras, bracelets, and pendants catching the firelight.

They were spaced out evenly between the torches, their arms raised stiffly over their heads as they droned some kind of chant. It was then that it occurred to me that they weren't speaking aloud at all, but that I was receiving their thoughts directly in my brain. With that revelation, all became clear. I leaned forward to look more closely into the bowels of the chamber far below from where I stood on the ledge and where the light of the torches didn't quite penetrate.

I began to notice details that had escaped me before: the constant sound of water sloshing about, coming from far below and echoing throughout the huge hall, and the almost overpowering stench of rotting sea things. As my eyes accustomed themselves to the light, they began to form a picture of that space below. Moonlight filtered through a low arch of rock to one side where the ocean lapped in and out, flooding the chamber floor; water dimly sparkled as it washed inward, lapping about the foot of a small mountain of rock and coral that slowly built itself into a thick bed of living mollusks, crustaceans, dead fish, and even frogs. I would've looked further, but just then my attention was drawn to a disturbance on the far side of the chamber. There was an opening there similar to the one I'd just come out of, but with no ledge. Two torches burned on either side of the opening.

Then I saw two of the creatures emerge with Carol between them. My first instinct was to go to her, but that was impossible with our relative positions being what they were. As it was, I had to watch as her naked form was led to the edge of the precipice. She no longer struggled, and I could see by her tangled hair and filthy skin, crisscrossed with fresh scratches, that the fight had gone out of her. She simply stood between her two captors, head bowed a little as they raised their arms and intoned something. I'd been so centered on Carol that I hardly paid attention to the thoughts that pushed their way into my brain. Then I heard something that jolted me back, something that filled me with the same dread I'd felt in reading some of those old books back in Labuan—the name of Cthulhut. I looked around wildly, the image of a woodcut rising back into my mind. I wanted to scream out, but something held me back. I fought it, and managed a weak, "Carol, Carol ...." She must have heard that pitiful call, more a plea for help than a call to action, because her head lifted and she spotted me.

Her lips parted. "Vic? Vic! Oh Vic, help me! Please, help me!" As if her words had activated it, there was a sound from far below. At first it was like water sloshing, then it was a moist crunching of shells beneath a sudden weight, a slithering.

"The blood of the woman will enliven the Great Cthulhut. Cthulhut. Cthulhut." The words droned through my brain, becoming stronger and stronger. "Release us from your bondage, O Great Chtulhut. We offer you this rare morsel in appeasement. Have mercy, great Cthulhut."

"Vic!" She was struggling now, as her two captors seized her arms and legs and began to lift her, kicking and screaming, over their heads. They approached the ledge.

"Carol!" I screamed one last time as they hurled her bodily into the abyss, trailed only by her last, raw, wrenching plea that ripped my soul to shreds: "*Viiiiiiiic!*" It ended when her body hit the mountain of sea creatures and tumbled a little way to the water's edge. I could see her broken limbs moving feebly in the uncertain light, and in an unemotional zombie-like state, I saw what had caused those earlier sounds as great Cthulhut flowed, a massive, gelid, tentacular mass, mercifully hidden even from the hardened gaze of his loyal servitors, crested the peak of shellfish, and allowed certain of his arms to reach for his offering. One slipped under Carol's body and encircled it, and as it began to drag her upward, her head must have lolled on its broken neck to face the creature whose appetite she was fated to sate. Her nerveless face yet twitched and I knew she was fully aware of what was happening to her. Unfortunately, this time, she couldn't even scream. But even in that catatonic state in which I found myself, somewhere there must have resided a safety mechanism, a psychic fail-safe device that protected me even when the rest of my body had shut down. I felt a tightness in my chest and a sudden pain that stole my consciousness.

I don't know how long it's been since that night. The night I died. All I know is that I've been somehow reborn or reanimated into a kind of living death, kept animate by the dreams of Great Cthulhut. Like my fellow treasure hunters, castaways, and explorers—Lopez, Donovan, Guerrera, Ångstrom, and the rest—I exist only to please Cthulhut, hoping that someday he may tire of us and release us from his bondage. Even now I hear his hellish call, and the last vestiges of my self control vanish … I weaken … I weaken … Great Cthulhut … Cthulhut … R'lyeh is your City … Cthulhu Fhtagn …

ABOUT ROBERT M. PRICE

Robert M. Price has edited *Crypt of Cthulhu* for fourteen years. His essays on Lovecraft have appeared in *Lovecraft Studies, The Lovecrafter, Cerebretron, Dagon, Étude Lovecraftienne, Mater Tenebrarum*, and in *An Epicure in the Terrible* and *Twentieth Century Literary Criticism*. His horror fiction has appeared in *Nyctalops, Eldritch Tales, Etchings & Odysseys, Grue, Footsteps, Deathrealm, Weirdbook, Fantasy Book, Vollmond*, and elsewhere. He has edited *Tales of the Lovecraft Mythos* for Fedogan & Bremer, as well as *The Horror of It All* and *Black Forbidden Things* for Starmont House. His books include *H. P. Lovecraft and the Cthulhu Mythos* (Borgo Press) and *Lin Carter: A Look behind His Imaginary Worlds* (Starmont). By day he is a theologian, New Testament scholar, editor of *The Journal of Higher Criticism*, and pastor of the Church of the Holy Grail.

THE SHUB-NIGGURATH CYCLE

Among the most familiar names in the Lovecraftian litany, Shub-Niggurath, the Black Goat of the Wood, the Goat with a Thousand Young, is never met personally in Lovecraft's stories, but is often referred to in rituals and spells. This deity mutated and was adapted as Lovecraft crafted and revised tales spawned by other authors. Here for the first time is a comprehensive collection of all the relevant tales concerning Shub-Niggurath.

5$\frac{1}{2}$" x 8$\frac{1}{2}$", 256 pages, $10.95. ISBN 0-56882-017-8; available from bookstores and game stores or by mail from Chaosium, Inc., 950-A 56th Street, Oakland, CA 94608-3129.

THE HASTUR CYCLE

The stories in this book evoke a tracery of evil rarely rivaled in horror writing. They represent the whole evolving trajectory of such notions as Hastur, the King in Yellow, Carcosa, the Yellow Sign, Yuggoth, and the Lake of Hali. Writers from Ambrose Bierce to Ramsey Campbell and Karl Edward Wagner have explored and embellished these concepts and thereby created an evocative tapestry of hypnotic dread and horror. Here for the first time is a comprehensive collection of the thirteen relevant tales; several are rare and (almost) impossible to find. Selected and introduced by Robert M. Price.

5$\frac{1}{2}$" x 8$\frac{1}{2}$", 320 pages, $10.95. ISBN 0-56882-009-7; available from bookstores and game stores or by mail from Chaosium, Inc., 950-A 56th Street, Oakland, CA 94608-3129.

MYSTERIES OF THE WORM

New Second Edition, Revised and Expanded. At the end of H. P. Lovecraft's life, the young Robert Bloch was an enthusiastic member of Lovecraft's literary circle. This is a new edition of the long out-of-print volume that collected most of Bloch's early work concerning the Cthulhu Mythos. The new edition includes three additional tales from the period—"The Brood of Bubastis", "The Sorcerer's Jewel", and "The Creeper in the Crypt", previously available only in scarce fanzines and anthologies. Bloch also has slightly revised the texts of three other stories. Seventeen tales, introduction by Robert M. Price, the original afterword by Bloch, and a supplementary essay by Lin Carter.

5½" x 8½", 272 pages, $10.95. ISBN 0-56882-012-7; available from bookstores and game stores or by mail from Chaosium, Inc., 950-A 56th Street, Oakland, CA 94608-3129.

CTHULHU'S HEIRS

Tales of the Mythos for the New Millennium. Nineteen new stories of the Cthulhu Mythos, never before printed. These range from an ironic tale of a cultist's conversion, to a first-person narration of possession by the thing from beyond itself, to what amounts to a retelling of the Lovecraft classic "The Dunwich Horror" from the inside out. These stories are by turn deft, horrifying, and hilarious, and give new life to the notion of the Mythos. Also, two rare stories are reprinted, one the definitive version of Ramsey Campbell's "The Franklyn Paragraphs." Selected and with an introduction by Thomas A. Stratman.

5½" x 8½", 288 pages, $10.95. ISBN 0-56882-013-5; available from bookstores and game stores or by mail from Chaosium, Inc., 950-A 56th Street, Oakland, CA 94608-3129.

THE AZATHOTH CYCLE

At the heart of the universe the mad god Azathoth pulses like a cancer. As with the physical universe it created, no purely reasoned argument, no subtle scientific proof, no brilliant artistry, no human love affects the unyielding will of Azathoth. As an entity it is of transcendent power and unthinking immortal sway. It can be avoided sometimes but never challenged. Here are fourteen tales concerning Azathoth by authors as diverse as Ramsey Campbell, Lin Carter, John Glasby, and Thomas Ligotti. The macabre poet Edward Pickmen Derby contributes his immortal "Azathoth", the title piece of his single printed volume. Introduction, exegesical essay, and notes by Robert M. Price.

5$\frac{1}{2}$" x 8$\frac{1}{2}$", 256 pages, $10.95. ISBN 0-56882-040-2; available from bookstores and game stores or by mail from Chaosium, Inc., 950-A 56th Street, Oakland, CA 94608-3129.

THE BOOK OF IOD

Henry Kuttner (1914-1958) was a friend of young Robert Bloch and a promising writer in his own right. He also became one of the Lovecraft Circle, submitting plot ideas and draft manuscripts to Lovecraft. He had an important impact on the development of the Cthulhu Mythos, especially with his contribution of a mystical tome, the *Book of Iod*. This collection of stories comprises all of Kuttner's Mythos tales (including one co-written with Bloch) and a story by Lin Carter about the infamous *Book of Iod*. Introduction and commentary by Robert M. Price.

5$\frac{1}{2}$" x 8$\frac{1}{2}$", 224 pages, $10.95. ISBN 0-56882-045-3; available from bookstores and game stores or by mail from Chaosium, Inc., 950-A 56th Street, Oakland, CA 94608-3129.

MADE IN GOATSWOOD

Ramsey Campbell is acknowledged by many to be the greatest living writer of the horror tale in the English language. This book contains eighteen all-new stories, all set in the ancient and fearful portion of England's Severn Valley which Campbell evoked in narratives such as "The Moon Lens." Included is a new story by Campbell himself, his first Severn Valley tale in decades. This volume was published in conjunction with a trip by Ramsey Campbell to the United States.

5 3/8" x 8 3/8", 288 pages, $10.95. ISBN 0-56882-046-1; available from bookstores and game stores or by mail from Chaosium, Inc., 950-A 56th Street, Oakland, CA 94608-3129.

THE DUNWICH CYCLE

In the Dunwiches of the world the old ways linger. Safely distant from bustling cities, ignorant of science, ignored by civilization, dull enough never to excite others, poor enough never to provoke envy, these are safe harbors for superstition and seemingly meaningless cutom. Sometimes they shelter truths that have seeped invisibly across the centuries. The people are unlearned but not unknowing of things once great and horrible, of times when the rivers ran red and dark shudderings ruled the air. Here are nine stories set where horror begins, each story prefaced and with a general introduction by Robert M. Price.

5 3/8" x 8 3/8", 288 pages, $10.95. ISBN 0-56882-047-7; available from bookstores and game stores or by mail from Chaosium, Inc., 950-A 56th Street, Oakland, CA 94608-3129.

THE DISCIPLES OF CTHULHU
Second Revised Edition

The disciples of Cthulhu are a varied lot. In Mythos stories they are obsessive, loners, dangerous, seeking not to convert others so much as to use them. But writers of the stories are also Cthulhu's disciples, and they are the proselytizers, bringing new members to the fold. Published in 1976, the first edition of *The Disciples of Cthulhu* was the first professional, all-original Cthulhu Mythos anthology. One of the stories, "The Tugging" by Ramsey Campbell, was nominated for a Science Fiction Writers of America Nebula Award, perhaps the only Cthulhu Mythos story that has received such recognition. This second edition of *Disciples* presents nine stories of Mythos horror, seven from the original edition and two new stories.

5 3/8" x 8 3/8", 288 pages, $10.95. ISBN 0-56882-054-2; available from bookstores and game stores or by mail from Chaosium, Inc., 950-A 56th Street, Oakland, CA 94608-3129.